RETURN OF THE
TEMPLARS

PROPHECY

Book II

PJ HUMPHREYS

RETURN OF THE TEMPLARS - PROPHECY

Book 2 in the series Return of the Templars
ISBN 978-1-9163167-2-0

Compiled by: Rod Craig
11.10.2020

Acknowledgements

Joanne, for her unwavering support and steadying hand through the entire journey of 'Prophecy'. For her ability to unblock the blockage when I am stuck, staring at empty pages — screen.

Brands with Influence, who had the vision for the book brand and for giving Return of the Templars a visual presence on the digital bookshelves. For their support, brilliant media, design talent and for helping us to get the message out.

Zostro, for their support in establishing the first book, Ark, in the Return of the Templars, on Facebook.

Jason Hulott, for sharing his knowledge of Asian and European traditional martial arts, traditional Japanese sword fighting, medieval martial combat and period combat of the Egyptians, Greeks and Romans.

Gregory Stevens, who was a monk in the Orthodox Church in the US, for nearly a decade, for sharing his views, thoughts and insights about a number of the subject streams in 'Prophecy'. And for being a willing sounding board for my enquiring mind.

Lucinda E Clark, for applying her grammar skills to the draft manuscript

Rod Craig, for his patience and attention to detail in formatting 'Prophecy'.

This book is dedicated to:

Every person who aspires to do the right thing; to every group, association, brotherhood and sisterhood that travel in hope and with good intentions. And to a small band of men and women who keep safe some of the world's most powerful secrets, so that one day they can be revealed, understood and used for peace and creating harmony.

'Secrets are made to be found out with time'.
(Charles Sanford)

Contents

Prologue
The Sound of Menace

On Christmas Eve 2007, Jonathan Rose's life changed forever when he was told his sister had been murdered and he began his quest to find her killer.

Before this, his old life had a gentle rhythm to it. However, on that fateful night, his life took on a new rhythm, one stripped of faith, belief and certainty, replaced with despair and anger. He fell out with God; he was angry with Him. He fell out with the church. He fell out with the world. His life, like his faith, crashed and splintered into a million fractured pieces. Back then, he needed a miracle to put those pieces back together again; halfway through 2008, he was given three of them.

For months in early 2008, he blundered around carelessly in the dangerous world of criminals, asking questions and stirring the criminal cesspool, looking for his sister's murderer. He was driven by hate; he was driven by revenge, but, to him, it was clear what he had to do: find her killer, bring her killer to justice. It was his *act of remembrance,* the only thing he had left in life that made any sense; the only thing that kept him going.

He thought he was alone, and, if he had been, he would have been dead before the summer of that year. But he wasn't alone. Jonathan Rose had angels watching over him; he had the Knights

Templar watching over him. The most secret religious Order the world has ever known. Shrouded in mystery for centuries, and long thought disbanded and extinct, the Knights Templar, those warrior monks, came out of the shadows from their secret base in Scotland to help the young American priest.

Four years ago, towards the latter end of 2008, Jonathan and the Templars lured the evil murderer, Salah El-Din, out into the open in a fierce battle at a deserted farm house in Cumbria, England.

However, Salah El- Din evaded capture by the Templars, and he'd evaded it every day since. He remained off-grid. Hunted, not only by the Templars but law enforcement agencies around the world. Despite the bilateral efforts, the Arab criminal had completely disappeared and their efforts went unrewarded.

Since Cumbria, though, Jonathan's life had settled into a new rhythm, and, for the last four years, it was something he had grown accustomed to, comfortable with, and liked. He had become a Templar. He was a Seer. However, it was now 2012 and the rhythm of his life was about to change yet again. It started with a failed operation in Abu Dhabi. It got worse with the disappearance of a member of the Higher Council of Knights Templar, one of the Nine Worthies.

If he'd had time to pause and listen, he would have heard the low menacing hum of it coming; the foreboding barely perceptible, but it was there. Like the faint sound of a far-off drum. Payne St Clair, the Templar Grand Master, felt it. The rhythm slowly grew: ever heading towards Jonathan and the Templars. And the rhythm had a name, and its name was **Abaddon.**

Revelation 9:11 – *They had as king over them the Angel of the Abyss, whose name in Hebrew is Abaddon ... (that is, Destroyer).*

Chapter 1
White Perfects

Date: July 1446 (566 years earlier)
Place: The Languedoc region of France

It was hot and the road was dusty; it was always hot and the roads were always dusty at that time of the year. They'd left at sunup and they wouldn't be back at the farm until way after sundown. It was the girl's first trip away from the farm. It was her first trip with her father.

The girl was excited, despite having to carry out double chores for the past three days, so that her mother would not be burdened with the extra work. Her mother would only have the livestock morning and evening feed to attend to, in addition to her usual chores of cooking, milking, tending the growing garden, washing the laundry down at the brook and parenting her younger daughter and two infant sons.

The farmers were a poor family. They wanted for much, had little and, like most farmers of that region, had seen their fair share of adversity and loss. The farmer and his wife had lost two children at birth and one to the smallpox that had blighted their disparate and remote community some years back. They toiled the unforgiving soil, grew what they could, grazed a limited number of livestock in the withered pastures and eked out a living. No member of their family had ever been to school: no one was ever likely to. They were too poor and needed all family hands to work – no matter how small those hands were. Their rustic farm was etched in hand-cleaved stone and burnt clay tiles and nestled in the patchwork landscape of the Languedoc, France. It offered a life, but only just.

The 15-year-old girl, Juliette Trevin, didn't know that her name was not Trevin. Her real name was Romée, which was probably the most famous name in all of France at that time – it had been for the past thirty-four years. She believed the farmer and the farmer's wife were her parents, but they were not her parents, they were her great aunt and great uncle.

The farmer didn't say much on their journey, he never really said much at all, often appearing distant, even aloof. However, he was a kind man. Hardworking. Diligent; he was a man of strong morals and standards. He loved his wife and his children and that included Juliette. She was the secret that he and his wife kept. They had sworn an oath fifteen years ago to keep her safe and to keep her existence a secret. Every day that had passed for fifteen years, they had honoured that oath.

Walking beside the farmer, the girl carried a sack with four chickens inside it. They were to be sold at Carcassonne market (*le Cité de Carcassonne*), so they could buy flour, salt and other provisions they needed. Her father, with the land ingrained on his weather-beaten face, always silent, stout and upright, carried a leather flask of water and the small hessian satchel his wife had packed that morning with bread and cheese. A small dagger, sheathed, was tucked tightly and neatly into his tunic belt. It wouldn't deter or stop thieves or vagabonds, but it would cut the bread and cheese.

That morning, before they left the farm, her mother had cut Juliette's hair short, so that she looked like a boy. A common practice in the back waters and remote places, to keep their daughters safe. Juliette was a little self-conscious of her new appearance. Her siblings had giggled until their father had cast them a scornful look. She'd dared not look at her reflection in the water trough, for fear of what she might see staring back at her. So, she'd busied herself and tried not to think about how she looked.

The farmer's wife had watched the girl through the kitchen window. The girl had skipped from task to task with excitement, as she'd readied herself for her journey. However, for the farmer's wife, there was no such excitement, there was only worry.

"I'm not so sure that was the wisest thing we could have done, Jon," she'd said to her husband, as he filled his flask with water from the kitchen pitcher. "Look at her Jon; look at her now with her hair short. People will know. People will surely know, won't they?"

The farmer sighed. Put a cork stopper in his flask, put the water pitcher back in the centre of the table, where it could always be found, and raised his head to look out of the window. He studied the girl. "People will not know her; it's been fifteen years now. Memories fade." He tried to reassure his wife.

"They will never forget that face, Jon, not her face, no matter how long it's been. Look at Juliette now we have cut her hair; she is the image of her. I pray to our Lord that we have not sealed her fate; we have worked so hard to keep her safe."

The farmer grunted and waved his hand in a dismissive gesture. "You just mind the babies and take care of our farm. You have much to do, too much to be fretting about something that's not going to happen." His tone then a little softer, "and, stop worrying. She will be fine; you have my word. Now, say your goodbyes to her so we can be off. We have a long road to cover this day."

They left five minutes later as the sun had broken the horizon and bleached the Languedoc sky with a cascade of reds, oranges and yellows; and a surrogate mother stood afraid, worried she might not see the child again.

Juliette and the farmer followed the hard, rock-strewn, arid, winding track, the *piste de terre*. It led them due east towards the main Carcassonne road, which was still some two to three hours away. Once on the main road, their journey would be easier because it was often used by many wayfarers, horses and carts, so it was more even under foot. However, for now the going was slow and, at times, awkward.

Juliette's mind wandered as she strolled along, her thoughts absorbed with what she might see when they got to Carcassonne. She daydreamed of Knights in bright silver and gold armour. Horses, white as snow and black as night, with chain mail throws resting on their thick woven numnahs, snorting nostrils and neighing commotions. Juliette, like most children, regardless of gender, wanted to be a Knight. She wanted a fine horse, black with a white star on its forehead and she would call it Galiano, Gali for short. She would have armour, shiny and glittering; and she would go off on quests and adventures and save villagers from evil men who lived in dark, gloomy castles; and save farmers from greedy barons and lords. For her, imagining such things was easy. She saw those pictures in her mind as clear as people see things that are in front of them. She could dream an experience and swear it was true. She could hear the words and sounds, smell the smells in a dream as clear as people lived their daily lives.

The sun shone into their eyes for most of the journey because of the direction they were travelling. It was mid-summer, and now mid-morning the temperature was approaching 35 degrees – even the birds had taken shade in the sparse Cypress trees that dotted their route like abandoned sculptures. The still day was engulfed in the haze of the heat and they toiled to walk in its presence.

Her father became aware of it first. A small dot in the distance. *A goat maybe, or even a stray cow,* he thought. *Too large for a feral dog or a wild boar,* he concluded. *A bush maybe, yes, perhaps a bush,* but he had the sense that it was coming closer to them and at the same pace they were getting closer to it. It troubled him. After so long walking alone, with nothing on the horizon, as far as the eye could see, seeing something now was slightly unsettling.

Ten minutes later, he could see that the thing was walking. *Mmm, not a bush then,* he thought. He strained to see. He fidgeted with the small knife sheathed in his tunic belt, knowing it offered little or no protection but for some reason he felt a little comforted by it.

After a while Juliette noticed it too. At first, she paid no mind to it. It was whatever it was and it had nothing to do with them. However, as it got a little closer, she began to feel anxious, and as the minutes grew, so did her unease.

"What is it, Papa?" she asked, her father's consternation palpable and his concentration on the thing that neared became more visible. He strained to see.

"Keep walking girl, we've far to go." He tried to remove the tension from his voice but he could hear it in his words – they were swimming in it. He knew there hadn't been many cases of robbery on the road but this was the first time he was travelling with the girl. This time there was another soul for him to be mindful of. He kept his pace, he didn't hurry, he didn't slow down. Eyes firmly fixed on the ever-closing spec before them and the promise he had made his wife to keep the girl safe. He knew he could turn right around and go home. The track led right back to their farm; it was the first building they would come across, the first sign of life. If they walked a good pace for two hours, the approaching shape might not catch them. He could get home. Lock the door. Stay hidden. He shook his head, as if to dispel the silly thought from his mind. He stayed his course and kept walking forward.

Suddenly the farmer stopped. He was agitated and unsure of what to do. The girl was happy for the rest; her legs ached, her feet slightly sore where her leather sandals rubbed and she was hot and thirsty. Her father squinted, straining his eyes. He held his hand over them to shield them from the glare of the sun, desperate for some sign of what neared them – as they neared it! He wiped his forehead with the sleeve of his coarse, brown tunic, and breathed deeply and ruefully. There was no one else around. No sound. No wind. No shade. No hiding place! He sighed again.

The figure moved ever closer. Its pace slow and steady but with long strides – which made it seem tall. It didn't veer, pause or linger. It didn't slow or increase its pace, it strode, solidly, almost stoically the farmer mused; its resolve and purpose of direction almost tacit.

Minutes went by but they seemed like hours to Juliette's father.

"Who is it, Papa"? Now she asked 'who' and not 'what' because it was now clear that it was indeed a 'who'. In the distance the stranger continued their unrelenting pace. Tall and proud, the figure gained ground ever closer.

"I don't know, girl. I can't make it out." Her father continued to strain his eyes in morning sun. "Stay still and we shall see …" He stopped speaking as if a thought had just come into his mind. "… and keep your counsel, girl. Say nothing if the person should happen to linger. We don't see many strangers come this way. Not now, not in these times, not anymore, not since ..." her father's words petered off as he focused on the stranger. "Just mind your words and your manners." He was visibly very unsettled.

The two now waited, the farmer and the girl. The road was the only road; there were no junctions between them, no side tracks. The stranger would walk their way.

The farmer gave the girl some water, which she drank in gulps, he sipped a little himself, then he took her hand. "Remember, Juliette, until we know we are safe, you are a boy." He pulled her close but tried to reassure her with a smile. It didn't work and all thoughts of heroic deeds and a white-starred horse called Gali, fled from Juliette's mind.

Ten minutes later and the figure was upon them; they could now clearly see that the figure was a man. Despite signs of fatigue and obvious signs he had been on the road for many days, he strode with such grace and confidence, it made his gait seem almost majestic.

The stranger was now only 100 yards away. They could clearly make out the flowing robes of a holy man. Once white, the thick woven cloth of his long, hooded robe, now carried with it the dust and toil of many roads and tracks. The stranger was an old man. He had a white, unkempt beard and white flowing hair, below shoulder length. His skin, olive in colour, was stained and leathery by the searing sun; his cracked lips parched like the roads he had travelled. He did not stoop forward or bend, despite his weariness. He strode straight and true. His eyes were as blue as the sky and as clear as spring water. He held his head up straight, proud with conviction and meaning. Around his robes a frayed rope belt was tied loosely, knotted three times at each end. It held a wooden cross. Around his neck, unusually for a holy man, he wore an amulet, a bronze disc with a five-pointed pentagon star in the centre. The farmer didn't understand its meaning or significance; the farmer didn't take notice of it.

Other than his worn sandals and a gnarly, old, elm wood staff he carried to aid his journey, he seemed to have no other possessions. No food, no water, no weapon, no implement for striking fire.

The girl felt her father's hand tighten slightly. Then he let out a gasp. "By the grace of our Lord God Almighty." Her father crossed his chest with the sign of the cross. "It's impossible. Bow your head, girl." He turned to the girl. "Bow your head." She lowered her head and went to speak. "Shhh, know thy manners and say nothing," her father said, "for we are in the presence of a Cathar holy man, one of the White Perfects." He let his daughter's hand go and then he lowered his head in reverence. "I thought they'd all been hunted down and killed," he whispered.

At last the stranger stood before them, they could make out his dusty, wrinkled, sun-beaten face, half in shadow from the hood that covered his head. He smiled warmly. He stood well over six feet tall and towered above the girl and the farmer. They were the only three humans for as far as the eye could see. No preying eyes, no over-hearing ears. The holy man bowed slightly; his appearance was shabbier and dustier now he was close up and in front of them.

The farmer cleared his throat. "Holy Father," he started, "by God's good grace, your kind still walk amongst us. Praise the Lord for his mercies and for giving us good fortune. We are indeed blessed. I never thought I would see one of your kind again." The farmer made the sign of the cross over his chest.

"We are indeed still here my friend, but only just." The holy man chuckled, his dry throat rasping his voice from the dust and the heat. "Our numbers are few these days. Most of us are indeed dead, God rest their souls, and there are many that would see us all dead. But for now, at least, as you can see, I am very much alive." He chuckled again.

"I have not seen your kind for … let me see now, it must be nigh on forty years," the farmer said. "Forty years," he repeated.

The holy man's face now took on a thoughtful look. "On our last count, I hear tell there were only twenty-three of us left. Twenty-three, where there used to be thousands." He shook his head at the thought of it. "No, wait, I speak wrongly. Let me see now," his thoughtful look deepened, "that count was done … yes, yes, ten years ago now, so the number must be lower. I must confess I suspect it is lower." The Cathar holy man raised his hand to shield his eyes and looked at the sun to estimate what time of day it was. He breathed a fatigued sigh and pushed sweat from his leathery, tanned brow. "Of course," he went on, "we should have all been dead because of the Catholics." The holy man paused, sad in thought, his face rueful. Off somewhere a crow screeched and it echoed in the still of the long, hot day.

"What did they do, sir, the Catholics?" the girl asked, intrigued by the holy man and forgetting her father's words to say nothing. Her voice snapped the holy man out of his thoughts.

"Why, they killed us, my boy. They killed us all but for a few.

10

They launched an Inquisition, the terrible Albigensian crusade, as it is known by now. They had one goal: to wipe us all out. And not just us, mind, but all practising Cathars: French men, women and children, all Christians alike. They murdered us by the tens of thousands." He laughed; it was an incongruous laugh. "Do you know that the Greek word *Katholikos*, the origin of the word Catholic, means universal. Imagine that, the Catholic Church accepting one and all: universal."

The farmer was apologetic that his daughter had spoken directly to the holy man. "Please excuse her … him, Father." The farmer slipped up, but he saved himself at the last second. "He is young. He does not mean to be impertinent."

The holy man smiled at the farmer, and then at the girl. "It's okay, my friend, don't fret so. It is healthy to be curious, it's the way we learn." He turned to the girl. "It was their crusade against us. It was the first crusade that wasn't against Muslims. The first crusade to attack fellow Christians. It was the first genocide France had seen." He paused and looked at the sun again and sighed. "Mmm, alas, the day's moving on and I'm afraid I've been talking far too much. I fear I have delayed you from your journey and conveniently forgotten about mine. I have many more miles to go and need to be on my way."

"I am one that is pleased your kind still walks amongst us, Father. It's a joyous thing," said the farmer. "You will always find a welcome at my door should you ever have the need, and any of your kind."

The holy man smiled. "Praise the Lord. You are a kind man. I'm pleased our presence can still bring joy to my fellow brethren of France." He was speaking to the farmer, but he was looking at the girl; there was something odd and yet familiar about her that he couldn't quite put his finger on. "Forgive an old monk for going on in the heat of the day without introducing myself. My name is Father Jacque Durand."

The farmer cleared his throat. "And forgive us, Father," the farmer said. "My name is Jon Trevin and this is Thomas Trevin, my son."

The girl smiled shyly, somewhat embarrassed by the lie – it seemed worse because it was being said to a holy man.

The holy man raised his hands jubilantly. "Ha," he cried out. "God is indeed merciful. What a splendid miracle, my search ends here then. I thought I had at least three more hours of road to cover before getting to your farm." He looked at the girl again and realised their ruse; now it was clear she was no boy and, by her looks, who she really was. "God is gracious, Jon, to save an old monk's feet. God is gracious indeed. I have found you."

The dust kicked up by the horses in the distance had not been seen by either the holy man, the farmer or the girl.

"You were going to my farm, Father, to see me?" the farmer asked, confused.

"Yes, Jon, yes, yes," the holy man said excitedly. "I am journeying to see you and—"

"But … I don't understand, Father," the farmer interrupted. "What would you want at my farm, with me?"

Father Jacque Durand raised his hand to his eyes again; something on the horizon had caught his attention. "I need …" he started to explain but didn't finish. He saw the dust. The farmer turned to see what the holy man was looking at. He too saw the unmistakable sign of horsemen riding towards them: and fast.

"Can you make them out?" the farmer asked, straining to see who they were.

The holy man sighed a woeful sigh. "Yes," he said, "I'm afraid I can."

"Should we be worried, Father?" he asked the holy man.

"Yes," he replied.

"Are they coming for you, Father?"

"No," the holy man said.

"Then who?" the farmer asked.

"They're coming for this girl."

The girl looked at the farmer.

"No, that can't be so. You are mistaken Father. This is my son—"

"But we both know she's not; she's not your son, neither is she your daughter. In fact, she is not a Trevin; she does not have your name. She is a Romée; she bears that name. I've come because we need her; we need her help, Jon."

The girl was scared. She turned to the farmer. "Papa … what is he saying?"

The farmer looked distraught. He turned to the holy man. "Please, Father, you don't understand …"

"But I do, Jon," the holy man said. "I understand better than you think. I have not come to hurt her, I have come to protect her and ask for her help." He stopped and looked again at the riders approaching at speed. "No time now. You must get her off the road before they get here. They will not spare you and they will take the girl."

The farmer put his arm around Juliette; she was shaking.

"Who are they, Papa? Why will they kill us?"

"I don't know, child," the farmer said. He took her hand and started to move away from the holy man.

The farmer turned and called back, "Who are they, Father?"

"They are Abaddon *Alqatala*, Jon," the holy man replied.

"What manner of men are Abaddon *Alqatala*?"

"They are assassins, Jon. They are Abaddon *Alqatala*; it means Abaddon assassins."

"Then are we done for, Father?"

"It's a good question, Jon. Quickly now, off the road."

The horses were frothing at the mouth and breathing hard, sweat running down their foreheads, withers and necks. Eight thudding hooves hitting the dry, parched, hard ground. The noise almost thunderous as they came upon the holy man. The two assassins were dressed like Arabs. "*Merde*," the Cathar cried. Moors, why did they have to be Moors?"

The two riders did not slow down as they neared the holy man; they did not pull on their reins. As they got closer, and in unison, they jumped from their worn, leather saddles, their long, radical curved shamshir swords – a lethal weapon from the scimitar sword family – already out and ready. They wore black turbans with the final folds of cloth wrapped around their faces so you could see only their dark, murderous eyes. They had long black tunics covering most of their bodies, revealing a glimpse of the white trouser fabric and dusty, brown leather riding boots. In their black waist belts, two Janbiya curved hand daggers each: sharp and deadly. A pale-blue cloak swished about in tempo with their body movements. The Moors used their cloaks as distraction; they were masters with a sword in one hand and cloak in the other, to cause maximum distraction. They did not speak other than to utter two things: *masihiun* – 'Christian', they said, and then, *tabut* – the name the Quran gives the Ark of the Covenant.

The holy man dropped his staff. He reached behind his head and slowly drew his sword from a scabbard strapped to his back and hidden under his hooded robe. It was a Katana sword – used by Samurai and Ronin for centuries but not seen in France. The slightly curved, single edged blade, had a white ribbed elongated handle to facilitate a double grip. He stood, face on to them, feet apart in a wide stance, left foot slightly forward, hips facing forward, a bend in the knee, his sword held high with a grip on the right side to the mouth, at an angle of 45 degrees, pointing backwards, his elbows tucked in. He was poised in the traditional Kendo style. "*Alkilab*" was the only word he uttered: "dogs". He started controlling his breathing and slowed everything down and shut everything out, other than them.

The assassins struck out at the holy man in long, arching, slicing movements. Like threshing blades their swords flew through the air with frightening speed and ferocity. Their blades were not made for thrusting and stabbing; to thrust they had to turn their hand over, so that the back of their hand would be facing their face and the blade would then be upside down, then they could thrust. They seldom used this, within a few seconds both knew it would be pointless, their opponent was too good to be fooled by the technique. They advanced using full arc slicing movements. Their swords would not cut deep but the wounds they inflicted would be much longer than a normal sword, sometimes 20 to 30 inches. Their movements flowed like a deadly synchronised dance. Edging forward; cloaks flaming like restless, raging fires in a deadly dance duet. They lurched forward; again, and again they tested his reactions and strength. They synchronised their attack, searching for his weaknesses.

The holy man was well trained, and for his age, he was quick and nimble – this took them by surprise but he was just one man, and they were two. The holy man breathed slowly, like a yogi mastering some feat of strength but showing no signs of effort. At times the holy man closed his eyes as he turned slowly on the spot, feeling their presence, feeling their breathing. He held the centre spot, digging his feet into the dusty road, to anchor, to balance. The circle he created in the dried earth was no more than 18 inches in diameter; as he rotated and defended each attack. Using two-handed strokes, he was able to block some of the long slice from the assassins and counter with a combination of thrusts and short diagonal cuts. With some of their strikes he didn't block them with his sword, he moved and deflected the blows to protect his blade. Swords are not indestructible and he knew that two swords raining down on his blade, would soon begin to dent the blade edge. He was smart; his skill was superior and this visibly unsettled the assassins. What they saw was a dishevelled old monk; what they were fighting was a master swordsman who advanced, blocked, deflected, cut, thrust, lunged, sliced and pivoted.

The first assassin felt the Katana blade; he fell foul to the holy man's subterfuge, a well delivered bait and switch. A move to the left but then a quick turn and a twist of the body and the holy man struck.

The sword came down from the left. His cry of 'Kiai' melding the body, mind and sword together. The diaphragm contracting and then, an explosive attack. It hit the assassin in the neck and, like rice paper, it drove through. The assassin fell to the ground, his neck almost sliced through, his head flopping over on a skin and sinew hinge; he hit the ground with a thud.

The farmer gripped his dagger in his belt. He so wanted to help the holy man. He wanted to help defend him but fear struck him motionless and he was glued to the spot. The girl watched; she could not look away.

The second assassin spotted the amulet worn around the monk's neck and now realised that the man they had tracked from Rennes le Chateau, was not just an old, worn out monk; he now realised that the rumours were true, that the few Cathar monks that were left had joined forces with the Knights Templar. Had he known, he would have insisted on four assassins.

He let out a yell, more to bolster his own resolve than scare his opponent. He lunged forward, slicing high left to low right, then high right to low left. Across, two, three, four body shots, and then diagonal; one carving motion after another, one, two three … eight, nine … on and on they went. His blade crashing down towards the holy man's body, torso and legs. The holy man blocked and deflected each of the hard blows. If any one of them had landed, they would have killed him instantly.

The assassin continued to advance but he was now breathing hard – they had been fighting for nearly ten minutes. The sun was unforgiving. Father Jacque Durand maintained his slow and low breathing discipline to regulate the amount of oxygen going into his blood vessels and heart, so he would not start to hyperventilate and lose stamina. He knew the battle would not be won through brute strength, it would be won by the sun. His body movements were using as little energy as possible; he moved rhythmically, graceful and deadly.

Having led with his left leg for the entire fight, the holy man suddenly changed stance to lead with his right leg. It was like fighting a northpaw, who just switched to southpaw. To change from a right to a southpaw meant that not only did he have to change feet, he also had to change hands, so his left hand was on top of his sword grip. Samurai swordsmen carry their swords on the left and draw right handed, even if they are left handed, they are only taught to fight righthanded. A Japanese teacher would not teach someone to fight left handed, but Father Jacque Durand had been taught by a master tactician. The change of stance was fast. He advanced, sprang, swiped, stabbed, checked, and punctured. Thrust after thrust, slice after slice. The assassin was bleeding and he was all but done.

He looked around desperately for an advantage point; he knew he was outmatched and risked death. He was breathing hard. Gasping. He needed to end it soon or it would end him. He made for the man and the girl on the side of the road. They were just ten feet way. He ran towards them, blade raised ready to strike. The farmer turned to run. The holy man chased after the assassin, catching his shoulder with a downward stroke. The assassin tripped, fell forward towards the farmer and the girl. He managed to roll, the forward motion pushed him to his knees, his sword raised again and held high and to the left, ready for a downward slice. He was about to swing it down with all his might towards the larger target first, the farmer.

From the left, the girl grabbed her father's dagger. She lunged at the assassin. She let out a yell as she drove it into him without any regard for her own life. The dagger hit the back of the assassin's neck and severed an artery. He never saw it coming. He grabbed at the area of the excruciating pain. He found the blade and pulled. Blood gushed out. His life ebbed out and then the second of the Abaddon assassins was dead.

Father Jacque Durand fell to his knees, exhausted. The girl now stood beside him. "By my Lord God Almighty," he gasped breathlessly, "you have your mother's bravery, girl. Thank you." She handed him his staff and he scrambled back on to his feet.

The farmer gave him some water and the holy man drank, his

17

breathing still fast as he fought to control the adrenalin and slow his breathing down.

"What's your name, girl?" he asked.

"Juliette, sir," she answered.

"Well, Juliette, I think it's about time that Jon and I told you what's going on, right, Jon?"

The farmer nodded, realising that the Cathar knew exactly who Juliette was.

"The lady that gave birth to you does not live on your farm," the holy man started. "The lady who gave birth to you saved our country France, God rest her soul. She had courage and she had the 'sight'. You have your mother's courage, I need to see if you have the 'sight' as well."

Juliette turned to her father. "I don't understand … who was my mother?"

Chapter 2
Two Roses

Date: Present day

By 2012 many things had changed for the Templars since they were formed in 1119 and sent out to the Holy Land by the King of France to protect Christian pilgrims. Back then, they were a fearless band of warrior monks. They were not in the shadows and they did not hide. They were known by all and they fought openly in the crusades. However, after their almost total destruction, on Friday the 13th, 1307, they went underground. They became a highly secret organisation: they only existed in the shadows.

In 2012, they were a fighting force that was skilled in modern day weaponry and tactics, but not all its weapons were modern. The Cathar monk, Father Jacque Durand, first changed one part of the Templars' fighting tradition. Until he came along, the Templars always fought with the long sword. This was the weapon that dominated their crusades but it was heavy and it was cumbersome. Knights would quickly tire wielding the heavy longsword, whilst wearing armour and in the heat of the Middle East; as the battle wore on, so the Knights would grow more fatigued. Father Jacque Durand was the monk that had found Juliette Romée on the road to Carcassonne and saved her life from Abaddon assassins. He also introduced the Templars to the Katana sword, the sword used by the Samurai of Japan.

Earlier in Father Durand's life, he had befriended, and was trained for three years by a Japanese Shinto monk. The monk, whose name was Kiyoshi, meaning soundless, was a Samurai warrior in Japan. He told the Cathar holy man he had worked for a local Lord, who was an evil tyrant. After years of doing his master's bidding, Kiyoshi said he grew tired of the killing and intimidation his master demanded his Samurai inflict on any villagers not paying their taxes. The villagers were poor and if it had been a bad growing season, many could not pay the steep taxes the local Lord imposed on them. Samurai worshiped Hachiman, the Shinto god of war, and enforced the local lord's barbaric and feudal justice.

Kiyoshi told Father Durand that one day he'd just had enough, so he left and wandered rural Japan as a Ronin – a Samurai without a master. He became destitute and starving. However, he was taken in by Shinto monks and nursed back to health and, as it turned out, to salvation. He became a monk himself, worshiped Inari, the Shinto god of agriculture, prosperity, finance and industry, and travelled the strange lands of the white Europeans, spreading the Shinto word: he had become a missionary and met Father Durand whilst in France.

From then on, every Knight Templar was meticulously trained in the use of the Katana sword. And, just as a sword had been part of the weapons of choice for the Templars of old, the sword remains part of the Templars' weapons of choice today, along with hand guns, rifles, machine guns and a whole range of other small artillery.

However, Templars also needed to be as skilled with technology as they were with their swords and modern weaponry. In 2012, the technology highway was fast becoming the new battleground and the fight against evil, injustice and tyranny was just as important there as on a battle field. The ability to hack a target's communication system, their digital data storage systems, and security surveillance systems was paramount. Understand digital processes, procedures and systems. Read them, disrupt them, copy them, use them, close them down. Wipe them clean or manipulate them. They needed speed of information so they could stay one step ahead of those criminals.

Whilst they attacked their enemies using digital means, they themselves had to make sure they were completely hacker proof. They needed solid security within their own communication and digital network; they needed their digital security to be as advanced and secure as it could be. Leading the security for the Knights Templar was a key role that guarded the lives of some 3,000 Knights. After the Salah El-Din mission, they knew they needed to find someone who could create a solid digital shield around them.

Dominique had installed 5G into their network. The Templars had had 5G nearly four years before commercial operators. It was many times faster than the 4G they'd been using but integrating the new technology took her and her team over a year. It improved the latency issues, and the delay issues that frustrated so many of them, and it vastly increased the responsiveness. They now had better coverage and more capacity and could now use billions of bits per second (GBPS) – a measure of bandwidth on a digital data transmission. However, Dominique knew it wasn't enough, not nearly enough. Every part of their systems needed attention and she really needed to add to their technical operative numbers.

Hacking was one of her primary concerns. Maverick hackers surfing the internet would occasionaly stumble on a Templar digital trail. Cybercrime was her worst nightmare. Whilst cybercrime was estimated to cost businesses up to $2 trillion per year, it could cost a Templar his or her life. She needed to reduce the digital 'attack surface' from hobbyist hackers and from their enemies. She needed to support their legacy encryption systems but also upgrade them at the same time. It was a mountain to climb for Dominique.

Her team was too small and her knowledge base was being stretched to the limit, the requirement on their resources was growing and technology developing and expanding at a tremendous rate. She needed to 'future proof' their infrastructure. She needed to decommission some of the older systems and replace them with new technology. She needed help and did not have the time or the increasing skill set to carry out the upgrade they needed: but she knew the very person that did.

Courtney Rose had undergone a number of major changes in the past four years. For a start, she was still dead! Four years ago, the name Courtney Rose had been entered onto the missing person's list with the Washing DC Police Department. Two hours later, her frozen, charred corpse was discovered. Her file was then transferred to two detectives working in homicide: her case had never been solved and she was still officially dead.

Courtney was four years older than her brother, Jonathan. She was not married. She was a Harvard graduate, with a double honour's degree in criminology, as well as a doctorate in computer sciences. She had worked as a desk-based FBI agent on one of the most powerful computers in the world. She liked science, math and puzzles. She had a mind that was logical, clinical and rational. After Cumbria, she had stayed on at the castle to help out. This meant spending time with Dominique and helping her with the communications network and implementing 5G.

There was small group of people who worked in the communications centre at the castle; there were also a number of satellite teams strategically placed around the world, working out of either safe houses or hiding in plain sight in office buildings.

The main communications control room in the castle, the heart of their operations, was called exactly that: 'the control room', or CR for short. Since Cumbria, Dominique had increased her head count in the CR – she'd gone from two to eleven but it still wasn't enough.

Courtney had become a Knight in 2010, and in 2011 she was asked to take over the role of Head of Communications from Dominique. This left Dominique free to become the 'Guardian of the

Seer'. Jonathan was the Seer, and she loved and teased him mercilessly. She kept telling him he had to do exactly as she said: always. Dominique was also given the role as Second Lead on missions; her father, Zakariah, was appointed as Mission Team Leader upon his return to the Order.

The first thing Courtney did was to increase the CR headcount even more. She then undertook a major IT upgrade. Part of the restructuring was to close down the Hyderabad satellite office that covered Asia and South East Asia. Until that point, it had been entirely run by one man, an Oxford graduate who had a first in Computer Science, specialising in Nanotechnology, Artificial Intelligence, Blockchain, Advanced Electronics and Gaming. His name was Bertram De'Ath. Bertram was a genius – albeit slightly eccentric, or perhaps very eccentric. He was born Bertram Hubert De'Ath, in Calcutta, India, in 1987. And whilst Calcutta changed its name to Kolkata in 2001, Bertram always insisted on using the old name and spelling. Bertram had a distinctive look: white teeth, deep black skin, curly unkept hair and acne. He looked 12 but he was 25 years old. His father had been a Templar and so had his grandfather. Bertram had got his brains from his mother's side; he lacked the combat skills from his father's side.

In 2012, Bertram was offered the new role as deputy Head of Communications, to be based in Scotland. His new role was to support Courtney and be her second in command. He accepted, and then closed down the Hyderabad office within three weeks. He then sent an email to Courtney with some ideas, caught a plane and arrived in Scotland.

Bertram was waiting for Courtney and Dominique in one of the meeting rooms. Courtney was reading his email on her tablet on the way to the meeting. Dominique was with her.

"These are good ideas, you know," Courtney said to Dominique. "What he's suggesting is pretty revolutionary, also brilliant. He wants to immediately create and then put everything on the cloud, our own cognitive cloud that will store and process all our data; this will be so secure it should help negate most of our concerns about hackers and cyber criminals. It will make our coms so much simpler, faster, and cheaper as well. We will have an internet that's more secure, and it will do so much more than ever before." She read on. "He is suggesting radical new ways of constructing our digital architecture, how we consume and create data, and operate networks across our software, hardware, and optical solutions. Damn, this guy's good," she said. "He wants AI, blockchain technology that will continuously measure application performance." She moved her eyes to the bottom of the email, to his name and details. "What's this guy's na—" she stopped short when she read his name. "It's De'Ath?" she asked.

"It is," Dominique replied.
"Are you su—"
"Yup, very sure. It's pronounced 'De'Ath'."
"You do know it spells death, right?"
"I know."
"Do you think he knows?"
"I don't know. Actually, I've never physically met him. We have always met virtually. I have never mentioned the name thing to him."

Jonathan Rose
It had been four years since they almost captured Salah El-Din in 2008. It was then that the Templars discovered Jonathan had the Seer's gift; it was back then that the Ark of the Covenant healed his lifeless body.

In the last four years many things had happened to Jonathan, but none more important than his marriage to Dominique St Clair, in 2010. The daughter of Zakariah St Claire and niece of Payne St Clair, Grand Master of the Knights Templar.

Only four people went to their wedding because Templars

24

rarely go about in more than twos or threes because of the risk, unless they are 'mission active'. Her father, Zakariah, her uncle, Payne St Claire, Zakariah's brother, Jonathan's sister, Courtney Rose were there and the fourth person was André Sabath, a man she had known since she was a baby. Sabath was her godfather and mentor. He was also one of the Nine Worthies who sat on the Higher Council of the Knights Templar.

The wedding was held in the birth place of her mother: Italy. Dominique was raised in Italy before being sent to Mary Thomas's, a private boarding school for girls in the heart of the Derbyshire countryside. After that she went off to finishing school in Switzerland. Dominique was independent and strong willed. She'd never had any interest in men or complicated relationships. Then she met Jonathan Rose, the ex-priest from Washington DC and everything changed. The Templar that everyone thought would never marry and everyone called *the girl,* was married to a man they all thought would never become a Templar, a man everyone called *the priest.*

Dominique had an impeccable upper-crust British accent; Jonathan was an American with a slight Washington lilt. She had the same drive, same focus and ambition as his sister, Courtney. Her skin was tanned due to her Italian heritage. Rarely without her mirrored Ray-Ban sunglasses. She was pretty, intelligent and had a presence about her that Jonathan loved. When he had first met her, he had a sense there was a softer side to her nature: he was right. She was small and petite, but could put most trained men flat on their backs without breaking a sweat. She had short, mousy brown hair, and was attractive. He teased her and said she looked like Kate Beckinsale in the *Underworld* film poster, clad in a black leather all-in-one suit looking menacing and ready for action.

She was a 7th Dan in karate, skilled with firearms who favoured a Heckler Koch .40 and a pump-action 12-gauge shotgun, designed for smaller shooters. She was a skilled Backgammon player.

Of late, on Thursday evenings, she liked to make toasted ravioli and drink Dolcetto red wine with Jonathan in front of the fire and talk about their dreams and aspirations, or watch old black and white movies together.

Eighteen months ago, Dominique and Jonathan moved into a small, remote, rented cottage just outside of the town of Kirkcudbright, in Dumfries and Galloway, Scotland. They loved the tranquillity and remoteness. Surrounded by moss and lichen covered drystone walls, the Scots call dykes. The walls, placed to delineate boundaries and corral cows and sheep, traversed the rolling, lush green, undulating hills that stretched for miles over the grazing landscape. The night sky was not diluted by millions of electric light bulbs and the bright majestic hues of thousands of stars in the Milky Way, hung like a gargantuan Christmas light display.

They moved in with few belongings that didn't have a qwerty keyboard, a circuit board, a barrel and a trigger, a blade, or something that would detonate given a fuse, or timing device. They did, however, move in with two South African Ridgeback puppies called Cleo and Simba. Adorable red wheaten male and female – brother and sister. They had a telephone landline installed, dialling code 01557, but no one had the number – it was just part of the ruse. Kirkcudbright was always full of artists and attracted many visitors; this added to the tourist traffic that swelled in the summer months. So, their comings and goings just dovetailed into the ebb and flow of people in and out of the seasonal town.

The Roses liked nothing more than walking their dogs on the beach on cold winter mornings, when very few people ventured out. However, there was always one person out walking her dogs, called Dusty and Nell, about the same time as the Roses, her name was Elaine Wall. She had become the closest to an acquaintance the Roses had, outside of Templar life. Meeting Elaine on the beach gave them a shot of normality, and, for an hour or so, as the dogs played and they chatted, it took them away from the secret, double lives they led.

26

Elaine was retired and lived close by with her husband. She had met him when she took a helicopter ride in San Francisco – he piloted the sightseeing rides under the Golden Gate Bridge. Elaine was blond haired, green eyed and of medium build. Originally from South Gloucestershire, she and her husband had retired to Scotland. She always had perfect, manicured nails and Dominique liked that, despite being retired, she always took the time with her nails and her appearance. Dominique even got nail tips from her. Elaine loved history, liked reading and walking her dogs; these ticked all the Roses' boxes. Her love of sunny mornings, nature, waking up every day, her distain for intolerance and cruelty, ticked the others for the Roses. Elaine looked forward to bumping into them and chatting to the young couple that she had come to like.

Jonathan and Dominique told Elaine they were education consultants and worked on high stakes, education reform programmes around the world. When they needed to travel, Elaine would always take Cleo and Simba for them. Elaine loved dogs and dogs loved Elaine.

The only other person they interacted with was their housekeeper, Morag Beverley Clements, a widow in her late 50s, who minded her own business and was thorough with her work. Jonathan and Dominique again used the ruse that they were education consultants. No one ever actually asked them what that meant. Dominique set up a false Facebook page, which was maintained by the Order, along with a website and company registered at Companies House, together with annual accounts that would withstand any cursory look.

Jonathan had developed new skills during those four years. He had become accomplished at self-defence. He had been trained by John Wolf, the 41-year-old Shawnee Indian Knight, before Wolf returned home to Kentucky, where he lived and worked. Wolf held the post of Protector of the Western Kentucky Indian Burial Sites, since he was 22 years old. His job was to protect the ancient Indian burial sites from weekend surface hunters, para-archaeologists, grave robbers and commercial operators. Wolf, like his father before him, was a proud man; the embodiment of the wild and rugged land on which he lived. He was Johnathan's favourite teacher because Wolf also had a wicked sense of humour and often they could be heard giggling like two schoolboys down the corridors of the castle, hatching some new dastardly plan to annoy Dominique or frustrate the Russian, or both of them.

However, it had been the Russian, Nickolin Klymachak, a hardened vet of the Afghan war, who'd trained Jonathan the hardest and therefore the best. Unlike the Indian, the Russian hadn't wasted his time with pranks and practical jokes. Nickolin had stayed on at the castle after the disappearance of Salah El-Din back in 2008 and had used his combat skills to hone the training of many Knights. There was always a stream of Knights arriving and leaving the castle: some for training or retraining; some for preparation and planning for one of the many missions the Templars undertook around the world. Some came to be close to their 'Charge', the Ark of the Covenant. Others came because they had heard of the sanction team that fought in Cumbria and wanted to meet the Russian, the Indian, the Girl and, the new Seer, the Priest. They were now minor celebrities in the Knights' ranks – although they each cringed at the thought and did everything possible to discourage the notoriety.

Jonathan was a reluctant student. He was always trying to find an excuse not to train. It was hard work. It was harder because Nickolin Klymachak was the teacher. At times, Dominique took on the role of his martial arts teacher. However, he tried to discourage this tutor because getting the stuffing kicked out of him by his wife did nothing for his self-confidence: he spent most of the lesson on his butt.

Jonathan also spent a lot of time with Payne St Clair, as they continued to seek the meaning of the encrypted messages hidden within the Ten Commandments, placed in the Ark of the Covenant.

Once a week, they would journey down into the bowels of the castle, through a maze of underground tunnels, dug out of the rock foundations of the castle centuries before, to where the Ark was now hidden and protected. The tunnels had been expertly excavated and formed. Supporting the ceiling, at 10-yard intervals, were the most exquisite vaulted stone arches, barrel, domed, ribbed and pitched vaults. In perfect symmetry, the stonemasonry looked like subterranean art: the proportions and balance, stout and strong, yet integral and beautiful. Having walked the tunnels many times, Jonathan still had not been able to memorise the way, despite hundreds of visits.

St Clair and Jonathan would walk by the light of the burning torches they carried and also the light from wall-mounted burning torches – Templars were strong on traditions. Jonathan knew the tunnels either led to the outside somewhere, or that there was a vertical ventilation shaft that had been constructed as the air was always clean, always fresh and cool and the flames of the torches would flicker as they walked. He never asked about it. He had learnt a long time ago that when St Clair wanted you to know something, it was for a good reason and he would tell you. When he didn't want you to know something, it was for an equally good reason and he would not tell you.

Jonathan liked a specific area they always passed through on their way to the Ark. It was a stretch of about 500 yards. Along the walls were small niches and, in every niche, an urn, ten inches high, black in colour, a rounded body but with a narrowed neck. Each had a lid on it. And on each black urn, the Templar red cross. St Clair had told him, when they had first walked the underground tunnels, they held the ashes of nearly every Knight that had fallen in combat. Centuries of proud and valiant men and women who had served their God and their Order, with total commitment and deep grace. St Clair always whispered a prayer as he passed this place – Jonathan had started doing the same.

Above them, as they walked, at intervals of every 300 yards, were a number of alloy steel doors hidden in the tunnel ceiling. They were big, six inches thick and they were solid and strong. Jonathan guessed they were to seal off the tunnels at given points if the need ever arose. He concluded that one of the uses of the underground tunnels was the Templars' escape route, should the need ever arise. What he didn't know was the harsh lessons the Templars had learnt in Jerusalem and in Acre, in the 13th century, before they were driven from the Holy Land for good by their nemeses.

About two miles in, one of the tunnels they followed would suddenly turn sharp left at a forty-five-degree angle. Jonathan always recognised this part because it meant they had arrived at their destination. The whole journey took them around 30 minutes. Without hand-held torches, it looked like the left turn ended, and there was just rock face; there were no wall mounted torches from which to cast a burning flame in this section of the tunnel, just the ones they carried. However, as they approached and their flame light hit the rock, a door could be seen nestled back in an alcove. A seven-digit code opened the reinforced, tungsten door to reveal a small, perfectly rounded room with the same exquisite stonework in the form of a cupola domed stone ceiling.

The Ark of the Covenant was kept in a dull, silver alloy box. St Clair always approached it with reverence. He would press the tips of his fingers against the side of the box so that his fingerprints were held flat, then he would whisper something, an incantation, a prayer that Jonathan could never catch. He thought it was Latin but he didn't know. Then, the sides of the alloy box would slowly fold down into small, one-centimetre concertina sections, taking the lid with it. They would then have to wait. Sometimes nothing happened and sometimes, after 20 minutes or so, blue smoke would appear and their patience rewarded. Small at first, but it would grow. A strange rumbling noise, like faraway thunder, would seep out of the empty space before them and echo in the rock chamber. Then a shimmer would appear, slowly forming a shape, hazy and glimmering, transparent. A square shape would begin to form. Gold, then silver, then a myriad of colours, all fusing into one another like a rainbow exploding in front of their eyes. The thunder would intensify. Jonathan's stomach would churn with the sound and the vibration it caused: and with the awesome sight of the stunning spectacle before them. At this point, St Clair, his voiced raised above the noise, would recite ancient words. The shape would grow more pronounced. And then, the Ark would fully appear. Magnificent. Glorious. Reverent in its own grace. Made of acacia wood and overlaid in pure gold. Four gold rings attached to it and on the lid, two gold cherubim faced each other. The cherubim wings spread upwards, overshadowing the cover.

However, disappointingly for both men, their progress was slow and it frustrated them. Often the symbols did not appear for weeks and there was no logic or reason as to why. Often, when they did appear, they would only stay for a short while, sometimes for less than a few seconds, at other times for a few minutes, five at the most, but never more. They both felt that they could do more, should do more, but they were in the hands of the Ark.

One of the discoveries that Jonathan and St Clair made was that if they took the two stone tablets out of the Ark, and moved them away from the Ark by more than a few feet, the mystical symbols would fall from their levitated, rotating orb shape and then disintegrate into nothing. They would just fall mid shape and disappear, as though they were linked to the Ark in some way for their energy. St Clair had long since believed that the Ark was the key to whatever the symbols meant. It was a symbiotic relationship, the tablets and the Ark – you can't have one without the other; it just didn't work. You can have a car chassis and you can have an engine but if they're not together, nothing works. The car doesn't exist; both parts are on their own. St Clair also had a theory of what the Ark was and what, ultimately, the mystical symbols were, but it was just a hypothesis he could not prove, so he said nothing. He waited patiently, as he had always done, for a Seer to come along and tell him the answer.

St Clair had known three Seers during his time as Grand Master of the Knights Templar. Two Seers, Dumoun and Philippe, who were not Knights but civilians, crossed over to the Abaddons in the early sixties. Their treachery cost the lives of many Knights and the Order entered into a bloody, dark time. Without them, the Templars' work had been slow. It was frustrating and at times counteractive, as the Templars struggled to understand the complexities of something that they often thought could never be truly understood because it was of a divine origin: it was from God.

Sophia was the third Seer that Payne St Clair had known. She was the wife of his brother, Zakariah St Clair, and mother of his niece, Dominique St Clair. A senior maths professor, she was able to make inroads into understanding some of the time paradigms symbols it began to reveal to her. Her deep comprehension of maths, physics, gravitational time dilation and relativity offered the Templars glimpses into what might be possible, and it was then that St Clair began to suspect what the two tablets really were and why the Ark was built. But Sophia died. She died because she was a Seer.

Despite slow progress with the Ark, everything was well in Jonathan and Dominique's life, then Abu Dhabi happened!

Chapter 3
The New Lionheart

Part 1: The Funeral in The Rain

Date: September 1989
Place: A graveyard in Essex, UK

It was a bleak funeral; it was a sad funeral. All funerals are sad but this one had twice the sadness because it was a double funeral. Two deaths. Two lives lost because of a freak accident on the M1 motorway, which resulted in the death of a young couple, a husband and wife from Saffron Walden, Essex, England. It made the regional news, but that was all. They left behind a son: he was seven years old. The deceased male had one living relative in the United Kingdom, a father who lived in Southlodge, London, just south of the river, and was well known for all the wrong reasons. The deceased had been estranged from his father all his life. His mother and her family all lived in Spain; they sent flowers but failed to show up at the funeral. The female had a number of living relatives but they all lived nearly 3,500 miles away in Cameroon, Africa.

The small crowd gathered around the graveside – an oxymoron because only five people and one child stood there. They were wet and cold. Standing motionless, umbrellas open and aloft, their heads down and expressionless as the sombre internment stretched on, accompanied by the relentless sound of the rain beating down on their umbrellas and the headstones. Rat-a-tat-tat, rat-a-tat-tat. Unrelenting. Miserable.

The vicar, a man of some years with alarming eyebrows, steadfastly held his Bible and intoned the final prayer, as the rain beat against his bald head. The two coffins were slowly lowered inside the bleak, muddy, black holes. One at a time they made their way to their final resting places. The four gravediggers, or 'Burial Ground Custodians' as their name badges announced, lowered the elm boxes with expert precision.

The Vicar raised his voice above the rat-a-tat-tat of the rain. "We commit their bodies to the ground ..."

Winifred Mabel Doris Rushton held onto the boy's hand. It was a small hand, a cold, wet, trembling little hand; it was the hand of a frightened little boy: now an orphaned little boy. In her other hand, she held her black umbrella, shielding herself and the 7-year old from the September downpour that was punishing the day and all those that had ventured out. The trees in the cemetery now bare, their green coats long since gone in the coming of winter, standing like dark and menacing rustic statues. To the boy they looked like eerie ghosts, bending and twisting as they too battled the rain and the wind.

The vicar raised his hands and gazed heavenly as he uttered the good Lord's name, dark potent skies His representative on this day. Winifred Rushton didn't need to listen; she'd been to enough funerals to know the lines off by heart.

"... earth to earth," the vicar began, "ashes to ashes, dust to dust. The Lord bless them and keep them, the Lord maketh His face to shine upon them and be gracious unto them and give them peace." The gathering just wanted the service to be over. They found the grieving exhausting and the weather sapped their resolve.

Winifred squeezed the small hand, the frightened hand. The little boy didn't look up, his gaze firmly fixed on the two coffins lowered into the ground. The two coffins which held his parents, those odd-shaped boxes that represented the parents he loved, the parents he ached to hold again. He watched, still and quiet, knowing that he would never see their faces again. He would never hear their voices, never smell their smell again and never feel their love. The seven-year-old boy saw the soil scatter across the coffins. And then, it was over; they were over. It was done; the funeral, the burial, the words, were all done. It had taken less than thirty minutes.

Winifred led the boy away; his head was down, his face expressionless. The vicar walked with them, wiping his glasses with a neatly ironed handkerchief trying to avoid the puddles growing by the minute on the uneven cemetery path.

"I'm sorry, Winifred, not much of a turn out, I'm afraid." He walked her to her car – an old Mini Cooper, not one of the new flashy ones, but one of the old ones, she was proud of that fact. It was bright red and little worse for wear; it could barely cope with her 18 stone, but it had done so for the last fifteen years. "I could only get three people to come; my parishioners are not known for venturing out when it's wet and cold; arthritis, sciatica and dodgy hips, I'm afraid, the burdens of an ageing congregation." His apology wasn't needed, he had done his best. The Vicar always did his best when Winifred or one of her colleagues needed help. Other than the vicar, Winifred and the boy, the other people who attended the funeral had come because he, the vicar, had asked them. They didn't even know the deceased couple.

"It's not your fault, Father." Winifred assured the vicar in her distinctive, colourful Jamaican brogue. He held her umbrella and she searched her handbag for the keys to her car. "Bless you for trying, at least a few people made it. She moved a book in her handbag. "Look, I've been to that many funerals, I even carry my own service book." It was titled, *Funeral Services of the Christian Churches in England, Fourth Edition.* "Ah, there they are," she said, finding her keys under the book, a hair brush, a packet of cigarettes and an inhaler for her asthma.

The vicar looked at the inhaler and the cigarettes. "Winif—"

"I know Father, I know." She unlocked the passenger door.

"What of the boy?" he asked.

She made sure the boy had strapped himself into the passenger seat then closed the door so he could not hear. Winifred thought about it for a second or two. Could she tell the vicar? He might know about the grandfather's reputation. Could she really tell him? Of course not; she wasn't even sure herself that she was going to do it and very much doubted if she'd get permission to even try it anyway. "We'll have to wait and see, Father; we'll figure something out, we always do."

"You certainly do, Winifred, and God bless you for it," the vicar said, as she squeezed her hefty frame into the small car.

Inside the boy sat silent. He was bewildered and still in shock from the trauma. He was in a place he didn't know and with people he didn't know. His life had broken and he had no understanding of it. He looked back at the grave being filled in by four men he didn't know, their shapes distorted because of the rain beating down on the passenger window. He didn't cry. He hadn't cried when the policeman pulled him from the wreckage of his parents' car. He hadn't cried as he watched them trying to free his parents from the front seats of their car. He hadn't cried when the car suddenly caught alight and then exploded, when the nice policeman had tried to shield his eyes from the blast, as he ran with the boy in his arms to safety. He hadn't cried when he saw the firemen run back from the flames as the car erupted into a burning fireball with his parents inside. He sat quietly. He didn't know how to feel but he knew he never wanted to return to the place where his parents were under the ground, the place where he had stood with people he didn't know. The place that scared him with the black, wet dirt and the hideous ghost trees.

Winifred Mabel Doris Rushton turned the key in the ignition and the old mini's engine fired first time. She smiled and patted it on the dashboard; fifteen years on and it had never failed to start first time: even in the wet and the cold. She pressed down on the clutch, moved the gear stick into first and slowly pulled away – windscreen wipers bobbing backwards and forwards erratically, trying to clear away the deluge.

All Winifred's hopes were now on the young boy's grandfather, a man called Billy Jack. She sighed at the mountain she would have to climb.

Part 2: The Pregnancy, The Solider, The Racist

Billy Jack was not a nice man by any stretch of the imagination. He was a racist. He was also a bully with a temper who drank too much and cared little for society: in fact, he cared nothing for anyone, but he hadn't started off that way.

Back in the 60s, 70s and 80s, Billy Jack had defended his country in the British Army. He joined young – very young – to get away from the poverty of Southlodge, London, where he had grown up with his parents and seven siblings. His father was an alcoholic who'd found it hard to get work as an illiterate man and his mother, scared and bruised from the beatings from her drunken husband, had cleaned houses and taken in laundry to make ends meet. It was a hard life and the cultural and social revolution the rest of the country and the world was experiencing in the 60s, just seemed to pass Southlodge by.

The other reason he left when he did was the death threats. His girlfriend at the time became pregnant. They were both 16. Billy was over the moon but his girlfriend's family were not. They were well-known criminals, full-time gangsters who lived north of the river. They didn't want their daughter to have anything to do with a boy like him, from south of the river. They decided they would send their daughter away to Southend-on-Sea to have the baby, they would not allow the gossip and shame upon their family. Then they would bring the child up as their own and he, Billy, would have no say in it, nothing to do with it, ever. One night they made their feelings abundantly clear. Billy and his two brothers were severely beaten, one brother was slashed across the face and his parent's council house was torched by two Molotov cocktails thrown through their front window. His father was out at the time drinking in some pub but his mother suffered severe burns and lost the use of her left arm as a result. Billy got the message. So, a few weeks later, he left home to save his family and his own life and he took his country's shilling and enlisted into the British Army.

Billy Jack was a good solider. He loved it. He loved the training, the square bashing, the firing range, the drills, the manoeuvres, the adventure. He loved the tough, harsh lifestyle of being a British paratrooper and he wore his maroon beret with pride.

In July 1967, he was sent to the Sultan of Oman to help fight the Dhofar rebellion. A few years later, he applied to join the SAS. He underwent the SAS aptitude test. Trained for and past 'selection' and 'continuation' and was assigned to A Squadron. There he thrived in the covert world of one of the world's most feared fighting forces. Where 90% of those who tried, failed, Billy Jack passed and succeeded.

In 1970, he was sent back to Oman to help in a coup d'état. The backward-thinking Sultan, Said bin Taimur, was deposed, went into exile in the UK and was replaced by his son, Qaboos bin Said. Billy Jack was assigned as protection for the young Sultan as he attended Sandhurst in the UK and then later, he was with him when the Sultan was commissioned into the Cameronians (Scottish Rifles), a British regiment.

Throughout the rest of the 70s, Billy Jack was mostly deployed under 'Operation Banner' in Northern Ireland, or, as it became commonly known, The Troubles. There a number of comrades were killed and he saw the horrors of war close up. He was truly tested to the full, his skills in close quarter, urban combat, his resolve, his elite force's soldiering, in the longest continuous deployment of British troops in history. Originally, their role was to support the Royal Ulster Constabulary (RUC), which involved supporting the police in security duties, such as checkpoints and patrols. However, as the troubles grew, so did the role of the British forces and Billy Jack's remit, like his fellow comrades, became more and more dangerous. Tensions were high, stress levels teetering on breakdown and service men and woman changed forever in the cramped, brutal and violent urban conflict of Northern Ireland. Billy Jack was no exception but back then, no one talked openly about the growing psychological damage the horror and trauma would cause. Hit squads, bomb disposal, riot control, street patrols, check points, house-to-house searches, under fire daily, IEDs, sniper and full-blown assaults. People from both sides suffered mental damage because of the horrors of the civil conflict.

In mid-March 1982, he was moved out of his tour of Northern Ireland and his Squad were put on a new deployment and they set sail. On the 2nd April, the Falklands war began. It lasted 74 days and ended with the Argentine surrender on 14th June. Two hundred and fifty-five British military personnel died in the conflict. Billy Jack lost six close comrades. Two burnt to death – Billy suffered second-degree burns, as did others, trying to save their comrades. A sniper bullet blew his captain's head open and three lost their lives in a brutal hand-to-hand combat skirmish. Only Billy got out of that skirmish alive – but not unscathed; mentally he was scarred and the damage would come back and haunt him in later life.

The other thing that happened in 1982, was that his son, David, who Billy had never seen, had a child with his girlfriend Marona and like Billy, they too were 16 years old when they became parents. They named their son Cameron, after his mother's country of birth, Cameroon. Billy's mum wrote to him, saying she heard that David had had a son and that he was soon to get married when he turned 17. Billy's mother had also never seen her grandson, David; none of his family had. David's mum had always told her son that his father, Billy, wanted nothing to do with him and had run away when she was pregnant and joined the army.

In 1986, Sergeant Billy Jack was demobbed from the British Army and left his regiment in Hereford for the last time. With nowhere else to go and only ever knowing army life, he went back to live in Southlodge, London. Billy tried to join one of the two SAS reserve regiments, 21 and 23 SAS, but the cracks regarding his mental health were already starting to show and there was no appetite by the powers that be to encourage the ticking bomb, Billy Jack, back into their fold. Post-traumatic stress disorder (PTSD) was beginning to raise its ugly and debilitating head in the ex-sergeant, but he had no way of recognising it; he also had no way of dealing with it.

A year after being demobbed, Billy was in full blown meltdown. It was the early days of post-traumatic stress disorder, the mental health condition triggered by witnessing or being involved in a traumatic event. Billy had been right in the thick of a large number of traumatic events for over 22 years. The memories of them had burrowed their way into his subconscious and now they were pushing outwards, affecting his memory, his state of mind, his tolerance, his sanity, his norms. Slowly, he was becoming someone his army buddies wouldn't recognise. Back then PTSD wasn't considered a disability by the majority – a lot of people did not recognise it as a mental disorder or even acknowledge it existed. Of the five main types, Billy was suffering the worst one: complex PTSD.

Afflicted, Billy had become a nasty man with no regard for people who were different from him and, due to his training, he had become a dangerous man. Whilst he had never been to prison, by the end of 1987, the police knew him well and he knew their detention cells even better. He had made the national news on two separate occasions. His name had been linked to a number of neo-Nazi groups in the London area. Since there was no war for him to funnel his growing aggression, created and fuelled by his PSTD driven metal health, he found his own war and did the only thing he knew, he fought. However, before he was trained, calculating and professional, now he was angry, nasty and violent, amplified by inadequate medication and drink.

He had become a racist and considered anyone not like him the enemy. Fuelled by the extreme racist views around him, he had been involved in some of the earliest black paybacks, so called because he and his kind took revenge on members of the area's black population. The irony was, he had many friends of different ethnicity and colour in the army. Deep down he was not a racist; he had become one in his desperate need to find an outlet for his boiling rage. The army had left a great hole in his life, to him it had been everything and everyone. Now it was gone. His parents were dead and his siblings had either died or had moved away, far away and they had all lost touch. He had no support, other than his racist friends, drink and the pills.

By 1989, his PTSD had taken its toll on the ex-solider with an exemplary service record: he was tired and lost. He was disillusioned with the movement he had become involved with. He had begun to hate their ideology. He didn't tell them though, scared he would lose the only family he knew; he went through the motions of their bigotry and racism. He didn't understand his PTSD. It had been left untreated. Now he attended very few meetings and marches.

The letter came on a miserable Wednesday morning, telling him his son, and his son's wife, had died in a terrible road accident. He was given the time and location of the service. He felt impassive. He'd had no relationship with his son, David. His PTSD had stripped most of his softer emotions away. He was sad for a son he didn't know. He didn't attend the funeral.

Part 3: A Mountain to Climb

Date: The second week in October 1989
Place: Social Services offices, Essex

There was nothing pleasant about Winifred's office. It was on the third floor of the council office buildings, down the end of a never-ending, windowless corridor that hadn't seen new paint since the 70s. It smelt of damp in the winter and smelt of damp in the summer.

Her desk and chair had seen many offices over the years and had been passed from person to person, office to office, until they found a permanent home with Winifred. The walls were of magnolia descent - that was the rumour, it was hard to tell these days. The only decoration on the walls was a picture of the council offices being refurbished in 1962, a poignant reminder that things tended to move slowly in local government. The metal window's glass had wire in it. It was broken in several places, thanks to bored brick-throwing youths. Her computer was the only thing in the office she considered of any worth. A request at the start of the year, one of 25 over an 18-month period, had finally reached someone who took decisions, a rarity in her department and so she was, as her colleagues liked to say, the only social worker with a computer worth stealing; which many of her file-cases had tried to do. It was secured to her desk with plastic-coated steel wire and two D clamps.

Winifred had four children of her own and was foster mother to three more, now all over the age of sixteen. She was a devout Christian; she went to church every Sunday and helped her minister whenever he needed her, which was often because Winifred was one of life's helpers, reliant, strong and caring. A doer who got things done. She was one of the nicest people around, a big woman with a big heart. A Jamaican immigrant back in the fifties, with a laugh to match her big heart. Winifred wouldn't see another person in trouble, or go short; she never passed a beggar in the street without reaching into her purse. Winifred Mabel Doris Rushton was in the ideal job; she'd been in the job for the last 15 years. Her only vice, she smoked ten cigarettes a day, more if she had a difficult case: today she was on her twelfth cigarette and it was only 3 p.m.

The little boy sat on the hard-wooden bench in the corridor outside Winifred's office. She could see him through her glass door. He sat silent and still. He didn't fidget, he didn't whine. When asked if he would like a drink, he accepted politely, an unusual trait from her normal cases. She already liked the boy. He was sweet and undemanding and considering the trauma of the last few weeks, he showed a quiet resilience. Winifred could see that his parents had brought the boy up well and it was abundantly clear that he had come from a loving, caring family. This made her decision all the crazier.

Her in-tray would have frightened the hardiest social workers, but Winifred ignored it. She would deal with it later because the young boy was her priority now. Her phone rang. It was her friend and supervisor, Connie Jones; she was on her way to discuss the boy's case. Winifred braced herself; *well*, she thought as she waited, *what's the worst thing that can happen, they can sack me, commit me to a lunatic asylum or, they can agree it; flying pigs and blue moons spring to mind*, she mused.

Connie arrived and Winifred explained it to her. Connie Jones sat with her mouth open.

"Seriously?" she asked.

"Yup," answered Winifred, deciding it best to keep her answers short.

"You want to ask the grandfather to look after the boy. *The* grandfather, Billy Jack, the racist who has a mixed-race grandson; a grandson he has never met, from a son he never met. That's the plan?"

"Yup." She stuck with her brevity like an invisible shield.

"Enough with yups, Winifred, have you lost your mind, girl?"

She has a point, Winifred thought, but said something different. "Maybe I have," she said, "but I just got a hunch that that little boy, that cute little boy out there," she pointed to the corridor and the child sitting on the hard-wooden bench, "just might find a way to that old white racist's heart. Look at him Connie, he'd melt the hardest of hearts."

"There are no other living relatives?" Connie asked.

"No, not in this country anyway. And the nurses took blood from him at hospital after the crash and I ran it through the police DNA database to see if there are any other living relatives, but it came up blank. I'm out of choices. It's put him into the foster system or it's the grandfather."

"Poor little bastard," Connie Jones said, as she reached for one of Winifred's cigarettes from the packet resting on the table. She lit it up, inhaled and then unwittingly blew smoke towards the no smoking sign above Winifred's head. "What has that little boy done to deserve this pile of crap. My God, sometimes you know, I hate this job." She paused and drew on her cigarette again, deep and hard. "Winifred," she said, through a haze of smoke, "I think you're stark raving mad but I have to agree with you, the boy has little option, whichever one we choose for him it's pretty damn shitty." She paused, looked her watch, then extinguished the cigarette and said, "Do it. I have to go." Then she got up and left.

Winifred breathed a sigh of relief. She thought about what lay ahead and breathed a sigh of dread. She took a cigarette and added to the accumulating fog in her office. She opened the file that had been sitting on her desk. The file gave details about the history of Billy Jack. She looked through the glass door at the boy still sitting still on the hard-wooden bench. *It's just you and me, kid*, she thought, *just you and me.*

Part 4: A Dirty Shade of White

Date: The third week in October
Place: Southlodge housing estate, south of the Thames, London

The maisonettes were shabby, ill-treated and forgotten about in everyone's maintenance budget. Graffiti was everywhere and art was not a hidden talent the people who had held the spray cans possessed.

Winifred sat with the car ticking over, trying to quell the feeling she would be better off a hundred miles away from there, at the very least back in Essex. The housing form said that Billy Jack lived on the third floor, number 16. She looked up, it wasn't an inviting sight. "Winifred," she said out loud, "get your scraggy, old black ass out of this car and go do your job, girl."

The stairwell had been visited by the same art-less painter or painters as the outside of the buildings. They carried the same graffiti tags: *Ollli, Mif, Tunc and MMV.* She moved quickly on and made her way up yet another flight of urine-smelling stairs. Panting and puffing on her inhaler in great gulps as she climbed the stairs.

Number 16 was another bland, inconspicuous door, identical to all the rest. They were either blue or green; number 16 was green. She knocked on the door and waited. She knocked again. Finally, the latch went. Then the chain was removed and the door opened. Why she expected him to answer the door in dirty trousers, his vest, wearing worn slippers and three days' worth of beard, she didn't know: too many doors had been opened to her with the owner looking like that. This one was wearing clean jeans, trainers, a neatly ironed shirt and was clean shaven. She'd forgotten he had spent over 22 years in the British army. She moved her head slightly to catch a glimpse of the inside. It looked clean and well kept. Then she was knocked off-kilter. She saw resentment in his eyes. She saw how her colour affected his demeanour. He looked angry; it was tacit. Winifred felt it. Years of racism had honed her antenna.

She took a deep breath. "Winifred Mabel Doris Rushton," she announced as she held up her Social Services plastic badge like an FBI agent at a gruesome crime scene. She used her full name like the girl, Mattie Ross, in *True Grit* used her lawyer's name 'Lawyer Daggett' to cause people to be put off guard by the seeming importance of the name. She had done this ever since watching the film, back in 1969. He didn't respond; he just stood there holding the door. *Perhaps he's never seen the film*, she thought. "It's about your recent bereavement." Still he said nothing. "You have a grandson, Mr Jack, a seven-year-old grandson, Cameron." He hadn't moved but she thought she felt a slight easing in his body language. "Well," she pressed on stoically, "I am assigned to his case. I'm his social worker and that means that I have to make arrangements for him. I have to find a place for him to stay, a place for him to be." Billy Jack still hadn't uttered a word or made any significant gesture. He stood motionless. Winifred took a gulp of her inhaler. "Look, he has very few options here. I really don't want to put him into the system but I really do only have two options. I don't think a care home is the best place for him right now and there is such a long waiting list for foster homes." She paused. "I don't think that's the best for him anyway. He's such a sweet little boy, brought up proper by your son and his wife. We always try to home children who have lost both parents with a relative. That's my second option and for Cameron, his best option. And, Mr Jack, you're it. He has no other relatives that are living in this country."

Finally, the man propping open the door spoke. "Do I look like a man who can take care of a kid? Just look at where I live, and I have no doubt you know my history. The kid's a half-caste, right?

The inference agitated her straight away; although she had promised herself that he would not get to her, he just had. "He's a seven-year-old little boy. His skin colour has nothing to do with who he is or his tragic circumstances. He's a human being. A boy. A child. A grandson. An orphan. Dealt a shit hand at such a young age."

"I'm sorry about his situation," Billy Jack said, "but you will have to find another alternative. I'm not an option."

Winifred was not disappointed at the rejection; in her job she had learnt a long time ago to always expect the worst and then you are never disappointed, and if the worst does not happen, you can be pleasantly surprised. "He is of your blood, Mr Jack. He's your grandson."

"I've never seen the kid, nor his dad. Not of my doing, mind," he quickly interjected, and Winifred picked up on this, the fact he wanted it known he had not abandoned his son. "I would have stayed, his mother knew that, I told her that. Her family, the Carriers, gangsters and scumbags every one of them. Run a borough north of the river. They badly beat members of my family. Mother's house got torched, she lost the use of her left arm because of that fire. If David's mother had wanted me to have anything to do with the kid, she could have stopped all of that but she didn't, so I left. I got no history with this boy. I assume David's mother doesn't want anything to do with him?"

"She married her third husband about two years ago and moved to the Costa del Sol, her mother and father too, although her father got extradited and is serving fourteen years for armed robbery. What I can gather is that she lost interest in David when he went to university. She has a high dependency on drugs and is in a pretty bad way. So, no, she has no intention of taking her grandson and to be quite candid with you, I would not let her."

"What, she's worse than me?"

"I didn't say that."

"But you would put him with me, you must be one crazy old nig…" He stopped short.

Winifred smiled, maybe a bit of a conscience after all, she thought. I can work with that. "My husband would agree with you there, Mr Jack, perhaps I am a bit crazy. Tell you what, agree to take him for two weeks, that's all, that's all I'm asking. That gives me time to try and find somewhere for him to go if you won't take him. Two weeks for the sake of the child."

"Where is he staying now?"

"With me," she replied.

"You got the room?" he asked.

"I have four kids of my own and foster three more, I don't have the room."

"You must like kids?"

"I like people, Mr Jack, and I want to be able to like myself."

"I haven't liked myself for a long time now," he said, looking straight at her.

"Well, Mr Jack, it's about time you started to, don't you think? So, do we have a deal?"

Billy Jack agreed to take his grandson, Cameron, for two weeks so that Winifred could find a home for him. The preparations were made, which involved Billy Jack sorting out his spare bedroom and ensuring there was a place for the boy to keep all his things, do his homework and sleep. He did all of this over three days. The boy was due on Friday afternoon, but there was a mix up with the timings at the office.

Friday morning came and Billy, as usual, was in the pub, the Bear and Hog, with a group from the Southlodge English Patriots, a banned movement. He was there because that's the way he spent every Friday morning. He was there because they were his family, because they were the only family he had. He was there because he was scared of being alone. He was there because he was wanted there.

Winifred was advised that the boy was going to his grandfather's at 11 a.m. on Friday morning. Billy Jack understood he was arriving at 3 p.m. Friday afternoon. On finding Billy Jack was not at home, Winifred knocked on the door of a neighbour.

"Try the pub, the Bear and Hog,' the neighbour helpfully said. 'He's there every Friday morning. He's there nearly every bloody morning. It's just around the corner."

Winifred took Cameron's hand and left the maisonettes, the crappy art and the urine smelling stairs and stairwells and made for the pub. "Come on, Cameron," she said, reassuringly, "let's go find your grandad. It's not far now. Come on, son, you can skip when we get onto the pavement if you want. I'll hold your hand."

When they got there, she thought about leaving the boy outside the pub while she went inside to get Billy but it was cold and she didn't want to leave a seven-year-old hanging about, even for a minute.

Despite smoking being banned in public places, the pub smelt of smoke as she entered. It also smelt heavily of drink and sweat. She found the stench oppressive. Inside it went quiet as Winifred and the boy entered. Winifred sighed deeply: everyone was white, not just white but *white*, white.

"You must be lost," the barman called to her as he stopped wiping a pint glass.

"She must be stupid," someone from one of the tables called. "You'll find a pub for your kind in the town. This one's not for you or your kind."

Winifred took a deep breath; her heart was pounding. "Oh, I'm not stopping, thanks all the same," she said, aware the boy was beginning to get worried. "I'm just looking for—"

"There's no one here you want. No one that has anything to do with your kind. No one wants you. No one here cares about you. You're not wanted. You and your kind are not one of us. Just because you keep weighing a pig doesn't make it fat." Laughter broke out. "And you can take the dirty shade of white kid with you."

A man with few teeth in his gums, tattoos on his neck and a shaven head, rose to his feet. He was just four feet from where Winifred and Cameron were standing. Two others stood up, then three more. Cameron started to cry, he was seven years old and had never experienced prejudice before: he was frightened. Billy Jack sat in the corner with his back to Winifred; he'd stayed silent throughout. How could he tell them he had a half-caste grandson? How could he tell them, all of these people? His brothers. His friends, his family.

"Ah, the benighted of Southlodge," Winifred said, as each one stood – this went over their heads but it didn't matter, it wouldn't have mattered whatever she had said. She was not white, neither was the boy, he was of mixed race, and colour to the ignorant meant more than just pigmentation, more than servility and common sense. "I just want to—" she wasn't allowed to finish.

"You just want to fuck off, you black bitch; that's what you just want to do and take that little fucker with you. For the last time, you're not welcome here. Now fuck off before I break a bottle over your head and slash the little fucker's face up." The man threw a chair in their general direction but the chair took a wrong turn, bounced and hit Winifred on the leg. She winced loudly. Cameron was sobbing his little heart out, begging to go, pulling on her hand. Beaten, Winifred turn towards the door. And that's when it happened, that's when Billy Jack finally let his racist family go; when he finally had enough of their poisonous ideology. When he finally found his real family. When Billy Jack found some salvation and his true self again. When Billy Jack became a grandfather.

The blow to his head hurt. The chair-throwing man fell to the barroom floor with a yelp. The vocal one, who had cursed, threatened and sworn at Winifred and Cameron, stood up and took a swing at Billy but he wished he hadn't. His mouth open and the words "you fuc…" starting to come out of his mouth, until Billy's fist hit him in the ear and his head started ringing; and then Billy's foot hit the man's groin with tremendous force and the man hit the ground, curled up into a ball, his nostrils flaring like bellows as he gasped to get air into his lungs.

Somewhat stunned, those who had stood now sat down quickly. They knew Billy Jack was a fighter, ex SAS. Billy stood in front of Winifred and Cameron. He picked up the crying boy. "Hey buddy, it's going to be alright, your grandad will take care of you now, don't you worry." Billy had tears in his eyes as he looked at the frightened little boy. He turned to the men in the pub. "So that you know, this is my grandson, Cameron, Cameron Jack. He's seven years old, for Christ sake. And this," he said, turning towards Winifred and smiling, "this is Cameron's friend, so she's my friend now." Cameron buried his head in his grandfather's shoulder. "Well, Winifred Mabel Doris Rushton," Billy Jack said, smiling, "shall we go?" Billy pointed towards the door and held out his hand.

"Mr Jack," Winifred said as she took his hand, "I would be bloody delighted to go."

Chapter 4
Saeed Al Bateat

Date: March 10th 2012

Place: Scotland

Jonathan had never been to Abu Dhabi, the largest of the seven Emirates of the United Arab Emirates (UAE). Jonathan was looking forward to seeing the rich emirate that held one tenth of the planet's oil and over one trillion dollars in investments abroad,

The meeting was to be held in Abu Dhabi city, downtown. The city, situated at the coast of the Arabian Gulf, south west of Dubai, is an island, similar to the location of New York's Staten Island. Whilst the meeting would be held there, it was decided that the Templars wouldn't stay in the downtown district, or in the city. Instead they booked accommodation on the diverse and popular tourist spot of Yas Island – one of over 200 islands around Abu Dhabi. Yas was just a 20-minute drive away from downtown, depending on traffic, National holidays, Eid and Ramadan. It was much closer to the airport, a straighter route and less traffic. Its downside was that it only had two ways on and off the island by vehicle and both ways could be blocked off quite easily. One of the routes passed Yas Marina and involved a two-lane tunnel to get on and off the island. Stage an accident in the middle and the whole tunnel got closed off. The other way on and off the island was a junction intersection to the main Abu Dhabi to Dubai road, the E11. If that were closed, there would be no way off the Island. The only other way to reach the mainland was by boat and a good knowledge of the mangroves. No one expected to need to leave the island quickly because the initial part of the mission just involved a meeting. Their contact, the man they were meeting, said he knew where Salah El-Din was. They wouldn't take unnecessary chances though; many had, then found out to their cost that Salah El-Din was a resourceful, elusive and a very dangerous man.

Yas island's transformation, initiated in 2006, had turned the bland, sand and mangrove island into a leisure, shopping and entertainment attraction. Add the building of a marina, a Links golf course, a Formula 1 Grand Prix race circuit, Ferrari World and a long list of future multibillion-dollar projects. Yas, meaning Jasmine Flower, had become a 'must' place to go to for all those that wanted to combine sun, with the pleasure of high-speed motor sport and endless shopping. The Templars wanted none of those things, but what they did want were crowds of foreign tourists, western-looking tourists because that would give them the cover they needed. Blend in and in plain sight. It was always safer to be able to disappear in plain sight should they need to abort their mission and leave.

There were several hotels on the island they could have chosen: the Rotana, Radisson Blu, Crown Plaza. However, the decision was made by André Sabath that Zakariah, Dominique and Jonathan would stay at the Staybright Suites. Six floors of one and two-bedroom serviced apartments, at the far end of Yas Island. Sabath had stayed there a number of times before and knew the area well. The Middle East was his territory; he had nearly 300 hundred Knights spread out across the Middle East and the Near East. The Staybright was closest to one of the two roads off the island, the tunnel exit. All the other hotels were within 500 to 2000 yards away from the Staybright, so there were plenty of tourists milling around the entire area at most times of the day and night. All they had to do is look like them, and act like them and there would be no need for anyone to be suspicious or take note of their presence. The Templars were masters of this type of camouflage, of hiding in plain sight: they had been doing it for centuries.

The library in the Staybright was a perfect place for their base of operations: to meet and plan. No one ever used it other than an occasional mother, or nanny, trying to amuse bored children. To the casual eye, it would look like they were planning their day trips around Abu Dhabi and the surrounding areas, forts, sand dunes and mango tracks. Sabath would stay with one of his Knights, a Templar who lived on the Sas Al Nahkl compound, just off the main Al Ain road and a fifteen-minute drive from Yas Island. The Templar worked under the cover as an expat oil worker, working for ADNOC, the Abu Dhabi National Oil Company. He was from the Lebanon and was stationed in Abu Dhabi with his wife and three children; they had been there for over three years.

At first it was strongly felt by all but Jonathan, that Jonathan should not accompany Zakariah, Dominique and André Sabath on the Abu Dhabi mission. He was the Seer. They wanted to protect him, keep him safe and out of harm's way but even St Claire knew this was not really an option, despite him wishing it was. Ensconced in an isolated castle in Scotland, sitting in his cottage in Kirkcudbright, or out in the countryside being trained by the Russian could only teach him so much. It would certainly not help him to develop the very thing he needed most, if he was going to be an 'active' Knight, a mission active Knight. It would not help him find, nurture and master a sixth sense. Only combat veterans ever get to develop and hone this: the sense of the unseen, that feeling that something is wrong, lying in wait, a sense of impeding danger, someone is watching, that thing called sixth sense. Abu Dhabi would be the first time he would have the chance to put some of the skills he had learnt, into practise. Abu Dhabi would be the first occasion where he could begin to listen to his feelings in a real live situation. They all knew he had to go – they all knew you cannot hone that one skill through simulation – but everyone was worried.

He was told it would be hot, getting up to well over 30 to 35 degrees Celsius and sometime in excess of 40 degrees. He was told not to wear shorts whilst out publicly, to be conservative in his dress and mindful of not being tactile out in public. Holding hands, kissing and embracing, would be frowned upon. He told his wife he had packed well and said that he had been mindful of her advice. Dominique checked his bag whilst he was out and found a pair of cut-off jeans and a T shirt that said 'Rolling Stones' on it, accompanied by their ubiquitous big red tongue motif designed by John Pasche. She took them out and hid them.

They had arranged to meet the contact at 4 p.m. at the Al Watan café, Al Fal street, just behind Al Kalidiya Park, in downtown Abu Dhabi. People would be returning to work after their lunchbreaks at that time – which tended to last for two or three hours as most people worked a split system because of the midday heat. They worked from around 7:30 a.m. in the morning, went home around 1 p.m. and stayed inside until around 3 p.m. or 4 p.m. and then returned to work until around 8 p.m. André Sabath had set the meeting up. He was one of the longest serving Templars. He was a member of the Higher Council of the Knights Templar and an Arabic speaker. He had made the arrangements with the man he had been talking to for a few weeks, a man by the name of Saeed Al Bateat, a Yemeni intelligence officer based in Abu Dhabi.

Al Bateat had contacted the UK's MI6 branch of their secret services. They in turn had reached out to the government's communications headquarters, GCHQ, and specifically to one of its senior members, Proctor Hutchinson.

Hutchison had, for the last nine years, also advised on the Communications Electronic Security Group (CESG) of GCHQ. CESG advises various UK government departments and armed forces on the security of their communications and information systems. Proctor Hutchinson had also been a member of the Order of Knights Templar since the age of 29, and for the last 19 years, one of the Nine Worthies, but of course, his employers were not aware of this fact. However, because he was named on a prior operation called 'Operation Roulette Wheel' – which was the large-scale manhunt for Salah El-Din in 2008 and the dismantlement and prosecution of his criminal organisation Unity – Hutchinson was contacted by MI6 regarding the message from Saeed Al Bateat.

The UK's secret intelligence services (SIS), like SIS's all over the world, uses private outside contractors from time to time. In the UK these have what is called Omega 1 clearance and they are each given a unique code name. What made the organisation, code named Pi, so different was that it truly was of an unknown source. In most cases, private outside contractors were usually setup and owned by ex-services people or those who used to work for one of the 'firms' MI5, MI6 etc. Pi was known to have advanced intel and a communications network that spread worldwide. Not all of the work was accepted by the secret organisation Pi and, on occasions, they provided intel to the intelligence and security services. Because they had been used on the Roulette Wheel project, and had in fact led the project, and the information from Saeed Al Bateat was connected to it, permission was given to reach out to them to again take the lead.

Proctor called his friend and fellow Templar via the usual covert route. He punched the seven-digit number into his private mobile phone. The number rang three times, then the call automatically routed to an address in Islington, United Kingdom. The computer, in an electronically protected shell (ESP) in Islington, checked the call's authenticity. Then it checked the caller's location against its worldwide GPS system. It matched the location where the caller was meant to be on that day's location list.

The fifty-old woman focused on the computer screen with careful scrutiny. As 'controller', her job was to ensure that no one from the outside was hacking into the system. She checked the meter on the cloaking software. It was normal. The software then directed the call to a private number in Scotland. The conversation would take place between the two men via the computer. The computer would cloak and scramble the conversation. If the EPS room's security was breached, the scrambler would protect the identity of the Templars and the contents of their part of the telephone conversation if they were talking to an outside person.

Proctor Hutchison gave a brief overview and then gave his friend the mobile phone number of Al Bateat. Nothing else was said between them but both men sensed the other's anticipation: the hunt for Salah El-Din was back on again. The Templars put a sanction out on his life four years ago and thus far he had eluded them. This was the first intelligence about him in four years.

Payne St Clair called the number Proctor Hutchinson had given him. He listened to the Yemeni intelligence officer. He thought the Yemeni's voice sounded young and confident. St Clair worried it sounded too confident, almost rash; he made a mental note.

"Are you Saeed Al Bateat?" St Clair asked him.

"I am," a young voice answered. "Who am I taking to?" he asked.

"Saeed, it doesn't work that way. You will get no information about us." St Clair's voice made it clear to the young Yemeni that he meant it. "Remember Saeed, you came to us. Does that work for you?"

"Okay, yes, that works but are you still searching for him?" he asked.

"Saeed, our coms are scrambled; I assume yours are not. This means if anyone is listening, they will not hear what I say, but could hear what you say, so please say the bare minimum. That said, I need to know who you mean by 'him'?" St Clair replied.

"The evil one," the Yemeni intelligence officer said. "Al-Malik al-Nasir al-Sultan Salah El-Din. The man from Har Megiddo, Israel. Armageddon. Are you the ones still searching for him?"

"We are," St Clair confirmed. "I want to be upfront with you, Saeed: if we catch him, we will terminate him. If that's what you also want, then our interests are aligned."

"They are aligned," Al Bateat said; "they are very much aligned."

"Why do you want to help the British?" St Clair asked him. "Why not talk to the Americans? He's also on their hit list. Actually, he's on many lists."

"I have friends in the Jordanian secret police. The Jordanians and us Yemenis do a lot of work together. I guess we are the smaller, less wealthy under dogs and we look out for each other among our neighbouring rich nations. I know that you guys helped them capture their traitor Abu Taha, four years ago—"

"Saeed, no detail. Remember, you are not using a secure line."

"Yes, *sadiq* ... yes, my friend, I will remember. He needs to be terminated. He's bad for my Arab brothers and sisters."

"And what is your business?" St Clair asked him. He already knew though; he just wanted to see how honest the Yemeni would be with him.

"My country's security is my business; and that also means this region's security."

St Clair already knew from the dialling code 971 that had flashed up on the panel that the Yemeni was in Abu Dhabi, but he had just confirmed he was in the Middle East by saying 'this region's security'. Again, St Clair made a mental note to tread carefully with the young Yemeni; he was not skilled in trade craft. In fact, he was downright sloppy. St Clair eased back on his seat; it creaked a little. "You've seen him, Salah El-Din?" he was desperate to know. It had been four long years since there had been any sighting of him. Back then he had been sighted in Russia. St Clair had sent a team of Knights but when they got there, Salah El-Din was long gone.

"He is back in Salalah," the young Yemeni said, "in the Sultanate of Oman, where his family moved to when they left their home many years ago. He has many, many contacts and friends there. It was in Salalah that he began in crime. Petty theft, then more serious crimes. It was there that he ran his arms deals, and human trafficking and drugs across the border into the Yemen. He has returned there. He has returned to his base and his criminal friends have been protecting him. He stays between safe houses and often travels with one of the nomadic tribesmen who trade in slavery."

"And you've seen him for yourself, or you have a confirmed sighting?" Now St Clair eased a little forward on his seat, this was the all-important question. He needed to hear it. He needed proof of identity.

"Myself. I have seen him myself. Yes, Sadiq, I have seen the evil one."

St Clair told Al Bateat he would next hear from a man called Sabath. Sabath would now deal directly with him. He told him he should never use that name on an open telephone line, and from now on, he should only refer to Salah El-Din as the target. Arrangements would be made for the men to meet and a plan made to confirm the sighting and then the termination would be arranged.

St Clair sent a message to a pre-set list of recipients from his mobile phone. All Templar mobile phones had high-spec integrated memory chips. They worked off their own virtual network and used short and rapid touch pad sequencing to announce instant voice messaging. They allowed person-to-person and person-to-team, with exchange of free form text messages. Lucid formatting, a full data download facility, fully secure anywhere in the world. The Nine Worthies would receive the message from St Clair. Plus, a number of other Knights would also get the message, including Zakariah, the Indian John Wolf, Luther Jones and Norman Smith, the Templar Sergeant at Arms. The message read 'confirmed sighting of Salah El-Din, make ready'.

Later that day, André Sabath and Al Bateat spoke for the first time. A date for the meeting was set up between them. They agreed

58

on Abu Dhabi as the location, easy to get in and out of, not far from Oman. Al Bateat said he was stationed there. Sabath chose Yas Island as their base – but he didn't tell the Yemeni where they would be staying. He only told him that that his mission team would leave for Abu Dhabi straight away. Al Bateat agreed he would call Sabath with timings for the meet once Sabath was in-country and when everything was in place and safe.

Through their protected coms network, Sabath then called one of the local Knights in Abu Dhabi, a man called Tarik Tahir. He briefed him on the situation and told him when they would be arriving.

Chapter 5

Abu Dhabi

Place: Abu Dhabi, United Arab Emirates (UAE)

They checked into the Staybright Suites on Yas Island, Zakariah in a one-room suite on the second floor and Dominique and Jonathan in a double suite just a few doors down.

André Sabath met them at Abu Dhabi Airport, he had flown in from the Lebanon the day before and rented a Toyota four-wheel drive. He drove them to their hotel. Once they had checked in, they all unpacked and began to settle into looking like and acting like tourists. Sabath, in his Arab dress, blended in with the locals.

Later, they were all sitting down stairs in the library, near to the inhouse restaurant, when Sabath's phone range. They all went quiet. After less than a minute Sabath hung up.

"Well? Dominique asked. "Are we on?"

Jonathan reached for the coins in his pocket and started messing with them – his nervous-tell.

Sabath shook his head. "The Yemeni's got no trade craft; this bothers me."

"What do you mean?" Zakariah asked.

"He's too cavalier for my liking. Mentioned our friend's name twice, on an open call, and mine once. Not smart. St Clair warned me about his bullish approach. We're going to have to watch him. However, we're on for tomorrow. Let's be vigilant, Knights."

"I'll give him one of our burners when we meet him," Dominique said. "It's programmed like our phones, so it's fully secure."

"Thanks, Dominique," Sabath replied. "Don't want him getting any of us killed, we all know how resourceful Salah El-Din is." He almost whispered the last part. "If he gets wind we are here, things will go bad very quickly and, as a four-Knight team, we are not set up for that kind of trouble. I would need to call in my Knights from home but it will take them hours to get a flight from the Lebanon and get here. We need to remember we are not a kill team, we are recon."

"Let's go slowly then," said Zakariah. "We are tourists and you are our local guide. We stick to the plan. Has Al Bateat told you the time of the meet?"

"Yes, it's all set," Sabath replied.

"Okay, great," Zakariah said. "Let's get ready then. Oh, and one more thing, Dominique, can you take those coins off your husband? He's advertising his tension to the world when he does that; it's such a nervous-tell."

Zakariah and Sabath walked off together.

"Will you stop doing that!" Dominique said to Jonathan.

"What?" Jonathan asked, surprised.

"That 'change' business."

"What 'change' business?"

"You rattle the coins in your pocket when you're nervous."

"I do not."

"You rattle the coins in your pocket when you're nervous. You walk flat-footed. Whenever you have to stand for some time, you always have to find something to lean against and you lean slightly forward whenever you're trying to make a point."

"I do not," he said, learning against a pillar and slightly forward, trying to make a point.

61

"I do love you," she said. "Sometimes you are so funny. Come on, Priest; let's go."

"Right behind you, Girl." He slapped her bottom gently. "You don't think we would have time to …"

"Jonathan …"

"Okay, just asking."

Place: Downtown Abu Dhabi, (UAE). The Meeting

What first struck Jonathan was that it was difficult to tell the good guys from the bad guys because virtually everyone dressed the same. The local Arabs in their long-sleeved white thobes and ghutra headcloth, white, or red and white chequered and black and white chequered. The itinerant migrant workers that made up around 80% of all workers in the UAE, either in their blue, dirty overalls or their Shalwar Kameez traditional day wear. The other problem was spotting trouble on faces, when there are so many around you; it was nigh on impossible, he thought.

Sitting facing the door of the Al Watan café, on Al Fal street, Zakariah, Jonathan and Dominique sat and waited patiently. Zakariah sipped a dark, sludgy Turkish coffee and Jonathan and Dominique aromatic coffee, much lighter in colour and laced with cardamom seeds. The waiter, a boy of no more than 15 years old, had served them quickly and had been delighted with his ten Dirham tip from the westerner female. He had given her a cheeky grin and went off whistling, hoping for another order soon and more money.

The Templars looked like western tourists enjoying their drinks and a few pastries, whilst chit-chatting about whatever they were chit-chatting about but it didn't look serious. On their table were bags from the nearby mall and bags from a souk just around the corner. Also, on the table, a tourist guide map for Abu Dhabi, a tube of sun tan cream, mosquito repellent spray and a tube of 'after bite'.

They looked like tourists, the ruse fully complete in the picture they presented sitting there.

They had been there for about four or five minutes and were starting to get a feel for the place, its ebb and flow. Every place had a feel to it and Templars were trained to try to tune into it. To try to use their sixth sense. It was loud and animated in there because most of the customers were loud and animated. Arabs tend to use their hands a lot as a form of expression and emphasis, so there was much hand waving and guttural Arabic throaty sounds. The other prevalent sound was slurping, many of the patrons slurped their drink – a custom in many parts of the Middle East and Asia. The woven smells of sweat, burning frankincense and other scented essences, strong coffee, sweet coffee and sweet pastries - there was no shortage of gooey Lebanese, sweet delights - hung heavily inside the popular café.

Dominique was uneasy because she was the only female in there, but more so, because Jonathan was on this mission. Her father, Zakariah, had suggested she stay behind at the Staybright Suites, because two men could get lost faster in a sea of men, should they need to run. A western lady running along the streets would draw too much attention in the predominately male-oriented, conservative society. She was having none of it. If Jonathan was there, she would be there to protect him, the Seer, her husband, her best friend.

None of Templars waiting in the café knew where they would be going next but they suspected it would be soon. They had learnt with Salah El-Din, when things started moving, things started changing. After they had made contact with the Yemeni intelligence officer, they hoped they would have enough information from him so they would be able to get eyes on Salah El-Din. Once they had done that, it would trigger the approved death sanction. Four years was a long time to be hunting someone all over the world and they were all tired of it. This time they were so close.

About five minutes after Jonathan, Dominique and Zakariah had entered the Al Watan café, a local man, who had been reading his

Arabic newspaper, drinking coffee and smoking a potent-smelling shisha in a hookah pipe, got up from his seat and ever so carefully cast a sideways look towards Jonathan, Dominique and Zakariah. Dominique picked it up. She rubbed her left, upper arm, the signal they had agreed to use if they thought they had been spotted.

The man, who looked in his mid 50s, had an intelligent look about him. He had been softly spoken when the waiter, the 15-year old boy, had asked for his order. As he rose, the man adjusted his red and white chequered ghutra and left a five Dirham note on top of a small plate. Directly the man went outside, crossed the street, and as he did so, he folded his Arabic newspaper, *Al Khaleej Times*, under his right arm – he had given the signal to another man waiting in a doorway 30 yards away. The Templars did not see the signal between the two men outside because their line of sight was obstructed by a delivery truck.

Another local man crossed that same street and entered the Al Watan café. Once inside he settled down and ordered chai. The Templars noted him and where he sat, then carried on chatting but still scanning the room. When the waiter left to get the man's drink, the man removed a package he had hidden under his long-sleeved thobe; it was about the size of a paperback book and three times as thick. After drinking his chai, he got up from his seat and left the café. No one noticed the package he'd left behind; it was tucked underneath the table on one of the chairs, and the white paper table cloth draping down, hid it from view.

Normally, a bomb will either have a command wire attached to it, a rocker motion sensor, or a timer. The timer on the bomb reached its pre-set time. The explosion went off four minutes after the man had left the establishment. Three people died instantly - those closest to the table where he had been sitting. Seven others were wounded, two of them, it would later turn out, also fatally. One of them was the young waiter.

Two minutes before the explosion, three Templars, Zakariah, Dominique and Jonathan, all heard the message come through into their secure, nano coms earpieces. "Knights go red. I repeat, go red, I'm at the back entrance: we need to get out, NOW." It was André Sabath. Five seconds later, Sabath entered through the back door of the café and led them out. No one took any notice when he entered the café. He looked like a local. Anyone that noticed them leaving just assumed that the westerners had met up with their guide. Once outside, Sabath led them away from the café as quickly as he could. The plan had been to park the vehicle three blocks away, once he'd dropped them off at the café, which he'd done and then wait for them. Sabath had negotiated the arrangements regarding the meeting with the Yemeni intelligence officer. However, Sabath did not want to be at the meeting because he lived and worked in the region and, as yet, Al Bateat was an unknown source to them. Sabath did not want to reveal his identity at this early stage.

The four Templars had only left the building two minutes before the explosion.

They heard three shots crack, which pierced the normal sounds and din of downtown Abu Dhabi. Normally, the Templars were good at inclusion, seeking each other's views on strategy and tactics. The rule, though, when the heat was on, 'convene and discuss', was replaced with 'command and control'. Despite being on the Higher Council and one of the Nine Worthies, it was Zakariah that now took command, not Sabath. Zakariah was the most experienced combat Knight there. He took immediate action.

Zakariah spoke to them over their ear sets. "André, take point. Find the fastest route back to the Toyota, but make sure we have cover. Dominique, follow Sabath. Jonathan, you go next. And keep low and keep moving. I'll follow and watch our six." Jonathan knew it meant their backs; Templars used the clock face for giving quick positional information.

The four Templars were fast over the ground, pushing forward and zigzagging. There was no way of knowing where the shots had come from, the sound ricocheted and echoed against the maze of buildings. It was too built up and every building ranged from three storeys to twelve. Every window, every laundry-peppered balcony, every corner and shop entrance could be concealing the gunman or gunmen. Only Sabath was armed, they'd decided that if they were caught and searched, it would be the three westerners who would get searched, and their punishment for carrying illegal arms would be punitive. It didn't matter now anyway, given their situation, any return fire would be speculative at best. Sabath, leading the way, running 10 to 12 yards at a time, zigzagging with no set pattern so the shooter remained uncertain which direction he would go. Then Dominique, Jonathan and, finally, Zakariah followed.

"How much further, André?" Zakariah called over their coms, after two minutes of hard zigzag running in 35-degree heat.

"About four minutes," André Sabath answered – he was already out of breath.

"Jonathan, don't bunch, stay calm; stay in the zone and remember your training," Zakariah reminded him.

Now locals and migrant workers were also running. They were scared and panicked. It didn't seem to be in any particular direction; they were as confused as the Templars as to which direction the gunfire had come.

When the Maghrib had come – the late afternoon call to prayer for Muslims – voices of Mullahs echoed from a hundred Minaret towers across the city and the reverberating sound wove its mystical enchantment across the rooftops. However, it was interrupted by the loud explosion, which shook the ground. Prayer then moved out of everyone's attention. The Al Watan café had just blown up. The public had only one direction to avoid, so they all ran away from the explosion and the black plumes of smoke now rising into the clear, blue Middle East sky. Fortunately for the Templars, that was the same direction as their rental, so they ran in the crowd.

"Stay amongst them," Zakariah called. "It's our only hope."

Another crack of gunfire, this time two shots. Two locals, some 25 yards off from the Templars, fell to the ground: dead.

Now Zakariah and Sabath, the two most combat experienced Knights, knew three things: one, the shooter, or at least one of them, was behind them. Two, the shooter had a rifle and not a hand gun, probably a 7.6 calibre round, deadly up to 1000 yards, in the right hands; and three, the shooter would be heading their way, because it was the only way to go.

"Faster, Knights," Zakariah called over their ear pieces. "We must go faster."

Jonathan was breathing hard. His fitness was better than it had ever been, thanks to the dedication of a number of Templars. However, the adrenalin pumping around his body sapped his energy and his leg muscles were being swamped with lactic acid as he zigzagged and snaked, hugging the doorways and trying not to look back. The training he had received from the Russian – Nickolin Klymachak, aloof, hard, stubborn, mean-looking with a body like iron and hands of leather – was now saving his life. He heard the Russian's voice screaming inside his head as he gasped for air and control over his body. "Escape and evasion, Jonathan. There are only two golden rules: don't let the urgency a crisis creates, crowd out the important things you need to do to stay alive; and secondly, RUN."

A KFC delivery man on an antiquated moped nearly ran Jonathan over. The Indian driver stopped, smiled – with the largest, white toothed grin – waved, and then drove on, oblivious to all the chaos and death around him. The absurdity almost caused Jonathan to break out laughing. Then a shop's window metal shutter came down: fast. Jonathan nearly jumped out of his skin.

Dominique turned around at the shutter sound and saw Jonathan. "It's okay baby, breath," she said over his coms. "It made us all jump. You're doing fine. Just keep moving. The Russian would be proud of you."

The heat was now getting to all the Templars, more so Sabath, who was the oldest and had not been an active combat Knight for many years. The Order's unwritten rule: no one over the age of 50 could be an 'active' Knight – active meaning combat-active on sanctions. This was not a sanction; it was a recon mission. It was a normal mission, so there was no age restriction. Sabath was beginning to question the judgment of that as he panted and struggled to keep his pace. He was leading them out; he needed to pick up the pace. The small, rotund figure with short-cropped silver hair moved faster.

The running crowd gave them cover but of course their assailant would guess that is what they were doing. Besides, nobody was going left or right, they were all going in a straight direction away from the bomb blast. If the Templars went either left or right, they would be the only ones and visible. Yet still the crowd ran in chaos and mayhem – people in the Middle East are extra anxious and nervous of loud bangs and gunfire because of the region they live in.

Finally, amongst the screams and the hysteria, the Templars made it to the Toyota. It was outside in a car park, by the Snow-White laundry, along with 20 other vehicles. They all jumped in. Sabath turned the ignition, the engine fired up first time. The other three kept low below the window line. He hit the accelerator. Wheels spinning and dust spewing everywhere, the rental sped backwards before a crunch of the gears, and then it sped off forwards. Sabath hit the back streets so as to lose any tail, and to keep out of the way of the police, fire and ambulance vehicles now hurtling towards Al Fal street. He headed towards Sheikh Zayed bridge. After ten minutes, he eased down on the accelerator and drove like everyone else: manically. Switching lanes without warning or indicators – everyone driving in the lane where the shade was best. He headed for Yas Island and the Staybright suites.

Sabath pulled up outside the hotel and three loitering valets were quick to respond and headed for the Toyota but Sabath let down the window and told them he didn't need them *la shukraan*. He turned back to Zakariah. "I need to go back; I need to find Al Bateat.

I got a text message from him warning me our meeting had been compromised and to get you out of there, quick. I've not been able to contact him since. I have no idea what happened but I need to try and find him. We need to find out what's going on."

"It's going to be dangerous down there," Zakariah said. "Are you sure you want to go back?"

"I'm sure, Zakariah; he might need our help. Plus, we need the intel about Salah El-Din; we have a sanction to complete. Zakariah, tell St Clair … well, you know what to tell him."

Dominique placed her hand on Sabath's shoulder. "You be careful, you hear? I want to see you back here soon." André Sabath was her godfather and mentor; he'd been the only person at her wedding who was not family; she loved him like a father.

Sabath looked at her through his rear-view mirror and smiled. "Go. I'll see you soon." His three passengers got out of the Toyota, somewhat sweaty and flustered. Alone, Sabath took a deep breath. It'd been many years since he'd been in live combat. Even when he led the raid on Salah El-Din's men in Egypt, in 2008, he'd stayed in the command vehicle and never actually went into their compound during the forced entry. He didn't know if he was headed back into a combat scenario now. He put the vehicle into first gear, nodded back to the three Knights, and then drove off at speed, with his gun at the ready on the passenger seat. He headed back downtown. He called Al Bateat again from his mobile phone; there was no answer, again. He called Tarik to meet him.

Zakariah, Dominique and Jonathan made their way inside the Staybright Suites, past the reception desk and to the two lifts at the far end of the building. Jonathan hit the button for the second floor. They would stay together. They would clear Dominique and Jonathan's room first, then Zakariah's, which was just a few doors down. Dominique was working her phone hard. Talking to the controller, between them they managed to book new flight tickets back to the UK, for that night.

69

"What happened back there?" Jonathan asked. "Does Sabath know?"

"We got spotted at some point, or Al Bateat got made, Jonathan," Zakariah said, "and no, he doesn't know what happened. He just got a message telling him to get us out of there. We don't know anything else but what I do know is that we need to leave. We need to leave Abu Dhabi; our cover is blown and we will remain in danger until we get out of here; I have a bad feeling about this."

"I've booked four new tickets. Our plane leaves at midnight but we should wait here for Sabath," Dominique said, still pushing buttons on her mobile. She looked up at Jonathan. "Don't worry; we'll find out what happened soon enough."

"You know when I say something has gone wrong, Dominique," Jonathan said, "and you always tell me that it hasn't gone wrong, it's just gone different? Well, I think this just went very differently wrong."

The Templars knew that the shots were different from the shots downtown; these definitely came from some kind of 9mm sub machine gun: they have a very distinctive sound. Then a number of screams rang out as the Yas Island tourists started to panic and run. Islamophobia just found another reason to exist.

"We have no choice now," Zakariah said; "we have to go. I will let Sabath know. Is the room clean?"

"Clean," Dominique answered.

"Then we need to go now; they're armed and we are not. Leave my room; there's nothing in there anyway."

Then another short burst of gunfire. This time it was closer. "They're coming down this hallway; they know our rooms." Dominique put the chain on the door and then went over and opened the balcony doors. They were two floors up overlooking the pool below. "We need to jump," she said. Another burst, more screams – a maid who had confronted them had just been shot.

Zakariah's phone beeped. "Sabath just text back," he said. He cracked the room door open slightly, door chain still on, watching for the gun man or gun men. "He says go; Tarik Tahir is with him. Tarik's sent his family to Saadiyat as a precautionary measure, until they find out what the heck is going on. Sabath has contacted his Knights in the Lebanon. Eight are on their way; they will be with him by nine tonight, so he will be protected. He said leave and leave now as all hell's breaking lose downtown."

"And the Yemeni intelligence officer, Saeed Al Bateat?" Domonique asked,

"Has he been able to find him?"

"No. He can't reach him," Zakariah said.

"So, what's our plan?"

"Expect the worse, hope for the best. Leave the bags, passports only. Put them in this plastic bag. We need to jump."

"What do you mean jump?" Jonathan said. His hand in his pocket searching for coins to rattle. There were none. He looked at Dominique.

"I took them out," she mouthed, and smiled.

Zakariah looked out of the patio doors and down onto the pool below.

Jonathan looked incredulous. "Don't you people ever do anything not dangerous? I'm not jumping out of this window." Two more shots rang out. This time it was right outside their door. Jonathan threw his passport to Zachariah, then he jumped.

Nobody noticed three people jumping from their balcony and into the hotel swimming pool because five other people were doing it at the same time. Not only were they at risk from the gun man or men, they were now also at risk of someone landing on their heads and drowning them! They quickly made their way out of the pool. Zakariah leading the way, Dominique clutching the plastic bag and Jonathan clutching Dominique.

They looked around for an escape route but they could not see any viable options. Everywhere they looked, there were screaming

71

people. They risked being split up or trampled if they got caught in the hysterical crowd. There were now hundreds of guests running around screaming, panicked and trying to get away from the gunfire. Their other concern was, if the gunmen – because now they were sure there was more than one – spotted them, then a lot more innocent people could get shot.

Another four shots. A body fell from a balcony on the second floor, their floor. The gunmen would soon figure out the Templars had jumped – it was the only way past them.

"I have an idea," Zakariah said, "just go along with it."

They started to run towards the Rotana, the hotel furthest away from where they were. It was about 2000 yards. Outside the Rotana, a group of hotel employees had gathered to see what all the commotion was about. It sounded like gunshots but they could not be sure. Fireworks, perhaps? Most of the hysterical crowd were running in the opposite direction, the direction that led away from the multi hotels' complex. As the Templars drew near to the Rotana, Zakariah grabbed his chest and started gasping. Dominique and Jonathan were right behind him: they quickly got it. Zakariah burst into reception through the revolving doors and cried, "I think I'm having a heart attack, I was in your pool and … help." The employees had followed him in. Dominique and Jonathan, now part of the act, started shouting for help.

The hotel manager, already spooked because he thought he heard gun shots, now began to panic: the death of a westerner from having been in his swimming pool, was all he could think about.

"*Yalla, yalla*" – quick, quick – the manager called to his staff. "Get him into my office and call an ambulance … and call the first aider … and do it now … now."

Out of sight, hidden, at least for now, inside the manager's office, Zakariah continued with his chest grabbing and groaning. Dominique and Jonathan played the concerned daughter and son-in-law brilliantly. The manager hovered, silently praying to Allah that the guest would not die in his office. The young first aider, an

Egyptian, who had only agreed to undertake the one-day first aid course because it meant an extra 50 Dirhams per month in his pay-packet, silently prayed to Allah that the guest would not die in the manager's office.

It was quick thinking by Zakariah because with only two ways off the island, he figured that the gunmen would have accomplices watching both roads, so he came up with a plan that would get them off the island unseen.

Finally, the ambulance arrived and Zakariah was stretchered in side it, complete with an oxygen bottle and mask, accompanied by a concerned-looking Jonathan and Dominique. It sped off at great speed, now passing several other ambulances going the opposite way to them – there were reports of gunfire and casualties.

Once off Yas Island and clear of any potential ambush, Zakariah took out a soggy bundle of Dirhams notes – he had about 2,000 dirhams – and persuaded a rather shocked ambulance driver and his crewman to drive them to the airport instead.

They checked in at the BA check-in desk; got a few odd looks from the BA staff: no baggage, damp and bedraggled passengers was not something they saw every day. The Templars made it through customs without a problem. They headed for their gate. No one bothered them, no one noticed them, the other passengers were too busy getting to wherever they needed to get to.

Seated in the business class lounge of Abu Dhabi International Airport, they were finally able to breathe easy. André Sabath had messaged as they were going through passport control, he said that he was still trying to track down Al Bateat and he would follow on tomorrow or the next day. He just wanted to know they were safe. Zakaria sent the message back '*Omnis Templars tatum*': All Templars safe.

The three Templars breathed a sigh of relief as they boarded their plane and saw the smiling faces of the BA crew: they felt they were already home.

The BA 326 midnight flight to Heathrow took off on time and the three Templars left Abu Dhabi with nothing other than their passports, phones and damp underwear.

Date: Earlier in the day of the meeting
Place: The Al Watan café

Saeed Al Bateat, the young Yemeni intelligence officer, had a feeling all day that he was being followed; actually, he'd had the feeling for a few weeks now. He couldn't shake it. It irked him because he couldn't figure it out and it wouldn't go away. Besides, he was on to a big thing, working with the British government and their outside operatives, and he didn't want anything to interfere with the biggest operation he had ever been involved with. Likely the biggest he ever would. So, he ignored the feeling. Al Bateat was young, and as St Clair had rightly deduced pretty early on in their call, he was rash. St Clair knew that this would make him clumsy in his trade craft, willing to take unnecessary risks and chances, and a danger to those around him: especially those whose life depended on Bateat's skill and judgement. They needed him but they would detach themselves from him as soon as they had the location of Salah El-Din.

Al Bateat was on his way to the meeting with Sabath's team at the Al Watan café. He was excited, almost exuberant. He had set it up. He had stumbled on Salah El-Din, a wanted man – wanted by most of the major enforcement agencies. His name would be known, known as the man that got Salah El-Din. He was already planning what he would do with the salary raise his promotion would give him; and planning which international schools he would send his two young children to when they were older, so they had opportunities outside their war-torn country of birth.

That morning he called home to speak to his wife and children – something the young Yemeni intelligence officer knew was breaking with security protocols, you never call home when undercover but he was rash. They were excited to hear their father's voice, and his wife was excited to hear he would soon get a pay raise. He spoke to them for about four minutes, then told them he loved them and hung up. Another Templar enemy was closing in on him; they listened in on the call; their operatives were already in place to plant the bomb once the Templars turned up at the Al Watan café and, the kidnap team were minutes away.

Al Bateat had stopped to buy some cigarettes on the way to the meeting, Marlborough reds, from a corner shop. He was a few miles from the meeting place with Sabath's team. He stood outside the shop in his locally tailor-made suit that was excessively generous in the leg and extra generous in the shoulders. He looked like a 1950's Omar Sharif. Black hair gelled back; black moustache but the rest of his face was clean shaven; deep brown eyes. He smelt of cheap aftershave and incense. He wore imitation Ray-Ban glasses. He lit his cigarette, checked his phone. No messages from Sabath; the meeting was still on.

The street was busy – the Abu Dhabi streets were always busy. Hustle and bustle passed him by. He took his imitation Ray-Bans off and wiped thin beads of sweat from his forehead that were heading for his eyes. Looking at him, people would think that he was an affluent, successful businessman: he just lacked the briefcase, the wealth and the success!

He threw the cigarette on the sandy ground, then lit another one. He was excited; he needed his nicotine fix. He wouldn't smoke at the meeting, despite the fact that smoking was allowed in any building, at anytime, anywhere in Abu Dhabi. He wanted to present himself as professional to the westerners.

The cacophony wrapped itself around the street scene. Then there was a distinct change in the decibel level around him, ever so slightly, but it was there. He looked around to see what might have helped temper the chaotic racket of downtown Abu Dhabi.

He saw them, the four men approaching towards him from

across the street. They were different somehow. They didn't hide the fact they were heading his way, their intentions written all over their faces and obvious from their body language: it was tacit and menacing. They were all in casual western clothes; all in mirrored sunglasses; and, from the way they walked and the position of their hands, they were all armed. They did not split up. They were together and walking at a fast pace, closing in on him. They looked straight at him. He did not need any trade craft or sixth sense to know they were coming for him. He was rash but not stupid; he knew his cover and the meeting were blown. He quickly texted Sabath to warn him to abort the meet and get his people out.

A black Lexus car pulled up beside him. The back door opened, curb side. The four men were now on him. Other people around instinctively knew that trouble was happening and they wanted no part of it. They parted and quickly moved away, taking their noise with them; they gave the event unravelling plenty of room.

Al Bateat pulled out his gun from his shoulder holster: 38mm, fully loaded with one in the chamber. He clicked the safety into the off position with his right thumb. His heart was racing. He spat out the cigarette and eased back towards the shop window so he could protect his rear. He felt light-headed. He tried to steady himself, to remember his training, but all he could think about was where he could run. He trained his gun towards the back door of the car. A man in the back of the car had a gun on him. The man shook his head in a 'no' motion. The gun aimed at him had a silencer on it. The man in the rear seat looked as if he would not hesitate. Al Bateat thought about his two young children and his wife. He wanted to be physically sick. His stomach churned.

The four men were now on him. One of the men quickly took the gun from Al Bateat with a quick twist and wrist lock. The gun fell to the ground, another man bent down to pick it up. Al Bateat noticed the three moons tattooed on the underside of the man's right wrist. Still in the painful lock, Al Bateat was led towards the car.

Al Bateat had been tracked for a long time but he didn't know it. His assailants knew everything they needed to know. They had been watching Salah El-Din for weeks and then Al Bateat popped up. They put a team on him. Bugged his phone. When they learnt that he was setting up a meeting about capturing Salah El-Din and the name Sabath came up, their boss knew he was meeting Templars. They were ordered to kill everyone at that meeting but to interrogate Al Bateat in case they had missed anything. Then they were ordered to execute him. The meeting place was known through Al Bateat's phone calls. The bomb team was in place. They would blow up the Templars.

The Yemini was bungled into the back of the Lexus - blindfolded. He was punched several times in the head and ribs to subdue him. He was driven to the industrial district of Musaffah, just off the E30, and to a disused warehouse some ten miles from Seeb, Abu Dhabi International Airport. It echoed inside. He heard planes take off and land, large planes. Other than the Al Bateen Executive Airport, near to the Eastern Mangroves, he knew there was no other airport. With the frequency of the planes coming and going, he knew where he was. Al Bateat was exhausted. He was scared. His hands were tied behind his back. He was bloody, still blindfolded and his feet were bound to the legs of the chair he was sitting on.

The torture began immediately. His blooded blindfold was removed. Through bleary eyes he saw his four assailants. He did not see the man from the car. However, there was a fifth man in the room, a man he had not seen before. It was obvious to Al Bateat that this man was the leader of the group, just by the way everyone treated him and by the way they looked at him: eyes down, tentative, paying him full attention.

He was dark skinned. His hands were scarred – the white scarring stood out against his dark skin. He wore a suit, dark blue, with a white open necked, button-down shirt. His shoes, black, were polished. For some strange reason they caught Al Bateat's attention straight away because you cannot keep shoes looking shiny in the Middle East with all of the tons of sun-bleached desert sand strewn on virtually every inch of the Emirate. On his face were markings; they looked like African tribal markings – puncture marks on the face, single puncture marks, side by side. Under each eye and from the cheekbone down in line with the mouth. The hot ash that his father had rubbed into his face, whilst he was having it punctured one hole at a time, when he was four years old, had lifted the welts and ensured the markings always remained. The man's eyes were almost ebony, his stare unsettling because it was devoid of emotion. He was nearly six feet tall, long braided hair to his shoulders. He weighed around 196 pounds and most of it was lean muscle. His forehead carried a scar, around five inches long; his nose carried another scar, three inches long and running horizontal across his nose. Al Bateat knew this man would kill him and not think twice about it if he did not cooperate.

"My name, Bo Bo Hak. I bleed you."

Al Bateat struggled to understand him. His lexicon was short and sharp, almost clipped, like pigeon English but with a French accent.

The torture started immediately and lasted for 25 minutes. He now had two broken ribs, his torso heavily bruised – the pain was beyond anything he had ever experienced before, beyond what he thought severe pain could ever feel like. He told them everything. However, he'd never known that the man in Scotland, or the Lebanese man, Sabath, or the people he was going to meet at the Al Watan café, on Al Fal street, were Knights Templars.

Al Bateat didn't understand why they had left him there. He didn't care that something was happening elsewhere that took them away; he just wanted to get out of there before they came back and killed him. He struggled and managed to get his hands free and slip the rope that bound them, then he untied the rope from around his ankles. The single guard left to watch him was lazy. A metal pipe across his head killed him instantly. He took the man's phone and money. Al Bateat made for the highway and flagged down a taxi and headed for the airport where rental cars were a plenty.

Later that night, after hiring a four-wheel vehicle, he would drive over 775 miles, which would take him a little over 13 hours. From Abu Dhabi he drove to Al Ayn, the southern end of the Emirates, and then through the night into the Sultanate of Oman. At Nizwa he turned right and pressed on. By early morning he was making good headway. The mobile phone he had taken from the guard rang. He'd forgotten all about it. The sun was beating down some 38 degrees and he was heading for the border with Yemen. He answered it tentatively. He recognised the voice; it was the African's voice, Bo Bo Hak. His message was short.

"When you smell the petrol, remember my face."

Al Bateat opened the window and threw the phone away into the desert. Had he not thrown the phone away, and had he called André Sabath instead and told him about his assailants and about the three moons they all had tattooed on the underside of their right wrists, Sabath would have told him not, under any circumstances, to go home. He would have told him to call his wife and tell her to go stay with relatives; to travel as far away as possible. Sabath would have sent his nine Knights back home to the Lebanon and he would have caught a flight back to Scotland. But Al Bateat didn't call Sabath and because of that things would change for everyone involved, and it would start with Al Bateat.

Al Bateat entered Yemen and drove straight home on the outskirts of Sana'a, the capital. He got home midday on the 17th, almost 24 hours since his ordeal had begun.

The next day, Al Bateat and his entire family burnt to death in a house fire.

Chapter 6

Zivko Cesar Gowst

Zivko Cesar Gowst was born in Serbia around 1933, no one knows for sure as his birth was never registered; he was half Serbian and half Egyptian. Zivko was born prematurely and he was a sick and weak child. Zivko was also born with the congenital disorder of albinism. He was instantly different because of his disorder and suffered terribly at the hands of those that were supposed to care, love and protect him.

Zivko's father, Stallas Gowst, was a callous, unkind man; a tyrant who made Zivko's life unbelievably miserable and unbearable. He was a despicable, strict disciplinarian; a puritanical Christian who bullied his son, his wife, his work staff and his household staff and treated them all with derision and contempt. He cared nothing for them. He cared nothing for anyone other than himself. He ruled his family and staff with strict, overbearing, draconian brutality.

Stallas Gowst was the proprietor of a right-wing newspaper. In 1933, when Zivko was born, the world was still three years away from the rise of Adolf Hitler but the coals of war were already stirring and their glow was getting brighter each day. Stallas Gowst did well from the sales of newspapers but he also made money trading in the growing black market that thrived throughout the Balkans. He traded anything and everything: goods, people, food, currency, arms, and jewels ... As long as he could make money out of it, he would trade it; he was a ruthless racketeer. Stallas was also a fascist who became a Nazi sympathiser as a young man, then a co-operator, then a Nazi when Hitler came to power. He worked long hours, had a string of mistresses, was rarely home, and, when he was, he did not see the boy. He would not see the boy. From the day that Zivko was born and Stallas had first set eyes on his sick, newborn albino son, he had not seen him but three times more before Zivko's sixteenth birthday.

At the age of 40, Stallas embarked on a tour of Berlin, Paris, England, Istanbul and Egypt. He was away for three months, maintaining his business dealings via land and ship telegraph. Whilst in Egypt's capital, Cairo, Stallas encountered the Coptic Orthodox church, a Christian-based church whose head is the Patriarch of Alexandria and the Holy See of Saint Mark. He worshiped at one of their churches and it was there that he met Zivko's mother. She was 16 years old and stunningly beautiful. Her mother was a devoted Christian and so was her daughter. Mother and daughter went to church every day. Her mother could also be found, several times a day, praying but never when her husband was in the house. She always ceased when he went into the room. She used to whisper over and over again, *alshaytan* – devil. Her husband was called Malik Abu Malik Ismail and he did not go to church; neither did any of his sons. On the two occasions that Stallas walked out with Malik, whilst he seemed to command respect from the people in the small town where they lived, that respect bordered on fear. He recognised the look; it was the same look he received from his staff and his workers. He believed that he and Malik were men of similar religiousness beliefs, but nothing could have been further from the truth.

Within a few weeks and through an interpreter, he had negotiated Malik's daughter's dowry and her hand in marriage with her father – paying a dowry price which would feed the rest of his family for a year. Her father believed she was going to a good home and would live like a princess in the affluent west. That's the story they had been told by this wealthy bachelor gentleman. Six months later, the girl, now seventeen, arrived in Serbia, with no other language than her native Arabic and an old, battered camel skin suitcase containing one change of clothes and a hair brush. Stallas and his young bride were married the very next day. However, her misery started before she left Egypt – she didn't want to leave. It got much worse the day she arrived at her husband's home.

Zivko's mother always felt alone: she quickly realised she was alone. She had no one to talk to and no way of communicating, other than some basic hand gestures. The weather was harsh, bitter and cold compared to what she was used to; she never felt warm. The culture was alien and the only people she had met – her husband's house staff – were brusque and suspicious of the foreigner. She found the language difficult because there were no common structures between the two languages and there was no teacher employed for her. No one to explain it to her, to teach her the words, the phrases, idioms and grammar.

Within days, Zivko's father was sexually brutalising his 17-year-old bride on a regular basis. Drunk, he would beat her, then he would rape her and her screams would go unanswered by the staff employed at the house. He portrayed himself as a man of God. He believed in the God of the old Testament, Yahweh: revengeful, harsh and cruel. It was an empty, loveless marriage, desperate and wretched for the young girl. He had bought a trophy wife, a young wife. He got annoyed as she constantly wept. She was just a child. He treated her like mud on his boots – as he did most people. She was an object to him; another one of his possessions to use as he wanted. She dreaded the rising of the sun and him waking. There was no fairness in her life, no genuineness, no kindness, no love and no way home. Her family and her God had abandoned her.

Stallas blamed his wife for giving him a defective son. He wanted nothing to do with the albino child. He was ashamed of the boy, but more than that, he was disgusted by the sight of him. He had

82

been told by the doctors that the genes had been passed down by one of the boy's parents. Stallas believed it was not his side of the family that carried the mutant gene, it was her family, her Arab family and he despised her for what she had given him. In Europe and North America, one in 20,000 people have albinism, in other parts of the world, the third world, it can be as high as one in 5,000. Stallas had never seen an albino. He considered the boy marked by the devil. It wasn't God's fault, it wasn't Stallas's fault, it was her fault, the women he now referred to as the 'Arab whore' or 'the monster's mother'. He was, like his medical advisors, ignorant of the facts.

From an infant, Zivko was hidden away by his ashamed father. He was kept in the nursery at the far end of the chateau, the 18th-century family home on the edge of a vast and dense forest full of wild boars, tall trees, poisonous mushrooms and long, grey shadows. Inside the chateau, at the far end of the house, hidden away, is where Zivko spent most of his young life. He slept, ate and lived there. He was only ever allowed out if his father was away on business and there was no chance of him coming back unexpectedly and finding the boy out of the nursery. His retribution on his house staff and his wife, would be punitive if this were ever allowed to happen. However, from about the age of four, Zivko had started to roam the hallways and corridors of the house late at night, when the household was fast asleep. A sickly looking, frail, ashen, ghost-like albino child, barefoot, wearing threadbare pyjamas because his father was so thrifty, listening outside the doors to snores, coughs, restless noises and sleeping people. He would sit in the drawing room and places he was never allowed to go during the day when people were about. He would sit and hold conversations with his imagery self. "We like it here, don't we, Zivko?" … "Yes, we do, Zivko, we like it here," referencing himself in the first person. Odd. Worrisome and unchecked, he took refuge and companionship with the only person he knew: himself, his inner self.

In the kitchen he would pretend to make a sandwich and then

in the dining room he would sit and pretend to eat it, holding a conversation with himself in the low scratchy, eerie whisper he had begun to speak in, in the isolation and darkness of the night. He would linger in the reception area where the coats hung. He would smell his father's coat. As a boy, the closest he ever got to knowing his father was the smell on his father's coat. No one knew about Zivko's nocturnal wanderings. When everyone was asleep and the darkness was at its fullest, he roamed freely. It was during these times that he glimpsed, all but briefly, what it would be like to be part of the family. Part of the house. Part of his father's life. It was cruel and yet it helped temper his growing psychosis a little. Alone, he learnt to walk silently over the creaky, bare floor boards, quietly mumbling and talking to himself.

The nursery was a cold and draughty combination of three rooms: a small bedroom for the infant, a sparse, barren room for the nanny, and a classroom. In the winter the nanny was allowed just one bucket of logs per day for the nursery fire – despite the house being surrounded by a large, dense and overgrown forest. In the winter, temperatures fell to freezing most days and cold blizzards from the Artic or Russia, drove the wind-chill temperatures well below zero.

In 1936, Zivko celebrated his third birthday and by October of the same year, Germany and fascist Italy had formed the Rome-Berlin Axis treaty and the world was about to change. These events would also change the shape of Zivko's life. His father, one of Hitler's greatest supporters in Serbia, would also eventually benefit from the impending war and benefit beyond his wildest dreams.

From the age of four, Zivko had Bible studies every day for an hour. The priest who taught him, also came on Sundays to administer mass. His father would not let his wife or his son attend the same church that he attended. He would not let his wife or his son beyond the grounds of the estate. His wife had not left the estate since arriving there many years before. Later in that same year, the war machine grew a little bit bigger when Nazi Germany and Imperial

Japan signed the Anti-Comintern Pact against communism and Russia.

By the time Zivko was five years old, it was 1938 and Hitler had annexed Austria into Germany: the eventuality of a war was now deafening across Europe.

In September 1939, when Zivko was six years old, Germany invaded Poland and World War II began. The usual priest stopped coming to the house, no reason was given. In his place a new priest, a much older man, arrived into Zivko's life. A zealot. He had no compassion. He was self-righteous. Holier than thou. He was also a deeply troubled man who wielded the words of God like razor wire. He breached the legitimacy threshold of preaching by beating the boy on his hands daily with a birch twig, if the boy failed to recite sections of the Bible they had learnt the week before. The birching, a corporal punishment dished out in the name of God, was pain enough. However, far more serious he started sexually abusing the young boy. When the priest came to the nursery, the nanny left and took her rest for an hour whilst the child had Bible studies. Left alone, the priest terrorised and raped the boy on a number of occasions. The introverted boy retreated further into his safe, dark place: his mind.

Zivko's mother had always spoken to him in Arabic – she knew no other language. A quick leaner – with an IQ of 160, a score that put him in the top1% in the world – Zivko was able to have basic conversations with her by the time he was seven years old. She would spend hours in the nursery with her son explaining about her wonderful homeland. About the people, the culture, the food, the history and of course the pharaohs and the pyramids. He was fascinated. His father kept an extensive library and one of Zivko's favourite pastimes was to creep in there at night when everyone was asleep and read the plentiful book collection by candlelight. There were a number of books on the Middle East, so he was able to see pictures of the things his mother described. He was always careful though to make sure the books went back exactly as he had found them. His father was a most meticulous man.

By the time he was ten, he was fluent in Arabic. He had also acquired a deep understanding of pronunciation and intonation, so not only was he fluent, he was accurate in local Arabic and classical Arabic. The young Zivko lived for those times when his mother was able to visit the nursery. However, those times were becoming less and less as her health was deteriorating. She was weakening from the hardships she suffered at the hands of her husband; and from the mental torment she felt listening to the terrible screams from her poor son. She was helpless to stop either and was slowly being eaten away by exhausting guilt, severe depression and debilitating sadness and loneliness. The lack of sleep dragged her even further down the road of despair. Her appetite was next to nothing and she was not getting the sustenance she needed to fight back. She had been married to her husband for just over ten years.

Now weighing less than six stone and looking more than 50 years old, despite only being 27 years old, most days she barely made it out of bed. Zivko would sneak down to her bedroom when his father was out and the house staff were busy elsewhere, and sit on her bed and talk to her in her native Arabic tongue and brush her hair for hours. When she slept, he would sit by the window talking to himself. Discussing with himself, like two people, all of the places they should take her, and all of the things they would buy her. Zivko was so introvertly institutionalised his reality was his madness.

Then, one cold, miserable November day, his mother mustered all of her strength, got out of bed, dressed, put some clothes into the small, battened, camel skin suitcase, her father had bought for her. She barely made it down the three flight of stairs. Weak and out of breath she walked unsteadily towards the front door and to freedom. She had never crossed that threshold since the day she'd arrived. If she wanted to go outside, she was only allowed to use the back entrance. As she approached the front door, her head swimming with nausea, she fell to her knees in the hallway, two feet from the front door, suitcase in hand, and took her last breath. Zivko's mother never made it to freedom. She keeled over and died.

Zivko was not allowed to go to the funeral, his father would not show his defective son to the world. His father wrote to her family as a matter of municipal process and as was required by the church but within days it was as if she had never existed.

Now the house lacked any love for Zivko. At the age of ten, he was truly alone and left to wander the rooms and corridors of the big house by himself at night. More disturbingly, he fell deeper and deeper into the dark passages of his young mind, where he also wandered. At the far end of the house, in the attic, Zivko found sanctuary. No one ever went there and no one slept near there. There he was free.

The smell had plagued the household for weeks. A search was made for a rotting animal carcass. Zivko's father was furious and blamed his staff for leaving meat out or their tardiness in their pest control duties. Living on the edge of a forest brought all kinds of vermin into the house. Their job, he reminded them, was to make sure none stayed but the smell was there and it was the smell of rotting meat. Zivko's father beat two maids to within an inch of their lives and after that, the household staff worked around the clock to find the source of the smell.

Two weeks after the hunt started, and several severe beatings later, the household staff found the source of the smell and the master of the house was called to see its origin. At the far end of the house, in a part of the attic that no one had been in for at least twenty years, they found a macabre sight. Butchered and skinned were over thirty rodents and seven larger animals, including four of the house cats. Their rotting carcases pinned to rafter joists; and their skins stretched and pinned to an old, faded wardrobe door. Their blood was held in a number of jars and it was obvious someone had been mixing their blood with other liquids. The stench was over powering; the sight sickening. A Russian migrant worker, who had been taken on a month earlier, was blamed for it. The household staff, fearful of getting blamed themselves, huddled together in secret and agreed the Russian would have to take the fall. He was severely beaten and thrown out without pay or even the few belongings he had come with. Had someone taken the time to notice, they would have seen young Zivko staring out of the nursery window, watching the Russian hobbling away from the house, bloody and bruised. Had someone take the time to listen, they would have heard him say, "Don't worry, Zivko, we will get more and find another secret place. We aren't worried, Zivko. We aren't worried because we know we will."

Zivko was never sent to school; he was schooled at home. He had no friends and, from birth and up to the age of 12, he had never met another outside soul, other than the priests, the household staff and a succession of mediocre teachers. From the age of four, he was schooled by a series of teachers who came to the house. Every two years his teacher would change as his studies' range increased in scope and depth. His studies started at 7 a.m. every day and finished at 6 p.m. six days a week – on Sundays, the Sabath, he would have mass alone with a priest.

During Zivko's eleventh year the paedophile priest stopped coming to the house. No one knew where he had gone or why; Zivko, however, did. His father didn't bother replacing him and so Zivko's religious teachings ended abruptly. However, it no longer mattered for he had long forsaken any Christian beliefs.

The trap Zivko had set for the priest, on what would turn out to be the priest's final day at the Gowst house and his final day on earth, was a success, despite the fact Zivko had never built such a trap before and, he had constructed it under the cover of darkness. It took him nearly two weeks to cut and shape the wooden stakes because of his lack of strength and his ill health. It took him six weeks to dig the pit, then place nine wooden, two-foot spikes into its floor. Almost a week to make a makeshift ladder and covering for the pit. Asking the priest if they could walk and continue his studies outside, he suggested a place at the edge of the forest where it would be shaded. The priest readily agreed. Seeing an opportunity to take the boy away from the house and away from the house staff, he was quick to put on his coat and take the boy outside. Leading the priest towards the pit, hidden on the fringe of the forest, Zivko mumbled to himself as they walked along. Old and somewhat hard of hearing, the priest did not hear the conversation.

"Not much further, Zivko, and we will see him without his coating. Yes, yes, Zivko, I know, we have the knife and we have made it sharp. Are you afraid, Zivko? We are happy, not afraid. Are you afraid? No, we are happy." The conversation with himself was in the low scratchy, eerie whisper he now used constantly.

Zivko hung back a little. The priest was keen to get to a place hidden by trees and out of sight, and so pressed on. Ahead the path turned slightly and ran between two thorn bushes. It was a worn path. Zivko had walked it over a hundred times to create the path's new line.

The priest felt the earth fall from his feet. The ground of loose leaves and twigs just gave way under him. Shocked and stunned he felt the searing pain all over his body. It took his breath away and he struggled to breath. He was upright but twisted. He tried to move but his body seemed pinned to the ground. Hunched, the priest was impaled by three of the nine wooden spikes. One through his foot – and clean through his boot. One went into his left armpit and out through his left shoulder. And the final one through his right hand that he had stretched out instinctively to break his fall. The stake in his foot hurt the most. He could not scream hard enough to stem his pain but he tried. Crying, he begged Zivko to help him. To call for help. To run to the house and fetch the house staff. He tried to twist. He tried to pull his impaled body up and away from its wooden spikes. Adrenalin rushed through his body. Blood gushed from his hand; it spurted like a geyser from his foot and out through his boot.

His muscles began to tighten; energy was seeping away, drained by shock, exertion and blood loss.

He saw movement above his head. He looked up. A figure moved. Through streaming eyes, he saw Zivko descend into the pit via a makeshift ladder. Swirling with pain he thought he was saved. He thanked the boy – but didn't consider how Zivko would have a makeshift ladder. The pit was only four feet by four feet wide. Zivko was close, next to him.

"Good boy. Good boy," he cried. "Bless our Lord for sending you to help me." He let out more screams. "Get help, now, son." His pain and desperation strangling his words.

Zivko stood expressionless.

"Not here boy, don't stay down here. Go. Get help from the house."

Zivko watched the priest writhe in agony. He reached out and touched the priest. He smiled a little with that same vacant look in his eyes he always had. The stare of an acute introvert; a boy lost in the dark passageways of his own mind. An eleven-year-old boy about to commit an act of a deranged psychopath.

"It's time then, Zivko," he said to himself. "It's time. We will see him now, Zivko, we will see him now. Yes, we will." Zivko pulled out his knife.

"What are you doing you crazy little bastard? What are you doing? Put that knife away and go and get help. Get help like I told you. I will whip you, I will beat you good, you albino freak. DO IT NOW."

"Shhh, priest, we have practised. We will do a good job, we promise, don't we?" "We do, Zivko, we promise. We have practised on the rats and cats and other beasts, haven't we, Zivko?" "We have. Zivko has. We have. It will be neat but, it will hurt." Zivko cut the priest along the length of his spine, from top to bottom. Then he cut along the priest's back waistline. "Vikings, priest ... they called it the 'blood-eagle'." He cut some more. Deep. "I want you to know, even though you cannot see, I want you to know what we are doing for you. We will pull your skin back." As he said it, he did it. In less than 60 seconds, as the priest roared and screamed with pain and fright, the skin on his back was peeled back and flapping over his shoulders.

"Now, are we ready?" "Yes, Zivko, we are ready. Now we must detach his ribs from his spine and open them out. Then, we will pull his lungs out." The priest passed in and out of consciousness. Zivko had a small saw on the pit floor already. He sawed through the ribcage, where it was attached to the spine and then opened his ribs outwards; then he pushed his hands inside and pulled out the priest's lungs.

Zivko completed his task within one hour and at some point, during that time, the paedophile priest died. Zivko filled in the pit in just four hours, just before the sun went down. He walked back into the house and to his bedroom at the far end of the building. That night he slept soundly; he didn't stalk the corridors of the house that night. He did not dream, he did not stir. Zivko Gowst slept soundly.

As for the myriad of teachers that came and went in the Gowst household, none were of good calibre. All were cheap, and most didn't care if the boy learnt or not; it was a job and they had a roof over their heads and they got fed. However, to the quality of Zivko's schooling, none of them mattered because he had schooled himself from his father's extensive library and often knew more about the subject than the so-called subject specialist. In that time, three teachers disappeared and never returned, just like the old priest.

In 1945 Zivko was twelve years old. Eight events that year would change the life of the young Zivko Cesar Gowst. On March 22nd, the US Third Army, under General Patton, crossed the Rhine River. On April 30th, Adolf Hitler committed suicide. On May 7th, Germany surrendered to the Allies and Zivko's father planed a trip to occupied Germany. August 6th, the United States dropped the Atomic Bomb on Hiroshima, Japan. August 9th, another atomic bomb was dropped, this time on Nagasaki, Japan. September 2nd, Japan surrendered to US General Douglas MacArthur and the Allies. On October 23^{rd,} Zivko's father travelled to northern Germany and became a very wealthy man. And finally, on December 16th, Zivko met his first outsider, when his grandfather – his mother's father Malik Abu Malik Ismail – arrived in Serbia at the house of his deceased daughter – and his obviously disturbed and introverted grandson. Malik had wanted to visit his daughter's grave and pay his respects for two years but because of the war and international tensions, he was not able to travel until now.

Malik was a strange man; he was kind to Zivko, but Zivko thought there was something about his grandfather that gave him an air of mystery, almost an air of danger, although Zivko never felt in danger with him, quite the reverse. He felt that something was slightly off-kilter but he couldn't put his finger on it. Malik stayed for a month. Zivko's father stayed at his town house in the city and only met Malik twice and both meetings were brief. His head housekeeper was told to cater for him but to get rid of him as soon as she could. Only Zivko was happy to see the visitor.

That one month was a happy time for Zivko, the happiest since his mother had died. At last, he had someone to talk to. Someone who did not ignore him. Someone who did not treat him like a freak, like the household staff, or despise and hate him, like his father. Someone who did not beat and abuse him like the old priest, shout and malign him, like the teachers. Zivko and Malik spent every second they could together. When the teachers came, Malik sat in the room with his grandson and the teachers' behaviour towards the sickly albino boy were a lot more temperate with Malik there. The grandfather was an imposing man because of his stature. Tall and well built. He looked odd, though, in his western clothes; they didn't suit him and he often fidgeted with their awkwardness. Whilst Malik had some basic Serbian – he had been learning for many months – Zivko and Malik spoke in Arabic so the house staff never knew what they were saying. It was a blissful time for Zivko and for that brief period, he experienced glimmers of happiness, leaving those dark recesses of his mind for the company of his grandfather.

It didn't take Malik long to work out what kind of man his daughter had been married to. He felt shame for allowing her to marry him. But he had agreed to it for the price of feeding the rest of his family for a year. He also quickly worked out what kind of father he was to Zivko and how the rest of the household treated the boy. However, Malik was no fool; he also saw the demons lying just behind Zivko's eyes. The disturbing, psychotic darkness that Zivko lived in was plain to see. When Zivko told his grandfather what the old priest had done to him, he said it without emotion. In its telling, he was cold and impassive. He talked about it as if it had happened to someone else and would break into a mix of the first and third person whenever he was describing any of the horrors he had endured. What Malik noticed most was how desensitised his grandson had become to those horrors. He saw how the boy had gone through the torturous and dangerous process of self-blame and recriminations, through to self-loathing, self-hate and self-harm. He also saw how he was now beginning to show signs of mimicking the cruelty. He had a way of harnessing that and helping the boy, but the boy was too young; he needed to wait – often you can become the evil that besets you.

In the final week of his stay, Malik gave Zivko two books he took from the red, ornate trunk he had carried halfway around the world. The first was a large anthology of Arabic and Arabic history. The beautifully handwritten tome was scribed by a craftsman; the lines, the twist, dots and swirls of the Arabic writing wove like patterned poetry. The second, a black leather-bound book, small with a sliver metal clasp. It was embossed on the front with three crescent moons, the same design as the tattoo his grandfather had on the underside of his right wrist. He called it *Al kitab – the book*. He told Zivko he should only read the second of the two books if he ever lost complete faith in his religion, Christianity. Zivko had already lost faith; in fact, Zivko hated religion because of his father and the priest but he didn't tell his grandfather. Malik also gave him a piece of folded paper. On it, neatly written in Arabic, was the address of a man in Cairo, called Samir Fancy. He told Zivko, if he ever read the second book and should he then want to know more of its origin and teachings, he should write to this man, he would help him. This man, he told him, knew of ancient times.

Malik left as he had come, without fuss. Expecting nothing. Gracious and polite. He was sad to say goodbye to his grandson and Zivko was sad to see his grandfather's taxi drive away from the house and down the long drive. Within days of Malik leaving, Zivko was back in those dark recesses.

Whilst Zivko's native tongue was Serbian, with his teachers he also studied Hungarian, Romanian, and English. By the time he reached sixteen, and thanks to his own nocturnal studies, he was fluent in all three, as well as Arabic. Each teacher was chosen by his father and each given the strict instructions to teach the boy and ensure he was thoroughly disciplined for any tardy or unpunctual behaviour. Often, he would be made to sit by the window, the sunlight piercing his delicate eyes causing excruciating pain.

By the age of 15, a long line of so-called medical people, charlatans, quacks, hoaxers and swindlers began to appear. His father, realising that he would not be able to keep Zivko prisoner within the estate forever and the fact that he was now extremely rich, although no one knew just how rich, spent money in a vain hope. He employed the medical experts to 'fix' his defective son. Many of the so-called medical experts gave him harmless herbal remedies that did nothing other than take away his appetite for a few days and make him feel sick. Others were not so harmless. A number of them injected liquids into his body to change the composition of his blood; others made him wear metal contraptions that restricted his movements and dug deep into his skin. Some used small doses of poisons in daily concoctions, which left him weak and bedridden for days, and one experimented with electrodes stuck to his head and lower back. This went on until he was 17 years old. However, it would not be the last of the experimental attempts to understand the deficiency of melanin in his body and the defective genes.

By the age of 21, Zivko had become bitter, manipulative, controlling, Machiavellian and as cruel as his father. He had turned into a wretched, spiteful, self-absorbed person with no concern for others. Because of what had happened to him, he hated the Bible, Christianity, men of the cloth and God. No longer could the household staff bully him; he bullied them, and he loved the power and control he could wield. No longer could priests abuse him, teachers dominate him and charlatans strap devices to him and run electric currents through his head.

On the day of his 22nd birthday, he received a telegram to say that his grandfather, Malik, had died in Cairo. Zivko decided the time had come to leave the house for good. It was time to leave the chateau that had imprisoned him all of his life and seek what lay beyond. To seek his life and not what others – his father – thought that should be.

He believed he could get enough money together to buy a third-class ticket for passage to Egypt, to see his mother's family. However, he also had another motive to travel to Egypt. Zivko had read the book his grandfather had given when he was twelve. The black leather-bound book with the small silver metal clasp, embossed on the front with three crescent moons, the same design as the tattoo his grandfather had on the underside of his right wrist. His grandfather had told him he should only read the book if he ever lost complete faith in his religion, Christianity. Zivko had read the book the first night he had been given it: and most nights since. The second reason he had for wanting to travel to Egypt was to meet the man who owned the name his grandfather had given him on a note: Samir Fancy.

Zivko decided he would confront his father and tell him he was leaving and no longer wanted any more to do with him. He would be leaving for Egypt and then he would go on to Africa, to the

French Congo, and seek his fortune in the gold mines he had read so much about. He had first learnt about them at the age of sixteen; from then on, he read everything he could and self-studied mining techniques, geological engineering, gold extraction processes: hard rock, surface mining, cyanide extraction. By the time he entered adulthood, Zivko knew just about everything there was to know about mining gold.

Once he had decided to leave, he'd resigned to take nothing from his present life other than the clothes on his back, the leather-bound book his grandfather had given him and his mother's ivory hair brush, with which he used to brush her hair.

He arranged for one of the household staff – a labourer from Hungary who helped around the grounds – to take him into the city using one of the cars in the garage. Zivko had never been taught to drive.

Zivko arrived at his father's residence around 8 p.m. The driver dropped him off out front and then parked up close by. Outside it was dark and drizzling with rain, and Zivko raised his overcoat collar to protect his white, weak frame from the cold. He paused outside the front door, shivered from the cold, then took a deep breath and rapped on the door lightly – partly because he was nervous. His father opened the door after a few moments – visibly annoyed at the intrusion. He was alone and drunk, he had a crystal glass goblet of red wine in his hand – his fifth that night. Inside the room a fire raged in the hearth and there was a smell of spiced *pljeskavica* – pork and lamb – in the background. Candles lit the hallway. Zivko was not invited in and stood outside in the cold and the rain.

"My God, if it isn't the desert whore's son. What the hell do you want … and how in the hell did you even get here?"

Zivko could count on one hand the amount of times he had exchanged words with his father over the years, and it was never him that had instigated the exchange. "Father." He didn't lower his head; custom would have been to bow the head low out of respect, and the slight to his father was a deliberate act that did not go unnoticed "We wanted you to know," he began in a low scratchy, eerie whisper, "that we shall be leaving in twelve weeks' time. We shall go and will not return." It felt good to face his nemesis. He was outwardly weak but inside his exceptional IQ gave him great power over people. Dwelling in the dark recesses of his mind gave him strength; dwelling there for so long made him a psychotic, dangerous, calculating narcissist and he liked himself for it.

"Good, I was intending to sell the property next year anyway and evict you all. So, go, you'll get nothing more from me, not one dinar. Go and be damned with your wretched, disease-ridden body." He paused. "And where the fuck can you go anyway? You defect. Eh, where can you go? Who the fuck would have you? Look at you, you disgust me. Everyone will despise you, freak. You brought shame to my name; your very existence killed your mother. Go, go and be gone with you, you pink-eyed reject. Always looking; always watching, aren't you? Good riddance to you." His rant over, his father downed the hefty glass of red wine, merely adding to his inebriated aggression. "Good riddance to you."

Zivko was irked. His temper rose slightly. "It was you who killed our mother, not me. If I'd been stronger, we would have protected her like she tried to protect us but I wasn't. We couldn't protect her; we were weak. You destroyed her, repressed and oppressed her, like you do everyone. You, and you alone, father, you killed our mother. You."

"Fuck you. And what's this fucking 'we', you fucking idiot?"

"You're a failure, Father. No wife, no children. Can your money keep you company? And where's the Nazi Party you loved so much, the Party that is hated by most of the world now? Where's your God from your church, your priests? You will die alone and we shall rejoice."

His father raised the glass goblet lurched forward but his foot caught the threshold step and it unbalanced him. He stepped back on his right foot to right himself and caught the edge of the bottom of the door with his foot and fell over. There was a low cry and sound like gristle being cut. He managed to roll onto his back. The glass wine goblet had snapped in the fall and the stem and base now protruded from his neck, blood gushing out. He gurgled and coughed and blood spat out of his mouth. "Help me, help me," he cried.

Zivko knelt beside him. He placed his hand on his father's head – it was the first time he had ever touched his father. He leaned down further and smelt him. He smelt the same as his coat that had hung in the hallway by the front door.

"Shhh now, Father." He was surprised how cold and clammy his father's skin felt. He pushed against the glass and it slid further into his father's neck "Poor Father; poor, poor Father." He started to sing "*Horst Wessel*", the banned Third Reich song. Softly he uttered the words, softly, as one would to a baby. "*Die Fahne Hoch! Die Reihen fest geschlossen ...*"

A large pool of blood gathered around his father's head, soaking slowly into the ornate door rug. His father, prostrate, eyes getting wider; a gaping gash in his neck, glass everywhere. His colour draining.

"I think ... we think you may have cut one of your main carotid arteries. If we remember our biology classes ... ah, Mr Vlado, a particularly nasty man you employed when I was around thirteen, but he's gone now, father. We removed his coat and we saw inside him and it was glorious. He cried; oh, how he screamed at us to stop. We saw inside him.

"Perhaps you could call your Lord. Call him for help; let me see him help you. Call him; Call HIM. CALL HIM, FATHER. *Die Fahne Hoch! Die Reihen* ... shhh. Your God never helped me. I called and called but he never came. The priest would not stop, I called for your God's help, I called you for your help ... *Die Fahne Hoch! Die Reihen* ... Shhh now, Father." Zivko pushed the glass stem still further inside his father's neck, more blood flooded out. His father screamed but Zivko placed his gloved left hand over his father's mouth, all the time humming the Nazi song.

Once his father had stopped breathing, Zivko closed the front door to the town house and left him lying where he had fallen. He made his way to the waiting car and informed the driver that his father seemed not to be in and they should go back to the chateau and they would try again another day. The journey back to the chateau was quite uneventful. Zivko said nothing to the Hungarian itinerant; he just sat in the back of the car and stared out of the window, quietly humming to himself.

Back at the chateau, Zivko instructed the driver to put the car back in the garage and then lock up for the night, he was going to bed. Zivko had moved into his mother's room a few years back. He had kept it exactly as it was when she had it – her clothes still hanging in the yew tree wardrobe and her vanity set still laid out upon her dresser. That night Zivko slept well, very well.

The next day, the alarm having been raised by one of his father's many lovers, the police arrived whilst Zivko was having breakfast. He appeared shocked when he was informed that his father was dead. It appeared, they said, that he had tripped in his hallway near to the front door and landed on the wine glass he was holding in his hand. There were two empty bottles of red wine on the side in his front room and wine mingled with the blood on the floor where he fell. They told him that, in all likelihood, his father had been drunk, tripped and pierced himself with the wine glass as he hit the floor – the fluted stem of the wine glass was still embedded in his father's neck. There was no sign of a break in, no sign of a struggle and no sign that anyone else had been there. That same day, the itinerant worker from Hungary, who had driven Zivko into the city to see his father, left the chateau. Zivko announced to the staff that he had told Zivko that he was going and moving on. The worker was never seen again. One week later, the police recorded a verdict of accidental death and the case of Stallas Gowst's death was closed.

Zivko believed that his father had made a will and further believed that all of the assets would be left to one of his father's mistresses, or all of them. However, what he hadn't figured on was the lawyers dealing with the probate, assigned by the authorities. The firm was Spiradon and Jana. Spiradon, as it turned out, had received the wrath of Zivko's father on numerous occasions. On one particular occasion, Spiradon had suffered greatly when Zivko's father had falsely accused Spiradon's son of theft. Zivko's father, a wealthy man of importance, was able to get the boy sent to prison for six months. The boy had been working as an intern at a rival newspaper, the editor being a friend of Spiradon. He'd been working there until he went to university to study law. He had handwritten a piece about Stallas's political activities; as a prominent businessman, Stallas was fair game. Whilst Spiradon was eventually able to free his son, after only serving three months in jail, the damage was already done. The boy was ashamed, despite being innocent and now he had a criminal record – he did not become a lawyer.

The other twist in the last will and testament of Stallas Gowst was the fact that Stallas hated Jews and Spiradon was a Jew. It pleased Spiradon immensely to think that Stallas Gowst would have been infuriated to find out that a Jewish lawyer had been appointed to investigate and recommend on his estate.

At the reading of the will, at the city premises of Spiradon and Jana, which Zivko did not attend but three women of low standing and ill repute did, the lawyer announced that Zivko's father's will, as produced by one of the aforementioned women, was null and void because it had not been signed. However, Spiradon already had a trick or two up his sleeve to get his revenge on Stallas Gowst – deceased or not – and Spiradon had no compulsion in manipulating the law to assert revenge because that's exactly what Stallas had done to him. Spiradon announced that the case must be tried in probate court and decided by the courts regarding who got what, what taxes or debts were to be paid. He promptly lodged the case with the clerk of the court that very day, so that the estate was now protected in probate. The manipulated wheels of justice were now in motion.

Zivko, still believing he would not inherit anything anyway, because everyone knew his father's feelings towards him and therefore he could not see a judge ever ruling in his favour, decided to leave Serbia that week. However, at the suggestion of Spiradon, he was ordered by the courts to remain in the country until the matter of the will was sorted out. Spiradon, through his long-established contacts with the clerks of the courts, was able to get the case fast-tracked. It was due for hearing in one week's time. Zivko stayed.

When the hearing began, the court room was packed. Most of the town had come out to see the circus they believed the proceedings would be. They all knew about Stallas Gowst's philandering, his brutality towards his family, his staff, his workers, how he treated Jews and just about everybody else. They all knew that he hated and despised his albino son, Zivko; and they all knew that the brutish man had many mistresses, and many of them would not be afraid in making a show of themselves if money was involved. The townsfolk sat in the gallery and savoured the moment as the proceedings began.

Spiradon, having been called by the clerk, announced that there was good news in the case of the last will and testament of Stallas Gowst. "It seems that Mr Stallas Gowst," he began, "had made two wills, one which was not signed and thus necessitated the need for these proceedings and one which, as it turns out, was indeed signed. If it pleases the court, I found the signed will and testament whilst tidying and archiving, for the purpose of the putting the estate in order, all of Mr Gowst's papers that he had in keeping at his offices. It became clear to our firm that both the will, rightly dealing with real estate, in this case the family home and its estate and a townhouse in the city, and the testament, rightly dealing with all his personal property, of which there are many and an inventory of which is contained within the testament, are, in our opinion Mr Gowst's true last will and testament."

Spiradon passed a copy of the will to the clerk who then passed it to the judge. The judge studied it for a minute or two, then announced, what would become a talking point for the next few years.

"And this signature," the judge said pointing to the last page of the will, "you are satisfied that this is indeed Mr Gowst's signature and you have no reason to believe it was signed under any duress?"

"I do believe it is indeed Mr Gowst's signature and we have no reason to believe he signed it other than willingly," Spiradon answered.

"Then," the judge announced, "it is clear to this court that the deceased, Stallas Gowst, has made a true and legal last will and testament and I hereby rule that the court recognises that this will represents the wishes of the deceased, as made by him in sound mind and body." He hit his gavel hard on his bench. "You sir," he said, turning to Spiradon, "are hereby ordered to formally read the last will and testament of Stallas Gowst, at your appointed offices, within five days of this day. And, as there is only one beneficiary to the decease's entire estate, a Mr Zivko Gowst, who is therefore the sole heir to the estate, you need not make it a public meeting."

Even the stenographer stopped in her tracks at the announcement that his son, Zivko, had inherited his father's estate. There was a gasp from the gallery. There were screams and shouts from three woman of a questionable standing. The court constable had to intervene and two male members of the public had to help the constable escort the ladies from the courtroom. The judge banged his gavel down on his bench again, rose, then left the court room.

Four days later, Zivko was at the offices of the court appointed lawyers, Spiradon and Jana. He had inherited everything. He promptly appointed them his own lawyers and instructed them to sell everything. He told them he would forward details of where he wanted the proceeds to be transferred in the coming weeks. Spiradon was glad that Zivko hadn't attended court the week before. Spiradon had never met Zivko before and was quite shocked at how disturbed the young man was. Stallas's son sat in front of him constantly talking to himself in a way that suggested he believed he was two people. It was blindingly obvious to Spiradon and his clerk, who witnessed the documents that needed to be signed for Spiradon's firm to be Zivko's lawyers and in absentia, his power of attorney, that the young man had some very serious issues.

It came as no surprise to Zivko that his father had a private bank account out of the country. However, whilst he had long suspected why his father had made a rather dangerous trip to Germany, on October 23rd, 1945, he hadn't any proof, until now. The lawyers gave Zivko the details of an account, held in Zurich, in his father's name. They told Zivko they had already notified the bank that all assets of Stallas Gowst, held by the bank, had now passed, in transfer, to Zivko Gowst, his only son and heir. The lawyers did not know what his father had there, but Zivko believed he did. He would be proven right.

Three days later, Zivko headed for Egypt, via Zurich, with only the clothes on his back, the book with three crescent moons on the front and the address of a man called Samir Fancy, which his grandfather had given him. He also had his mother's ivory handled hair brush, he kept everything in the small battered, camel skin suitcase brought to Serbia, from Egypt, two decades before.

Five years after Zivko had left Serbia, a chance discovery was made by contractors clearing an area of forest on the old Gowst estate. In all five graves were unearthed. The grizzly sight that awaited them was the same in each. Four feet down, wooden stakes buried into the ground and, on each, a mangled body. Four were identified as priests, the fifth was unknown. The coroner told the authorities that it would take approximately eight to twelve years for a body to decompose in that type of soil and that's why they were able to see the faces of the

deceased. They all had the same distorted, petrified, haunting look –
the coroner likened their look to the painting by the artist Edvard
Munch: The Scream.

Chapter 7
The DNA of Heroes

Place: A remote castle in Scotland

Majestic, steeped in history and imposing, Castle Glennfinch sits isolated and remote in the picturesque wilds of Northern Scotland. The area doesn't see many people. It's off the beaten track, deterrent enough, but also, there are no tourist attractions close by to entice visitors. It has no amenities close by either, no shops, petrol stations, hospitals, no airports; there is no reason for people to go anywhere near it. It doesn't have historical decay and rustic charm; it isn't on the tourist guides and it doesn't have the corruption of human visitors. It is not stifled by their noise, their presence or their predilections for litter. If someone happened to stumble across it, and made their way to the main door of the castle, they are either met by the housekeeper or his wife, neither are known for their welcoming nature; or they are greeted by a man who appears a little eccentric and looks a little like Sean Connery.

Unwanted strangers wouldn't see beyond the castle's high, solid stone walls and into the maze of hidden courtyards. They wouldn't see the men and women of the Order of Knights Templar, going about their business in total anonymity; nameless and faceless modern-day warriors; a secret organisation doing good and fighting evil, just as the Order has done for centuries: pious and brave. Neither would they see the communication systems, a complex network that maintains and drives their entire global infrastructure of over 3,000 Knights. They wouldn't see the training grounds: scenario areas, practise kill zones, extraction and infiltration practice areas and underground firing ranges. The numerous stores, rooms and containers, full of state-of-the-art equipment and resources used to ensure that the modern-day Knights are well equipped. Military field craft, including ground coverage, urban and rural, seek and destroy strategies; escape and evasion, entry and extraction, shock and awe and advance infiltration techniques and stealth soldiering. Combat techniques and fighting skills, unarmed combat training and self-defence, combat with knives and of course, swords. Firearms and weapon training, small arms, rifle and machine guns. Explosives. A myriad of intense training to ensure that the Knights are highly skilled in modern-day combat. They wouldn't see the man overseeing it all; they wouldn't see the Templar's Sergeant at Arms. Planning, directing, watching, leading, showing, to ensure that the Knights remained the most efficient and effective private fighting force in the world.

They wouldn't see the prayer meetings, the Bible studies; room after room full of old books, ancient scrolls, manuscripts and codices, collected and studied over centuries. Secrets and mysteries in print; answers to historical questions on paper and parchment; truth and the facts of the last nine centuries.

The castle, restored in 1972, has 30 updated and refurbished dwellings on the sprawling estate – they were completed in 2003. Outsiders would consider them tied cottages or perhaps they would guess they might be summer 'lets' – following the trend of many estate owners to generate new and much needed income. However, for the Templars, those 30 cottages are their first line of physical defence of the castle. They are run, operated and manned, as fully equipped garrison posts. Electronically protected – linked to the control room at the castle. Heavily armed, fitted with perimeter sensors, sound sensors, night scopes, infrared cameras and range of small arms. The garrison posts are their ring of steel protecting the castle and their holy 'Charge', which lies within. Two Templars live and work in each of the cottages. They are the 'eyes on the ground'; they are the 'frontline'. Every three months, new Templars come and take their turn at the outposts. This rotation is also used to bring Knights into the headquarters. To train them in the castle on new technologies, for new missions. To debrief them on completed missions, and to brief them on future planned missions. To bring them up to date with a myriad of operational changes. For them to meet other Templars they have not met before – to build comradeship and unity, a family. It is also used as rest time, down time, a contemplative time. A time to see their 'Charge', to kneel before it, genuflect and be in its grace. Medical examinations for fitness and tests of various kinds, are also undertaken. The rotation is a finely tuned operation, planned and delivered by a finely tuned military Order that continue to hide in plain sight.

There are places inside the castle that are consecrated ground. It is a sanctuary; it is as sacred to the Templars, as the Temple Mount in the Holy Land – the Ark's first resting place, built by King Solomon. There, inside the Templar castle, hidden deep within its subterranean passageways, is where the most iconic, religious artefact of all time – the Ark of the Covenant, the Templar's 'Charge' – rests in its holy grace.

The castle, with its two-metre-thick walls, is a solid and safe sanctuary for the Templars and has been for decades. It is surrounded by hundreds of miles of Scottish wilderness. On three sides are bracken-covered hills and on the other side, a dense spruce forest. Past the spruce forest is a mixture of little-used tracks, grassy plateaus, ranks of dry stonewalls and rambling glens.

The castle has all of the modern amenities, state of the art electrical and gas back-up systems; 35% of its energy consumption is from solar energy. It has food stocks and medical and operating facilities. It has many features you wouldn't find in normal life, but you would find in some leading technology and military instillations. The only non-Templar staff employed on the estate are a local family. Their ancestors had served the Templars when they first acquired the castle centuries before and the family have looked after the Order ever since. They clean and cook for the Templars; act as a public face. Deal with anyone appearing unannounced at the castle; deal with the payment of bills and repairs. They keep the Templar's secret. They keep the castle's big secret.

The Templars are Brothers in Arms and refer to each other as brothers. Of the 3,000 Knights, 80% are male, and 20% are female. They are Knights, regardless of gender; the term brother means brother Knights. They are a family, a unified, secret Order.

Date: March 19th
Place: The castle

It had been three days since the aborted Abu Dhabi mission. Al Bateat was missing; he had either gone to ground and was in hiding, or he was dead, they still didn't know. André Sabath was still there looking for Al Bateat. Sabath had eight Knights with him, who had flown down to from the Lebanon, plus he had the Knight he stayed with at Sas Al Nahkl, who lived in Abu Dhabi. No one was unduly worried; Sabath and his team were highly experienced.

Proctor Hutchinson, a senior member of the British Government's communications headquarters, GCHQ, was monitoring all coms for any news of Al Bateat or Salah El-Din. The only lead they'd had on Salah El-Din was by way of Al Bateat; without his help, there was no way to locate the criminal and complete the death sanction. They needed the Yemeni or they would be back where they had been for the past four years - nowhere!

The Templars still didn't know if it was Salah El-Din that had attacked Zakariah and his team at the café in Abu Dhabi and again at their hotel on Yas Island. At that moment, with what little information they did have, nothing made much sense about the events that had unfolded in Abu Dhabi. Things just didn't add up for both St Clair and Sabath. Something was off; they were both experienced enough to know that and it worried them a lot. They started to think that maybe there were two groups in play there. They knew that if Salah El-Din had discovered what Al Bateat was planning with Sabath and the team, then he would have gone to ground; it was his modus operandi, his MO. He had done it before. Time and time again he had just gone to ground and it had proven very successful for him over the years. It not only kept him alive, it had helped him grow his illegal organisation, Unity, and so prosper. They knew he would not have carried out a pre-emptive strike like the bombing. Even if he did, then certainly not one so public, unless there was great gain in it for him, which they couldn't see where there was. Also, whilst not averse to murder by bullet, they thought the hotel shootings were excessive and not normally his style; it was more gangster style.

Their thoughts kept going around and around in the same circle and with the same questions: why would Salah El-Din carry out those two strikes, especially the bombing? They kept coming back to the fact that there were only two possible answers: either he did carry out the strikes, and his MO had now changed, which was bad news because it meant he would strike anywhere and at any time; or, the second possibility, he didn't carry out the strikes and that meant someone else did: but who, and why?

Sabath had reported in and spoken to St Clair several times during the first two days after the failed mission. He called on the 17th and 18th. They spoke at length on every call. St Clair offered to send more Knights but Sabath didn't see the need. On one of the calls, St Clair brought in Proctor Hutchinson and Zakariah, so they could share their thoughts on possible scenarios. On both days, whilst St Claire was busy in the control room, trying to figure things out,

Proctor Hutchinson briefed the other Worthies by phone. They all agreed that Sabath and his team should stay in Abu Dhabi and see if they could pick up any information about either the bombing, the shooting at the hotel or what had happened to Al Bateat. However, thus far there was no trail to follow, no leads, no information, despite their best efforts. They knew that the first 72 hours was the vital timeline in any investigation; after that, the trail starts to go cold and it becomes much more difficult to follow. They were all frustrated but thankful that Zakariah and the team had made it out safely and back to Scotland.

Then the day of the 19th came and everything changed: Sabath did not call in that afternoon. St Clair grew worried; by 10 p.m. he started making calls – Abu Dhabi was four hours ahead, so by 10 p.m. it would have been 2 a.m. for Sabath. At 11 p.m. that night, Proctor Hutchinson called St Clair. Proctor Hutchinson's news was not good. He told St Clair that information had just come into GCHQ that Al Bateat, and his entire family, were now dead; they had died on the 18th. Hutchison told St Clair that the local Yemeni police investigators were saying it was murder. There was evidence the house had been dowsed in petrol, the charred wrists and ankles of the bodies, two adults and two children, had been bound with fence wire. Al Bateat's body was discovered ten feet away and it was thought he'd been forced to watch his family burn to death.

St Clair had kept the Nine Worthies informed of developments throughout the day and had called them several times. With the news of Al Bateat's death, and the fact Sabath had not reported in, St Clair knew he would need to call them all together. He had to call the Nine Worthies, the Higher Council of the Order of Knights Templar, to the castle. It was now too serious not to, despite the risk. They rarely met face-to-face; it was too dangerous. St Clair, routing his calls as always via the controller in Islington, made calls to a number of destinations all over the world. The Worthies were now gathering and they would be there, in Scotland, by the 21st.

For days, St Clair hadn't spoken much to anyone, not since the return of Zakariah, Dominique and Jonathan, from Abu Dhabi. They didn't know why he was so quiet – he hadn't told anyone about Sabath, other than the Nine Worthies and Zakariah, so no one knew the burden and worry he was carrying. No one knew that Sabath and potentially nine Knights might be missing but people understood their Grand Master enough to leave him alone. He needed thinking time. They all knew this was his way; whenever anything lay heavy on his mind he would go deep into thought. He also had a great sense of humour and was at times mischievous, but not now. They gave him space.

St Clair and the Templars were always dealing with new threats to their 'Charge' and to their Order and to their anonymity because of the interest in the Templar legends. There were hundreds of rumours, speculations, hypotheses, assumptions, guesses and, occasionally, some truth. There were thousands of associations, groups and individual people around the world that sought to prove that Templars still existed, or to prove they never existed. Trying to prove they took the Ark, or they didn't; or prove that they found the Spear of Destiny or had the Holy Grail or any number of other Bible relics. Millions of dollars spent trying to find the so-called Templar treasure. From virtually every corner of society, their past was studied and scrutinised and their Order and their secrets, investigated with forensic vigour.

Templars also had many enemies, dangerous enemies. Numerous people, organisations, criminal factions and even governments that would see the Templars demise, that would take what they had … what they protected and what they knew. St Clair was always mindful of the threats. He took them seriously; all Templars took them seriously. He had lived with those threats ever since he became a Knight of the Order and even more so, when he became the Order's leader, their Grand Master.

However, St Clair felt that something had changed, but he just couldn't put his finger on it and it bugged him. If Jonathan Rose, their Seer, had paused and listened, he may have heard the low menacing hum of it coming – coming his way; coming their way. Payne St Clair, the Templars' Grand Master, felt it. He knew something was out there and it was different. Ever since Abu Dhabi, he'd had the feeling of foreboding, barely perceptible, but it was there. Like the faint sound of a far-off drum.

Date: March 21st
Place: The castle

It had been exactly five days since the mission in Abu Dhabi had been abruptly aborted and their Knights barely made it out without casualties.

The 21st was full of showers but still laced with the smells and sounds of spring. St Clair was lost in thought as he headed for his favourite place. He made his way up the dimly lit, spiral stone stairs – steps worn with age and use. The sunlight fighting its way through the showers and seeping through the open embrasures. St Clair turned the large iron key and the oak door creaked as he pushed against it. He walked out onto the battlements and breathed in deep. He leaned on the waist-high parapet wall, pulled up the collar of his Barbour trench coat and buried his hands inside his coat pocket. St Clair loved the castle. He loved Scotland. Scotland had saved the Templars in 1307, when they were all but wiped out. It had welcomed them, given them a new home and then, like the rest of the world, it forgot about them as the Templars slowly retreated into the shadows.

As was his way, he was there, on the battlements waiting for them to arrive - he always waited on the battlements. He had called them on the 19th; now two days later, the last of them was arriving. However, one – Proctor Hutchison – would not come because they decided it would be better if he stayed in GCHQ monitoring the coms from the Middle East; he would join by video. One was about to retire, Norman Smith, the Templars' Sergeant at Arms. He was away setting up a home near his sister in Cornwall – he had lived in the castle for forty years. It was decided he would not take part in the meeting. And, one of them was missing: André Sabath. St Clair and Sabath had been friends for over 30 years and Sabath was St Clair's closest friend.

St Clair had also called Jonathan late on the night of the 19th and asked him to come to the castle on the same day as the Worthies. He would meet with him after his meeting with the Higher Council. It was time to tell Jonathan about the prophecy of the French maid and, of course, about the new Lionheart.

St Clair's first meeting of the day

The five Worthies were inside waiting for him. Some had arrived late the night before, on the 20th, and some in the early hours of the morning. The Higher Council of the Order of Knights Templar had gathered and St Clair, their Order's Grand Master, was about to join them.

The fire, already raging in the hearth of the great hall, gave out a welcome warmth, which extended beyond the hall; its light and heat always intoxicating as they seeped down the corridors. As was his habit, before he went in to meet the Worthies, St Clair paused outside the door to the great hall and checked his dress in the tall, 17th-century French mirror, hanging on the stone wall. Like all Templars when they attended formal meetings and gatherings, they wore their white battle dress to signify purity, symbolizing their abandonment of darkness for light, evil for good. He adjusted his white surcoat, centralising the distinctive red cross of the Templars. He breathed deeply and quietly asked God for his guidance. Once, perhaps, sometimes twice a year, the Worthies would meet. It's all they would risk: they had too many secrets to protect. He turned the black, iron ring handle and entered the great hall.

Tapestries depicting medieval adventure and stoic heroism

decorated the tall stonewalls in the great hall. History radiated from every direction. Carved into the stone hearth were the words, *'Nil nisi clavis deest, Templum Hierosolyma, clavis ad thesaurum, theca ubi res pretiosa deponitur'*. (*Nothing is wanted but the key, the Temple of Jerusalem, the key to the treasure, a place where a precious thing is concealed.*) It is the same Latin inscription that once adorned a precious jewel held by the Royal Arch of Freemasonry many centuries ago. The Templars were pious people, dedicated to the holy vows of righteousness; warrior monks, who worked in the shadows, dedicated to the sacred science of the Qumran – the original Nazarene church.

Payne St Clair, as the Order's Grand Master, took his seat at the head of the table. Normally, four Worthies would be seated to his left and four Worthies to his right. However, only two sat to his left and three to his right. On a large plasma screen, which looked decidedly out of place in the medieval surroundings and décor of the great hall, via video, Proctor Hutchinson sat waiting for his Grand Master.

The Worthies waited in silence, at their head hung the *baussant*, the black and white chequered war banner of the Knights Templar. They too had already donned their white surcoats for the initial welcoming ceremony of intoning chants and secret gestures. Now they sat around the long mahogany table that dominates the great hall of Glennfinch Castle.

They completed the ceremony of welcome and then each one took the Eucharist, the embodiment of Christ. Then St Clair rose from the high-backed Jacobean chair to address them. He was a tall and proud man; he personified reverence and dignity.

"Brothers, by God's grace we are called again. May our Lord watch over this Council and give us the wisdom we will need. And Lord, please keep our brother Sabath safe and his brave Knights, wherever they may be. Amen."

The Worthies lowered their heads in respect and a meaningful and concerned "Amen" was repeated by the Worthies – resounding in a rich deep tone around the stone-walled room.

St Clair raised his head. "Brothers," he began, "if you will permit me. Firstly. I would like to deal with the two positions that we have to fill quite urgently. As you know, Norman Smith, our Sergeant at Arms and one of our Council, is retiring at the end of this week. At the age of eighty-two, I think he deserves a long and healthy retirement. He has served our Order well over a number of decades. He is currently away setting up a home near his sister in Cornwall. I think Norman will find the transition difficult because he has lived in the castle for nearly forty years but I am sure we all wish him well. I have already given you my recommendation for a new Sergeant at Arms. You have a copy of his file that Courtney and Bertram sent to you last week. I think he will make a good addition to our Order and certainly has the background to be the person responsible for all our military supplies and weapons held at the castle, and those held in the cottage garrisons on our perimeter, and finally, those held throughout our operational cells in other countries. I would like us now to formally take the vote."

The Higher Council always voted the same way, no matter what the vote was about. Once the vote was called for, they would either remain seated at the table, signifying they were for a proposal, or they would leave the table, signifying they were against it. No chair was moved and the vote to appoint a new Sergeant at Arms was cast and the proposal agreed.

"Thank you, brothers," St Clair said, "it is a great weight off my mind that we shall have a new Sergeant at Arms because we are going to need him. The second vacancy is also due to a retirement. However, in this case we have had a candidate on our list for some time, in fact a very long time. We just need to convince him because he is not a fan of us Templars. You also have the report on him, which you have all read. My second proposal, therefore, is for him to take up the position of Master of the Blade."

Again, no chair was moved and the vote to appoint a new Master of the Blade was cast and the proposal agreed.

"Next, my brothers, is the serious matter of the replacement for Norman onto our council, so we are back to nine. I know some of you have suggestions, all good Knights and anyone of them, in my opinion, would make a great council member. However, I would like to propose that we hold off on the selection. It would take too long to make the formal appointment and carry out the initiation ceremony. We can't afford the focus shift, not in regard to item three of our agenda, our last item. My proposal, therefore, is that we postpone the appointment for now." Again, Payne waited to see if any chairs were moved back. He kept his head low and, as always, as the proposer, he would not vote. With no chairs moved, he announced that the vote had been passed and a postponement approved.

St Clair raised his head. "Brothers," he began, "item three and our last item. You have all received the detailed report compiled by Zakariah, on the failed Abu Dhabi mission. Of course, we now know that Al Bateat and his poor family were murdered. I briefed all those who came in late last night, so for those who arrived this morning, it saddens me to report that as of this time, André has still has not reported in, or responded to any of our calls or attempts to reach him. We have failed to locate him. Along with André and Tarik Tahir, the Knight from Abu Dhabi, there are the eight Knights who flew down from the Lebanon to support him. Other than you, and Zakariah, no one else knows about André and the Knights. I didn't want to alarm everyone but I think now we need to tell our people and I will begin today."

The concern about Sabath and his team was visible on the faces of the Worthies. The vows they had all taken as Templars were absolute. They left no room for compromise, once pledged, they were forever followed. Their commitment to their vows reflected everything they did. Their life was dedicated to the sacred science and the protection of the Order's 'Charge'. They had all made many

116

sacrifices over the years, but their lives were not their own, they had already given them to the Holy Order of Knights Templar.

"However," St Clair continued, "we do have news to share with you. We have more pieces to the puzzle of what happened. Proctor, would you tell our brothers what we have now learnt."

The plasma screen flickered slightly. "Thanks, Payne," Proctor said. "We don't know everything that happened, but I can now tell you that Al Bateat's mobile phone calls were all bugged. His mobile and house phone in the Yemen and at his apartment in Abu Dhabi. The Yemeni authorities confirmed this to British intelligence today. However, and here's the kicker, he was bugged twice. Different kit. They think, and we think, that two factions were listening in at the same time, without him knowing. We have to assume that at least one of them, maybe both, would have fed the calls through a monitoring algorithm that would have been pre-set with key word-flags because that's what we would have done; it's what we always do. When Al Bateat made his initial call to UK intelligence services and then to me, he used the name 'Salah El-Din', which would have been flagged. When he then had a conversation with André Sabath, we know he used André's name, despite being told not to. That would have been flagged. In the conversation he had with Payne, he said that 'I have friends in the Jordanian secret police … I know that you guys helped them capture their traitor Abu Taha, four years ago …' That would have been flagged. Plus, we have also been told by the Yemenis that Al Bateat reported in to his superiors several times during the build-up to our team arriving. We have to remember that their firewall is less robust and fairly easy to bypass. We have no idea what he said on those calls and what was overheard. We are assuming the worst."

St Clair carried on with the briefing. "Whoever was listening in to his calls, clearly would have known everything we were planning and, where and when. So, this is what we think happened. Al Bateat was watching Salah El-Din. But there was also another faction that started to watch Salah El-Din, for some other reason that we don't know yet."

The Worthies were surprised at this news. They knew that if it were true, it complicated things tremendously: another party in play, an unknown group in addition to Salah El-Din, was not a combination any of them relished.

"They would have discovered Al Bateat's surveillance," St Clair continued. "And, they would have quickly realised that he was not very experienced because he spoke openly on his mobile phone and his tailing technique would have been poorly executed. So, they bugged Al Bateat's equipment and probably had him followed, to find out what he was up to and why he was following Salah El-Din.

"Brothers, we all know Salah El-Din; we know what he's like and what he is capable of. We know how bad Al Bateat was at trade craft. Salah El-Din would have found out about Al Bateat's surveillance of him and would have bugged his equipment to find out why he was following him. That's our two factions. Salah El-Din bugged Al Bateat and the second faction who was watching Salah El-Din, bugged Al Bateat. So, earlier when I said that whoever was listening would have known everything, that means Salah El-Din would have known everything. He would have known about the Abu Dhabi meeting and that we were meeting to plan a trap for him, he would have been long gone by the time Zakariah and his team landed.

"We thought the team were safe on Yas; they were not because we have also now found out that artist impressions, of a number of our Knights, were circulated to a large number of hotels in Abu Dhabi, including Yas Island. Money was offered to anyone who saw any of the faces on the sketches. We hadn't realised that the hotel had been under surveillance almost as soon as our team had arrived. The hotel concierges in most hotels had sketches of Jonathan's face, along with Dominique's and four other Knights, one of them was of me. They had obviously been drawn-up by an experienced composite

118

artist; we had copies faxed to us. Neither Zakariah's likeness or Sabath's were among the sketches. We believe it was Salah El-Din that circulated them and offered the reward because all the Knights in the sketches were at Cumbria in 2008. Salah El-Din saw Jonathan and Dominique in Cumbria, but of course not Zakariah, who was fighting down at the farm house, whilst we were at the top end near to the entrance And, André was in Egypt raiding Salah El-Din's safe house. Those six Knights' faces would have been etched on the criminal's mind from that gun battle in Cumbria, back in 2008.

John Edison, who lived on the island of Barbados, had known St Clair since the very first day St Clair joined the Order. He had worked with him when he had been an active Knight, now over seventy, his mission days were over but his mind was still as sharp as it had ever been. He saw his Grand Master was deeply troubled, he guessed it wasn't only about their missing brothers and the seriousness of the situation, St Clair was always dealing with difficult scenarios – it was his job.

"You want to tell us something Payne," John Edison said. "I can see it in your eyes there is more than this. You called us here for another reason. You could have told us all this via the telephone."

St Clair sighed. He didn't want to say it; he didn't want to allow himself to think it was true but, he knew better. "Ah, John. I …" he started ruefully, then paused a little before carrying on, "… I we think that, perhaps, it was Salah El-Din that took shots at Zakariah and the team at their hotel. I think he just used local thugs instead of his normal crew because it was such a sloppy job; it was stupid to make it so public. But I don't think that it was Salah El-Din that planted the bomb at the meeting point with Al Bateat. And, I don't think he had Al Bateat and his family killed. I think it was the second faction."

All the Worthies' eyes were now on their Grand Master but it was John Edison who asked their question for them.

"Who then?" Edison moved uneasily on his chair. He wanted

the answer but, like the others, he didn't because by St Clair's demeaner they all knew the answer that was coming.

"I am worried that they have André, that they have him and the rest of our Knights. I think, brothers ... I think that this is the work of Abaddons."

It went deathly quiet. The only sound was the cracking and spitting of the wood in the hearth, as the fire raged on. Finally, John Edison spoke again.

"But we have not seen or heard from them for a long time, not since the conflicts after Sophia. Why have they resurfaced now? What has triggered their actions? We have taken great care to stay hidden. Why now?"

"Proctor, will you?" St Clair said, prompting his friend to give them the answer.

Proctor spoke. "Our best guess is that they were planning to lift Salah El-Din from Salalah and discovered Al Bateat trailing him."

"I don't get it, Proctor," John Edison said, "if they knew everything, why would they try and kill us, with the bomb? Wouldn't they take us alive if they could?"

"Because," Proctor replied, "we don't think they wanted us alive, there was no point; they would just kill us and be rid of a few more Templars."

"Why?" John Edison asked.

"Because," Proctor said, "they don't know about Jonathan; they don't know that we have a Seer. If they did, they would not have planted a bomb, they would have set some kind of trap to take our Knights to get to the Seer."

"So, what does that mean?" John Edison asked. "Where do we think André and his team are?"

"I'm afraid we think they are either dead and their bodies have not been discovered yet, or they have them. If that's true, André and his team are in real trouble and so is Jonathan because if they took the Knights, they probably know about Jonathan by now."

"Then we must all stay here," John Edison said. "We cannot risk being in the open if you are right. We have to reduce our exposure. We have to protect the Seer and the Ark."

St Clair's second meeting of the day, an hour after his meeting with the Worthies

Since moving into their cottage in Kirkcudbright, Jonathan and Dominique did not go into the castle every day. However, they were there a few times a week and would go whenever called.

Jonathan knew St Clair was worried, despite his best efforts not to show it. To Jonathan, the Order's Grand Master walked around the castle with a heavy burden. He didn't know what bothered St Clair, but it was there. It crept into his expression at times; it festered and lingered in conversations they had on their way to the Ark but never clarified. The castle's atmosphere seemed more edgy because of St Clair's demeanour. Dominique didn't know what was going on either and as always, she would tell Jonathan to wait and see, they would be told soon enough, when St Clair was ready, he would tell them. And then on the night of the 20th, St Clair telephoned and asked Jonathan to be at the castle the following day for a meeting. It was to be only the two of them. Jonathan was intrigued.

On the 21st, Dominique drove Jonathan to the castle. It was raining, a March shower. St Clair always called them blessing showers. He was thankful for all things and had a great way to look at them. The rain was a blessing because it watered the crops, plant life and animals; "Why would we not be thankful for that?" he would say.

"Another of those blessing showers," Jonathan called to Courtney. He was now standing outside the large, arched, double oak door – the main entrance to the castle – in his jacket and Red Skins cap. He'd already made the ten-yard dash from the car to the cover of the doorway.

Courtney locked the car and ran across the courtyard holding her umbrella. "I know he does, Jonathan, but have you ever noticed, you never see St Clair in the rain."

Once inside, Jonathan went off to find St Clair and Dominique went to chat with Courtney and Zakariah.

Jonathan and St Clair had been talking for about ten minutes. St Clair asked him how he felt about the Abu Dhabi mission; what had he learnt during that time. He asked him how he was getting on with his training. Jonathan explained that it was going okay but he was frustrated that some of the things he found difficult to master and a few things he didn't like. St Clair smiled and told him that Einstein famously said that if you judge a fish by its ability to climb trees, it will live its whole life believing it's stupid. Not everyone can do certain things but they can other things. He told him to find the things he felt he was good at, that he liked. He said that working hard for something you are not good at, don't like or you don't care about, is called stress. Jonathan was enjoying the chat, then St Clair dropped the bombshell.

Jonathan didn't quite know what to say. "Joan? Stake? French girl?" There was more than a hint of incredulity in his voice.

"Yes, *that* French girl," replied St Claire, smiling.

"And you think I am related to Saint Joan of Arc?" Jonathan asked.

"Don't forget her maladies."

"Maladies?" he said.

"Yes. Her Maladies, that's the best bit."

"Madness, is that what you mean?"

"As a hatter, some say," St Clair said.

"Some?"

"Some say different though," St Clair replied.

"Different?"

"Yes, some say she was a visionary who had visions. She heard things. She had what some doctors call 'crazy wisdom' or, 'theia mania' – divine madness."

"Divine madness. So, not psychotic behavior, strange, outrageous outbursts but wisdom?"

"Jonathan ..." St Clair began. Jonathan knew that tone, a bunch of facts were heading his way. "R.D. Laing said that madness may not be a breakdown, it may be a breakthrough; think about that. Put it another way, from an outsider's point of view, it would look like madness, but is it? A psychiatrist unfamiliar with divine madness cannot distinguish between these two. However, for those that seek answers, like us, that so-called madness is a divine gift, a mystical experience that is the gift of the Seer. When Joan was just a young girl, she used to hear voices calling to her. She believed it was God telling her she had a duty to her country."

"So, she was a Seer?"

"No," St Clair said.

"Wait, I thought you said she had a divine madness?"

"She did but she was not a Seer; not as we know the term: someone who sees writings and symbols on the Ten Commandments."

"Then why are we talking about Joan of Arc?"

"Because her daughter was."

"She had a daughter?"

"She did," St Clair said.

"And who was her daughter and how do you know she was a Seer?"

"Juliette Romée."

"Wait again. Joan was Joan of Arc."

"Actually, most people think her name was Jehanne Romée. She certainly took her mother's maiden name of Romée. It was a fairly normal thing to do back then and especially around the area that she came from. She even used it when testifying. And, she was from Arc.

"Her daughter was born the year Joan was executed," St Clair continued, "but they were able to get the newborn child away before

123

the authorities came for Joan. So, you are DNA linked to her daughter, a girl that took the name of Juliette Trevin throughout her young life, but her real name was Juliette Romée; the daughter of Joan of Arc.

"You have to remember it was unsafe for that child to bear her mother's name. At her trial, Joan was ordered to answer over seventy charges, which included heresy, witchcraft, and dressing like a man. The French king could have saved her but he had no intention of being seen to help a heretic and a witch, despite what she had done for France: saved them. The Maid of Orléans, that was her nickname, was considered a heroine in France for her role during the Lancastrian part of the Hundred Years' War. She said she was acting under divine guidance, when she led the French army in their great victory at Orléans, in 1429, that thwarted the English attempt to conquer France. Despite this, the French burnt her alive, at the stake at Rouen, Normandy. She went from being one of France's most celebrated saviours, to a witch they burned. Then, many years later, when she was long dead, she was canonised in 1920 as a Roman Catholic saint."

"And how did the Order know that her daughter, Juliette, was a Seer?"

"The Prophecy told them. After the Cathars were nearly wiped out, they joined with the Templars and revealed the prophecy."

"Wait again, firstly, the Cathars?"

"I will explain more later but for now, the Cathars had the prophecy about Juliette hidden away in France. A Cathar monk and Knight of our Order, Father Jacque Durand, finally found her in the Languedoc, France, on the road to Carcassonne. The fifteen-year-old girl, Juliette Trevin, didn't know that her real name was not Trevin; it was Romée. She thought the couple she lived with were her parents, but they were not her parents; they were her great aunt and great uncle. They were protecting her and it took our Order a long time to discover she was in fact real and then to locate her.

"We were just in time because two assassins had been sent to kidnap her and kill her surrogate family and if it wasn't for the skill and swordsmanship of Father Durand, they would have perished and she would have been kidnapped. So, we were blessed to share the prophecies with our Cathar brothers."

Jonathan made a 'Time out' sign with his hands and then said, "Wait… 'prophecies'? There's more than one?"

"The first prophecy was about Joan of Arc and her daughter," St Clair said. "It reads, 'The daughter of the maid of Pucelle, shall have the gift to read the sacred words of God from within His Ark'. Joan referred to herself at her hearing as 'Joan the Maid', in French, *'Jehanne la Pucelle'*."

"How many prophecies do you have?" Jonathan asked."

"Ten," St Clair informed him, "but that's not the important thing right now."

"It's not?"

"No," St Clair said.

"Then what is?" Jonathan asked. "What could possibly be more important than that?"

"That you are related to Joan of Arc's daughter."

"What do you mean, related?"

"We share half of our DNA with our mother and half with our father; a quarter with one grandparent and so on and we can trace all of this because of a DNA marker. Deoxyribonucleic is the molecule that contains the genetic code of organisms. DNA is in each cell of the organism. It's 'blood line sequencing' of lined descendants."

"Heck. So, you have my DNA and you checked a DNA database and you got a —"

"Hit," St Clair informed him.

"I'm not even going to ask you how you got my DNA."

"We have two hits, actually," St Clair said. "Oh, and it was Dominique: she stole your toothbrush, the morning after the first night you stayed here at the castle, four years ago. She took it and had it analysed; we do it to everyone."

"Of course, she did; it's normal behaviour around here. So, if I have this right, me and another person are related to the daughter of Joan of Arc?"

"No." St Clair smiled. Now he sounded excited. "Here's the great part about all of this because we got so, so lucky. We got two hits: Joan's daughter and the Lionheart."

Just then the door opened and Dominique walked in. Jonathan jumped.

Dominique smiled at him. "Just checking how long you will be."

"Oh, I guess about a lifetime," Jonathan said. "Come in, you've got to hear this." He replayed the last 30 minutes' worth of conversation. "We got up to the Lionheart." He turned back to St Clair. "I assume you mean Richard?"

"Yes, him. Richard the Lionheart."

"Jonathan's related to Richard the Lionheart as well?" Dominique asked.

"And all this from a toothbrush," Jonathan chipped in and gave his wife a look.

"No. Of course not. Not Jonathan. Cameron is," St Clair said.

"Who's Cameron?" Jonathan and Dominique asked at the same time.

"Cameron Jack."

"Who's Cameron Jack, then?" Again, they asked in unison.

"He's a thirty-year old ex-army intelligence officer, who also spent five years in the SAS. He was the British Kendo and Iaijutsu champion some years ago and still holds the *Iaido* record for the fastest sword draw and number of cuts. Today he teaches sword craft and martial arts and lectures."

"And?" Again, they said it in unison.

"And, he lives with his sixty-two-year-old granddad, Billy Jack, in London."

126

They hadn't noticed that Zakariah and Courtney had walked into the room.

"He lives with his grandad?" Zakariah said, having been in on the news beforehand. "You never told me that."

"Yes," said St Clair, surprised that they were surprised.

"GRANDAD?" Courtney asked.

"It's a long story."

Just then there was a crash outside the door. Courtney looked away from the others and down at the floor – she knew what it was.

"You've not sorted him out yet, then?" St Clair asked.

"No. I keep trying but I've never met anyone so clumsy," Courtney said. "It might take a while, or in fact sometime longer than a while."

Just then the door opened and Bertram Hubert De'Ath, Deputy Head of Communications and clumsy eccentric, appeared from around the door. He was dressed in a green tartan, tweed cloth suit, with a waist coat and a fob. He wore brown scuffed shoes and hair that looked like it had been up all night. His black square glasses had a piece of tape over one of the hinges — the broken one. He was apologetic.

"Erm, sorry. Really sorry about …" at that another crash. He dropped the six phones he was carrying for the second time. "Don't worry, don't worry, they are all fairly breakproof."

"Is that even a word?" St Clair asked.

"I'm sure it is. Somewhere. Yes. Well, almost positive it might be-ish," Bertram answered. He knelt down and starting picking up the mobile phones. Then he stopped and looked at Jonathan's coat on the back of a chair. "Whose coat is that jacket?" he asked. "Not everything that covers you does you a favour but I have to say, I rather like the look of that."

"I think that jacket might be Jonathan's coat," Courtney answered. "I thought we said three o'clock, Bertram."

"Ah, well. I don't have a watch."

"Zakariah looked at him. "You don't have a watch and you are the Deputy Head of Coms and all things technical."

"It broke," Bertram informed him.

"It broke?" Zakariah said.

"The alarm went off and I hit it because I was sleeping."

"Sleeping?"

"Yes, tired people make bad decisions. I had to go back to sleep, so I hit it. A little too hard, I'm afraid; Mr Russian Klymachak said I could have his but it's very heavy."

Zakariah shook his head, then whispered to Courtney, "What is it with the Russian and Bertram? They are like the odd couple. He's hard, stubborn, says very little; a hardened special forces vet; six five; survivor of the Gulag system and Siberia. And Bertram, well... I sometimes feel I'm on the set of a Marx Brothers' movie when I see them together."

"I don't know," Courtney said. "The Russian just took him under his wing when Bertram came here and they have been friends ever since."

"Don't worry, Bertram; we'll get you a new one," St Clair said. "Now, why don't you tell us what you want?

"I thought we would use the time whilst everyone was here," Courtney said, "to give you all your new phones. So, I asked Bertram to call in at three o'clock to take you through the new functionality he has developed."

"Good idea," St Clair said. "Bertram, show us what you've been up to."

Bertram was visibly excited. "Ah, good, jolly good, Mr St Clair, Jolly, jolly good."

"Bertram." Courtney said.

"Ah, yes, must focus," he said and then gave them each of them a mobile phone.

Jonathan took his. Looked at it. Looked at it a bit more then looked at Zakariah for help. Zakariah shook his head, as if to say "I have no idea."

When he was sure everyone had admired his new invention,

Bertram began. "Well. Well, I am very excited by these babies because I think of them as my bab—"

"Bertram." Again, Courtney had to remind him to get on with it and not meander and bluster.

"Yes. Well, first, they use our full five G network, great coverage. All of it is on our cognitive cloud, so safe and secure. Miss Picking will be happy."

St Clair turned to Courtney and whispered. "Who is Miss Picking?"

"Daisy Picking," she said.

"Do we have a Daisy Picking? I don't remember a Daisy Picking," he said.

"We don't," Courtney confirmed. "When he first got here, he wanted to know the controller's name; he was obsessed by the shadowy lady in Islington, as he called her. He wouldn't stop going on about it. We told him very few people knew her name for security reasons but he kept going on. So, Dominique, and I told him her name was Daisy Picking. It was that or Nora Bone."

"And he didn't see through daisy picking, picking daisies? St Clair asked."

"Nope."

"I thought he was clever."

"He is," Courtney told him, "exceptionally and stunningly so; he is a math-a-magician but he is also somewhere on the spectrum."

"Somewhere pretty far north, I would say," St Clair said.

Jonathan interrupted the whispering behind him. "Mine doesn't have many buttons," he said. "My buttons are missing. I only have three buttons. Where are my buttons?"

"No one has more than three buttons, Mr Rose."

"Jonathan."

"No, Bertram," Bertram said.

"No, I mean call me Jonathan, not Mr Rose."

"Ah, okay. Will do, Mr Rose. Actually, this is a perfect Segway into …"

"Bertram." Again, Courtney had to get him to focus.

"Sorry. Yes. Mr Russian Klymachak, he's my friend, you know, he says sometimes I can cause unnecessary certainty, but very slowly because I blather a little and I go the long way roun—"

"Bertram." Now there was some exasperation in Courtney's voice.

"Well, we don't really need buttons anymore, Mr Rose," Bertram announced. "We use LISA." He said this with such introduction that some of the Templars were waiting for someone called Lisa to enter the room. Then he clarified it. "Lips in synchronised animation: LISA."

Jonathan looked at the others. Besides Courtney, he could see that there was no point asking any of them for any help.

"It is locked into your eyes, you see. It has a biometric retinal scan. Your eyes turn it on. No 'on' button needed or 'off' button. It lies dormant until you let it read your eyes. Look at it and then, you're good to go. Once it's live, just tell it who you want to call, message, search for, or anything else you want to do. It's just like any other digital, hand-held mobile phone.

"So, you may ask, and I'm sure you are, the three buttons, what are they for then? Well, press red for emergency: it means can't call, can't speak, come and get me. Help. Each phone is set to alert a number of people, including Miss Pickings. It's like the red pull cord in a retirement home for the elderly."

The Templars looked at each other. St Clair mouthed, *retirement home*? And they all shrugged.

"Green means all is well and used if someone is calling you but you are unable to take a call at that time but will call them back," Bertram continued. "It means don't panic. It means I'm okay, just a bit busy right now."

"And the black button?" Zakariah asked. "The small one on the side, the one that's indented?"

"Boom, Mr St Clair number two," Bertram answered.

"Boom?" Zachariah said. "What do you mean, boom?"

"If you press the black button for five seconds, it will beep, then you have twelve seconds before it blows up. Your phone is also a bomb. It has a kill blast arc of fifteen feet in all directions; very powerful."

Jonathan stopped messing with the buttons straight away. They all stopped messing with their buttons immediately, and checked to see everyone else had too.

"In addition to the voice command function, we realised that there will times when you don't want to make a sound. In this case you can switch to audio negative mode. This simply means you call someone by miming their name with your lips in front of the screen. Say the name of the person you want to call, or persons if you want a conference call with, or what you want to search for, or anything else.

"Also, you can hold your conversations with your brothers without speaking because the screen reads your lips. This function allows you to use your phone when you are in a tricky jam and can't make a noise or you don't want people around you to hear what you are saying. Just mime it. Of course, the person at the other end will hear perfectly well, although you will sound a bit like Stephen Hawking. And, you get the same in reverse. As they speak to you, your phone will change their voiced words to text if you ask it to. So, you are completely sound free.

"It has an extended battery life. It's waterproof up to ten meters. You can switch the camera to infrared so you can see in the dark on the screen, so you can use it as night vision or to take night pictures. It's fully encrypted. So, if you lose it no one can read any data on it. It has a natty little device that will allow you to open digital locks. For example, hotel rooms that use a touch contact key configuration or most cars that use electronic fobs, or doors that use digit sequences.

"The phone is intuitive and predictive, so it learns how you use your phone, the more you use it, the more it gets to know your style and will begin to give you shortcuts that should be fun and save you time. It has up to ten thousand dollars on a prepay function. Lastly, it has a tracking device. This means we have updated the GPS system we were using and now we have almost global coverage. If you have the phone with you, we can find you and find you real fast. My friend, Mr Russian Klymachak, says it's a marvel."

"He's right," St Clair said. "That's great, Bertram, but my concern is that the two things that get taken first if you are captured or arrested are your weapon and your mobile phone."

"Ah. Good point, Mr St Clair. Miss Courtney asked me to develop a solution to that very problem, and here it is. Now. This will do the trick." Bertram produced a credit card.

"We all have credit cards, Bertram; I was speaking about the tracker," St Clair said.

"Indeed, Mr St Clair, I'll be right there in a minute now. Each card has a credit limit of fifty thousand dollars and works in most ATMs around the world. You can, of course, carry it in your pocket or, you can sew into your trousers, skirt, dress, shorts, socks, shirts."

"Bertram," Courtney said. "I think they got the sewing thing. Tell Mr St Clair what he really wants to know."

"Yes, yes. Indeed. If you put the cart too far in front of the horse, the horse will not see the cart."

St Clair was trying to figure out if he'd just been called a horse.

"We are trying out the hidden sewing thing and Mr ..."

"Bertram," Courtney said.

"Ah, indeed. It has a built-in tracking device. The card is polymagnitite multilayer skins, compressed together, with nano circuitry imbedded within the centre skin layers. It has a built-in nano chip tracker, which means we can find you almost anywhere. Keep the card with you and we will find you. It transmits by bouncing its signal off any nearby satellite, and there are thousands of satellites in the sky; this is what gives us the range and coverage. Its battery life is around three months; however, it will constantly recharge through either body warmth or solar, the sun. If it is exposed to either of these, then it will transmit without pause indefinitely."

"Damn it," St Clair said.

Bertram looked upset. He thought he had done something wrong. "Mr St Clair?"

"No, not you, Bertram. If only we'd done this a week ago." Bertram was not in the loop as yet and so did not know about Sabath, nor did the others, other than Zakariah. St Clair decided it was now time to tell them.

"As of yesterday, André Sabath is missing, and so are nine of his Knights. We have no way of finding them and are completely in the dark as to what happened. So, you see, Bertram, I just meant that this new invention of yours just may have given us a solution to a very grave problem, if it had happened a week earlier. That's all I meant."

"It will, Mr St Clair.'

"I know, Bertram, that's what I just said."

"No," said Courtney, "he means he did do it a week ago. Tell Mr St Clair, Bertram."

"It's Mr Sabath," he began, "it's what I was trying to tell you. He came to say goodbye to me. He's such a lovely gentleman; he always brings me ginger biscuits because he knows that I—"

"Bertram," St Clair said, "let's see if we can focus on this now. It's important."

"Oh, yes. Of course. Sorry. Mr Sabath said he would not be back for a while so Miss Courtney suggested I give him his phone and card and show him how to use it."

"And?" St Clair asked, now slightly impatient.

"And that's what he did," said Courtney. "André was our first 'go-live'."

"And the card?" St Clair said. "And the card with the tracker?"

"Mr Sabath took the phone and the card whilst sipping mint tea with me and eating ginger biscuits," Bertram said. "We've been following him about ever since. He's certainly racking up his air miles. Oh boy, isn't he just."

St Clair hugged Bertram and Bertram looked utterly confused. He then told Jonathan, Courtney, Dominique and Zakariah to come back in hour. Next St Clair sent word to the Worthies to meet back up in the Great Hall and to Proctor Hutchison to be back on the video call in ten minutes.

They all left the meeting room and went off to do various tasks. Jonathan and Bertram were walking along the hallway together chatting. Jonathan didn't really know Bertram; they hadn't spent much time together and Jonathan thought it was time he found out more about him.

"Your father was a Templar, I hear?" Jonathan said.

"He was, Mr Rose, in India," Bertram said.

"You know you can call me Jonathan, don't you?"

"I will, Mr Rose. He lived in Calcutta."

"I thought Calcutta changed its name and is now spelt k.o.l.k.a.t.a?"

"It is, Mr Rose," Bertram said, almost skipping along, his white teeth flashing out from his deep brown skin and his curly, unkept hair flopping about. "Don't you think Mr St Clair looks like Sean Connery?" he suddenly said, from out of the blue.

Jonathan stopped him. "I wouldn't," Jonathan said, "I really wouldn't. He doesn't like people saying that."

"But," Bertram giggled like a naughty schoolboy telling a little rude joke, "he jolly well does. I keep thinking he'll say 'my name is Bond'…"

"He may well look like him," Jonathan said, "but, I'll tell you, when I first met him and I alluded to it, he said, and I quote, 'I've no time to bandy words with you. Tell me your business and get to the point. I know how you Americans like the sound of your own voices'."

"Brilliant," Bertram laughed. "I know, let's see if we can get him to say," Bertram's voice went down an octave or two, "Hello, Mish Moneypenny; is M in? I've come for my game of ten-ish." Bertram almost fell over laughing at what he'd just said.

The was a cough behind them. It was St Clair.

Jonathan turned around, but Bertram wouldn't; he froze. He whispered to Jonathan out of the corner of his mouth, "Is it him?"

"Yes," said Jonathan.

"What's he doing?" Bertram asked.

"He's staring at us with one eyebrow raised."

"*The* eyebrow thing?"

"Yes," said Jonathan, "he's doing *the* eyebrow thing."

"Is it the left one?"

"It is."

"He has quite the stare on him when he does that."

"He does, Bertram."

"Anything else?" Bertram asked.

"He's rolling his eyes, out loud."

"Loud?"

"Very."

Bertram had a think, and then said, "I feel a bit of a stinker. Is he still there?"

"He's still there," Jonathan said.

"Well, thank you for the chat, Mr Rose Jonathan," Bertram said in a loud voice, "but I really must insist I get on, I have lots to do, I can't dally here chatting." And with that, Bertram ran.

Jonathan and St Clair burst out laughing.

St Clair's third meeting of the day, and his second with the Worthies

The meeting was short. They all agreed what needed to be done. They closed their meeting in the normal way with prayers and this time, with Templar battle ceremonies. They decided that they were better in their individual places of domicile, where they would be of better use than holed up in the castle. When they left, they would be protected by the Knights assigned to protect them. They needed to work their channels now and put all Knights of the Order on full alert. They all departed late that night. Separately and under the cover of darkness, the Worthies left Scotland as they had arrived, unnoticed, without suspicion; just everyday people going about their everyday lives; which of course, they were not, and their lives were not!

As St Clair headed for the control room, to review the day's data on their numerous operations, his mobile phone rang. He was pleased this new model didn't go live until the weekend – he would need some time to digest Bertram's disjointed instructions and he was tired. The call was from the controller in Islington.

"Sorry, I know it's late," she said, "and you have been in meetings for most of the day but it's our man in Panama, says its urgent. He thinks he's found the party who owns the companies he's been investigating. He can also now confirm the original source of the money. Says it came into play on October the 23rd, 1945, in Germany."

"Germany, again. That was his original hunch. Is he still on the line?" St Clair asked.

"He is," she replied.

"Good, can you transf—" St Clair stopped. "Tiff?"

"Yes, Payne?"

"Do you like the name Daisy Picking?"

"You mean as opposed to Nora Bone."

"Ha, they told you."

"Yes, they told me. The two girls, Dominique and Courtney, came up with it."

"Brilliant, I love it."

"Me too. I love their wit and their sense of humour and fun;

it's good to have young blood in the Order again. Here's Morgan Clay for you. Goodnight, Payne, don't work too late." She connected the two men.

Morgan Clay was a Templar 'ghost man'. A term used mostly in the world of espionage to describe a person who infiltrates an organisation and is able to stay there gathering information without being discovered or killed. The title fitted Clay perfectly.

"Where are you?" St Clair asked him.

"Still in Panama," Clay replied.

"How you holding up down there?"

"I'm doing okay," Clay answered.

"I could do with some good news, my old friend," St Clair said hopefully.

"Then you've come to the right place." Clay couldn't see him smiling but he knew he would be.

"You think you found him?"

"I'm close. I need another few days but I think I am there with it. Payne," now Clay's tone lowered. "I need some help; it's getting a bit hairy here and I'm about to make it worse."

"Who're you thinking of?"

"I'd like Wolf," he asked.

"The Indian … you must be expecting some heavy fall out?"

"Could be," Clay said. "I need to do some nocturnal breaking in and they're not going to be very pleased. Some real bad guys around here, Payne. Was thinking around the 28th. Once we go in then I'm finished in the law firm; it will be too hot to go back so I need to make sure I have everything I need before then."

"He'll be with you," St Clair said.

"Any news about André?" Clay asked St Clair.

"We just found out he might have a tracker on him."

"Wow. Keep the faith, brother, the Lord will provide," Clay said.

"Always brother, always."

Chapter 8

The Lionheart & the Swordsman

In just one day, Cameron Jack's childhood went from perfect to tragic.

Cameron could barely remember his parent's funeral. He couldn't remember the church, or the people who were there, who they were and why they were there. He remembered though, the sound of the rain, the rat-a-tat-tat sound beating down on that dreadful day. He vaguely remembered some of the words the priest said whilst they were all standing outside in the rain 'We commit their bodies to the ground …' but nothing more than that. What he did remember were the trees in the cemetery. Bare, their green coats gone. He was seven years old and the trees stood there like dark, menacing shapes. He'd battled with nightmares about them for nearly two years after the funeral; not the accident, not the funeral but the trees, the hideous, dangerous trees. The seven-year-old boy saw the soil scatter across the coffins. And then, it was over; they were over.

Then, fate intervened on that small, vulnerable, confused little boy. Two connected events coincided that would change the course of his life. Those two things that turned, what could have been a life in care and foster homes, into a happy and loving life – although it got off to a bit of a rocky start.

The first was his good fortune in being assigned to a social worker called Winifred Mabel Doris Rushton. She entered his life when he needed someone like her most. She was the person who held his small, cold hand at his parents' funeral. The social worker that had his case file on her desk. The social worker who had a heart of gold. The social worker who was never willing to give up at the first hurdle, or give up even at the 100th hurdle. She wasn't prepared to put the little boy into care, not unless she had explored all the options, no matter how crazy they may have seemed to others. Winifred worked tirelessly for Cameron, and, as his temporary protector, she had sworn to do it until she found another to take her place. Until she found him a new home, a forever home.

The second thing was his grandfather, a man called Billy Jack. Winifred and he had driven to where his grandfather lived. He couldn't remember what day it was or what month it was. His grandfather lived in a block of old, shabby maisonettes on a dangerous looking estate. However, when they got there, his grandfather was not in. A neighbour came out and being assured Winifred was not the police, told them where he would be and so Winifred took him to the pub where the neighbour said his grandfather was. Cameron remembered the smell of smoke, drink and sweat, as they entered the pub. He didn't like it. He had never been in a pub before. He remembered the hostility from the people inside but he didn't know why they were like that. He remembered a man with only a few teeth and tattoos on his neck and a shaven head, standing up. A chair was thrown towards them. He remembered crying; he was scared. He wanted to run out and he thought that Winifred also wanted to run. Then another man, he did not know, stood up and he remembered thinking that the man looked like his dad but older. The man who looked like his dad walked over to the angry men who were stood up, hostile and aggressive. Then, as Winifred still tells the story, the man, that he later found out was his grandfather, sorted them all out with short thrift. Then the three of them left, all holding hands and he remembered feeling safe for the first time since his parents had died.

Cameron Jack went to live with his grandfather that very same day. Six months later, with Winifred's help, they both moved from the flat in the dingy maisonettes, and the crime-ridden estate. With the intervention of Winifred, they secured a two-bedroom council house in the W11 area of London, an area called Notting Hill. There Cameron was happy. He had his own room, which was bigger than the one in the maisonette; and for the first time in a long while, he started to feel normal again; not lost, alone or different.

Billy Jack was also happy in Notting Hill. He was away from the bad crowd he had got in with. He had left the old Billy behind, a man he now utterly despised. Every day, Billy resolved to make amends and be the best person he could be. He had not seen his own child, Cameron's father, David – not of his doing. Now he was determined to be a good grandfather and a friend to his grandson. To try, in some way, to make up for his shortcomings as an absent father. He was under a new doctor in Notting Hill. Ironically, and fortunately for Billy, the doctor was a veteran; he had been a navy doctor for 20 years, so he fully understood Billy's condition. With his new mix and balance of medicines and the support and understanding of a caring doctor, his PSTD started to wane, so much so he was able to manage the condition without the rage and anger that had distorted his personality and driven him to actions that now appalled and embarrassed him.

When Cameron was 12 years old, he went to the local secondary school. It was a good school and it had a great reputation. The school had great teachers, facilities and opportunities and Cameron flourished. He was a good student, smart, studious and interested. Even at that age, there was something about his character. He wasn't shy or aloof, but he wasn't one to bawl and shout, or draw attention to himself. He was well mannered but his teachers could see that he was developing a steely determination. He was a popular boy. He got good grades and rarely got into any trouble.

He and his grandfather were close as grandson and grandfather, but they were also great friends. Occasionally, Cameron encountered racial abuse because he was of mixed race. Billy Jack had been a paratrooper and then a sergeant in the SAS, so he took it upon himself to teach the young Cameron self-defence – of the most effective kind. This would change everything for Cameron at the age of 12 years old and then, in 2012 at the age of 30.

Cameron was a natural fighter because he let his brain control the combat, not rage. He learnt quickly from his grandfather. Whilst he wasn't yet strong, he was pinpoint accurate with any blows he dealt, and he was lightening quick – much quicker than Billy. Within months, and driven by his steely resolve, he was soon able to look after himself. He seldom used his newly developed skills, preferring to walk away. However, if he did have to use them, it was swift and, for his abusers, somewhat painful. From Billy's tutelage Cameron progressed to the local Judo club on Thursday nights for three hours, and then he also joined a Shotokan Karate club just around the corner from where they lived and trained on Tuesday nights for another three hours. He went through the belt rankings with great speed. Then, on Saturday mornings he attended a Kendo club, the Japanese martial art of sword fighting skilfully practised by Samurai in times of old. It was just a bus ride away from the house. Billy saved hard so that his grandson could be properly kitted out for his Kendo classes and Cameron soon became one of its star pupils. Once he'd achieved black belt, second Dan in Karate and Judo, he gave them up to focus all his free time on Kendo. He was a natural fighter; he was a natural swordsman. Cameron loved this traditional Japanese martial art. He started at the lowest rank, seventh *kyu* but quickly he advanced through the grades: sixth *kyu*, fifth, fourth *kyu*, right the way through to first *kyu*, and then, by the time he was 16 years old, he'd achieved 1st dan. Cameron defied the odds because no one remembered anyone ever gaining their grades so quickly before.

Cameron read everything he could about Kendo. He read

about Japan, its customs and traditions and how they had shaped the Samurai code – as if they were one. The values displayed in martial arts, along with the discipline required, the honour, the courtesy, the lack of hubris and bravado, fitted Cameron's calm, respectful manner – but his manner also had that steely, no nonsense determination. Billy started taking Cameron to competitions when he became good enough to compete and he started to make a name for himself in the junior ranks as a swordsman of stealth, with great natural and explosive power but also as a great tactician.

In addition to his schooling, and his martial arts, his grandfather also made sure that Cameron went to church every Sunday – this was at the request of and involved some major prodding and cajoling from Winifred, who had stayed in their life and remained great friends with Billy Jack. She often attended church with them, bringing her extended family along whenever they could make the trip from Essex. Sometimes, Billy, who had bought a car not long after moving to Notting Hill – a mini, at the great insistance of Winifred – drove himself and Cameron to Essex to have BBQs at Winifred's house in the summer months.

Cameron's achievements at school continued. He loved maths, geography and English; however, he loved history more. He was absorbed with any part of history that involved warfare, especially those wars that relied on bladed weapons, or where bladed weapons played a major role. This included the years right up to the Second World War – with officers' sabres and solders' bayonets. He became a medieval history buff because he considered it was the zenith of the sword.

At the age of 16, luck would again smile on Cameron Jack, when a priest, visiting their local diocese, told Billy about a competition being run by a philanthropist that might interest his grandson. The philanthropist, who supported a military museum in France, and several inner-city Kendo dojos in Japan, was running a competition. The rules were simple: define the most effective bladed weapon in history and say why you believe it was. The prize was a trip to Japan. It was 1998 and Cameron, a sharp-minded 16-year-old Kendo fanatic, applied every fact he knew and produced a detailed, considered submission. He won.

The trip to Japan was fully funded by the philanthropist; it included airfare, hotel costs, food and some spending money; and it was for two people and so, naturally, Cameron asked his grandfather to go with him. They applied for Cameron's passport the very next day they got the news.

When the day came to leave for the airport, the pair set off like two schoolboys – albeit technically one of them was. They were both full of excitement and wondered what it would be like there. Billy had travelled far and wide whilst serving in the armed forces, however, he had never been to Japan or the Far East. The plane journey was long; longer still by the fact Cameron couldn't wait to get there, it seemed endless to him but he amused himself with books on swords he had brought along to read on the journey. Billy slept a lot and amused himself with endless inflight films and a few crosswords.

When they arrived, they both instantly fell in love with Japan. They loved the Japanese people, the sights, the smells, the sounds, the food, the culture, and the architecture. The shear politeness of the people overwhelmed them – especially Billy, who had grown up on a rough, London estate. He found them nice natured, accommodating and respectful. Because of Cameron's interest in martial arts and especially Kendo, the priest who had brought them the news that Cameron had won the competition arranged for Cameron and Billy Jack to visit one of the inner-city dojos the philanthropist supported. They were to visit a dojo, run by a very famous Kendo teacher, a master swordsman and a grandmaster. He had been Japan's top swordsman for almost two decades, before he retired from competition to teach, his name was Hinata Satō.

The day after they arrived, a Saturday, and full of excitement, they jumped into a taxi to go to the dojo – showing the taxi driver a piece of paper with the name and address of the dojo, written in Japanese, thanks to the help of the reception staff at their hotel. The taxi journey was short, no more than 20 minutes. Their hotel was in Chiyoda City, an up and coming location just north of Tokyo city. They needed to get to the dojo in Katsushika city. The taxi crossed three rivers to get there, the Sumida river and then the Arkawa river, and finally the Ayase river, despite it only being ten miles away.

As they got out of the taxi, they knew they were in the right place because of the sound coming out of the dojo. The cry *"kiai"* is used to meld the body, mind and sword together. It allows the diaphragm to contract when a blow comes, but also to allow an explosive attack. Short clipped *"kiais"* boomed out of the dojo. Young and old voices alike echoed from behind the dojo walls. As they entered the dojo, Cameron told his grandfather that Kendo still wasn't even an Olympic sport, when Judo was, despite Kendo having many, many more practitioners than Judo and more outside of Japan than inside Japan.

Once inside, they saw the regimented discipline of many martial art students being put through their paces. Billy watched in awe at the speed and accuracy of the fighters. He already knew that in Kendo there are no coloured belts as in other martial arts, so a beginner looks exactly the same as an advanced fighter. However, Cameron knew who was who, despite no belts; he could tell their levels by their skill. Billy was in no doubt who the man in charge was. Hinata Satō was the dojo owner, the teacher, the Sensei – he was the man that was very much in charge. Hinata Satō was a 10th dan grandmaster. He looked to Cameron to be as old as his grandfather, who he considered old. In fact, Billy was only 48 years old when they were in Japan in 1998 and Hinata Satō was 83 years old! Hinata Satō had white, medium-length hair, receding on the top, revealing a shiny forehead. He sported a white goatee and strangely, his eye brows were black. He was small and whispery in stature. He didn't look like a swordsman, he looked more like a bank clerk or a doctor.

Billy leaned over and whispered to Cameron, "He looks like Mr Miyagi from the Karata Kid film." Cameron told his grandfather to shush, in case he was heard. "But he does," Billy continued, "Wipe on, wipe off, wipe on ..."

"Grandad," Cameron whispered but laughing.

Despite his looks, there was an air about the old teacher. The pupils gave him great reverence as he walked past them, looking to catch his eye and show off their skill. He strutted about, a wooden practise sword in his belt. He wasn't wearing any protection, like all the others, although Cameron knew that as a grandmaster, he doubted very much anyone in the dojo could get anywhere near to him to strike anyway. The noise inside the dojo was loud and intoxicating. It reverberated off the bland, white walls. Billy was fascinated. Cameron desperately wanted to practise with them. For him it would be a dream come true, something he'd thought about ever since learning they would be visiting an actual Japanese Kendo dojo.

Hinata Satō was expecting the English visitors. He walked over to greet them. He bowed and they bowed back. He was courteous but he had a stern edge to his voice and his body language. Both Billy and Cameron were extra polite. Hinata Satō showed them around and introduced them to various students, taking time to explain what they were doing. He referred to his top student as *deshi*. Cameron explained to Billy that this title normally meant he was the one who would most likely take over from the Sensei of a dojo when the time came. Hinata Satō's deshi was a man in his mid-forties and very much in the mould of his master. However, he was taller and stockier than his master. He wore the same outfit as all the others in the dojo, there was no distinction. His black hair was swept back. He wore it in a bun on the top of his head – a chonmage, the traditional Japanese top knot. He was clean shaven, neat in appearance and had deep, almost cold eyes. He too carried a wooden practise sword in his belt, along with a smaller one. He too was courteous. To Billy and Cameron, he looked like he would not suffer fools easily. The man said his name was Tanjkna Sugata. He bowed graciously. Billy made the mistake of saying, 'I am very pleased to meet you, Tanjkna'.

"Calling someone by their name, without using a title, is bad manners in Japan. It is *Busahō* – discourteous," Tanjkna Sugata said in perfect English. He bowed gracefully again as he spoke, which almost took the sting out of his words but the sting was still there. And in that moment, Billy got it. Billy got the culture applied to martial arts in Japan: you can be just as effective in making your point, perhaps even more so, but still be gracious and courteous. Tanjkna Sugata was charming, almost seemingly submissive but assertive all in one sentence and one body movement. It was difficult to take offense at such politeness.

Cameron, having used Japanese etiquette in Kendo for nearly four years, bowed. *"Sumimasen, Sugata-san, Sumimasen."* Knowing the word for sorry saved the day for the English visitors; it saved face.

Hinata Satō referred to his other pupils as *gakuseis* – pupils or students – but Billy made sure not to speak to any of them, he didn't want to make any more faux pas. Hinata Satō's English, like Tanjkna Sugata's, was very good, which made it easier for Billy and Cameron to get a deeper sense of the workings and etiquette of the dojo. Hinata Satō showed them some of the training and explained it, in some detail. He made it interesting and seemed genuinely pleased to be showing off his work. He also told them of the many competitions that his pupils had won and whilst modesty is all important in Japanese culture, he found it hard not to brim with pride at their accomplishments.

"My students range in age, size and ability, as you can see." He looked across the dojo at the trainee warriors. "Not all older and bigger people are better fighters. Look at me." He laughed. "I look like Mr Miyagi. Wipe on, wipe off." He laughed again.

"No, no, absolutely not," Billy protested. "You look nothing like him, no one would ever think that, surely not. No."

"See there," Hinata Satō continued, pointing to two small,

young boys, "those two students are the youngest in the class, they are twins, they are seven years old. And the oldest, that man there," he said, pointing to a rather bent old man who was making an attack move on his much younger opponent, "he is eighty-seven years, four years older than me." Hinata Satō laughed again.

"According to our Kendo tradition, we wear long *Hakama* skirts, *Keigoki* tops. Very important, Mr Jack," he said turning to Billy, "are their facemasks. They are called *Mens*, and made of iron, steel or titanium. You see, also part of the *Men* is a throat protector and flaps to protect the shoulders. *Kote*, those are the wrist protectors that you see. And finally, the *Do*, a breastplate that covers and protects their stomachs and part of their chests. In Kendo, you score by hitting, actually tapping with your sword, either the face, the throat, the waist or the wrists, so they have to be protected. And of course, they all have their Shinai. These are flexible bamboo swords we use in Kendo for practising fighting where there is contact. The wooden swords we also use," he pointed to the one he carried, "are for practise without contact because they are heavy and can create much damage."

A number of experienced and higher graded people were holding mini training sessions around the dojo. These were people who Hinata Satō entrusted some of the teaching and mentoring. They were helping to train people in the lower grades, those at seventh *Kyu*, the beginners, and those at sixth *Kyu*, one up from beginners, fifth and fourth *kyu*. In those groups there were many raised voices, drama and emotion as their stand-in teachers encouraged them to use the controlled, yet explosive power of the shout "*Kiai*". In almost a clipped barking tone, their teachers shouted commands of "*Hajime*" – begin, "*Seretsu*" – line up, "*Otagai ni Rei*" – bow to your peers ... In parallel lines, the pupils, all dressed in black, faced each other. Their swords in hand ready for the command. Billy was fascinated, Cameron mesmerised at the techniques they were using, far different from those that he used. Ready for combat, yet composed.

147

Concentrating. Their *Shinai's* poised. Then, upon command, there was lots of striking, with a hearty tapping and pushing: *Tai-Atari* – body checks or pushes; sword against sword. Lots of swift blows to the four score areas on the body. The action was fast, furious but controlled. Some fell in the melee of combat but quickly got up, their opponent moving back to allow them to get to their feet. And then, they were off again, striking blows and blocking strikes.

A group of seven students and one teacher, standing quite close to Billy and Cameron, were practising movement, balance and timing. It was almost soothing to watch these deadly movements delivered like a mixture of a waltz, salsa and rave! All wrapped up in surges of attacks and defences.

Hinata Satō led them past each group, his commentary focused on his guests but his ever-watchful eye was on his pupils. Occasionally he would stop to correct a student's position around their opponent, or stance before or after an attack. These students were visibly very honoured when he spoke to them. He was their teacher, their grandmaster and, to the younger ones, he was a living legend.

At the far end of the dojo, Hinata Satō stopped. He turned to Cameron.

"Young Cameron, I have been told by the man who arranged your visit that you are a student of Kendo."

"*Hai*, Satō-san." Cameron bowed."

"Then, if you will permit, I want to show you and your grandfather our annex dojo."

Of course, intrigued, Cameron and his grandfather followed Hinata Satō and Tanjkna Sugata, into another room. There were only four people in there. It was much smaller than the main dojo, about 30 yards by 30 yards and it was almost library-esque quiet, compared to where they had just been. Neither of the four students, who were mature in age, appeared to be in charge. Like synchronised dancers they were practising a pre-set number of movements but Cameron

148

didn't recognise any of them. He knew the traditional seven katas with the long sword and the three katas with the short sword but this sequence of movements was alien to him. For a start, some of the striking blows were at an opponent's legs, or the upper arm, not the four strike points.

"Today, most Japanese people do not own a real sword, they are not allowed to," Hinata Satō started saying, as Cameron and Bill were taking everything in. "They have to get special permission, like your gun laws in Great Britain. If you own a sword you must register it with the *Nihon Token Kai*, the Japanese, Sword Association and you must show its historical or cultural significance.

"Once, nearly everyone in Japan owned a sword, most of them were passed down from their ancestors. But then the second World War came. The Japanese Imperial army carried swords, they were a sign of rank. When the war was lost, and Japan was occupied, the American General, General MacArthur, ordered the confiscation of all weapons. Many of our ancestral swords were thrown into Tokyo Bay by the Americans and other Allied troops, or they were melted down for their metal. The Occupational Forces were even allowed to take our swords home as souvenirs. A great many of our swords were lost or destroyed.

"Now to Kendo. It is like Judo and Karate, it is a sport. In Kendo we don't stab, thrust, slice, we tap the sword on four score areas, and we practise with specific wooden swords."

The people in front of Cameron and Billy were practising with two swords. This room and its occupants were different to what they had already witnessed in the other room, the main dojo. Cameron suddenly figured out what kind of dojo this was. He had read about them but had never attended one; these types of dojos were secret, the practise was largely an underground movement. However, his grandfather didn't realise this was different.

"You know what this is?" Hinata Satō asked Cameron.

Cameron nodded.

"I don't," Billy said confused.

"Ah, this is Kenjutsu," Hinata Satō replied. "As I told you, Kendo is a sport and has all the killing techniques removed. Kenjutsu is a battlefield art. It has all the nasty killing stuff left in." He smiled. "This place, here, this is true *Ko-ryū*, *Ko-ryū* meaning school of traditional arts, it's the old style, before it became a sport. This is the real Samurai dojo.

"Do you want to train on this method, with Sugata-san?" Hinata Satō asked Cameron, who was still transfixed by the strange kata being performed before them.

Cameron was almost too excited to speak, but he managed to get it out. "To train with Sugata-san would be my honour." He turned to Tanjkna Sugata and bowed. "To train Kenjutsu, the Samurai way, would be my privilege Satō-san. He bowed again."

Hinata Satō smiled and then nodded to Tanjkna Sugata. Tanjkna Sugata led Cameron away to prepare for their training session. Hinata Satō turned to Billy. "In Kendo, as you saw, we use bamboo swords. As I have explained, you are only allowed to strike the body of your opponent on four parts, the head, the throat, the wrist and the waist. You are only allowed to strike these parts with the last section of your sword and only on one side of your sword, which represents where the blade edge would be." Billy knew this; he had taken Cameron to enough Kendo classes, had been there every time Cameron achieved a new grade and had driven him to and from enough competitions. He did not interrupt the old teacher though.

"In this dojo you will see three differences. First, you will see *Iaido* used during the combat. *Iaido* is the art of the quick draw. Who can draw their sword the fastest and strike, often becomes the victor. Like your cowboys." Hinata Satō laughed at his own joke but Billy didn't; he also didn't have the nerve to tell the old man that there weren't any Stetson-clad cowboys in South London; the old man was an ocean and a continent off. "It takes quick movements," the old man continued, "smooth control, moving the sword from its *saya*, you

150

call scabbard, to strike your opponent in less than a second. The whole movement is drawing the sword, striking the opponent, wiping the blood from the blade and then, placing the sword back into the *saya*.

"Second," he said, "Cameron will fight with two swords. Samurais carry two swords, their main sword, their Katana, and a smaller sword called a Wakizashi. The Wakizashi is used when a Samurai is fighting close to his opponent. Oh, and also of course, the wakizashi is used in the ritual of *seppuku*, suicide." Again, the old teacher laughed. Again, Bill didn't laugh.

"And thirdly, Mr Jack, they will wear more protection because in this dojo they are able to strike any part of the body, as would a true Samurai in battle. This is full combat, this is Kenjutsu."

Billy must have had a horrified look on his face. "Relax, Mr Jack, it is as easy as wipe on, wipe off, wipe on, wipe off." Again, he laughed. "Your grandson is a fine fighter, I have been told, and he will be with Sugata-san, my best pupil ever. He has trained hundreds to know Kendo and he has trained some select others in Kenjutsu." He didn't expand on the 'others'. "Cameron will be safe with Sugata-san. He will learn. He will know how the Samurai feel. He is a young lion heart, your grandson."

When Cameron and Tanjkna Sugata entered the dojo, the four others moved to the sides and knelt down to watch. Billy's heart was pounding; he had never worried for his grandson before in any of the competitions. He didn't know why he was so anxious now. He thought that perhaps it was because he didn't know these people, or they were in a strange place. If anything went wrong, he didn't think his SAS unarmed combat skills would be too effective. Besides, all around the walls of the dojo were really sharp-looking Samurai swords, and he was the only one there that had never used one.

Cameron and Tanjkna Sugata bowed to each other.

"*Kamae*," came Tanjkna Sugata's command.

"He is telling your grandson to assume his stance."

151

Then Tanjkna Sugata barked the order to begin. "*Hajime.*"
And Cameron and Tanjkna Sugata started the face-off movements of
two fighters circling each other.

"See, Mr Jack, your grandson is fearless. He has Bushido: this
is the Samurai's code of honour. It is our moral compass, as you say
in the west. It is like a code of conduct that is in all Japanese's martial
arts. It teaches our warriors how to behave. It has eight virtues,
including honesty, righteousness, self-control, respect, courage...
See how your grandson moves to the rhythm of the battle; to the beat
of the combat and even though he has not practised in full combat
before, see how he is aware of the strike points, not just four but
everywhere. See how he is concentrating on Sugata-san's movements,
no matter how slight. He is watching, listening and feeling. He moves
naturally, his sword is in concert with his body."

It was obvious to Billy, when the strikes and blows began, that
Cameron was outmatched and in a real combat situation with Tanjkna
Sugata; he would have died at the onset. Tanjkna Sugata was a master
Kenjutsu practitioner and held the record in Japan for the fastest
Katana sword draw. Yet, despite all this, Cameron was indeed
fearless, not stupid, but fearless. Billy thought he looked like a male
ballerina, a lead dancer. His poise was solid, his movements flowing
and his fight tactics mature. Step, step and step, thrust, pivot, breath,
concentrate; step, step, headshot, twist and then, wrist, back up and
head shot, down and across the legs. Billy watched the elegant dance
of two men in combat and to him it was beautiful sight because it was
graceful and because it was his grandson. And then, as quickly as it
began, it had ended.

"*Yame*," Tanjkna Sugata shouted.

"Tanjkna Sugata has called stop," Hinata Satō told Billy.

"*Osame-To.*"

"He is telling your grandson to put away his weapons." They
will now do *Chiburi*. They pour a little water on their blades and then
wipe it off with rice paper, if they were on a battlefield, it would be

152

wiped off using the clothing of a fallen opponent. Here it is symbolic but good discipline, if you put a blood-stained sword back in its scabbard, the blood will congeal and act like glue and cause the blade to lock, making a fast draw, vital for survival, difficult to achieve.

"*Rei.*" Both men bowed to each other.

"*Men-Tore.*" Both men took off their face guards.

"Seiza." Both men now sat in the formal sitting position.

And then, the training session ended and their first visit ended.

Billy and Cameron visited the dojo every day of their stay. In fact, they did nothing else other than attend the dojo, where Cameron trained and Billy watched. All plans of sightseeing went out of the window. Cameron trained six hours every day with Tanjkna Sugata and even sometimes with Hinata Satō. Always two swords, always using *Iaido* – fast draw – and always Kenjutsu, full body combat. Cameron was also trained one hour a day using a different sword. This sword was a solid white oak and, in the right hands, could kill a person and break a Katana sword. It was deadly and Cameron and Tanjkna Sugata had to wear special gloves with steel threads running through them. And every time he practised, Billy would watch and wonder at the boy's skill and dexterity. It was a proud grandfather who watched his grandson's growing artistry, confidence and maturity.

After that first visit to Japan, and every year after, Billy saved hard throughout the ensuing years so that every year they could return to Hinata Satō's dojo, in Katsushika city, Japan. Cameron's skillset grew under the expert guidance of Hinata Satō and Tanjkna Sugata. He became a much more accomplished swordsman and tactical fighter. His passion, however, was full contact and he found it hard back in the UK to practise this style as virtually no one knew it or had the skill. He longed for the time to come around for their trip to Japan. His relationship with Tanjkna Sugata grew. Throughout the year, Tanjkna Sugata would also video call Cameron and walk him through different training excises and whilst this was never going to match actually being back in that dojo in Japan, Cameron was grateful to Tanjkna Sugata for his time and his knowledge. The pair's relationship grew as Tanjkna Sugata became the master and Cameron his most accomplished student.

By the age of seventeen, Cameron had moved up a number of levels in the Kendo rankings and moved from regional competitions to national competitions. Finally, he won a place at the national championship. He attended his first national championship at the age of seventeen; at 18 years old, he won the UK national championship. That same year, he won the European championship. Then, Cameron Jack dropped out of competitions altogether and was soon forgotten about. He now spent all of his free time practising Kenjutsu; developing and honing the skills that Hinata Satō and Tanjkna Sugata had taught him.

During these years, and despite his obsession with sword fighting, he was still achieving good grades at school; his A levels were high enough to secure a place at a good university. Billy was delighted that Cameron would go to university. Cameron's passion for history had grown during his school years and so he applied to Queens, London, to do a degree in medieval history, it was a three-year course. He began his degree in the year 2000, at the age of 18 years old. He was lucky: his parish priest told him they had funds that would pay for his degree course and accommodation, so Cameron didn't have to sufferer the burden of student debt, like hundreds of thousands of others. Cameron studied hard and was a popular student at university.

He finished his degree course in 2003, at the age of 21, with a 'first' in medieval history; he then promptly joined the army. This came as no surprise to his grandfather because Cameron had been talking about it since the age of seven, ever since his grandfather started telling him stories of when he was in the army. Cameron joined the British Intelligence Corps, as an officer. The Corps was responsible for gathering, analysing and disseminating military intelligence, as well as counter-intelligence and security.

Of the six specialist areas the Corps delivers – All-source intelligence aviator, Human intelligence, All-Source Intelligence, Counterintelligence, Signals intelligence/electronic warfare, Imagery Intelligence – Cameron specialised in counter-intelligence. His job was to command and coordinate, to assess risk and act to counter that risk; and use intelligence systems, to reduce that risk and uncertainty in various theatres of war and conflicts. He loved the work. He spent time working alongside the FBI in Washington and also worked closely with the CIA in Iraq. He found he really liked Americans; he liked their humour and he liked their grit.

In 2007, at the age of 25, he followed his grandfather's footsteps yet again and applied to the SAS. He passed selection and was initiated into the world's most feared fighting force of the 20th and 21st centuries.

Then, in 2011, at the age of 29, Cameron was medically discharged from the British Army due to a leg injury from an IED in Iraq that left him with a slight limp. He left the army with the rank of captain.

Throughout 2011, Cameron, with the help and support of his grandfather, opened up his own Kendo dojo in London. However, privately he still trained full contact and he struggled to get full satisfaction out of his dojo. He loved the students, especially the younger ones, he loved their enthusiasm and commitment, but he had trained full combat and with two of the best swordsmen there were and he knew that very few things would ever match up to that. Cameron also gave lectures all over the country on medieval history and on martial arts, to help supplement his earnings.

As he entered 2012, Cameron was focused on building the membership at his dojo and also expanding his lectures on the circuit, at private functions, colleges and universities.

Chapter 9
Recruitment

Date: 24th March
Place: The remote castle in Scotland

It had been eight days since the failed mission to Abu Dhabi. Six days since Al Bateat, the young Yemini agent and his family, were horribly murdered in a gruesome house fire; and six days since André Sabath had last called his friend, Payne St Clair.

Sabath had called from Abu Dhabi on the 17th, 18th, and the morning of the 19th, then nothing – he had gone dark, and so had his nine Knights. It had been three days since the Worthies had gathered at the castle and then left to return to their places of domicile to prepare for what they feared was about to come. They all left as they had arrived: separately and covertly.

It was now the 24th. It was late March, so it was still cold out, although the castle had full central heating, so it was warm inside the Templar's headquarters. St Clair had called another meeting with Jonathan, Courtney, Dominique, Bertram and Zakariah. It was early evening; everyone had already eaten. They were all gathered in one of the meeting rooms, except Bertram and Courtney; they were late.

The castle had a number of meeting rooms. Some could accommodate 3 to 5 people, others 10 to 15 people. They were all furnished with comfortable and efficient conference furniture. Long teak or walnut tables, black, high back comfortable swivel chairs with castors. The rooms were mainly plain white walls, a few had oak panelling on the walls, about five feet high, capped off with a dado rail – nothing too fussy and all tastefully done with functionality at its core. A plasma screen was available in every meeting room for video conference calls, along with a central tele-conferencing telephone unit in the centre of every conference table. All of it, like the rest of their coms, protected by the new fire walls and scrambling technology that Courtney, Bertram and their team had installed. All the castle windows were stained glass – they would cast a thousand vibrant colours into the castle in the summer months. In case there was an attempt to use electronics to listen into or use long range satellite technology to visually see through the windows into the castle, all the windows had a high-density reflective coating to block signals. They also had three masts on the roof of the castle that were heavy duty jamming devices.

Around their meeting room, there was an assortment of flipcharts, a large wipe board, an assortment of pens and marker pens, writing pads and small sticky notes. On the back wall a teak wooden cabinet, on which were tea and coffee-making facilities and a water dispenser. Whilst the Nine Worthies, the Higher Council, always held their meetings by candlelight, tradition important to Templars, all other meetings and all other rooms, used electric lighting.

St Clair, Zakariah, Dominique and Jonathan sat around the conference table chatting, waiting for the others to arrive. No one sat at the head of the table, the chairs were never placed at the head of any conference table in the castle; they were always placed around the sides. The only time someone sat at the head of a table was in the great hall when the Higher Council met, and then at the head of the table would be the Templar Grandmaster, Payne St Clair. The other times were when they gathered in the banqueting hall, which they used for formal ceremonies; new Knights knighted, or promotions or retirements.

The meeting room had sunken ceiling lights and modern wall lights, which assisted the array of over 20 candles, some scented, and all loosely gathered in the centre of the conference table, flickering away each time someone walked past them. St Clair still liked candles at his meetings; he said it gave atmosphere to often grave subjects.

They had been chatting for about ten minutes when Courtney arrived, her hair still wet – she'd been in the shower five minutes before. She had a large mug of coffee in her hand but Bertram was not with her. She apologised and suggested to St Clair that perhaps he should proceed with the meeting as Bertram had gone to get changed. She told them that they had worked really late the previous evening, until 4 a.m., all of that morning and all of that afternoon to upload a mass of data –10,000 terabytes.

St Clair agreed they should start. Courtney could brief Bertram on anything he missed. He then thanked her for all the hard work done by the Templar IT team, in keeping the flow of information flowing in and for keeping their Knights safe by keeping all their coms covert and without leaving digital footprints. The others agreed it had been a monumental task her team had undertaken and completed in such a short space of time.

It had been three days since St Clair had last got them all together and spoken to them all collectively. Then he revealed that Jonathan's DNA was directly linked to that of Juliette Romée, the secret daughter of Joan of Arc. He told them that the Cathar monks' prophecies scroll had predicted, she too was a Seer: in fact, she was the first Seer.

They all wanted to ask more questions about Juliette Romée, the Cathars and the Prophecies. In the room, other than St Clair, only Zakariah knew about some of the prophecies. However, as always, they all knew that if St Clair wanted them to know, then he would tell them, and if he didn't, there was a reason. They waited to see what St Clair would say.

St Clair also reminded them that whilst the Templars had been conducting monthly scanning searches of global DNA databases, they had found a DNA match to Richard the Lionheart. The others were still pretty aghast and really excited about that news. They didn't know what it meant but they were all really keen to find out what St Clair had in mind. Again, they would first wait to hear what St Clair had to say. But they all hoped today was the day he would tell them.

St Clair stood up and paced a little - he had been sitting looking at a computer screen for most of the day. The flames from the candles in the centre of the table flickered slightly.

"A young boy had his blood taken at a hospital in Essex, where he was admitted for observation, after he was involved in a car crash. Unfortunately, both his parents died in the car crash, which happened in the south of England. Cameron Jack, the little boy who survived, became orphaned, so he went to live with his grandfather. After we made the match with the DNA, we decided to keep a watching brief on the boy and, well, that's what we have been doing for twenty odd years now. We've intervened in his life a few times, but only to help and of course, without him or his grandfather ever knowing about it.

"I guess, the relevant interventions you need to know about is the fact that our Order paid for his university and accommodation fees; André arranged it through an intermediary at Cameron's local parish church. As we requested, they told him the church had paid for it. He went on from university into the British army, Intelligence Corps and then he passed selection and joined the SAS.

"We also paid for him to go to Japan when he was younger, along with his grandfather, Billy Jack. We arranged for them to visit the dojo that was run by the man who trained all of our Knights in Kenjutsu for nearly fifty years. Zakariah, Luther, André, Dominique, myself, and many others, were all trained by him; his name is Hinata Satō-san, the Templars' Master of the Blade for a long time. And then, after Hinata Satō-san retired, Tanjkna Sugata-san, his understudy, became our Master of the Blade and took over the training of our Knights.

159

"Cameron and his grandfather went to Japan once, under our patronage. We created this made up philanthropist persona, that supposedly ran a competition, the prize, a trip to Japan. Of course, it was a non-existent competition because there was only one entrant." St Clair smiled. "The reason we did it was because the boy was an exceptional talent with the sword, he was gifted at Kendo, so we wanted to help. They went to Japan every year after that, under their own steam and with their own money. So, the boy began training with two Templar Masters of the Blade, Hinata Satō and then Tanjkna Sugata, and they taught him Kenjutsu. As you all know, Tanjkna Sugata-san retired at the beginning of this year so, we desperately need a Master of the Blade and we want to offer Cameron the role. Tanjkna Sugata-san has sanctioned the appointment, and so has our Higher Council."

"Is he in then?" Zakariah asked. It was an innocent question that would reveal St Clair's somewhat shaky plan.

"Not yet," St Clair replied.

"Yet?' Zakariah said, knowing his brother well, and that there was probably more to the word 'yet' than he was letting on.

"Well, he's not a fan," St Clair said. "He doesn't like us much."

"What do you mean not a fan and much?" Zakariah said with more suspicion.

"He calls us, well, not us obviously because he doesn't know about us, so to be more precise, he calls our brothers of old, egocentric, adventure seeking, thrill loving, money centric, murderers, hiding behind closed castles. He says history books are romanticising Templars. He lectures on it sometimes, on us."

"And do people listen?" Dominique asked with more than a hint of concern.

"He is qualified," St Clair said. "Holds a first degree from Queens, London, in medieval history. Plus, he won both the UK and European Kendo championships, so he knows a thing or two about history and the art of sword warfare. People listen."

"Anything else we need to know?" Zakariah asked, looking at his brother – all eyes were on St Clair.

"Yes, we've not actually spoken to him," St Clair announced. Then a new voice entered the conversation.

"Mmm. So, he knows nothing about our plans for him, nothing about what you have been doing for him, and he really doesn't like us. And … he doesn't know we exist anyway. Makes you want to just howl at the moon, right, Mr St Clair?" Bertram said. He had been standing in the doorway for a while; he was also carrying a tray of lemon drizzle cakes for everyone.

"It's like riding the ragged edge. It's like the canter, so called because of the Pilgrims having to run before the gates of the city of Canterbury closed for the evening, as they flocked to the tomb of St. Thomas Becket. You had to run before the gates close. Hence canter is from Canterbury. Now we need to canter towards …"

Zakariah turned to Courtney. "Riding the ragged edge?"

"He and the Russian have been listening to gangster rap together, she replied. "Bertram," Courtney said with a slight scowl, "pleniloquence, we spoke about this."

"Ah, yes, indeed; I'm being a little verbose again. Enough cantering, then. Please, everyone, have a cake."

"No," said St Clair.

"You don't like cake?" Bertram said. "They were homecooked by me; I just got them out of the oven."

"No," St Clair said again."

"Ah, I see, Mr St Clair, sweet stuff; indulge and you'll bulge, stuff and you'll puff, eat …"

"No, Bertram, you are right: we have to get on, we have to canter," St Clair replied.

"I'm getting a bit lost here," Zakariah said. "Can we get back to Cameron Jack, how are we going to recrui—" he started to ask the question.

"Courtney," St Clair interrupted. "We will recruit him via Courtney."

161

"Me?" Courtney said, surprised her name had been brought into it.

"He's very pro-American," St Clair told her.

"I hate to burst your bubble there, St Clair, but so are a few hundred million other people."

"He spent some time training with the FBI in Dallas, Texas and then worked closely with the CIA in Iraq," St Clair said.

"Again, bubble burst because so have many others, including those that we ending up fighting against—"

"Actually, that would be most of them," Bertram interjected, but everyone ignored him.

"He's clever; he matches your intellect, Courtney," St Clair added.

"And?" she said.

"Well ... he's ... he's single." St Clair informed her.

There was a three-second pause, and then, "Oh no," Courtney said, "you are not pimping me out. No way. What, you've got to be kidding me, St Clair, really?"

"Here's a photograph of him." St Clair moved to her side and showed her a photo of Cameron Jack in his military dress uniform, smiling."

Courtney looked at the photograph. Then she looked again. Cameron Jack looked a lot like Orlando Bloom but with dark blond hair. He had high cheekbones, pale-blue, almost turquoise eyes. He was about 5 feet 11 inches tall, medium build and looked like he weighed around 12 stone. He looked like a man who was calm under pressure, an honourable man. A man who would be good company. She liked his smile; it was warm and genuine.

"Well, okay then, I'll do it, but I'm doing it for the Order," she said.

St Clair smiled. "Good, then our plan is simple, Courtney: you will go and see our Mr Cameron, at one of his scheduled lectures. We have found out he is talking at a Hertfordshire college in two days' time, on the 26th. The plan is for you to engage him after the lecture and then, when you think the time is right, to tell him everything. Trust me, over the years I have found the best way to introduce us, is just head on."

"I know," Courtney said, "Zakariah did that very same thing to me four years ago, as I sat at a table sipping a nice cappuccino outside La Bohèmes. That was just before someone started shooting at us; I died at a railway track and my whole life changed forever."

"Splendid," St Clair said.

Dominique stepped beside Courtney. "Come on, sis, I'll help you pick out an outfit. St Clair can finish briefing you tomorrow; it's late and you've been up for nearly two days."

Courtney took Dominique's arm; then she took the photograph from St Clair. She turned to Dominique, "I was thinking, that pencil-lined skirt we got when we were in Milan last fall, after we concluded that Italian mission, oooh, and even that ..."

Dominique winked at St Clair as if to say, she'll be fine now.

Once Courtney and Dominique had left the room, St Clair poured tea for Jonathan and himself. The others had brought their own drink preferences with them. Jonathan had once drunk copious amount of coffee, daily, now he only drank tea – a St Clair influence, one of many. Bertram ate more cake and drank green tea.

The castle floor was flagstone flooring throughout the lower ground floor, but an array of ornate rugs, scattered over the floor, took away the blandness and coldness of the Scottish stone. They heard his footstep. Luther had a distinctive gait, they all knew when he was approaching. He liked cowboy boots, despite coming from Coventry, and his boots had metal toe and heel tips. His steps echoed as he walked, then were silent as he walked over a rug, then echoed again when he was back on the bare stone. Cowboy boots, black denim jeans and usually a sweat shirt or hoodie was Luther's go-to wardrobe.

Luther Jones had been an active Knight for many years. He had saved Dominique in South Africa in 1996; had he not been there,

163

she would have died. He was Zakariah's mission partner. When larger numbers of Knights were required they would form the lead – 1IC, and Luther second support lead at 2IC. The understanding between them when on a mission, was legendary in the Order. Rarely would they need to use coms to let each other know what the other was doing; instinctively they would know. They had worked together for so long and in so many dangerous situations that their sense of one another was highly tuned. Luther was a stocky ex-SAS serviceman. He joined the meeting.

"I have already briefed Luther," St Clair began, "so he is fully up to speed with where we're at. The good news is that Cameron's grandfather, Billy Jack, is an ex Paratrooper and ex SAS sergeant. Luther and I have decided that he will go and see Billy Jack." St Clair turned to Luther. "I'm assuming he was gone by the time you got to Hereford?" Bertram gave him an inquisitive look. "SAS headquarters," St Clair said.

"He'd left but I knew of him," Luther said. "He had a good rep; the older guys used to talk about him."

"But you guys will know you've both been in 'the' regiment, right? Despite never meeting."

"We will, Payne; he will know in the first two minutes of our meeting. I also have some names he knows well."

"Good, that's settled then. Courtney will meet with Cameron at his scheduled lectures on the twenty-sixth, at the Hertfordshire college. And you will go and see Billy Jack at his home in Notting Hill at the same time. We have two days to prepare. Luther, as you know, and now you all will know, the council have already voted that we want Billy Jack to be our next Sergeant at Arms, if we can persuade him to join us. Luther, it's pretty important we get him; we need a safe pair of hands and I don't want to be worrying about our arms and supplies situation."

"I'm on it, Payne," Luther said.

"Good, then let's pray for good fortune in two days' time,

when you and Courtney meet your marks. We need a new Master of the Blade, because of what we are about to go into, he could make the difference on the death toll. And we need a new Sergeant at Arms because he will have to make sure we are both fortified, armed correctly and our Knights are protected for the conflict that is now coming our way." He looked at them all. "And Knights, make no mistake: it is coming our way."

St Clair bowed his head; the others followed suite. "Heavenly Father …"

"Erm, Mr St Clair," Bertram interrupted.

"Is that you, Bertram? You see I have my eyes shut?"

"Yes. Yes, it is me, I mean I, me, Mr St Clair."

"Phew, Bertram, for a minute there I thought the good Lord was speaking to me. Yes, Bertram, what is it?"

"I know to eschew interruptions whenever possible but especially during prayer. Well, always in prayer, and I guess also when—"

"Bertram," St Clair said. It was a stern pronunciation of his name.

"Well, I was wondering two things really, Mr St Clair," Bertram said, "and I think I would really like to pray on them tonight but I need to know what I'm praying on."

"I'm still with you, Bertram." The others also nodded.

"Well, firstly, we know that Mr Sabath's tracker is currently in Romania because, well, we have been tracking it and, if Mr Sabath is still attached to it, that's where we'll find Mr Sabath."

"We're all praying hard that that's the case, Bertram," St Clair said. "As you know, we already have assets in place, a small recognisance team, led by the Russian, Nickolin Klymachak, your friend, I believe?"

"Ah, a very good chap, Mr Russian Klymachak. I miss our natters and our strolls and especially listening to our gangster rap collection and do you know—"

165

St Clair didn't let him go on, and on, and on. "The recon team has been scoping out the location for nearly two days, ever since you gave us the news that André had his tracker with him when he left Scotland. We are also trying to find out who owns the property where the signal is coming from. It is an old mining town, now disused, and stands on about six hundred acres of land, with numerous abandoned underground mines dotted around.

"Morgan Clay is in Panama. He has been there for some time trying to follow the sparse leads we have that might lead us to an enemy; and we now suspect it's the same enemy that has André Sabath and his Knights. We put together a team of forensic accountants to work with him, way back, and of late they've been making good progress and we are hopeful for a breakthrough. The Indian, John Wolf, has gone to support him because, as Clay put it, they are about to break into a lawyer's offices and he would feel safer with Wolf by his side. So, let me ask Luther to give you the answer to your first question. Luther?"

Luther turned to him. "Yes, Bertram, yes to your question. Yes, we are going to get Sabath and his Knights. We have been assembling an extraction team. That's why I was late for the meeting, I was talking to the Russian out in Romania about terrain, possible entry and extraction points. He's been sending two or three sit reps daily."

Bertram looked confused.

"Sorry, I spent too long in the armed forces, situation reports. We know that the tracker's signal is coming from this disused mining town in Northern Romania and now, thanks to the recon team, we have a pretty good idea of the layout of the target site. They have the Faro Lidar predictive analytics scanning equipment. Basically, it uses pulse laser sensors to scan terrain and buildings. It's high-grade military equipment. It basically gives us high resolution 3D imaging drawings. The Russian's been sending this data back to us.

"I have been training the extraction team for a few days now based on the images the Russian and his team have been sending back and we are about ready to go. I will lead Alpha team, the extraction group and we are waiting for conformation of who will lead Bravo team, the support and cover team for Alpha. We are going to go and get our friend and his Knights; we are going to bring our brothers home."

"Then," Bertram said, "I now know one of the things I will pray for tonight. Thank you, Mr Luther, sir."

"And the second?" St Clair asked.

Jonathan stood up. "He wants to know who we will be fighting? Who is the enemy? Who's got André and why, because it's what I want to know, what we all want to know? Is it Salah El-Din?"

St Clair did the opposite to Jonathan, he sat down. He looked at Zakariah and then at Luther; they both nodded in agreement. "Jonathan," St Clair said, "you may need to pour yourself some coffee instead of tea. Zakariah, would you mind?"

"Four years ago, Jonathan," Zakariah began, "I told you that we had an enemy that has been fighting our Order since the beginning, for almost 800 years. They were already there in Jerusalem when the first Templars went there. We have been fighting them ever since; they have been fighting us ever since. They are incredibly dangerous. They are evil, barbaric, cunning, seemingly well-funded but they are very, very skilled. They fight in an unconventional way and this makes them really hard to defeat. They are called Abaddons. You asked me four years ago, Jonathan, why you knew that name but you couldn't place it; do you remember our conversation?"

Jonathan nodded; he remembered it vividly because it was the week after the battle with Salah El-Din, in Cumbria, and he thought then that there could not be anyone worse than that criminal: but he was wrong.

Bertram spoke up. "It's from the Apocalypse of John, the Book of Revelation. Revelation 9: 1 to 11 … And he opened the

167

bottomless pit; and there arose a smoke out of the pit, as the smoke of a great furnace; and the sun and the air were darkened by reason of the smoke of the pit.

"And there came out of the smoke locusts upon the earth: and unto them was given power, as the scorpions of the earth have power … And they had hair as the hair of women, and their teeth were as the teeth of lions.

"And they had tails like unto scorpions, and there were stings in their tails: and their power was to hurt men … And they had a king over them, which is the angel of the bottomless pit, whose name in the Hebrew tongue is Abaddon …The king of the pit, the king of an army of Locusts."

Zakariah continued. "This is the same enemy that kidnapped my wife Sophia, and left Dominique for dead. They were the Abaddon *Alqatala. Alqatala* is Arabic for assassins; they were Abaddon assassins. The same enemy that tortured my wife. They smashed her elbows, broke both ankles, and her ears, eyes and lips had been removed. Then, they disembowelled her." He paused and St Clair and Luther both shared the same memories as Zakariah. Bertram had not heard this before; the others had. Bertram was visually shaken and shocked.

"Payne, Luther, Dominique, myself and hundreds of other Knights have been fighting the Abaddons for a long time," Zakariah said. "We have fought them many times and in many different ways and every time both sides came away with heavy casualties. The Abaddons have only three missions in life: one is to destroy the Templars, which they have been trying to do for eight hundred years; the second is to kill God worshipers and finally, get the Ark."

St Clair did not add anything to what Zakariah was saying, but he wanted to. He wanted to tell them his greatest fear but he couldn't; he just thought it: *and if they suspect the truth of the Ark, like I do, if they suspect its real purpose, they will destroy it the second they get it, or it will destroy them.*

168

"Despite it being eight hundred years, we really don't know much about them." Zakariah's words snapped St Clair out of his thoughts. "It exasperates us. How do you beat an enemy you don't know; when you don't know where they are, or where they will appear next? However, we do know that in the beginning they originally emerged from an elite division of an army of over two hundred and fifty-five thousand slave soldiers in the Middle East, in the twelfth and thirteenth centaury.

"Ah, crusade time period," Bertram said. He had rallied.

"Actually, they are one of the keys to our history," St Clair answered. "This army was no ordinary army; some say they were the most skilled and feared barbarian army of all time. They were slave-warriors; captured young, at an age of between twelve to fifteen, enslaved, then trained and hardened and unleashed to fight for their lives. Remember, this was medieval Islam, full of warring tribes, Moors and invading crusaders. Life was hard and bloody for a slave; their life was only theirs as long as their sword or lance pierced the man in front of them before he pieced them. In time, they rose up against their masters and overthrew them and slaughtered them. They defeated our brothers, drove us out of the Holy Land and then, when the Mongols invaded, they drove them out too." St Clair let the magnitude of their battle skills sink in for a while. He wanted Bertram and Jonathan to know the seriousness of an enemy they faced. He wanted them to know what was coming at them.

"So, they finally drove the Templars out of the Holy Land, in 1291, from our stronghold fortress in the city of Acre. As far as we can make out, as their self-regulating, self-governed army grew, and they achieved more and more wealth and more and more lands, mostly around Egypt, but also some further afield, they started to settle down and become a more normalised tribe and develop social structures within enclaves. It was then that the elite guard, those who always rode first into battle, the most hardened of warriors, those most feared, broke away, not wanting to become house-dwelling towns-folk. They disappeared into the hills of the Holy Land. Then rumours began of pagan rituals. Their ire and barbaric nature not reserved for Christians alone, they also murdered and pillaged Muslim and Jewish communities. They were said to be anti-God. Of course, they were not called Abaddons back then; they were called Mamluks, an Arabic word that basically means slave. Your history books are full of them.

"We have Canon law, there is Halakha law – Jewish, Sharia Law – Islamic, and then we have Abaddon law: kill the God worshipers. At some time during that period, they started to follow Abaddon and they took his name, and it was to him, their new Lord, that their allegiance was sworn. He was their Lord Abaddon, and they were his right arm of punishment, retribution and death.

"As for Abaddon himself, the Bible tells us little, other than what Bertram just recited, Revelation 9:11. That's it. However, we can piece a number of things together that add a little more insight into our enemy.

"We know that during the time of the 'Great Tribulation', God cast out Lucifer and a number of angels, cast them down to the pit, as it says, 'imprisoned in the lowest level of Hell'." These are the fallen angels. We see them in Abrahamic religions, angels expelled from heaven because they sinned. And, it is said, that these angels tempt humans into sin. Many believe that about one third of the angels in Heaven joined Lucifer in the rebellion against God.

"In Isaiah 14:12-15 it says 'How you have fallen from heaven, morning star, son of the dawn.' Of course here, it is referring to Lucifer. It goes on to say 'You have been cast down to the earth … You said in your heart, I will ascend to the heavens; I will raise my throne above the stars of God … I will make myself like the Most High. But you are brought down to the realm of the dead, into the depths of the pit'.

"The bible calls them demons, not fallen angels and says that the demons continue to serve Lucifer, Satan, in his attempt to lead the

170

world away from God and into sin. But, the Bible says that Jesus will ultimately banish Satan, and his demons in the eternal fire.

"In our scriptures, Jesus also talked about a 'period of tribulation' before his second coming. There are those, I am one, that believe that Abaddon was a fallen Angel. He was cast down with Lucifer and the others for their sins in heaven. So, his followers believe it is their duty to cause that 'sin' and their duty to inflict that 'tribulation': mayhem, death, destruction, wreak havoc and pain and they believe that as long as they do that, there will not be a second coming. If they stop, the second coming will come. That, my brothers, is what we are up against."

It was getting late; the candles were still burning brightly and their flicking flames danced to a silent tune. For Jonathan and Bertram, this was new; to Luther and Zakariah, it was not. Everyone was tired, it had been a long day – it had been a long week and everyone was on high alert. Everyone was concerned about the disappearance of their brothers. Some had families, of course they were worried sick and desperate to know where their loved ones were. St Clair wished he could tell them, he couldn't; all he could do was prepare his Knights to go and get them. He needed to tell the meeting more.

"Jonathan, you asked me a couple of days ago to explain what part the Cathars played in all of this; well, this is their part. The Cathars had all but been exterminated in twelve forty-four, so they joined with the Templars. In time, both organisations started to trust each other and eventually they shared their deepest secretes. The Templars finally revealed that they held the Ark of the Covenant. The Cathars matched that revelation. They told the Templars that there was a way to communicate with the Ark, and to do that they would need a Seer. They had a scroll of ten ancient prophecies, which they had hidden at their stronghold, Château de Montségur, in the Languedoc, France but managed to get them out in time before it was destroyed and their brothers burnt at the stake. They had translated

171

them from their original language and into French. They showed the Templars. The first prophecy read, 'The daughter of the maid of Pucelle, shall have the gift to read the sacred words of God from within His Ark.'

"It wasn't until Joan of Arc referred to herself at her hearing, as 'Joan the Maid', in French, 'Jehanne la Pucelle' did the prophecy make any sense. Of course, at the time I am talking about, there was no daughter because there was no Joan.

"Then, in 1412, 168 years later, Joan was born, and in 1420 to 1431, they knew exactly who the maid was; now they just had to find her daughter. They finally tracked her down to a place where she had been hiding in for 12 years. Unfortunately, the Abaddons somehow found out about the Ark, the prophecies, the Seer.

"As I told you last time, a Cathar monk and Knight of our Order, Father Jacque Durand, finally found the girl in the Languedoc, on the road to Carcassonne. The 15-year-old girl, Juliette Trevin, didn't know that her real name was not Trevin; it was Romée. She thought the couple she lived with were her parents, but they were her great aunt and great uncle. They were protecting her, keeping her safe from her mother's persecutors. It was Abaddon assassins who tried to kidnap Juliette Romée, Joan of Arc's secret daughter. She was only saved from the abduction by the bravery and swordsmanship of that Cathar monk, Father Jacque Durand."

They all wanted to ask the same question, but it was Jonathan who asked it first, because he had asked it three days earlier and had not got a reply then.

"You told me last time that there were ten prophecies."

St Clair nodded. "And you want to know what else they say?"

It was Jonathan's turn to nod. "I do, I suspect I'm not the only one here that does." Bertram and Luther nodded their heads; Zakariah had seen them.

"We have ten," St Clair began. "The first, as you know now, says 'The daughter of the maid of Pucelle, shall have the gift to read the sacred words of God from within His Ark'. The second," St Clair turned to Zakariah, "this has to be yours, brother."

Zakariah sighed. "The second," Zakariah said, his voice calm but rueful, "beware, the slave warriors will take the Seer, a cherished one with Italian tongue, the Seer will be killed'." Zakariah's head dropped down a little remembering Sophia. They all felt for him.

"You knew Sophia's death was a possibility?" Jonathan asked St Clair; he could not and would not ask it of Zakariah.

"Every Seer is a target, every one of them." St Clair emphasised the words 'every one of them' to drive home the message. Jonathan reached for the coins in his pocket. "She had been a Seer for over ten years and she had been safe all of that time. Never once did they try to kidnap or kill her, never once. Back then, we thought, hoped, that they had faded away; perhaps hoped they had all but died out. We heard nothing from them, about them, in all that time. We were naive, but not anymore; we are not any more. The biggest problem though, was that the translation was wrong, of course we didn't know it, not until it was too late. The prophecies are written in the ancient language of Aramaic; the language Jesus would have spoken. The Cathars had translated them into French centuries ago, when they first discovered them. Then Templars translated them into English in the fourteenth century, when they fled to Scotland after the Templar persecutions and executions in France in 1307. The prophecy, 'Beware, the slave warriors will take the Seer, a cherished one with Italian tongue, the Seer will be killed', was not what we had in the English translation we were all reading. The English translation we had, read, 'Beware, the slave warriors will take the Seer, a friend speaking Latin, the Seer will die.' The phrase 'a friend' was translated into English from the French version that read 'ami', which is the French masculine word for friend. However, when we finally worked out the translations were not accurate, we had the Aramaic version checked by a world-leading expert. What that Aramaic actually said was, not 'ami, friend', but 'cherished one'. So, we were thinking it referred to a male friend, who spoke Latin. And, of course today we would say, speaks Italian. What we should have read was a 'cherished one who spoke Italian' as their mother tongue. Remember, the prophecies have no dates, so they can be and have been, hundreds of years apart."

It went silent for a while as they realised that a simple mistake in the translation destroyed so many lives and perhaps Sophia's death could have been averted. They could have all been standing there, in that warm meeting room, with its coffee and tea-making facilities and its electronic gadgetry, with another Seer; Dominique would still have her mother and Zakariah would still have his cherished wife. Jonathan now finally knew why Zakariah had left the Order and become the fallen Knight. He thought it was solely because Zakariah beat himself up because he had decided to stay on in South Africa at the end of his mission there. Had he not and had he gone home, maybe, just maybe he would have been able to save his wife. But now Jonathan knew that was not the only reason. Had they had the right translation, she would still be alive.

Jonathan spoke again. "And the next prophecy?"

"Well," St Clair said, "now you enter the picture, Jonathan. It reads 'A Knight will fall. A new Seer will come from the house of God and the fallen Knight will return'." They all looked at Zakariah and Jonathan. "That's why we had Bill Meeks follow you when you first started digging around in Washington DC," St Clair said. "We didn't know for sure, but we hoped you might be the one and so we kept a watch over you. After Sophia, we have had all of the prophecies re-translated by an Aramaic expert.

"Ever since Sophia, our mortal enemy has been trying to get the Ark and our Seers, and destroy us; they want us all dead; they want all God's worshippers dead. And now, with the disappearance of André and his Knights, we have to assume two things: one is that they have André and our other brothers; and secondly, they probably now know about our present Seer and they will do everything in their power to get him." He looked at Jonathan.

174

They all looked at Jonathan.

Jonathan felt that familiar sickness in the pit of his stomach because he had just realised he was the new target. He reached for the coins in his pocket. "You really have no idea who these people are, St Clair?" he said desperately.

"No, we have one slim lead and that's why Morgan Clay was already in Panama and John Wolf has just gone to help him but no, you're right, we have no idea. We are desperately trying to find out where their base is and who is running the Abaddon Order, if we can get him, or her, we might stand a chance but we don't have anything, their leader is a ghost. We just refer to him as FB."

"Facebook?" Jonathan asked, somewhat surprised.

St Clair, Zakariah and Luther all smiled.

"If I may, Mr Rose," said Bertram. "I think Mr St Clair is referring to a Faustian Bargain."

Luther turned to Zakariah and said, "Told you he was clever."

"He is, and he makes pretty damn good drizzle cakes," Zakariah said.

Jonathan looked lost. Bertram helped him understand. "Faust sold his soul to the demon Mephistopheles, in return for worldly knowledge and pleasure. To strike a Faustian bargain means you are willing to sacrifice anything for limitless power and knowledge; literally you sell your soul to the devil."

"Yup." Luther turned to Zakariah. "He's a clever lad all right."

Finally, standing there in that room with the others, Jonathan felt the low menacing hum of 'it' coming. The foreboding, barely perceptible, but yet it was there, in the pit of his stomach. Like the faint sound of far-off drums carried on the wind. Payne St Clair, the Templar Grand Master, had felt it. He knew what was coming. The rhythm slowly grew: ever heading Jonathan's way. And the rhythm had a name, Payne St Clair, Zakaria and Luther knew it, now Jonathan, Bertram knew it. and many other Knights were about to know it.

"Wow," Bertram said. "Double wow. Very disagreeable personalities those Abaddons, with apocalyptic tendencies. A true sense of the savage nature of humanity…"

"Shall we stop him?" Luther said, turning to Zakariah.

"Naw, let's see how long Payne puts up with it," Zakariah replied.

Bertram vented on. "… their nature, *quod erat demonstrandum* …"

"Are you sure?" Luther asked again. "I have no idea what he's talking about."

"It's Latin," Zakariah said, "thus it has been proven, the nature of them has been proven."

"… homogeneous murderers, who cause a frisson of dread, untrammelled by…" Bertram's words a seamless line of syntax.

"Bertram," St Clair interrupted, finally not able to take any more, "I think we get your point." Luther shook his head, as if to say, 'I don't.'

"Brevity, then Mr St Clair," Bertram said. "What I mean is, they are in fact, our very own crown of thorns."

St Clair nodded in agreement. "Our crown of thorns they are indeed, Bertram; well said."

Bertram replied, "I now know what the second thing I must pray for tonight is; thank you, Mr St Clair."

"Well, Bertram," St Clair said, "why don't we all pray for those two things together; hopefully He will hear our combined voices, we're going to need His help on this one." He turned to Luther. "If you can get our Sergeant at Arms and Courtney can get our Master of the Blade, and all by the twenty-sixth, which is just two days away, then I intend for Operation Mairano to get Sabath and his team out of Romania, to go live on the twenty-ninth. That will give our two new Knights, assuming we get them, just the 27th and 28th to familiarise themselves with the plan for Mairano and indeed us. Either way, we need to get our brothers out of their captivity, they've been there far too long already. I am worried that we have Easter coming up on the 6th to the 9th and Passover on the 6th to the 14th. The problem we will have if we wait until then is that everyone will be out of their normal, predictable routines and into holiday mode, which means travel chaos and unpredictability for us. So, we need to go now."

St Clair lowered his head and the others followed. "Heavenly Father ..." he began.

Chapter 10
The Jacks

Date: The evening of 26th March, 7 p.m. Two days after the meeting with St Clair in the conference room
Place: Hertfordshire College, city centre

Courtney had arrived early so she would be guaranteed a seat. The hall was full, around 100 people; the audience were mainly students. She found a seat at the front, so she could hear and watch his body language, in the hope that she would have some insight by the time they met and spoke

The large projector screen at the front, already had the first slide projected onto it, it read 'Swords and their role in the history of mankind.' The word 'mankind' had been crossed out and handwritten above it was 'man & womenkind'. A sense of humour, she thought. Courtney was a trained FBI profiler so she gathered every slither of information she could to help her understand the man she hoped she would be speaking to in an hour or so.

The lights dimmed slightly – great effect, she thought. The screen at the front flickered and there was a picture of a Samurai warrior, a Roman centurion, a Mongol warrior and, a Knight Templar. *Oh my God*, she thought, *really*, as she fidgeted on her seat. Then a voice came out of the speakers. From the back a man started to walk to the front. He was confident, thoughtful and engaging, just as she had envisaged he would be.

"I am always asked," Cameron Jack began, "who were the greatest fighting force in History? I suggest it depends on who you are."

At the front of the stage four swords lay on a table: the Templar long sword from the middle ages; the Samurai single-edged Katana sword; the Roman centurion short, stubby sword, *gladius hispaniensis*; and the Mongol slightly curved scimitar sword.

Cameron picked up the Samurai sword.

"Many a man has drawn his sword first, only to be killed by that action because he was not good enough. They killed themselves by drawing it." He let this sink in for a second or two. "Swords can give life or they can take it away. If you win, the sword gave you your life; if you lose, the sword will take your life. He held the Katana out in front of him.

"My favourite for many reasons." He said. Then wielded the sword and preformed 9 katas in a graceful and effortless series of movements. "See," he said when he'd finished, "I'm not out of breath. The Katana sword is light; it makes it far less taxing during combat. With the long sword, for example, it is much heavier and many a soldier died, not through their skill, or lack of it, but because of fatigue during a long, bloody battle. If you have not killed your opponent in the first minute of a sword fight, the likelihood is the winner will be the one who is less exhausted at the end of it. The loser will be the one who tired quicker as the fight wore on. They will be the ones who start to make mistakes as their reactions start to slow down. As it nears the end, they struggle to defend against a sharp, dangerous, long and hardened piece of steel being lunged at their body, hurtling and thrust towards them by someone with only one thought: I have to kill that person or they will kill me. We, of course, are talking about judicial combat, or as it is most often called, trial by combat, be that duelling or a full battle. Today people fight for points; in medieval times, people fought for lives, their lives."

Cameron spoke for over an hour and through it all, Courtney's assessment of him never changed: confident, thoughtful, clearly a man of honour, engaging and very knowledgeable. His audience loved the presenter. They took copious notes; others had their mobile phone recorders switched on; holding them aloft so as not miss anything. Every now and then, Cameron looked in her direction. She was obviously older than most in the room.

He had been talking for about an hour and Courtney, like the rest of the people there, was thoroughly enjoying the presenter's style, but also the content; she found it fascinating. It was into the last segment of the lecture and Cameron had called for any questions – and there were many. Courtney raised her hand and waited patiently as he went through answers dealing with sizes, weights, battles and head counts, tactics, styles, stances et al.

Then he pointed to her. "Yes."

"What would have happened, do you think," she began, "if the Roman centurions, the Mongols, the Knights Templars and the Samurai had not in fact fought with the weapons they did; what if history had them using the other's swords? So, the Romans had arced blades of the Mongols, Mongols had long swords of the Templars, the Samurai had short swords of the Romans and the Templars had the Samurai Katana swords."

A number of people started nodding in the audience; they hadn't thought of that proposition before and liked the juxtaposition it created in their minds.

"My point is," she continued, "if there were, say, equal-ish numbers on each side, is it less about the sword and more about the skill, tactics and strategy of the particular army or, is the sword that important?" She could see that he relished the question because he was being challenged.

"Good point, Miss?" he asked the *Miss* as a question.

"Rose, Courtney Rose."

He got her DC accent straight away; he had spent time

working with members of the American intelligence services. "Well, Miss Rose."

"Courtney, please."

"Well, Courtney, firstly, most swords are created to fight the same kind of sword, and there's a good reason for that. So, if those armies had fought their enemies with a different sword, outcomes might well have been different in some cases. Secondly, even if an army does have similar numbers, or even greater numbers, there are many examples in history were the few have resisted or beaten the many. Three hundred Spartans at Thermopylae against the Persian army. However, often, the winning ingredient is down to mindset: tenacity, not willing to give up, bravery, self-confidence, faith and belief in a cause, often the righteousness of what you are fighting for. A charismatic leader. Of course, all of that can be struck off the list of why someone won, as soon as a greater or more advanced weapon is introduced into the combat zone."

"The siege of Acre, Mr Jack?"

"Cameron."

She smiled. "The siege of Acre, Cameron. Give Katana blades to the Templars and the long swords to the invaders." St Clair had briefed her so that she had enough to be able to engage him in face-to-face conversation.

"You mean the Mamluks."

"I do indeed mean the Mamluks," she said.

"Great question, Courtney, because it is recognised as one of the most important battles of that period and although crusades, in a much, much reduced form, continued for a while longer, when Acre fell, the crusades lost their momentum."

He moved more to the front of the audience and now addressed them. "For those who are not familiar with the siege of Acre, here are the headlines. The Templars, and indeed many other Knights, for example the Knights of St John, the Teutonic Knights, had been in the Holy Land fighting crusades for many years. The

Templars had been there from around 1120 to 1291, so a long time. Can you raise your hands if you know about the Templars?"

Nearly every hand went up, even Courtney's!

"After they had been defeated and removed from Jerusalem, their final stronghold was the port city of Acre. There they built a fortress, a big fortress. And it was there that they really perfected their doomsday strategy: emergency evacuation because of the possible threat of attack and because they had so much to flee with. The Templars had that thing that lawyers use; it's called 'abundance of caution'. This basically means that you put protection and cover in place, then you go overboard with it. If you apply for a mortgage, for example, and a lender thinks you might be a bit of a risk, the lender requires extra collateral."

A hand went up. "Do you believe that they have the Holy Grail and that stuff?"

Seriously, Courtney thought, *this is getting surreal.*

"I don't know what they had, but we do know they had something pretty valuable. As it turned out, they were right about a possible attack because that's exactly what happened and they had to flee to Cyprus, the closest friendly Christian country.

"The Templars were in Acre for nearly one hundred years. However, in 129, four years after the loss of Jerusalem, a barbaric yet highly disciplined and organised army attacked the Templars in their strong hold of Acre: the Mamluks. Nearly a quarter of a million militia assembled with one objective: destroy Acre and kill or drive the Templars out of the Holy Land for good. They were a mixture of Muslims, Christians and a handful of other religious beliefs, including some pagans. They were not driven by religion; they were driven by power.

"The attackers pushed into the city and began to annihilate everyone that got in their way. In the chaotic street fighting, men, women and children were struck, sliced, punctured and hacked to death. The onslaught was ferocious, bloody and barbaric. With the might of their force, and using giant catapults and battering rams to beat down the high, fortified walls of the Templar stronghold, they breached the fortress walls. Thousands of attackers fought toe-to-toe with the Templars, the attackers with their curved swords and the Templars with their long swords and body armour.

"I think Courtney's point is, if the Templars had not worn so much heavy armour and used the lighter Katanas instead of the heavy, cumbersome longswords, would the outcome have been different? What do you all think?"

There was much debate as young minds suggested several different scenarios. The interactive debate went for several minutes, without a natural conclusion.

"Courtney, we've not heard from you. What do you think?" Cameron asked, as the audience debate got stuck with just two people, who were louder and dominating the floor with their opinions.

"I think that some things are meant to be, and sometimes, no matter what you do, you cannot change what's meant to be. When the call comes, the call comes."

"Well," Cameron began, "I think the Templar Grand Master, Guillaume de Beaujer, may have wished you wrong; his call came because he was killed at that siege. I heard that a splinter group of Mamluks broke away when the Mamluks slowly started to form their own towns, systems of governing and started to become less a nomadic fighting force and more a conventional society."

"Interesting," Cameron said, "but I have not seen any evidence to suggest this is true."

"And the Templars escaped?" a young student asked from two rows back.

"Ah," exclaimed Cameron, "and this I do know because it's where the doomsday strategy comes in. Large numbers of Templars did indeed escape the siege and they took with them whatever treasures they had hidden in their fortress. In 1994 a tunnel was discovered that led from the central lower area of the Templar fortress and out to a hidden wharf where boats were docked. Only five per cent of that underground network of tunnels has been excavated.

"Acre is considered one of the most important battles from that period and although the crusading movement continued for a number of centuries, the fall and capture of the city marked the end of any more crusades to the Holy Land."

After the lecture there was a queue of young students wanting to speak to Cameron. Courtney guessed that most of them were history students and nothing would engage them more than a graphic account of an historical event. There were also a few martial arts students, easily identified because they didn't ask one history question; it was all to do with stances, katas and which were the best styles. They were the ones touching the swords after the lecture.

Finally, the queue subsided and Courtney saw her chance. Cameron was putting the swords back into a large black holdall, along with some notes. She knew he had arrived by train and as far as she could tell, having followed him from London, he meant to go home that night and not stop over because he did not have an overnight bag, nor had he dropped one off at any hotel earlier in the day. He saw her coming and stopped packing his things away. He put out his hand with a warm smile and shook her hand.

"Thanks for the great question. Sometimes these things can get pretty boring with too much focus on dates and places." He looked at Courtney and for some reason he already knew he liked her.

"I take it you're not a fan of the Templars," she asked him.

"Ah, I'm busted. I'm afraid I'm not, as you say, a fan. As a historian I should be objective, and I try to be; after all, I wasn't living when they were living but I do find the very nature of crusades, their crusade, somewhat flawed. To think you could just turn up in that melting pot of religion and take what does not belong to you … it just irritates me."

"Not a noble cause then?"

"I fail to see how it could have been noble."

"Five minutes, Mr Jack," a janitor called from the back. He was sweeping up and starting to turn the lights off.

"Ah, it seems we'll be kicked out." He started packing his things away again.

"There's a Chinese restaurant around the corner," Courtney said. "If it's not too forward, perhaps we could grab a quick bite to eat. I would love to talk to you some more?"

Cameron looked at his watch; he was torn. "I was kind of hoping to catch the 9 p.m. train. I'm not being rude but that's the last one out of here tonight so, if I don—"

"I'll take you wherever you decide you want to go," she said. "I have a car."

He smiled. "You don't know how far that might be, Courtney; you should be careful what you offer."

"What, like Notting Hill, where you live with your grandfather, Billy."

Cameron stopped doing what he was doing and stood directly in front of her. "Who are you, Miss Rose?"

"Well," she began without the slightest suggestion of lying, "to be fairly candid with you and why not, you're an ex-army intelligence officer, so I guess you would know if I was lying, I'm an ex FBI operative, now a member of the Knights Templar, who needs to speak to you about coming to Scotland with me, to fight the same foe that ransacked Acre, in 129. Oh, yes, and I've been dead since 2008."

Time: 8 p.m. that same night
Place: A two-bedroom house in Notting Hill, London

Luther had watched the house all day. He had seen Billy Jack come to the door with another man. He guessed it was his grandson, Cameron Jack; he fitted the picture the Templars had of him. The man got into a waiting taxi and then Billy Jack went back inside the house. He had followed Billy as he walked to the local shops. Luther watched him go into the newsagents, then a small supermarket. Then he returned to the house carrying a grocery bag. Later, Billy Jack went around to his next-door neighbour's. He was in there for about 30 minutes before returning home. It was now dark. Luther had a room at a nearby hotel. He had arrived late the night before, checked into the hotel and slept well. He'd been on his feet all day and there was a warm bed waiting for him three stops away on the underground. He decided he had observed Billy Jack long enough; it was time to make contact.

Luther knocked on the front door – there was no bell. It was chilly and Luther pulled his jacket collar up around his neck. The curtains were drawn in the large bay window of the front room. The lights were on. Inside he heard the TV. He knocked again.

The voice was low – not whispering but low. "Stay still." The voice was behind him.

Luther felt the cold knife blade on the back of his neck. "Wasn't thinking of moving. Nice move by the way."

"Thanks." Billy Jack frisked Luther.

"I don't have any weapons," Luther told him.

"Best to check," Billy said.

"You're so right," Luther said. "Can never be too careful but I just came to talk."

"Well, you should have knocked earlier, instead of following me around all day."

"Ah, you spotted me?" Billy just smiled, but Luther couldn't see the smile. "Just wanted to be sure about you, Billy."

"Are you sure now?" Billy asked.

"I am," Luther said. "Apologies but I'm only here because we need to talk to you quite urgently, so forgive all the cloak and dagger stuff."

"I don't know you," Billy said, "and I have no need to talk to anyone."

"Lofty Downs and Pancho Harris send their regards."

This surprised Billy; he knew the names straight away. "You were with them in Nigeria?" Billy asked.

"Nice try, Billy, but they were in Chad, not Nigeria; first in when we went in to save the hostages at the British Embassy siege there, back in the late nineties."

"You were with them?" Billy asked.

"I was," Luther answered. "Billy, we've never met, you'd left a few years before I got to Hereford, but I heard all about you from the boys; they said you were a solid bloke."

Billy removed the knife from Luther's neck and opened the front door. "If you were with Lofty and Pancho, then you must be Luther Jones, the third man of the Alpha lead team, the first guys in?" Luther nodded. "I thought I recognised the surveillance MO today, Northern Ireland?" Luther smiled. "Well, you'd better come in Luther, it's chilly out."

Luther was soon warm; the central heating was on and Billy broke out the whiskey. Luther instantly liked Billy, not just because they'd been in the same regiment or he still had honed street craft but because Billy had suffered from PTSD and had turned his life around, despite PTSD not being commonly recognised.

"Nice place, Billy," he said as he followed him into the kitchen.

"We do okay." He poured whiskey with a little water each. "How are Pancho and Lofty?"

"As crazy as ever. Lofty is doing security work, here in London, and Pancho … Pancho is running an outward-bound centre up in Lancashire. I don't think those two will ever slow down. How about you, Billy? How have you been keeping?"

"Not bad. Was a full-time parent for a number of years, well, full-time grandparent … he is my grandson. His mum and dad died but he's all grown up now, ex regiment himself, a Rupert, came out Intelligence Corps."

"Officer, eh, not bad, and brain Corps; must be clever that lad of yours," said Luther.

187

"Sharp as a tack, and turned into a really smashing guy."

The conversation was amiable, the house was warm and the whiskey was a single malt, so it went down well. The two ex SAS soldiers sat and talked in Billy's kitchen for over an hour about who they knew in the regiment, where they were now and what they were up to. They talked about missions, successes and failures. Luther enjoyed hearing about some of the work the guys had got up to in the Sultanate of Oman and operations in the Falklands, before he joined. Those stories were legendry in the regiment and Luther enjoyed talking to someone who, was not only there but someone who was a bit of a legend himself. They laughed about some of the colourful characters the regiment had and some of their more outrageous antics. The regiment was made up of tough men doing tough and dangerous work and it needed and attracted a certain kind of man; both Luther and Billy were such men. The two men sitting opposite each other had never met, but instantly became brothers because of the bond of their regiment, *the* regiment. They could have sat and talked all night, talked and drank all night but Luther had been set a task by St Clair and he needed to come through for him. It was the fifth whiskey and he decided it was time.

"Billy, I have a job for you."

Billy looked at him inquisitively. "Been a while since anyone wanted to give me a job. I'm sixty-three you know?"

"I know, Billy," Luther answered; "it's your skill set we need: your training and your combat experience."

Billy was certainly intrigued; he'd not had so much military talk since he'd left the Forces and he'd enjoyed it again. He still felt young and agile. Occasionally he trained with Cameron at his dojo, so he was reasonably fit. He also knew he needed to find something to occupy his time. For years he had focused all of his efforts on trying to be the best surrogate parent he could be to his grandson. However, when Cameron left for university, Billy felt very lonely and missed the company of his grandson. Then Cameron left for the Forces and

Billy again faced life alone. He had friends in Notting Hill but it was never the same without Cameron. Even though Cameron was back home now, and had been for about a year, he was either at the dojo, practising his own full combat style, or giving talks up and down the country. Billy was willing to listen to what Luther had to say.

"Okay, I'm all ears."

It took Luther over an hour and a half. He started with the history of their Order, their demise in 1307 at the hands of the King of France and a ruthless and feckless Pope. How they went into hiding in Scotland; helped the Scottish army against King Edward. He explained about their modern-day secret operations and gave examples of active missions over the last 20 years. He outlined their operations in Scotland. He told Billy about their 'contractor' status with the British Government.

That, from time to time, like secret intelligence services (SIS) all over the world, the UK's SIS used private outside agencies that have Omega 1 clearance to carry out certain classified assignments. Pi, which was their code name, had substantial clearances. He then told Billy about the Ark of the Covenant and the story of Salah El-Din. He explained about the Seers and about Jonathan. Then he detailed the aborted mission in Abu Dhabi and, finally, the disappearance of André Sabath and his Knights from the Lebanon.

Billy didn't interrupt. In fact, he didn't do much of anything other than listen. Now that Luther had finished, Billy poured himself a large glass of whiskey and drank it. Then he did the same again.

"And this stuff, this stuff that you guys have been doing; it's been going on right under everyone's noses for—"

"Centuries," Luther said.

"Scotland, eh?"

"Scotland." Luther confirmed.

"Sergeant at Arms?"

"We need you."

"And I'd be working with you?"

"You would, Billy, and a whole lot of other people – great people, dedicated and committed to the values of our Order, sworn to protect the innocent and our 'Charge'. It's full time, 24/7. It's a way of life. It's a calling. It's like the regiment."

"Damn, Luther, I haven't felt this excited since the day I passed my basic training and became a full paratrooper. I'm in. Of course, I'm in. However, I've got one problem: my grandson. How the hell do I tell him I'm moving to Scotland?"

"Oh, I wouldn't worry about that, Billy," Luther said. "If I was a betting man, I might be tempted to place money on the possibility that your grandson just might be on his way up there himself right now."

Chapter 11

Le Fantome Blanc (The White Ghost)

Date: 1955
Place: Zurich, Switzerland

When Zivko left Serbia, after inheriting all of his father's money through court probate, he headed first to Zurich, where he had been told that his father held an account.

There was no immediate money from his father's estate for Zivko to rely on. He had instructed the lawyers, Spiradon and Jana, to sell everything in Serbia that his father owned and he told them that he would advise them where to send the proceeds once he knew. Of course, all that would take time. He had no intention of waiting around in Serbia until his father's estate had been sold and the proceeds transferred to him. However, he did have money for the long journey ahead of him, a journey that would take him through a number of countries, principally Switzerland, Italy, Egypt and then into the French Congo in Africa. The money he did have, he'd taken from four priests and a number of other unfortunate souls he had disposed of over the years – the priests, he found, always had the most money. Plus, he had also been stealing from his father's housekeeper's food and house allowance for years.

In his jacket pocket was a letter from the courts declaring Zivko the inheritor of Stallas Gowst's estate. The letter was stamped and attested by the law firm Spiradon and Jana, who had already been in touch with the bank in Zurich about the change of ownership through inheritance. It had come as no surprise to Zivko that his father held a private bank account, he had long suspected why, he was about to find out if he was right.

It was 1955 and Zurich was a hive of activity, very different from the isolation he had known all of his life. The newspaper his father owned and therefore the only one Zivko ever got to see, was parochial, politically right-wing, and full of bluster, opinion, gaslighting and bad reporting. The newspapers in Switzerland carried international issues and events: He read that a place called Disneyland had opened in California, America, that year; the American President, Eisenhower, had had a heart attack; Austria's independence was restored from Germany and Albert Einstein died. On the radio, which he had never listened to because father had forbidden them in the house, Zivko heard rock and roll for the first time; it was new release called 'Rock around the Clock' – he didn't take to it much.

Upon leaving the only home he had ever known for the last time, he had taken a taxi to the local train station and from there he took a train to the capital, Belgrade. Next, he boarded a sleeper train that travelled right across the country; he changed trains to cross Hungry; and again, when he got to Austria; and then finally Zurich, in northern Switzerland. His journey took almost a week.

Everywhere he went people gawked at him. His looks disturbed them; his albinism often frightened young children – and not just young children. At times their reactions were of inquisitiveness, curiosity, but for the most part, their reactions were of alarm, mistrust and disgust. He, as always, ignored the looks and the comments he received. He was isolated within the dark recesses of his mind; it was his sanctuary where his consciousness and his id dwelt side by side, not as one person as in 99.9% of the world's population, but as two people, symbiotically co-existing; two deeply disturbed personalities.

However, Zivko was not used to the magnitude of alarm his appearance was creating. He was used to it on a small scale because he had never been around that many people before. Rarely had he ever left the grounds of the estate, and if he did, it was normally only at night. The figure of a fairly unkempt man, in an old-fashioned black suit, a white shirt with a starched, round collar, black tie, and emanating from this dark, drab attire, a pale-skinned, no complexion, pink-eyed, white-haired adult, talking to himself in a rasping, cold whisper, upset most. Zivko was lucky on his trip not to have been approached by the police, mugged or even attacked.

Upon his arrival in Zurich, he checked into a rodent infested, back-alley hotel because he did not have much money and because he saw no need to squander what he did have.

The day after he arrived, he woke early. Dressed. Washed in a primitive, chipped ceramic bowl with a pitcher of cold water. He brushed his hair in front of the mirror with his mother's hairbrush. He sang his mother's favourite Arabic song, "*Habibi, Habibi*" – *my love, my love* – as he brushed. Then, when he'd finished, he chatted with himself, whispering, "We hate them, Zivko, don't we? We are as reviled by them as they by us. Them, the duplicitous whores, the masses that sting us. Them, with their mundane, meandering, average existence of hypocrisy and mediocrity. '*Habibi, Habibi*'."

He had an appointment at his father's bank at 10 a.m., which had been pre-arranged by his lawyers, eight days ago. It was a 20-minute walk away from his hotel to the bank. He was punctual. Upon arrival, he was asked to wait in the seating area. He was offered tea or water; he declined both. He was an attraction to the other customers and a distraction to the staff: an odd-looking man with worn, crumpled cloths, pallid skin, pure white hair, pink eyes, who was constantly mumbling to himself. Zivko was talking with himself but had learnt over that week that if he spoke quietly, so it was almost inaudible, he didn't attract so much attention; plus, he didn't want anyone hearing *their* conversation.

After confirming that all his paperwork was in order, Zivko was shown into one of the secure rooms in the basement vault of the bank – most of the bank tellers turned to see the odd-looking man walking behind the bank manager and the assistant bank manager.

Zivko was told that the room had nearly fifty safety deposit boxes and one large safe; he was given the combination to the large safe. Once inside the room, the lock clicked and the door was locked behind him. He was alone now; he had full privacy. There were no cameras in the room. With the numbers of the combination in his hand, he turned the combination dial, slowly, until each number clicked. When he opened the door, he stood quite still. There, inside the large safe, was his father's hidden wealth.

There was a wad of American dollars, all used notes. He counted the money out on the table in front of him. There was $25,000 in $1.00, $5.00, $10.00, $20.00, and $100.00 dollar bills. In addition, and taking up all of the room, were 160 gold bars, each stamped '5 kilo'. Each gold bar was three inches wide and six inches long and each weighed 11 lbs, about the same as a large water melon. The total weight in gold was 125 stone, or approximately three quarters of a ton in gold. He had no idea where it had come from or how his father got it there. Each bar was worth $6,240; collectively the gold was worth one million dollars.

Zivko held a bar in his hand and looked down at it. He had no emotion; he had no sense of elation regarding his good fortune. He stared at the rest of the bars in the safe. The conversation he had with himself was about not wanting to change *their* plans. *They* agreed *they* would still go to Egypt and then to Africa. *They* would, he mumbled, use the money to buy mines in the Congo and increase *their* wealth.

Zivko had just become a Serbian millionaire. And for the next five decades, until 2012, he would turn that money into an amount that would make Zivko Cesar Gowst a Serbian billionaire. That day, standing in the vault room of that Zurich bank, his long-held

194

suspicion of why his father had abruptly gone to Germany, in October 1945, was confirmed. Each of the gold bars were stamped with an embalm, a large swastika; it was Nazi gold, gold the Third Reich had stolen from the Jews and smelted down.

The gold would allow Zivko to amass a bigger fortune; however, because it was Nazi gold, each time he sold any, no matter how careful he was, it would leave a trail – almost imperceptible, but it was there.

Date: 1955 to 1957
Place: Cairo, Egypt

Two days later, Zivko took a train that journeyed across Switzerland and then down through Italy to Gioia Tauro, in southern Italy. There he boarded a ship, on a third-class ticket, that took him around the southern tip of Italy, past Malta and then on to the port of Alexandria, on the West Verge of the Nile Delta, Egypt.

Despite his new-found wealth, Zivko did not change his travel plans; he did not change his third-class ticket on the boat nor did he opt to fly part of the way, which he could have done. He saw no need to be wasteful with his money and he was in no rush to get anywhere. However, the journey was long and tedious for Zivko. Very few passengers on the ship involved themselves with the mumbling idiot, for he must be an idiot, they all concluded because he skulked around the ship talking to himself. An unkempt, pallid-skinned, white-haired, halfwit with pinkish eyes that warranted no attention, conversation or engagement. For the few that did attempt to engage him in conversation, they found him to be articulate, extremely well read and smart. However, they struggled to get over his appearance and his low, scratchy, and somewhat eerie whisper of voice. Even if they could breach those prejudices, and a couple of people tried, including the captain of the ship, they could not countenance his disturbing behaviour of talking to himself as two people and referring to himself in a mix of the first and third person.

A few days out, and at the request of the captain, the ship's doctor asked to see Zivko, to determine if he was a danger to the other passengers and crew. The meeting went well and was amiable. The doctor's report suggested that, whilst he foresaw no threat to the crew and passengers, he did diagnose Zivko as having a mental health disorder that was affecting his thinking and his interaction with people. He suggested that Zivko was suffering from Schizoaffective disorder, one of four schizophrenia disorders. He noted his symptoms: he heard voices – which was himself, or his 'other self', and thus was delusional; he showed signs of mood disorder, hypomania and some depression; and finally, he displayed signs of suspicion and mistrust. The doctor hypothesised, for he was a general practitioner, not a clinical psychologist, that a traumatic, a series of traumatic, or systematic deep trauma had caused the condition. In his conclusion, the doctor wrote, *to admit someone suffering from this condition normally has three questions attached to it: do they pose a risk to themselves or others, I believe not; can they take care of themselves, I believe so, clearly he has and is doing so; and finally, would he benefit from hospital treatment, yes, but we are not a hospital and where this ship is heading, I would doubt they have the capabilities.* The doctor was not aware of the trail of bodies Zivko had left behind in Serbia. The corpses of priests and others, whose bodies were meticulously sliced open from the back, and skin, muscle and ribcages pulled open from the spine and out towards the shoulders to imitate the wings of an eagle.

Zivko was left to finish his sea voyage without further requests to meet the doctor. The crew nicknamed him the Ghost because of his pasty, pallid appearance and, of course, the similarity with his last name, Gowst. It would not be the last time that this name would be used when referring to him.

As the voyage progressed, he left his cabin less and less

during the day, the sunlight of the Mediterranean Sea growing ever stronger as they steamed closer and closer towards Africa and the Middle East.

After what seemed like an interminable amount of time to Zivko, and to most of the passengers, they sighted land and the large port of Alexandria, Egypt. The ship's crew moved into action as they began to ready the ship for docking. Everyone had a job to do, some several jobs to do. The passengers were kept out of the way below decks, until the ship had been docked and secured.

The passengers disembarked, the mayhem and chaos of Egypt hit them as soon as they started walking down the gangplank. The sights, sounds, smells hit their senses like a small earthquake. They had seen nothing exciting for days. The scenery had been the same every day, the routine, smells, food … it had all become very boring and predictable. They were mustered into single file as they stepped off the gangplank and onto the quayside. An officious, rotund Arab with a pencil moustache herded them to a corrugated building marked 'Customs'. Once inside, everyone struggled to get air into their lungs, the slow, rotating ceiling fans did nothing to ease the heat corralled inside the building. Each passenger was vetted by one of the customs officers, their passports and reason for their visit checked.

The young customs officer that dealt with Zivko was mesmerised by the odd-looking, passenger in front of him. He was not sure if the passenger was ill with some disease and maybe it might be catching? He asked Zivko what the purpose of his visit was; the customs officer's English was slightly suspect, having been learnt from American westerns on TV. Zivko answered in perfect Arabic. The customs officer was taken aback. Doubly so when Zivko explained that he was half Egyptian; that his mother had come from Cairo; that he was now visiting his mother's family and paying his respects to his deceased grandfather.

Other customs officers stopped what they were doing. The sound of Arabic coming out of a foreigner's mouth in their country was rare enough but that it was perfect Arabic, including local idioms and dialect, amazed them. The other passengers now wished they had taken the time to befriend the oddball, as he could have helped them have an easier time getting through customs.

Zivko was 22 years old when he arrived in Egypt. He had intended to stay for a week with his mother's family and then he would journey down through Africa, by train and road, and into the French Congo; he would then start his mining career; it was 1955. All his plans revolved around this. He even had train timetables and route maps that he had studied on the interminable sea trip, which would take him across and out of Egypt and across Africa, in seven days' time.

After taking a taxi ride from Alexandria, which took a gruelling three hours, he finally arrived at his hotel in Cairo. He had booked the hotel via the ship's telex, two days out from the port in Italy. A telex cable was waiting for him at the reception desk of his hotel from his lawyers, Spiradon and Jana – he'd also sent them details of the hotel he would be staying at for a week whilst in Egypt. The cable from the lawyers informed of him that all of his father's assets had now been sold and the sales process had achieved the amount of $28,000 dollars.

Two days later, Zivko wired a telex to them and told them to transfer all of the money to his mother's family. He gave them the bank account details where they should transfer the money. Only a second cousin in the family had a bank account; all of the others were all too poor and so had no need of bank accounts. The money was transferred.

Zivko had visited with his mother's family for just two days, after his arrival in Cairo. On his third day in Cairo, Zivko Cesar Gowst disappeared. He did not turn up to the family event in the *majlis* – front parlour, where he was expected to attend, at the home of an extended family member. A goat had been slaughtered in his honour and much fuss hand been made about the preparations but he never showed. Every trace of Zivko had gone. His hotel room had been cleared, his bill had been paid in full; he had checked out and retrieved his passport. The family checked with the police and they confirmed that he had not presented himself at any border or customs crossing, so they assumed that he was either still in Egypt, or dead.

In 1957, nearly two years later, Zivko re-emerged out of the blue. A man answering his description presented himself at the Argeen border crossing on Lake Nubia. His passport was stamped and he was recorded as leaving Egypt and crossing into Sudan.

Now Zivko was well dressed. He travelled in black, handmade tailored suits, finely cut and stitched by Egyptian tailors. His habit of talking to himself had all but gone, although it occasionally resurfaced if he got angry. He was more confident. He did not hide away. He now wore expensive sunglasses. Black, very large; often people mistook him for a blind person. When he left for the Congo, he had two companions in tow. Both were Egyptian and both wore traditional Egyptian garments. They did not speak to the other passengers. They had a hard, stern look. They never left Zivko's side and always watched everyone else. They looked menacing. They always sat either side of Zivko; he was never alone.

The journey took a long time. It was hot and it was very uncomfortable. The flies were intolerable. The hours passed slowly; the track was endless, monotonous and tedious; and the railway stations were chaotic, shambolic places. The food was bad, the sanitation even worse. Zivko had a berth; the two Egyptians slept outside his carriage. Zivko spoke to no one, other than the two Egyptians, and no one spoke to him. If anyone tried to talk to him, they were blocked or ushered away by either of the Egyptians.

Date: 1957 to 1967
Place: French Congo

When Zivko first arrived in the French Congo, at the age of 24, he was not aware of the prejudice against albinos; and not just prejudice: like in many parts of Africa, albinos were actively hunted, maimed, their limbs cut off and organs harvested. Often, they were just murdered. He learnt quickly that in some areas of Africa, people believed that certain body parts of albinos can transmit magical powers and, as a result, albinos had been persecuted and killed or dismembered for centuries. Even graves of albinos had been dug up and desecrated. Albinos were often shunned by their communities. They were viewed as spirits.

Zivko knew none of this before he went, but he soon learnt. Had Zivko gone to Africa first, he would not have survived and would have been dead within a month, but he changed in Egypt, things changed. He changed to such an extent that in the Congo's harsh and dangerous climate, and given he was an albino, he would actually thrive. They saw an albino; what they got was a cruel man and an evil man: bitter, angry, spiteful and revengeful. He was wealthy, powerful and he was dangerous. His two Egyptian minders protected him; he suffered no fools; he would allow no person to get in the way of his goals.

Sometime during his two years in Egypt, Zivko had sold a number of gold bars – he had kept them in the same bank and vault where his father had hidden them. His tractions were dealt with through one of the assistant bank managers. His name was Alberto Keller, and he was a year younger than Zivko. Zivko neither trusted or liked the main bank manager. The bank had sold the bars through an intermediary because of the stamp they carried. The bank had only offered the sale of the gold bars to three people. They would not risk any more than that because the repatriation of Nazi stolen plunder – gold, art and other artefacts – had become a full-time crusade for a number of private and commercial victims and government watchdog committees around the world. The bank took their 2.5% commissions for transacting the sale. From the proceeds, Zivko purchased three hard rock gold mines and paid hefty bribes to a number of politicians and mining commission employees. He also purchased another mining lease but this time it was not in Africa, it was in Europe.

In the ten years that Zivko was in the Congo, he made a lot of money to add to his already substantial hoard. He mined for gold using the rule that most of his workforce were 'born to be collateral damage'. He was just another user and abuser in a long line of people that had exploited the locals and used the greed of politicians and local law enforcement. His mines were dangerous places because he cared little for safety protocols and procedures, and so spent little on the safety of the local workforce. His fatality rate was one of the highest in the country; he cared not.

The French Congo, established as French in 1882, had seen many tribal wars. It was a harsh and unforgiving place. Its lands produced a significant amount of the world's cobalt, copper, diamonds, titanium, tin and gold. It was said that billions in gold lay under the ground in the French Congo and Zivko wanted to harvest as much as possible. However, he didn't have it all to himself. There were many others who were already mining in his area and some were as powerful and a few as rich. They would also stop at nothing to take his land leases and therefore his gold. Looters raided his mines on a regular basis. Punishment was swift and largely terminal but, for many of the poverty-stricken locals, it was the only option they had to stave off starvation. He also had to deal with local, French-speaking criminals, who despised the foreigner for taking their gold, although they had no intention of digging it out themselves, or sharing it with anyone else.

The French-speaking locals called the albino foreigner *le Fantôme Blanc*, the White Ghost, or just Ghost; it fitted his appearance. The Ghost spoke in English with a strong Eastern European accent and in a low rasp – it sounded like fine shards of glass being stepped on, then tapering off to a whisper at the end of every statement. Whilst he now spoke far less to himself, when he did, it was disturbing and frightening for the locals. They already thought of him as a spirt because of their prejudices with albinism. They were steeped in tribal folklore, tradition and archaic beliefs. He would seldom come out during the day, and if he did, he always wore a black suit and a white starched shirt and black tie, regardless of the heat. He always wore his thick, black sunglasses; most never saw his pink eyes but the odd few that had were quick to tell what they saw. He was always accompanied by the two Egyptians, they carried scimitar swords in their waistbands. The swords, curved blades that broadened towards the point, looked dangerous, and the men that carried them, equally as dangerous. There were rumours of missing locals who'd had their heads decapitated, men that had worked in Zivko's mines and had disagreements with their mine bosses. Their families complained to the authorities but nothing ever came of it.

There had been a number of attempts on Zivko's life, despite the fact that he had local police, politicians and other useful people on his payroll. In his part of the Congo, it was practically lawless and the mining community cut-throat – literally. The two men who had accompanied him from Egypt had sworn to protect him: the men that bore the three crescent moon tattoos on the underside of their right wrist … the same tattoo as his grandfather had … the same tattoo that Zivko now had.

During Zivko's second year of the ten years he spent mining in the Congo, he was brutally attacked. His Egyptian bodyguards failed to stop the assailant, and he got to Zivko. The assailant was a local, a man by the name of Azrael. He had been given that name by five Jewish surveyors and geologists, two decades before. They had been brought into the Congo, by a French mining company, to help them survey and test new ground for possible ore extraction – which included gold. Azrael's job had been to protect the five Jews from the lawlessness in the region – and they'd needed it because the area's crime rate was one of the highest in the world. The name Azrael is the Hebrew name for the Angel of Death; he who separates the body from the soul … the Grim Reaper. It fitted the African well and the name stuck.

Azrael had deep facial scar patterns running on both sides of his face – across his cheekbones. They were a result of ritual scarring, as practised across Africa, and indigenous people in Central America, North America and Australia. In Azrael's case, they were created by pulling his skin up with fish hooks, then cutting the flesh with a sharp knife and covering it with hot ash. It was done when he was a baby. Tribal legend has it that he didn't cry. His scars looked like Seal's Lupus facial scars. The locals called the act of applying hot ash *cicatrisation*, French for healing – but with scarification.

Azrael was a huge man, six feet five and weighed around 18 stone. A tough and powerful man who feared nothing. Even the tribal leaders did not cross him and would not tangle with him. Married with fourteen children, he provided for them when others with just one child failed. He was up for hire, a poacher, a mercenary and, at times, a thief, an extortionist, a murderer. He was feared because of who he was, because of what he did and because of how he did it. He carried a machete but not just any machete. Azrael's machete had been forged specifically to his instructions. It was longer than a normal machete and broader. He had wielded a machete ever since he was four years old. As he grew in size and stature, so his machetes got bigger and bigger.

In 1958, a year after Zivko arrived in the Congo, Azrael was hired by a Venezuelan mining company, with interests in the area, to remove Zivko: permanently. They had offered to buy the mining leases from Zivko, which he held, but he would not sell. They tried to cut off his supplies but he just got them from other places. They tried to bribe the authorities but Zivko just paid them more. Finally, they decided that a more permanent solution was required; so, they hired Azrael to kill the man the locals called the Ghost.

Azrael's style of assassination was always the same: under the cover of night, his victim, hampered by much reduced vison, would have to deal with the unknown sounds in the dark that would fuel their anxiety and feeling of dread and foreboding. He always carried out the assassinations alone. It was always done face to face, never from behind and, it was always with a machete: and it was always brutal. He planned the assassination at the next three-quarter moon, enough low ambient light to make out where he was going but not enough to be easily seen.

Zivko spent most of his time at the largest of his three mines. Rocks extracted from the mines, dug from seams of quartz, were crushed in the rock crusher, fed into a trammel that spun and washed the rocks, then out into a sluice box with running water. The gold, heavier than the crushed rocks and water, fell to the bottom of the sluice's ridges. Once done, the material in the sluice box, the concentrate, would be gathered and sent to the gold room for the final part of the separation process, extraction. The gold room was the most secure building on the mine site.

Zivko's gold room was part of three, stone-built buildings, the rest were all wooden constructions and mostly supply stores. His work forces slept outside. Zivko's living quarters was above the gold room. As for Zivko's two Egyptian bodyguards, one slept outside, directly outside the gold room door, the second slept outside his room.

The three-quarter moon was in the night sky. Azrael crept past the weary, sleeping mine labourers. It was 1 a.m. and the workers would need to be up at 4 a.m. He knew, because they were tired and exhausted from another hard day, they would not wake to sound the alarm if he moved with caution and stealth.

The bodyguard that slept outside the gold room was asleep in a sitting position, his back resting against the door; the key to the gold room door attached to his belt. It was the only way into Zivko's room upstairs, where he also kept the gold deposits, before selling it to gold brokers. Azrael did not want to fight the first guard. He knew there was a second and he did not want to alert him, or give Zivko time to make an escape, out of one of the top windows. A rock hit the sleeping gold room guard with force and split his head. He keeled over and hit the dirt floor. Azrael relieved him of the key and opened the door.

It was hot inside the building. The windows were always kept shut because of security. Azrael's nostrils flared at the smell of stale and rancid sweat. He gingerly made his way through the machine-lined gold room. He ignored the gold that was still lying about in test pans. Using the dull, yellow light from the moon, creeping through the grimy gold room windows, he carefully made his way up the stairs and up to Zivko's bedroom.

The first two boards at the top of the stairs creaked. Zivko has loosened them as another safety measure. His life was always in danger, either from other mining companies, illegal prospectors, local criminals, or those that meant to amputate his limbs and harvest his organs for their so-called magic powers.

The second Egyptian woke at the sound of the boards to see a mountain of man standing in front of him. His scarred face growled at him. The man's right hand held a long and powerful-looking machete. The Egyptian called to Zivko, and at the same time stood and withdrew his sword, the scimitar, sharp and now ready; it was a familiar presence in his hand. He and the other bodyguard practised with their swords four hours a day and in their own country, they were known as expert swordsmen. But, now this guard was about to be put to the test as Azrael forced a left shoulder, to right hip downward thrust of his machete at the guard. The Egyptian just managed to put his sword in the way to block the deadly blow but it knocked him against the door because of the force behind it. Azrael spun the machete round with a flick of his wrist, and the machete was back into an attacking position. The guard rallied and quickly moved into a wide stance defensive position. He too spun his sword, first moving his wrist round to the right and then, round to the left. He wanted Azrael's eyes on the sword so that he could sidestep round to the flank and attack on the African's unprotected side.

The bedroom door opened and Zivko stood in the doorway with a colt revolver in his hand. The hammer was back and it was fully loaded. He just stood there looking at Azrael; he had never seen anyone like him before. He looked like a demon who had come in the night to take away his soul – Azrael was living up to his name!

Azrael grabbed for a six-inch spike he kept in his belt – he carried six of them. He preferred a metal spike to a knife or dagger because it was more accurate. Used correctly, it could puncture a lung, an organ, an artery, the heart and because of its shape, he could easily bypass bone that often restricts a knife's penetration. Azrael took the spike from his belt and in one smooth motion he windmilled his left arm round and back towards Zivko. Zivko's left eye squelched as the spike was driven in. His revolver dropped to the floor, followed by Zivko. He screamed. He clawed at his face in an attempt to find and remove the thing that was causing the excruciating pain. He pulled the spike out – his eye was already dead. He fumbled around for the revolver. He found it and stood to his feet, this time with the revolver pointed towards Azrael.

The African ignored Zivko; he knew that if the albino was going to shoot, there was nothing he could do about it now. His focus was on the Egyptian who was trying to sidestep so that he could lunge his sword into Azrael's kidneys.

Zivko kept the revolver pointed at the African, his aim straight and true, his eye bleeding and discolouring fast and the pain almost unbearable but his hands were motionless holding the gun, — no shaking.

Azreal turned to face Zivko again, but his attention was not on Zivko, it was on the Egyptian. By turning around, Azrael's back was now fully exposed. The Egyptian thought this was a mistake by his adversary and saw his chance. The Egyptian raised his sword with two hands, in parallel with his head and moved the weight onto his lead leg. From the stairs, the other guard, sword in hand, stumbled onto the landing, his head bleeding badly, his balance precarious. The second guard saw his colleague stumble up the stairs and towards them. He began his move and took his chance to finish off the large African for himself, before help arrived. His sword started down towards Azrael's lower back. He could visualise the strike and then the bloody, gory aftermath.

However, the African had deliberately turned his back on the Egyptian to lure him in. Now Azrael spun his machete round until the handle was facing toward Zivko in the doorway — his blade facing behind him. He took a step back slightly and then he crouched in one movement, his left leg slightly in front. He learned forward a little. The Egyptian closed in for his strike. At the last second Azrael forced his right leg back as hard as he could, it smashed into the lead leg of the Egyptian and his shin shattered. The Egyptian collapsed forward and Azrael forced his blade backwards and upwards, using the falling, forward motion and weight of the Egyptian, he plunged his machete into his stomach. The Egyptian fell to the floor: he lay screaming with pain.

In a seamless, full movement, Azrael spun round again, taking another spike from his belt as he did so, fell on one knee and, at the same time, his left hand buried the spike into the cranium of the dying Egyptian. He took a second to catch his breath. The first guard was nearly on him. He looked at Zivko but the albino in the doorway just stood and watched him. He could have killed him at any time but he hadn't, yet.

Azreal dived forward on the ground and rolled. The first guard brought his sword down and nearly severed Azrael's left arm but he managed to dodge the blade. Azrael rolled to his feet and stood face to face with the first guard. The men locked blades. The Egyptian thrust, pushed, sliced; he was blowing hard. He fought, trying to overpower the African. Azrael stood square on and blocked every blow, every attempt to cut him up. The Egyptian's blows were now wild; he hacked and chopped as he ran out of breath and energy. His head swirled with the concussion from Azrael's attack with the rock.

207

Azrael saw Zivko out of the corner of his eye and couldn't understand why the albino mine boss still hadn't shot him. He didn't have to wait long.

Outside shouts started up. The mine labourers had awoken to the sound of swords clashing and their boss's scream. They knew enough not to get involved; there were rumours the murderer Azrael had been seen in the camp. They kept a safe distance away.

Now the Egyptian was lunging widely. Every attack with his sword was draining him even more. He was the better fighter of the two Egyptians but he was failing fast, the blood, from the split in his head, running down his face.

The sound of the revolver shot could not be mistaken; it echoed in the gold room, it echoed in the still and heat of the night. Zivko shot Azrael in his right arm. Azreal switched the machete to his left arm quickly and looked at Zivko. Zivko had lowered the gun and stared at Azrael. Then Azrael understood: Zivko had just equalled the odds. He had shot Azrael in his machete arm, so he had to use his other arm. The second guard had a gushing head wound; now he had his. Azrael smiled at Zivko and Zivko, the Ghost, smiled back.

Azrael turned his attention back to the Egyptian. Blood dripping from his right arm, he tucked his right hand into his trouser pocket so his arm would remain as still as possible and he would not agitate the wound. Plus, it would keep the arm out of the way. Azrael struck a blow towards the Egyptian, who barely made it out of the way. The Egyptian now knew that Azrael was able to use the machete with either hand. What then followed was a flurry of vicious attacks from Azrael; it was like a frenzied onslaught. He pressed forward with each stroke. He gave no ground, he gave no quarter.

The Egyptian, now back against the wall and all but spent, looked to Zivko for help.

Zivko looked at the African first, then he looked at the Egyptian. He just shrugged his shoulders.

Azrael smiled, just as he brought his machete down and across the face of the Egyptian in a slicing motion, splitting his face open. Then, he plunged the machete into the Egyptian's heart.

Date: 55 years later. March 2012, present day

Life had been good to the net worth of Zivko Cesar Gowst. He was a wealthy man – a very wealthy man. His health though, had not been good. The onset of old age was just one of a number of issues he suffered of late. He'd always suffered ill health, ever since he was a boy; he continued to suffer ill health into adulthood, middle age and old age.

The eye that he'd lost in 1957, in the French Congo, had never been replaced with an artificial one. The socket remained deeply sunken and majorly discoloured, deep in the hollow, which only increased the perception of how far back the socket went. He never wore an eye patch – people needed a strong stomach when they first saw it. Because of his albinism, he'd had white hair from birth but he'd been bald from about the age of thirty. His pale and ashen face supported cheekbones that stuck out because his lower cheeks and mouth were sunken in. His teeth had long since gone because of periodontal disease in his gums, mostly as a result of poor diet when he was young. As a boy, his father's hatred for him and his frugal nature meant that he often only ate potatoes and occasionally bad meat. His diet continued to be unhealthy when he reached the French Congo. With his poor nutrition and complications with his albinism, periodontitis took his teeth. Again, he did not replace them.

Zivko also suffered from photophobia. His eye was sensitive to sunlight but not fluorescent light; because of this, he always wore sunglasses outside and was never seen without them. The pain without them was too intense. In later life, he also began to suffer from nystagmus, a condition that made his only eye make receptive, uncontrolled spasm movements, especially when he got tired.

You could not miss Zivko Cesar Gowst: well dressed in a black suit, a wide brimmed, black fedora to keep the sun from his bald head and black sunglasses to protect his eye. When he took his sunglasses and fedora off, people found him quite grisly to look at.

In old age, when not in the Middle East, Zivko Cesar Gowst, now 79 years old, spent a lot of his time in Romania attending to his experiments. There, people were poor and cheap to buy: life was cheap in some parts, which supported his experiments.

He spoke the language and because of its geography, if he had a need, he could get out of the country via any of its boarders: Bulgaria, Serbia, Hungry, Ukraine, Moldova. The ease of getting out of a country had been the main factor in most of his decisions for nearly fifty decades. Of course, his spiritual base was in the suburbs of Cairo. In fact, it was his main base and had been since the day he had stepped off the boat at the age of twenty-two, after he forced a glass stem farther into his father's neck, killed four priests and a number of other unfortunate souls.

When Malik visited the young Zivko, he had passed onto him three things: the first was a large anthology of Arabic and Arabic history. The second was a black leather-bound book, embossed on the front with three crescent moons. The same tattoo the men wore who burnt Al Bateat and his family to death. The same tattoo that Zivko now had. Malik had also given him a piece of folded paper with the address of a man in Cairo called Samir Fancy. Zivko met Samir Fancy in Cairo, two days after getting there and had then spent nearly two years with him.

Zivko inherited gold from his father; he mined gold for ten years in French Congo and he also increased his wealth through offshore banking diversions, tax evasion, through clever smoke and mirrors and money laundering in Panama.

He was likened, by some of his men, to Howard Hughes: eccentric, reclusive, with an obsessive-compulsive disorder and in chronic pain because of degenerative arthritis. Zivko had chronic pain because of the experimental medical procedures he had endured over the years at the hands of his father's doctors.

When in Romania, he spent up to five hours a day in a germ-free, clinical atmospheric dome that was maintained at a certain temperature, which acted as an antiseptic environment. He had his skin treated three times a day with a lotion of Aloe Vera, llamas' milk, bees' honey and antiseptic components, like chlorhexidine gluconate, hexachlorophene, boric acid, Lugol's iodine and formaldehyde. The smell was distinctive, overpowering, ghastly and resembled the smell of a mortuary. He had also become a polyphasic sleeper, only able to sleep short intervals; this drained his energy levels and slowed his reactions and speech at times.

From the age of 23, three things had fuelled his existence: his insatiable greed; the contents of the leather-bound book his grandfather Malik had given him; and finally, the meaning behind the three crescent moons tattooed on the underside of his right wrist, put there by his friend, Samir Fancy.

Chapter 12
Abu Dhabi Capture & Rendition

Payne St Clair knew that the Abu Dhabi mission had been a disaster for the Templars. What started out as a mission to locate Salah El-Din had quickly turned into a nightmare, the ramifications of which he believed were still not truly known. He was furious that the recklessness of a young Yemini agent, Al Bateat, had sealed the fate of a number of lives, including those of Al Bateat's wife and two young children, in a horrific house fire. The trail of bodies started to mount, and they grew.

Initially, St Clair was glad André Sabath had stayed in Abu Dhabi, along with the Knight Tarik Tahir. Tahir worked undercover as an oil worker, working for ADNOC, the Abu Dhabi National Oil Company. He was also a Lebanese Christian, like Sabath, and lived in Abu Dhabi with his wife and three children. Sabath had been staying with them during the lead up to the mission. When the mission was aborted and Al Bateat disappeared, Sabath called in eight of his Knights to help. They flew down from the Lebanon that night, the night of the 16th. Other than a text message from Al Bateat to Sabath on the 16th, warning him to abort and get his people out, neither St Clair or Sabath had heard anything from him since: Al Bateat had gone dark.

From the 17th to the 19th, the Templar ten-man team scoured

Abu Dhabi trying to locate the young Yemeni intelligence officer. Everyone was still hopeful they would find him and be able to resume the search for Salah El-Din and complete the sanction on the criminal's life – the Templars had been searching for him for four years.

Even on the 17th and 18th, no one was unduly worried that the Templars left in Abu Dhabi would be in any danger. Sabath and his team were highly experienced and they all felt they would find Al Bateat sooner or later. Sabath had called in a number of times over those two days, and St Clair had spoken to him and nothing seemed amiss.

However, by the 19th, and despite Sabath's and his team's best efforts, they hadn't located Al Bateat. Sabath had called St Clair that morning to say that he had a hunch and they were going off to follow it up. He said he would call again at noon UK time. He never did.

Sabath and his team had come to believe that Al Bateat was probably gone. They thought he'd probably left in a hurry. If this was right, they knew he would not have gone back to his apartment, so they decided to check. They had found his address from a contact who knew him. Sabath and his team checked out his apartment. An Al Zubai newspaper from the 16th was still open on the kitchen table, next to half a cup of stale coffee and an empty packet of cigarettes, lying next to an over spilling ashtray. They found his car documents in a draw. They now had the registration, make and colour. They checked for his car in his space, in the underground residents' garage. It wasn't there. Sabath and two of his Knights checked with the police. They were told that the car had been impounded because the displayed parking ticket had expired. The car had been removed from Downtown Abu Dhabi and now lay in the police car-pound. No one had been to pay the fine and collect the car.

Based on this information, the Templars started checking the car rental places. They gambled that, if he was running, he would have headed for the Yemen and it would be safer for him to go by road through the Sultanate of Oman, than use the airports.

The Templars finally hit lucky around noon on the 19th, three days since Al Bateat had last been heard from. Sabath was supposed to call St Clair at noon but he stuck with the lead and made a mental note to call him later.

At one of the car rental places, just outside of the Arrivals terminal in Abu Dhabi International Airport, an employee remembered Al Bateat because, as he put it, he looked as if he'd either been in a car crash or had been pretty badly beaten up. The employee said it was obvious that he had a problem with his heart or his ribs because he was holding his chest all the time he was there. He had told Sabath he remembered that the man had been dropped off by one of the government taxis. The Templars also got a still shot of Al Bateat from the rental company's CCTV video. Now they knew what he looked like. They posted a reward amongst the taxi drivers; it was enough to get everyone interested and to get every taxi driver telling every other taxi driver. A thousand dollars if they'd picked up a Yemini, and they would say from where.

By 3 p.m. on the 19th, Sabath and his team had identified the industrial district of Musaffah, just off the E30, as their target location. It was just a five minutes' walk from where the taxi driver said he'd picked up the Yemini man who was cut and bruised. There was nothing else around, so it had to be the place. They suspected that he had been held captive there, because of the fact that he had been badly beaten and there seemed no plausible reason why he would have gone there of his own accord. They put wo and two together and made four: showing up at the rental car company meant he had escaped.

Pretending to be interested in letting one of the empty units, on the industrial estate, the estate manager had shown Sabath and three of his Knights around the vacant units for lease – there were five. The third one was the one they were looking for. There was blood on the floor; there were also other obvious signs that this was the place. The estate manager missed them all. They asked him if they could take some time to look around, take measurements to see how they might fit all their machinery in the unit. Happy to oblige, and with thoughts of signing a possible 2-year lease, he left them to it and went back to his office ten minutes away. They had promised to drop the keys off and discuss lease terms when they had finished.

Date: 4 p.m. on the 19th
Place: Mussafah Industrial Estate, Abu Dhabi

Outside it was just beginning to cool a little. It was 4 p.m. The man watching threw his cigarette to the floor and stood on it. Then he lit another. He'd watched four of them go into the unit with another man who wore a cheap suit; the others were dressed in casual western clothing, not local Arab clothing. It was the unit where he and the others had held and tortured the Yemeni prisoner. The unit the Yemini had escaped from and from where they had to remove the body of one of their own, the guard the Yemeni had killed with a metal bar. He saw four of them go in with the man in the cheap suit but two other vehicles, both 4 x 4s, lingered close by. After a few minutes, the man in the cheap suit, a middle-aged Indian, he took to be a person showing the others around, emerged from the unit and left in his car. The others were still inside.

The man watching, an Egyptian with three moons tattooed to the underside of his right wrist, called his boss on the mobile phone. His boss answered immediately and told him to stay where he was, to keep watching them but to stay out of sight. If they moved, he said, follow them. He told him that he would be there with the others in less than ten minutes, then he hung up. The Egyptian tucked himself further behind a parked transit van. He stood in front of the passenger wing mirror, which he used to watch the 4 x 4s and the entrance to the unit behind him. He fidgeted with the revolver tucked into the back of his belt. He lit another cigarette and waited for them to arrive.

215

* * *

Sabath and his team searched the unit and very quickly worked out what had happened. It wasn't difficult to figure out because whoever had Al Bateat, they hadn't cleaned the scene. Near a metal chair, in the middle of the room, they found a black rag, which they took for a blindfold because it was the right length and shape. The ends were crumpled as if they had been tied, and it had spots of dried blood on it. The ends of a length of rope, which lay on the floor near by the chair, were still tied to each other; another lay near to it, untied. They assumed this is where he had worked his hands free and slipped the rope and then untied the rope around his ankles. Behind the door, a metal bar lay on the concrete floor, next to it was a large, dried blood stain. They figured this was Al Bateat's escape weapon. One of Sabath's Knights picked it up: it was bloody. They knew it would have taken a lot of trauma to produce that much blood, so they knew it would have been a head blow. They surmised that the blood belonged to a guard and that's how Al Bateat had escaped.

He pulled up in a black Range Rover with five other men inside. He was dark skinned and spoke in a rough French accent. On his face were puncture marks, scars. His forehead carried a scar, around five inches long; his nose carried another scar. His eyes were almost ebony, his stare unsettled his men. He was nearly six feet tall. Bo Bo Hak barked at his men; they sprang into action. They made for the two parked 4 x 4s that held the six Templars. The man who had been hiding behind the transit van and keeping watch, ran over to join them. They all had silencers attached to their hand guns. Bo Bo Hak rarely carried a gun. He drew his machete.

With a final glance around the unit, Sabath picked up his walkie-talkie to call his men in the 4x4 outside. The walkie-talkie crackled. He tried again; it crackled again. Nothing.

216

A noise came from outside the door of the unit. It echoed in the emptiness of the building. One of his Knights went to check it. Moments later there was a low moan. Sabath called out to his Knight; nothing came back.

Bo Bo Hak appeared in the doorway. The large, imposing African had his machete drawn and held it firmly in his right hand. Two of his men came into the room holding the Templar who had gone out to check on the noise: they held machetes to his throat; his head was bleeding. Sabath tried the walkie-talkie again. He still couldn't raise his Knights in the 4 x 4s. He went for his gun, so did Tarik Tahir who was standing next to Sabath. Bo Bo Hak tutted and signalled to his two men. They immediately pressed a little harder against the Knight's neck with their razor-sharp machetes. The Knight tensed, his arms restrained.

"If you move, they will slice 'im," he said, his French accent and pigeon English making him hard to understand.

From behind the door, a Knight lifted the metal bar he'd been holding; the metal bar that hours earlier had been Al Bateat's escape weapon. The Knight was a trained swordsman – all Knights were. He spread his feet slightly to widen and bolster his stance, so he could twist around the door when he attacked. He figured he had one chance because he had been hidden behind the door and had the element of surprise. He stepped out and brought the metal bar down hard towards the head of Bo Bo Hak. Bo Bo Hak's men were slow to respond: Bo Bo Hak wasn't. He turned his machete over to protect its blade from the impact of the metal bar. The machete met the metal bar before it had time to move six inches from its lofted position. Bo Bo Hak's reflexes were like coiled springs. The crash of metal on metal rang out. The Knight tried to force the bar down, past the machete, by twisting his position, so he could smash the man's legs but Bo Bo Hak redirected the blow. Almost scooping the metal bar and forcing it down towards the ground. Then he brought his right foot back and pivoted round, bringing his machete from just above his right shoulder and down at a 60-degree angle. It went through the Knight's left arm like the arm was rice paper and sliced it clean off. The Knight leaned forward and let out a scream. Seconds later, his mouth was still open but nothing was coming out of it: he had gone into shock and was gasping for air, his head hanging down, spittle dribbling from his mouth.

"No!" Sabath cried, but he was too far away.

Bo Bo Hak spun around 360 degrees with his blade held high and because he was a tall man, he had the angle and accuracy to hit the back of the Knights neck and drive his machete through to sever the head clean off — because of the angle, a small swordsman's blade would have exited through the jaw.

The whole attack seemed to play out in extreme slow motion to Sabath but it took less than five seconds. There was blood everywhere. The Knight with the machete at his neck started to panic; he looked around widely and scared.

Sabath bent over, trying to get his breath, trying to hold back the rage but he was lost; he didn't know what to do. He was trapped, the life of the Knight with the machetes at his throat and Tarik, the Knight standing next to him, were in his hands. His thumb went for the bottom on the walkie-talkie once more. He shouted at it, "Where are you?"

"Dead," Bo Bo Hak answered. "Them dead." There was no emotion in his voice, no emotion in his eyes, it was though he was talking about an insignificant thing. Three more of Bo Bo Hak's men had entered the room and were now holding Sabath and Tarik Tahir. They took the Templars' guns, and bound their wrists firmly with plastic zip ties. Then one of the men took out syringes from a small leather case and jabbed them into the Templars' necks. After only a few seconds, Sabath's sight started to go hazy and his head started to swirl.

Bo Bo Hak was now stood in front of Sabath; he towered above him. He spoke inches away from Sabath's face. "We left the Yemeni man here 'cus the gunfire on the Yas. We know it is you team there. We went to finish them, 'cus our bomb didn't. We too late, you friends gone, Yemeni gone." Again, no emotion; it was all said in a matter-of-fact kind of way. "But we killed them, gunmen on Yas, they work for 'im, so we killed them, we bleed them with blades. We will get 'im soon and we will bleed 'im, bleed Salah El-Din.

"Here, I left man here to watch, knew you work it out about Yemeni man, you men come look, and my man sees you all. My master said no kill you, now. Before yes, blow you up, yes, but now no, 'cus explain him I did what we got from you' man in 4 x 4, on that street. You man said you 'ave got Seer. My master, him said him wants talk with you and see what more you tell him. He wants more talk. He waiting. We take you there, Templar."

Sabath's vison was now almost gone. The last thing he saw was the machete being removed from the throat of the Knight. Then Bo Bo Hak pulled a six-inch spike from his belt and drove it into the top of the Knight's head. He fell dead.

Sabath didn't see the bodies of his six slaughtered Knights in the 4 x 4s. He didn't see the severed fingers of one the Knights, the youngest, who was only 22 years old, strewn on the floor of the vehicle, after being cut off, one by one by Bo Bo Hak until the young Knight told him who they were and revealed the existence of the Seer.

Bo Bo Hak's men carried the drugged bodies of Sabath and Tarik Tahir to their waiting vehicle.

Date: 22nd March 2012, three days later
Place: Romania, an old disused mining town

Sabath woke up. He was now a continent away.

He was aware of an odour. It was the only thing he was conscious of – nothing else; not where he was, when it was or how he had got there, wherever there was. The odour was a sweet yet distinctive smell; he knew it but he couldn't place it. He wasn't sure if he was awake or the smell was in his dream, if he was indeed

219

dreaming. His head was conflicted and unsure. He tried to focus and reason but the mist in his head made it difficult.

André Sabath's thoughts were wrestling in the mist in his brain. He was mildly aware he was alive but he knew he was in trouble. He knew he needed to focus but found it difficult to understand how to do that. There was no compass, no set of logical thoughts that would help him out of the mist. He felt like a drowning man deep in dark, murky water, who doesn't know which way is up. He couldn't remember if he had known where he was before the mist; or what had happened or if something actually had happened. But it must have, he thought, because the mist had come.

The thought that he was in hospital kept drifting in and out of his brain. He wondered why, and then, slowly, it came to him: he could smell it. He could smell a hospital smell; he could smell carbolic acid, a hospital disinfectant, and he could smell iodine. He didn't know why he was in hospital but it reassured him somewhat. If he was in hospital then he was safe.

He lay still. He didn't know he was lying down, but it felt to him that he was. He was not conscious of himself breathing; he could not feel it or hear his breathing, but he knew he must be. He drifted in and out of consciousness.

He opened his eyes. There were a number of hospital beds in the room, he thought people were lying in them but he wasn't sure through the mist. Both his arms hurt, one more than the other, and he felt extremely nauseous. He knew it was good he could feel pain because it meant he was still alive. Then, again, he passed out.

Did I just hear a voice? he thought. *Was that outside or inside my head?* He attempted to open his eyes and found he could once more. Through the mist he saw two men he didn't know sitting at a table, directly in front of him. They were shouting and laughing but the sound was distorted. Sabath tried to bring them into focus but struggled with it. *Why are they there?* he thought. *Why are they there and why am I here?*

220

"One hundred Leu," the taller of the two men at the table said. It was a gruff voice with an accent. *Northern or Eastern European,* Sabath thought. *But why do I think that? Do I know? I must know.*

"Okay," the other man said. His accent was definitely Middle Eastern; Sabath knew it straight away.

There was a scorpion and a silver dollar in a downturned drinking glass in the middle of the table in front of them. The scorpion was exploring the sides looking for a way out. Confused by the clear sides, it couldn't figure out what was preventing it from moving forward. Sabath didn't know why there was a scorpion there. It confused him. Everything confused him.

"When you do it," said one of the men, "it can't get away. If it does, the silver dollar is mine and you owe me one hundred Leu. You can't get stung either. If you do the silver dollar is mine and you owe me one hundred Leu. Oh, and of course you'll likely die." His laugh was also as gruff as his voice.

Leu, thought Sabath; *currency. But from where though?*

The smaller man held the downturned drinking glass. He seemed to take deep breaths. Then, gingerly, he slowly lifted the glass. When he'd lifted it up about two inches, his fingers darted inside and retrieved the silver dollar. The scorpion's tail snapped downwards just milliseconds after the man's fingers were out of the way and he'd slammed the glass back down.

Both Sabath's arms still hurt him. He was aware of a low humming sound; he didn't know if it was in his head, connected to the nausea or coming from elsewhere. He lay there for an age trying to focus on it. It was odd because he heard it, just, but he also felt it: a low vibration. *A generator,* he thought. *No, it's softer; softer than a mobile phone vibrating.* Then he made the connection. The low humming sound was connected to the small, almost imperceptible vibration he felt in his left arm. He moved his eyes away from the men with the scorpion in the centre of the room.

He saw the tube in his left arm. His eyes followed the tube: it was attached to a saline drip. He looked at it, almost mesmerised as the droplets dripped in slow motion down to the restrictor. *Hospital,* he thought, *I am in hospital but why?*

His right arm ached. He tried to turn his body but he couldn't. He turned his head. The two tubes in his right arm led to a large, white machine by the side of his bed. Buttons, lights and dials did something but he didn't know what. *But which hospital; where?* He kept seeing images of the Sheikh Zayed Grand Mosque in Abu Dhabi. He tried to clear his head. *Abu Dhabi,* he thought; *am I in Abu Dhabi?* But it didn't feel like the Middle East; it was far too cold and the ambience was all wrong. The sounds were wrong.

He heard what seemed to be muffled voices, two maybe three people. One of them, a man, was crying, then he screamed.

"Alkahin!" – priest.

What was that? Sabath thought. *Was that Arabic?* He recognised the word but it didn't register. Then someone in the next bed to him started moaning deliriously.

"Linişte" – quiet, one of the men with the scorpion shouted. He'd stood up to scowl at the person in the next bed to Sabath.

Was that Romanian? Linişte, that's Romanian for quiet. Why am I hearing Romanian? He was confused and his brain and thinking muddled. Then he heard the Arabic again; again, it was a scream but this time he understood it immediately.

"Alkahin!"

Sabath tried to twist his body to see where the Arabic voice was coming from. His body didn't work. He couldn't move. He thought he must be conscious now, so he couldn't understand why it was impossible for him to move. *Focus,* he told himself, *it's just my brain not sending the right signals, focus.* He tried to move again. This time he felt the metal chains locked to his wrists and ankles and the thick leather belt around the chest. Sabath passed out again; it all went dark.

Chapter 13
Smoke & Mirrors

Morgan Clay was a Templar "ghost man". In fact, he was the most successful ghost man they had ever had. A ghost man can never afford to do things well because that would draw attention to them. Also, they cannot afford to do things badly because that would draw attention to them. They just do; mediocrity their greatest weapon.

Morgan Clay was average looking, average height, with average features and average ways. Outwardly, nothing ever changed about Clay. He was the kind of man you could see every day for a year and not be able to describe him when asked. He used to be British Secret Service. He'd spent thirty years defending the Crown. Then, one operation had gone bad. He'd infiltrated a known IRA cell active in London. He had spent fifteen months penetrating deep into their UK organisation. He'd been getting close to their source of funds there – which was his mission. Despite his warnings, his superiors badly misjudged a situation. He was nearly killed as a result of their stupidity and ineptitude.

He was told he was wanted at a meeting. The two Irishmen picked him up and drove him to a secluded area near to the Dartford tunnel, on the Kent side of the river. Clay had been in the business long enough to know that this was no meeting, that this was a murder squad, but he couldn't be sure and had to play it out.

He didn't see where the two shots came from. He only knew the two terrorists were about to put a bullet through his head. He heard two shots and the two men fell dead – their guns in hand, safety off. This was his first introduction to the Order of Knights Templar and he'd been with them ever since.

Templars fought their battles on three main fronts: digital, financial and physical combat. Morgan Clay had been involved in many digital and financial elements of their missions but never in combat. Whilst he had undergone basic combat training, like all Knights have to, he did not then progress on to 'active Knight' training; this meant advance combat and weapon skills. However, like his friend Payne St Clair, he knew that following the money was often as powerful as pointing a gun to bring down an enemy. Besides, you need to know where your enemy is before you can point a gun at them.

Using state of the art technology, forensic accounting and good old-fashioned sleuth work, they fought their enemy by attacking their financials. Upsetting their money flow. They had learnt a long time ago, that if they followed the money, they would find its owner. Disrupt their money flow, with the sole intention of causing their target to make decisions they wouldn't normally make, and thus make mistakes they would not normally make. This is what the Templars had done four years ago, with Salah El-din. By following his estate bosses, who were selling his drugs on the estates of Northern England, they disrupted the money. This eventually led to Salah El-Din coming out into the open – a mistake he had never made before and a mistake that had almost been his downfall.

Morgan Clay started looking for the Abaddon money source in late September 2004. The Higher Council of the Knights Templar had tabled it on the agenda many times over the years but it always seemed futile because there were simply no clues, no leads, no starting point: just blanks and dead ends. The Abaddons were an enemy that were as elusive as the Templars themselves. They were evil and they were barbaric; they had been at war with the Templars for nearly 800 years. Their evil had rained death on adversaries and innocents alike. Their victims were slaughtered, regardless of religion, although they hated Christians most of all. They were vile, malevolent and immoral. A mercenary tribe that survived centuries and adapted. They were not capable of moral actions or of remorse; they were followers of the demon of the pit: Abaddon. And the Templars had failed to eradicate them through centuries of fighting.

However, in 2004, a transaction took place that drew Interpol's interest. They in turn alerted various intelligence communities around the world, including the British. Proctor Hutchinson sent the intelligence briefing to his Templar brothers in Scotland. No one paid particular attention to it because they received such intelligence briefings daily; no one but Morgan Clay. There was just something about it that seemed off to him. He couldn't put his finger on it but he was dogmatic and he was meticulous, so he wouldn't let it go. He dug around for a while and the more he dug, the more his suspicions were aroused.

When these led him to Switzerland, he really started to focus. Switzerland is best known for having a neutral position, and, indeed, they have become the symbol of neutrality. Clay knew it was rumoured that Switzerland hid gold for the Nazis and also bought it from them. And, after the war, it was said, they failed to return billions of dollars of stolen gold. In a 1946 treaty with Switzerland, the Swiss agreed to return $58 million of the Nazi gold received during the war. Some say that this was only 15% of the gold and there is speculation that they received $425 million in looted gold, worth some $4.25 billion at today's prices. Gold from the death camps was sent to the German central bank (Reichsbank), where it was re-smelted, and was sent to Swiss banks – victim's gold mixed in with bank gold.

In 2004, a number of five kilo gold bars were sold privately. However, a routine stop-and-search at customs, on a French railway border crossing with Switzerland, revealed the gold bars hidden in a series of crates marked 'machinery' – the crates were bound for Algiers. What made the seizure an Interpol issue was that the gold bars were stamped with the insignia of the Third Reich: a swastika.

Morgan Clay had always suspected that the resurgence of the Abaddons in the mid-fifties was linked to some major financial event. The only thing that the Templars knew for sure about the Abaddons was that around the mid-fifties, the Abaddons suddenly became more prevalent. Their recruitment went up, their numbers increased and they started to see their presence on a number of continents. Before that, they seemed mainly contained to the Middle East and Near East. There were a number of assassinations that the Templars believed were the work of the Abaddon *Alqatala* – Abaddon Assassins; and there were a number of bombings that would have taken a lot of sophisticated planning and a lot of money to implement. Clay knew the funds had to come from somewhere and the only major event anywhere near the 50s was the Second World War – it was within a ten-year window. So, Morgan Clay took note of the intelligence briefing because it was connected to post-war financial activity: vast sums of money in Nazi gold. He knew hundreds of tons of Nazi gold remained unaccounted for. He now had a hunch that caused an itch that he needed to scratch.

In 2005 and 2006, Clay continued to look for any references to Nazi gold coming onto the market. It was difficult and painstakingly slow because everyone was obviously tight-lipped about any of the covert transactions. He got his break in 2007. After four years of frustrating work trying to track down the source of the Algerian shipment, in 2004, he finally found where it had come from: a private commercial bank in Zurich, Switzerland. Clay flew to Zurich, with John Wolf as his back up. He was not welcomed with open arms but, with the help of a number of Templars living in Switzerland, and to some degree the imposing stature of John Wolf, he finally arrived at the door of a retired bank manager. The retired bank manager was now 73 years old, suffering from cancer and living in a small village outside Zurich. His name was Alberto Keller.

Keller was extremely guarded but he had kids and he had grandkids; he was dying and he did not want his legacy to be about the Nazi gold. He had seen enough people from the banking community hounded, ridiculed and reviled for their part in Switzerland's open wound. After all, he had not been the person in the bank that had agreed to the deposit from Stallas Gowst, a Serbian business man. The decision had been made by his boss, back in December 1945.

He told Morgan Clay and John Wolf what he knew. He also told them that Stallas's son, Zivko Gowst, had inherited the gold from his father in 1955, after his father's death. He told them that Zivko, an albino and a weird, odd, sickly looking man with a most unsettling voice, he recalled, had sold most of the gold in 1955 and 1956. He told them that the bank's transactions were always carried out by wire, and, during those years, it was always to an address in Cairo – he no longer remembered the address.

This really got Clay's attention because the origin of the Abaddons was Egypt. He now believed they had their first connection with them. It also fitted the timeline with the Abaddon resurgence. Keller then told them two more things that were of vital importance. He'd been told by the bank's manager in 2004 that the final and remaining gold bars had been sold to a private buyer in Algeria, and Gowst closed down the account shortly after, so he was certainly still alive in 2004. The other thing was the name of the law firm that represented Zivko Gowst; they were a law firm in Serbia called Spiradon and Jana.

Morgan Clay was making headway, albeit slowly, and somewhat tenuous, at that stage. But then, in 2007, he was given a new mission that put his investigations on hold. His new mission was to infiltrate the offices of Salah El-Din's UK headquarters. There he spent over a year slowly fitting in and slowly becoming accepted. Not standing out. Gaining their trust, slowly. Slowly infiltrating the corrupt empire of Salah El-Din. Whilst suspicion had prevailed on all newcomers there, he had succeeded in infiltrating the corrupt world of 890-923 Knightsbridge Court Crescent. His mission inside Salah El-Din's headquarters lasted until the end of 2008, when the Templars were successful in shutting down the criminal's activities across a number of continents – but they did not get the criminal himself.

In 2009 he was put back on the trail of the Abaddon finances. He learnt that in 2008, Alberto Keller had died of lung cancer. No one else at the bank knew anything more about the gold; Keller was the last source of information in Switzerland. So, Morgan Clay turned his attentions to Serbia. There he would follow the information Keller gave them and track down the law firm of Spiradon and Jana.

Once again, John Wolf was chosen as his companion and protector. In the summer of 2009, they both took flights to Serbia: Morgan Clay via Heathrow International Airport, London; and Wolf, via Louisville International Airport, Kentucky. They met in Belgrade, stayed one night to meet up with a number of Templar Knights who lived in Serbia. The reunion was an enriching affair. They prayed together; renewed old acquaintances; caught up on all the news. Wolf had to tell the story of Sabath's raid in Egypt and how he got their scrolls back; and the battle with Salah El-Din in Cumbria but especially about the American priest, Jonathan Rose, and how the Ark performed a miracle for Payne St Clair and his Knights that day. He then had to tell it another three times. The Knights, nine men and four ladies, finished the night with some beers and much laughter.

The next day, Clay and Wolf hired a car and drove to the city where Alberto Keller said Spiradon and Jana were based, back in the fifties. He didn't know if they were still in trading. Clay and Wolf were lucky because the law firm of Spiradon and Jana – now Spiradon, Horvat, Jana and Isena – was still in operation.

All of the people who had dealt with Zivko Gowst, back in the fifties, were long dead. However, the present Spiradon at the law firm was Tamas Spiradon, the grandson of the original Spiradon, the very person who had dealt directly with Zivko Gowst back then.

Tamas Spiradon was a youngish-looking man but was in his late 30s. Articulate, as lawyers can be, he was well dressed and exuded an air of efficiency but approachability at the same time. He was obviously well educated. He greeted them with a friendly smile as he showed them into one of the firm's rather smart-looking meeting rooms. He was intrigued to know why they were asking questions about the area's most notorious family. He was willing to talk to them because the Gowst family had harmed his grandfather's life and his own father's life. They drank the coffee that had been brought in by a warm-smiling secretary, who offered them biscuits. They politely declined.

"You've come a long way, gentlemen," Tamas Spiradon began the conversation in earnest after the pleasantries. "Tell me what you would like to know; this firm has no dealings with Zivko Gowst, not anymore. However, all of the confidentially restrictions and covenants in our agreement with him have long since expired. So, we are not governed by any restrictions. I am also not inclined to withhold anything I know about that family out of any sense of service or loyalty, because of what they did to my family."

Clay took out a notepad and pen. "Do you mind?" he asked the young lawyer.

"No, please, make whatever notes you wish," Spiradon said accommodatingly.

"Perhaps," Clay began, "a good place to start then, is what wrong did Zivko Gowst do to your family?"

"Not Zivko," he corrected. "It was his father, Stallas Gowst." He was a horrible human being. A tyrant and a bully who owned a right-wing newspaper. My father was working as an intern, at a newspaper owned by one of my grandfather's friends. It was a competing newspaper. My father was there for the summer; he was

229

going to university that September to study law and become a lawyer." He paused for breath and sipped a little at his black coffee. "He wrote a piece for the newspaper about Stallas Gowst, Gowst didn't like and, well, he was a wealthy business man with many friends. He falsely accused my father of theft. My father was sent to jail for three years. Whilst my grandfather was eventually able to free him, it took him three months and it nearly bankrupt him. It destroyed my father's life."

The young lawyer paused, he sipped at his coffee a little again. Clay saw the consternation on his face. He was putting his thoughts in order. There was a gentle knock at the door and the secretary came in with a file. She gave it to Spiradon and he placed it on the table in front of him. He thanked her and smiled. She asked if anyone needed more coffee; they all declined.

Wolf asked if his grandfather or his father were still alive.

"Sadly no; both dead now. My grandfather led a good life. My father, not so much. He made a good career for himself in the newspaper business and retired as senior editor, but he always wanted to be a lawyer and he left this earth unfulfilled and bitter about what had happened to him. So, ask whatever you want, gentlemen; I am more than happy to share anything I know."

"Did your grandfather know what was in the bank account in Zurich?" Clay asked.

"No," the lawyer said. "Not even a suspicion. My grandfather and the firm were never involved in any disposal of any of the assets, other than Stallas's estate and business assets here in Serbia." Spiradon went on to explain about Zivko's upbringing in a tyrannical household. "His father, Stallas, was a brutal, cruel man. Everyone knew he hated his son. He was embarrassed by him. Hated the fact he was imperfect, as he saw it. Zivko never left the estate and rarely left the house. Did you know his mother was an Arab, from Egypt?" he asked the Templars.

Clay and Wolf looked at each other. Another connection.

"We didn't," Wolf said.

"By all accounts she was treated horribly by her husband; he beat her. Like the boy, she never went out. People say the 'dark-skinned' woman, that's what they called her, died of abuse and a broken heart. Zivko was devoted to her; it broke him, if he wasn't broken before."

As the lawyer spoke about Zivko's childhood, Clay and Wolf began to get a picture of Zivko Gowst's early life in Serbia. They knew that if the story continued like this, he was a prime candidate for insanity and they would find him in some mental institution. The lawyer went on to tell them that his grandfather had told him about the rumours that Zivko had been sexually abused as a child by at least one priest, and that he had been mentally abused by a number of others. The abuse included a line of no-good teachers employed by his father. Clay and Wolf looked incredulous when the lawyer told them about various so-called doctors that had experimented on the young boy, without success. He told them the Gowst family were the talk of the town back in the day and indeed they were still infamous today.

"Everyone here has heard the stories about the Gowst boy who acted in a most strange way: a pallid child who held conversations with himself. The Gowst household staff were not discreet at all. However, and this is hearsay, I guess the thing that the boy is best known for are the bodies."

Clay and Wolf shifted a little on their seats. It came out of the blue and they were not expecting this. "Bodies?" Wolf asked.

"After Zivko had left Serbia, I guess around nineteen fifty-five – he would have been about twenty-two years old – my grandfather, this firm, was instructed to sell the house and the estate by Zivko. This they duly did. However, a few years later, when the new owners were making improvements to the house and upgrading the grounds, they discovered the bodies."

"Bodies?" Clay asked the same question as Wolf.

"Yes, a number of bodies were found in pits that had been filled in, in the woods on the Gowst estate and near to the house. I think we are up to four or five bodies. They all died the same way."

Clay and Wolf were about to get their third connection.

"They tell me it's called the blood-eagle, leastways that's what the papers called it. You cut—"

"—the victim's back," Wolf continued. "You cut deep in and all the way up the spine and then fold their skin and muscle back out towards their shoulders. Then you detach their ribcage from their spine and also prise it out towards the shoulders, like an eagle with its wings spread out. Blood-eagle."

The Templars now had that third connection. There had been rumours for many, many years that there was an Abaddon, a man some said would blood-eagle his victims.

The fourth connection came when Spiradon told them that, apparently, many in the town had pointed the finger for the murders at an old Arab man who'd come visiting the Gowst household when Zivko was about twelve or thirteen. The old man never left the house but the taxi driver who had picked him up at the station, told everyone about him. The house-staff also spread the gossip. They told people that the old Arab man and the Gowst boy spoke the devil language together.

"Some say he was the boy's grandfather, some say he was an Arab murderer; I tend to believe the former. So, you see, it's not hard to tell things about the Gowst family. As I told you, they are both famous and infamous."

Clay asked Spiradon if Zivko had ever been back to Serbia.

"No, not to my knowledge, and I think if he had been back in these parts, we would have heard about it. It's not like he could hide his appearance. Plus, I suspect his semi madness will not have improved any. I would guess it might have become worse with time and age. That is, if he's still alive. He would be well into his seventies now, I guess."

The meeting lasted a little over two hours. It ended with Tamas Spiradon telling them that the only transactions they'd carried out for Zivko Gowst, after they had sold the Gowst estate and Stallas Gowst's business assets, was to set up an offshore company in Panama for Zivko. He gave them the name; the company was Al'umu Alhabiba Inc. Clay now had his big lead.

By early 2010, Morgan Clay, with the help of one of the Nine Worthies, John Edison, assembled a team of forensic accountants in Barbados, where Edison lived. They started looking into offshore companies in Panama and other surrounding offshore havens, Tortola, in the British Virgin Islands, Grand Turk, in the Turks and Caicos Islands and St Kitts, any that might be associated with the name Al'umu Alhabiba Inc. The company had been deregistered, so they were looking for trace elements of transactions associated with it that they knew would have been expertly hidden.

Like the everglades, the money trail in Panama and the Caribbean twisted and turned, appeared then ended abruptly. From nowhere another trail or link would reveal itself and all energy would be put into that. Desperate for progress. Desperate to find the source of the money for their elusive enemy. They all knew that if they could locate it, they had a chance of stopping or disrupting it. If they were good enough, it also might lead them to the Abaddons themselves.

Morgan Clay had had many dead ends that would have tested the resolve of even the most patient, but Clay was dogmatic and with the support of St Clair and John Edison in Barbados, he ground away at it, month in month out. He felt he was so close but he could never crack the final piece of the jigsaw.

Since mid-2011, Morgan Clay had been working at a law firm in Panama City. The law firm was well known for setting up shell companies for criminals and other nefarious factions. His infiltration into the organisation was, as always, seamless and without fuss or attention. He was just the guy who sat at the end, near to the water dispenser, who worked in the Debt Collection Department; and who, most thought, had been there forever. Morgan Clay had done what Morgan Clay did best: he beavered away, slowly gathering information and passing it on to the team of forensic accountants in Barbados.

Clay liked Panama, the Central American country stuck between Colombia and Costa Rica and the section of land that joined North America with South America. He liked the people and he liked the culture. It was famous for numerous things but two mainly: the world-famous Panama Canal that cuts through its centre; the second, and the reason Clay was there, was the country's propensity for shell companies and being one of the world's most popular tax havens.

Clay knew that most people visiting Panama for the first time expected to find a fairly poor, backward county, partially engulfed by jungle. This was true in part because up to 40% of Panama was covered by jungle, but it was also a country whose skylines were peppered by enormous, ubiquitous skyscrapers, with many casinos, restaurants, cafés, nightclubs and numerous other fancy and costly establishments and trappings of wealth and prosperity. It was here that Clay looked for answers to the problem that had perplexed the Templars for years: where did the Abaddons get their money?

He and the Templars knew that Panama's notorious, shadowy network of companies was there to hide the financial affairs of companies, corporations, politicians, kings, princesses and princes, the rich, the famous, the shady, and the criminals. Criminals guilty of kidnapping, extortion, murder, racketeering, arms dealing, fraud, drug lords and cartels. Everyone knew what was going on; most of the world's major law enforcement agencies knew that Latin American drug lords had been laundering their money in Panama for years – wash, rinse, repeat! Stolen money, ill-gotten money that someone didn't want recorded or tracked, they wanted it hidden. A haven for tax evading and money laundering. He knew that people went to Panama because they could avoid the tax and financial rules in their own countries and do things there they could not do in their own

234

countries. Clay saw contempt of the system on full view and on a daily basis; he saw contempt underlined with a 'screw you' kind of attitude'.

The process, Clay discovered, was fairly simple. Law firms set up shell companies. The tax haven masked aggressive tax planning, tax minimisation, tax evasion and tax avoidance using covert financial manoeuvrings by operating in the grey area of the law. A great place to hide money and to increase it if you need to fund a barbaric, murderous organisation, which started 800 years ago. Lawyers set up companies, trusts, foundations and other types of potential money filtering/laundering vehicles. The law firm that Clay worked at did exactly this. They created the kind of companies their shady clients needed in order to channel their money, away from the eyes of the law. The law firms in Panama were the architects of subterfuge, smoke and mirrors. They hid their clients' identities in the shell companies. They were masters at avoiding revealing the ultimate owners of the money, so the owners could avoid liability, inspection, investigation, scrutiny, prosecution and prison. Smoke and mirrors, a major preoccupation for them.

Clay's employer had set up thousands of shell companies and bank accounts, so that money could flow through numerous and unabated transactions, the owner of the money instantly anonymous. Clay discovered that local people were paid as nominees, with no knowledge of what they were signing. They became nominee directors of shell companies, without any idea what those companies were doing or their probity. The nominees would end up signing thousands of forms for thousands of shell companies. They got paid for their names or, if unwilling to cooperate they were coerced or threatened. They were frontmen and women, so the real owner never appeared on the company register. Local people rented their names.

The Templars knew that financial secrecy was the new Jerusalem. Andorra, Bahamas, Belize, Cayman, Monaco, St Kitts and a number of other countries were waiting with open arms. Clay chose

Panama because the trail, albeit almost non-existent, seemed to lead there and, it was one of the oldest tax havens in the world and a favourite of many. He discovered that experts suggested that as much as half the world's capital flowed through offshore centres. And that tax havens had 1.2% of the world's population, holding 25% of the world's wealth, including 31% of the net profits of United States multinationals. They estimated that $13 trillion to $20 trillion was hidden away in offshore accounts. His job was simple: to find the money in Panama of their most dangerous enemy – a camouflaged needle in a corrupt haystack.

Clay sensed he was about to made a major breakthrough there. After all those years he felt he was about to find the answer he and the Templars had been searching for, for years. However, he needed back up.

He'd called his friend, Payne St Clair, three days after Sabath had gone missing, and asked for help. He could have asked for Knights who were with John Edison in Barbados. However, whilst they were good, he'd become used to John Wolf. He needed stealth and surprise to make his plan work. There were many good Knights he could have asked for but he knew that the Indian was a tenacious, clever hunter. Besides, Wolf was his favourite Templar, opposite to him in almost every way but he admired Wolf for his commitment to his people, the tribe from which he came. So, he'd called St Clair to brief him and to ask for the Indian. Wolf was now on a plane from his home state of Kentucky.

Clay had worked tirelessly on the trail of the Abaddon money, as he always did, to expertly unravel the unfathomable. He believed he was about to link two things that would lead them to the Abaddons. His research took him to World War II. Ultimately, more than 50 countries were involved in that war. In 1933, Hitler began preparing his Third Reich to take over Europe but he needed weapons, and to buy the weapons and feed his troops, he needed wealth. The need for wealth stayed a priority for him throughout the war.

The Nazi party stole tons of gold from banks across Europe and plundered and stole vast troves of priceless artwork. In the years following the defeat of Hitler, individuals, families, organisations, foundations and movements sought to locate their stolen assets and repatriate them. Some were recovered; much more was still missing.

Then Clay came across the name Gowst, when he and Wolf went to Zurich and Serbia. Clay had discovered that in October 1945, Stallas Gowst, Zivko's father, had made an unexpected trip to Germany; Zivko would have been 12 at the time. This was unexpected because it was still dangerous to travel and you needed permission and you needed papers - somehow, he got those. No one knew why he visited Germany.

Clay discovered that the Third Reich had hidden their stolen treasure in secret locations all over Germany. They kept meticulous records of where it was, and what it was. Secrecy was paramount to ensure that looting didn't happen to their war machine's money. As soon as people began to realise that the war was ending, the looting began. Vast amounts simply disappeared. The allied forces were busy trying to establish a social structure that would cope with the loss and devastation caused to Europe, including the German population. They were tracking down factions still fighting; chasing deserters. Clearing ammunition dumps and land mines. In regard to the lost wealth of others, it was fairly low on the list and for those who were given the task of finding any stolen gold and art treasures, they were always playing catch up – the looters were way ahead of them.

Clay's tenacity and skill led him to papers from allied forces that detailed a specific mine, some two hours outside the northwest German city of Bremen, near to the coast, and six hours from Berlin. During the war it was a disused mine. But there the Nazi party stored a lot of their stolen gold and valuables, as they did in many mines all over Germany.

The stronghold in the mine was an underground room, nearly half a mile down a vertical lift shaft and two miles in, deep underground. On a large metal door, marked *"Gefahr"* – *danger* – someone had painted a skull and crossbones on it, giving the impression that either it was structurally unsafe inside the room, or there was poison or explosives in there. In the room, approximately 70 feet by 90 feet, with 10-foot high ceiling, the Nazis had stored a horde of stolen treasure. There were 4,000 gold bars, weighing close on 50 tons; each bar stamped with a swastika. Hundreds of pieces of precious art work. Over a thousand trunks, suitcases and boxes filled with various currencies, jewellery and table silverware.

Clay discovered that Stallas Gowst had kept meticulous records for the Third Reich. He was one of a number of highly trusted individuals who kept the secret inventories. Stallas kept the inventory for the Bremen mine. Clay now had proof that, along with a number of SS accomplices, they relieved the mine of some of its gold, and Stallas placed his share into the safe and friendly hands of a Zurich bank in Switzerland.

Clay knew that selling those gold bars in 1955, could have been the source of funds that created the resurgence of the Abaddons in 1955, when Zivko sold most of the gold – plus Zivko's numerous Middle East, and especially his Egyptian, connections. Then, add in that Clay had found a copy of the ship's log and the doctor's report on him. So, Clay knew that Zivko had actually sailed to Egypt after visiting the bank in Switzerland and now had a report on the nature of the man. He also knew that Zivko disappeared in Egypt for two years before turning up in the French Congo as a mine owner: more money. Then there was the offshore company that his lawyers in Serbia had set up for him, in Panama, all those years ago. Al'umu Alhabiba Inc, translated to 'Beloved Mother'. And it was this company, despite being deregistered years ago, that finally gave Clay an undisputable connection. It was this company he thought was about to unlock the link between nearly 800 companies and large financial payments into the Middle East. His gut told him Zivko was their source of the money. If he was, and they found him, they had found the Abaddons.

*   *   *

Date: 28th March

Place: Panama International Airport

Clay pulled off Avenida Domingo Diaz and headed for the Arrivals building at Panama's Tocumen International Airport. Waiting in the car park he saw a large guy learning up against the wall; it could only be John Wolf. Clay pulled the rental car over.

Wolf threw his bag into the boot of the car and the two men made their way out of the Arrival's car park and onto the highway. The city lay just ahead, full of bougainvillea-lined plazas, trendy shops, cafés and bars and myriad of businesses. It was a city alive, full of neon lights, full of people shouting and singing, screaming and crying. Drunks staggering, weaving in and out. Police car sirens blazing away, bouncing and echoing off the buildings and skyscrapers.

Clay's accommodation was outside of the city – although it was still very close to the centre. The city would have been too showy for the Templar ghost man; and it would have potentially raised his profile too much. He made a left and they headed towards Casco Viejo, a 15-minute drive from the city and known as old Panama.

It was hot and sticky out – about 30 degrees Celsius. Morgan Clay had the air conditioning on full inside the car. He handed Wolf a bottle of water.

"You want to be briefed?" Clay asked.

Wolf smiled and gulped down some of the cool water. "Just give me the short version; I don't have the same enthusiasm for numbers as you." He looked out the window at the beauty of the place; he soaked it in. "Pretty place."

"Dangerous place," Clay said, "but it can save you millions."

"Start my briefing there," Wolf said; "I like the savings millions bit."

"The basic outcome of banking in any tax haven is that you'll

239

pay much, much less tax by virtue of the fact that the tax percentages in tax havens are ridiculously low, some even at 1%," Clay began, whilst watching the road in front of him. "There are all kinds of savings to be had; all kinds of ways you get to keep your money. You can more easily launder your money. You can have intercompany loans from a tax haven company to a normal company you own elsewhere. Your shell company charges interest, real big interest, and instead of paying tax on the interest gains, it leaves your country and you pay a small withholding tax, and you pay virtually nothing via the tax haven company once it's been received."

Wolf nodded. "Makes sense for them, I guess. And you need me why? I haven't brought my calculator."

Morgan Clay smiled. "You don't own a calculator."

Wolf smiled back.

"We'll be breaking into the offices of the firm where I have been working undercover. They have some serious clients and those clients have some serious muscle and some of them are here in town. They are stationed here, watching the lawyers, watching their clients' money and everyone is trying to stop the authorities from watching them. It's risky, in fact very risky, but they have information I can't get any other way. We have our team of forensic accountants on the paper trails; they have vast forensic accounting and investigate experience to chase the money. They are in Barbados, under the guidance of John Edison; he oversees them for me. We put them there because we feared if we had them here, sooner or later someone would have found out and then the game would be up. Besides, I would never have got working visas for them all, no matter how many connections we have. We could not risk bringing them in on tourist visas. It took me nearly a year to get my working visa. Not only that, the unscrupulous law firms and their clients' henchmen would have been all over us, but for obvious reasons so would the local government who really don't want to see an end to something that brings big bucks into their economy."

Wolf wiped sweat from his forehead as Morgan Clay turned off the highway and followed a road that would take them to the outskirts of Casco Viejo. He fiddled with the air conditioning but it was as high as it would go.

"Remember, it is not a crime," Clay said. "It is not a crime to move trillions out of the reach. OECD, the Organisation for Economic Co-operation and Development, allows companies to set and move profits to wherever they want. It is legal for corporations to do what they do, and this allows the criminals to hide their money within the same accepted system. The British Virgin Islands has just over thirty thousand residents but have half a million registered companies."

"Who are we going to break into?" Wolf asked.

"A law firm called Durant, Martinez and Escudero," Clay said. "The one I've been working at for the past year. St Clair got some great references for me."

"He's like that," Wolf said, and smiled.

"He is," Morgan Clay said. "The name of Durant, Martinez and Escudero kept coming up in our research, time and time again. There's really not much on them. When you first look at them they look clean, which should always raise suspicion in places like Panama. However, they have never been served a warrant and have no outstanding investigations. The firm and their owners appear to be squeaky clean, but of course they're not. Most folk round here will tell you they are one of the most successful law firms in the city; they will also tell you, they are one of the most corrupt. They also have cast-iron digital security. Even Dominique and Courtney couldn't break through their firewalls. We looked at that first. So, it's back to good old-fashioned breaking and entry." Clay increased speed to overtake a city vehicle.

"The three partners are real shadowy types, Wolf. They have connections with all the bad people here in Panama, or I guess some would say the right people. They have ten clients. That's it, as far as I can make out. Problem is, I have no idea who those clients are and between them, they have nearly three thousand shell companies that have been set up for them. However, I only get to see the front face of the latest ones. The trick is being able to follow them back to the very original one; that will give you the money sauce and the real owners of the company.

"We've been investigating a number of the law firms here, and are learning how they work and how they use the system to save their clients millions. There are only two law firms here that represent clients in the Middle East. The one that seems to do the most transactions are—"

"Let me guess," Wolf said, "Durant, Martinez and Escudero, your current employers."

"Got it in one," Clay said. "Trouble is, you wouldn't believe how many financial transactions flow in and out of the Middle East and Panama every year and across thousands of shell companies."

Morgan Clay pulled the rental into a parking spot. He always parked his car a number of streets away from where his rented condominium was and he always alternated his parking location each time he drove back home. He flipped the boot so Wolf could grab his bag. They walked the short distance to the complex, a quick ten-minute walk – both men checking behind them every minute or so; it was the only thing that might have given away the fact that they were both highly trained covert operatives.

It was still hot, and it was humid out. Around them old colonial buildings stood, white, blue, cream and yellow facades, with Juliet balconies adorned in an assortment of potted plants and pruned miniature bushes. The sky was clear and smelt of sweet floral aromas and cooking smells; the air hung heavy, lacing the senses with an explosion and fusion of old Panama.

Once inside, Clay flipped the switch and the lights came on.

"Nice place, very trendy." Wolf was being facetious. Morgan Clay would never get a smart and trendy apartment; it didn't fit with blending in and not standing out. Do nothing that people can remember you by, he would tell any Templar that asked him about his trade craft.

Clay closed the curtains, checking the road outside before doing so. Then he went from room to room scanning them with an electronic detection scanner for any planted micro cameras or listening devices. When he was satisfied, he poured himself and Wolf a drink, added a little ice, then clicked glasses with Wolf. "To André and his Knights," he said.

"To André and his Knights," Wolf said. "You are all in our prayers."

Clay then opened a tall side cabinet and pushed against a false back. He reached in and brought out five hand guns, plus ammunition, 9mm calibre rounds.

"Nice," said Wolf. "Used?"

"No, they're clean. Serial numbers ground off." Then he brought out a digital code reader, two night scopes, and a 14-inch bone-handled knife and leather sheath.

"You didn't?" Wolf said lighting up.

"Bone handle, fourteen-inch … your favourite, right?"

"Just like the one I have at home. Thanks, Morgan."

Then Clay brought out two Katana swords. All Templars are trained in swordsmanship to a high standard and many carry them on missions inside their scabbards, affixed to a back-body webbing.

"That'll please St Clair," Wolf said, admiring the fact Clay had managed to get the Katana swords. "When do we go?"

Clay fed 9mm bullets into the gun magazine he was holding and then expertly checked there was one in the chamber and that the safety was on. "We're waiting for St Clair to call. You hungry?" he asked Wolf.

"I'm good," he replied. Then Wolf strapped the lightweight titanium sword scabbard to his back and placed the sword inside, with just about an inch peeking out of the top of his lightweight coat. They packed the rest of the equipment, including black spray paint cans and ski masks, into a small black holdall and waited.

"You get your new mobile phone from Scotland?" Wolf asked.

"A few days ago; it came via John in Barbados.

Wolf held the instructions he had been given along with the phone. "You read these, Morgan?"

"I did."

"You remember them all?"

"Only one," Clay replied.

"Which one?"

"Don't press the black button," Clay said.

"Me too," Wolf said. "Who the heck thinks of these things?"

"I'll give you one guess," Clay said, smiling.

"Bertram," Wolf said.

Two hours later, Clay's new mobile phone rang and it startled him.

"Clay," he shouted at the screen.

"Morgan, you sound stressed. Is everything okay?" It was the controller in Islington.

"You've heard about this black button thing? This phone just rang and I nearly jumped out of my skin; Wolf took cover."

The controller laughed. "You know you have to literally press the black button in and hold it down for a full five seconds, don't you? Plus, when you look at the screen to turn it on, you don't have to hold it an inch away from your face and shout; it will pick your features out and recognise you from three feet away. You made me jump when your face jumped out of my screen." She laughed. "Now, you boys have fun with your new toys, and don't break them." She laughed again. "It's Payne for you." She connected them.

Thirty minutes later, the two Templars had left the apartment building, walked back to the car, via a different route and were now on the outskirts of Panama City, with its bright lights and hectic night life. It was mid-week, so, whilst lots of people were out in the bars and the clubs, it was not as crowded as it was at the weekends. Clay navigated the city with ease, he was used to it by now. He didn't jump any lights and he kept to just under the speed limit. No one paid them any attention.

Wolf suggested parking two blocks away from the offices of Durant, Martinez and Escudero, they could then case the area and have alternative exit routes back to the car.

The Templars walked past the offices a couple of times, separately. It all seemed quiet. The offices of Durant, Martinez and Escudero were on the third floor of a three-floor office building. An import and export business was on the first floor, and an ailing insurance company business on the second that was about to go into receivership. The Templars stood over the road to the offices and tucked into a doorway, watching. Still all was quiet.

Wolf slid a black ski mask over his head and Morgan Clay did the same. They crossed the street quickly. Wolf sprayed the CCTV camera with the black spray paint, whilst Clay attached the digital code reader to the front door security lock. It took the code reader five seconds to unlock the door. They were in. They put their night-scope on: their world turned grainy green. Wolf headed for the second of the security cameras and sprayed their lenses. Clay had the alarm box door open and the code reader attached to its circuitry. The code reader's lights, ten of them, lit up in sequence. One by one they turned from red to green as the code reader determined the alarm code. All lights were now green, the alarm was disarmed. They headed for the lift. Using Clay's employee swipe card, they hit the button for the third floor.

Again, the code reader read the alarm code for the door to the law firm's offices. Once inside they stood still and listened, all the lights were off and there were no sounds. After a few minutes they decided it was clear and Clay led them down to the end of a large open-plan office. Next to a large conference room was an office with the name 'Mr Escudero – Partner' on it. Clay ignored it and turned his attention to a smaller office next to it.

"His secretary," he whispered to Wolf. This time there was no digital code pad; this time it was only a security door lock. Clay took out a small leather bag. Inside was a lock picker's tool kit. He had the door open in seconds.

He made for the wooden desk. He pointed to the second drawer down, which was locked. Wolf took out his 14-inch knife and prised it open. Inside Clay retrieved a small, black book.

"We may be in the twenty-first century but she was born in the fifties," Clay whispered, pointing to a photograph on her desk of herself and Mr Escudero presenting her with a bouquet of colourful flowers, with an assortment of balloons with Happy 50th Birthday printed on them. "She keeps all the codes and passwords in this little book. She thinks nobody knows about it. She keeps it quiet because she's breaking every company security protocol there is. Thank goodness for older people who don't trust technology."

"Or their memories," Wolf quietly replied."

They left the secretary's office and Clay used his lock picking skills once again and soon they were in the partner's office – Mr Escudero's. Clay made straight for a hidden wall safe.

"You've been busy doing your watching thing again, I see," Wolf whispered.

Clay opened the secretary's black book and found the code numbers to her boss's safe. He opened it. Inside were a number of external hard drives, 16 in all. Clay took each one of them out and looked at the labels. Finally, he selected the one he wanted. He took out a small tablet computer from the holdall and connected the external hard drive to it.

"The download will take about six minutes," he said. "Courtney and Bertram are waiting in the control room to receive the data, they will start decrypting it straight away. They are also going to send a copy to John Edison and the team in Barbados so they can get to work on it."

Wolf looked at the label on the external hard drive that was joined to Clay's palmtop by cable; it read 'Gowst'.

The sound of the lift moving made Clay jump. He turned around sharply. Wolf was already out the door and heading up the centre of the open office. "Phones," he called, "go dark."

Clay placed the tablet on the floor and put a mouse pad over it so it shielded the light from the screen. He crouched down beside it and opened his mobile phone. He removed the night-scope. The mobile locked on to his eyes. The biometric retinal scan flicked and his phone was open. He switched it audio negative mode with text only. Now he would be able to mouth the words at the screen and the recipient, Wolf, would see text instead of hearing a voice. He also switched the camera to infrared so he could see the screen in the dark. Two shots fired out. He took out a 9mm pistol and waited. He looked at the time left for the data transfer. It seemed like it was taking forever. He wanted to go and help Wolf but their primary mission was to transfer the data to Scotland.

Gunfire again, this time 10 to 12 shots rang out. Clay's mobile vibrated. The message came in: *'ready?',* it was Wolf. Clay looked at the time left to data transfer. He mouthed back at the screen: "70 seconds," the text message then sent. His phone vibrated again a couple of seconds later, the message read: *'Damn'*.

There was the sound of breaking glass, furniture and walled partitions being broken. Then, another sound. Clay put his night-scope back on. A figure was less than ten yards away. He knew it wasn't the Indian; it was too small. It went quiet. The tablet whirled as it made its final transfer protocols. The figure had heard it too. The figure – holding a sub machine gun – moved towards the office where Clay was.

Clay unplugged the external hard drive and read on the screen "download completed". The light from the screen seemed to light up the whole office. He turned to see where the figure was. Now there were two figures; one was in the doorway, machine gun at his shoulder. Clay's mobile vibrated. He looked down, it said: '*duck*'. Clay threw himself on the ground. The second figure opened fire, spraying bullets everywhere. The figure in the doorway fell.

"You good?" Wolf shouted. "Are you hit?"

"I'm good," Clay called back.

"Good, are we done?" Wolf asked.

"Scotland has it," Clay said, "so yes, we're done."

"Then, time to go," Wolf said, "We must have tripped something. I don't know if there are any more of them. Two are dead back there, plus this one. These guys are all heavy muscle and they're carrying automatic weapons. We need to go."

They ran through the open-plan office. They took the stairs – they wouldn't risk the lifts; besides, two bodies were hidden in the lift shaft. Outside and a hundred yards away, they took off their ski masks and stopped running but walked at a fast pace towards the car.

Clay put the car in first gear and pulled away, both Templars breathing heavy. Clay stayed within the speed limit. They stayed vigilant. They checked their wing mirrors and watched Panama City shrink into the distance. Then Clay starting laughing quietly.

"What?" Wolf asked.

"Whilst all of that was going on, I just couldn't get the imagine out of my head of you, standing there firing away, sending me a message and thinking to yourself, I hope he doesn't press that bloody black button when he answers me."

They both burst out laughing.

Chapter 14
Extraction

Date: 29th March, Extraction Day
Place: An old disused mining town, Romania

Romania had seen its fair share of internal strife, civil war, external war and external strife. Parts of the country were debilitatingly poor and people there live hard lives. The Leu, the Romanian currency, didn't have much value on the world stage and Romania's status as a country, was not considered a major force across Europe. The Eastern Orthodox church claimed 81% of the population and religion was often the only thing that gave them hope. The country was mostly famous for the Carpathian Mountains, the Black Sea, salt mines and Transylvania: Bran castle was said to have been Dracula's castle because it was the only one that resembles Bram Stoker's description. Romania was also a place a person could hide away in relative anonymity.

Sabath woke for the second time since his rendition. It was now nine days since his capture and six days since he last woke but, of course, he didn't know that. Nor did he know that since he had woken last time, he had been put into an induced coma because some of his organs had started to shut down and they were more manageable if he was in a coma. Now he had been brought out of it again.

249

He struggled to focus his eyes. There was a man on a chair in front of him, just looking at him. Sabath's eyes still didn't focus well. Both of his arms still hurt him. He made out the saline drip tube attached to his left arm. He was aware that there was no low humming sound this time. Nor did he feel the vibration of the low hum in his right arm like before. He looked down and the two tubes were still there but they were disconnected from the large, white machine next to him. However, now he was connected by a third tube to the man sitting in front of him. Sabath opened his eyes wider. He tried to move his body but he felt the same restraints as before. He looked at the tube; blood flowed through it. The man in front of him leaned in towards him a little. There was no expression on the man's face – it was empty. Close by a man in a white gown watched Sabath. *A doctor*, Sabath thought.

"Where am I?" Sabath managed to say, his throat extremely parched, his lips dried and cracked.

"Romania," the man on the chair in front of him said.

Sabath didn't know that the man in the chair had his skin treated three times per day with a lotion of Aloe Vera, llama milk, bees' honey and antiseptic components, like chlorhexidine gluconate, hexa-chlorophene, boric acid, Lugol's iodine and formaldehyde. However, what he did know was that there was an overpowering, ghastly smell about the man, like the smell of a mortuary. "You are in Romania."

Of course, thought Sabath. *I heard the word Leu … Romania currency*. "I heard …" he said as he tried to remember what it was he had heard before. "… I heard … it was Arabic. Before … I think it was Arabic." He paused waiting for the mist to clear. "I heard the name '*Alkahin*'."

The man in the chair moved a little closer. "Priest."

"Yes, *Alkahin* means priest," said Sabath. "I heard … no, no. I heard a scream. Someone screamed the word '*Alkahin*', priest."

"Your friend," said the man in the chair. "It was your friend; he was the one screaming. He screamed a lot."

The man in the chair pointed to the end of the room. Sabath turned his head. He couldn't make it out; whatever it was it was too far away. It hung there, motionless. The man in the chair raised his hand and a second man holding a set of controls pushed a green button. A small, overhead traveller crane, which ran the length of the long building, creaked, then started to move forward on its rails. The man pressed another button and the hook and block moved sideways until it was in the centre of the crane and travelling slowly. The crane moved ever forward down the centre of the room, its load about ten feet above the floor.

Sabath couldn't make out the object hanging from the hook. It made its way towards them. Then it stopped just before Sabath's bed. He looked at it. It was a body. Its hands were tied to a length of iron bar, attached to the crane hook and the feet were strapped together. The arms were spread out as far as they would go in a crucified fashion. Naked. Bloody. Beaten and torn. The body was lowered down by the man holding the controls, until the feet were just six inches above the floor. Then he lifted the head.

The man in the chair leaned in again. "Yes, see, your friend."

"My friend?" Sabath said, confused. He didn't recognise the features.

"Your friend," said the man in the chair again. "Yes, yes, your friend Tarik Tahir. Your Lebanese Christian friend from Abu Dhabi."

Sabath looked. The face looked like a hideously distorted image of Tarik, his friend and Knight. Sabath's breathing became shallow and rapid; his heart rate quickened. He was not a well man but he didn't know how ill he really was. His body wanted to retreat within itself, from the horror dangling in front of him.

The crane operator now turned the body around, rotating it on the crane hook. Sabath started retching. His Knight had been blood-eagled. He hung in a crucified position, with his entire back, ribcage and lungs leveraged open and peeled back out towards his shoulder blades.

The man in the chair showed no emotion. He spoke in English with a strong Eastern European accent and in a low rasp. He had pallid skin, pure white hair, and one eye, his right eye, was pink. His left eye was gone, the uncovered socket deeply sunken and discoloured. "We saw inside him, and he told us everything. We did," he answered himself. "We want the Seer, the Abaddons want the Seer, Christian. You will give us the Seer or we will see inside of you."

André Sabath had already passed out.

Place: The outskirts of the old disused mining town, Romania

The six-man Templar recon team had watched and waited for days. Their forward observation post (OP) was over a mile away from the target, an old disused small mining town, consisting of three dusty tracks in and out, eleven buildings, six unused and dilapidated buildings that looked dangerously unstable and five other structures that had signs of repairs and activity. Mountains, moorlands and thick forests surrounded the old broken-down mining town – mountains, moorlands and thick forests pretty much covered most of Romania. The location of the town was not chosen for its easy access; quite the contrary. It was difficult to access; in fact, it was isolated. The town was only built because of the seven gold mines in the mountain just above it. It had once thrived. At its peak the town boasted a population of over 60 people; now the only miners there were the dead ones lying six feet under in the town's graveyard. Even the town's name had been forgotten and the sign welcoming visitors had rotted away years ago.

Generators fed lights and equipment in the five buildings in use; wood fed stoves for cooking and heat. The spring well in the town had dried up years ago and the nearest water supply was an underground spring near to the rusting sluicing trammels at the mouth of the seven mines. A buried water pipe fed water from the mines

252

down into the town, a distance of over three miles. It was constantly in need of repair because bears and other vermin dug it up and chewed the pipe to get to the water they could smell, even when contained within six inches of earth and a plastic pipe.

The mountains, to the right of the town, were some of the most elevated in the region. Lush and green, with an abundance of foliage and trees: Scots pine, grey alder, silver fir, growing tall and strong. Except for the mountain that housed the seven mines, that mountain bore no trees; it was barren and scarred. The mines were over three miles away from the town, accessible only via the old mule track that led out from the right side of the town. The track had been used by miners to ferry equipment and supplies up to the mines in the mountain, known locally as *Muntele Gri* – grey mountain. The mines in *Muntele Gri* were abandoned years ago, along with the town, and hadn't been mined since the late 80s. The place was secluded and practically hidden from the world.

The Templar recon team's forward position was always manned by two Knights, with three Knights back another mile at the base camp, situated deep in the woods and well undercover. Rotation of the OP was every 24 hours and always an hour before sun up.

From the base camp they controlled the Faro Lidar predictive analytics scanning equipment. The pulse laser sensors scanned the terrain and buildings to produce high-resolution 3D images that they studied and sent back to Scotland for further analysis. The Russian manned the coms for the recon team and Bertram manned the coms between them back in Scotland. They spoke to each other several times a day and they kept everyone informed, who needed to be informed.

During the day there was good visibility on the target location; at night they used night-vision equipment to monitor the activity in the five buildings. They struggled with this, however, because they found the night vision grainy and the translucent green that coloured everything made it hard to give any definition or depth of field for distance through the scopes.

The recon team were pretty sure that Sabath was being held in the building just in front of the old church; the old church was the last building at the back end of town on the right. Sabath's signal, from the credit card tracker, was still emitting and its location was pinpointed in or within ten feet of the church. However, they figured that he was not in the church because it had virtually no activity. They assumed that this was where his clothes were being stashed, with the credit card hidden in them. However, the building before the old church, that looked like it was an old workshop or plant maintenance shop, had nearly all of the activity and a number of electric cables going into it. It was also the building that seemed to receive most of the supplies.

Sabath's tracker signal from his mobile phone had long since disappeared. The Templars assumed that his abductors had disposed of it back in Abu Dhabi. They had no idea how many Knights had been captured with him and therefore how many were with him now — because they had not been issued with their credit cards.

The leader of the Templar recon team was the Russian, Nickolin Klymachak, a hardened vet of the Afghan war and imprisonment in the barbaric Gulag system by a corrupt and failed judicial system. His upbringing, his culture and the unimaginable hardships he had experienced in the Gulag, and then his escape – across 200 miles of snowbound wasteland between Perm 35, the Gulag jail he had been incarcerated in and the nearest civilisation – made him one of the toughest Knights the Templars had. Only ten people had ever managed to escape from the camp Perm 35, in its fifty-year history and of those, no one had ever managed to get more than five miles. Wolves had eaten six, two had been mauled to death by bears and two had been found frozen solid, no more than three miles from the camp. Nickolin did it and he survived it. It had taken him just over six days, walking at an average of thirty miles per day in sub-zero temperatures, laden with a heavy pack containing extra spare clothes and food.

The five Knights that were on the recon team with the Russian knew they had to be on top of their game because the Russian was on top of his, always: he was known for it. Nobody was scared; they had the Russian as their mission leader and they had been told that Luther Jones would lead the Alpha team, the extraction group. Bravo team, the support and cover team for Alpha, was going to be led by a new Knight, who they had not met and did not know. They had been told that his name was Cameron Jack; he'd only been Knighted two days ago in Scotland, but he was ex British Intelligence Corps and SAS. He was also their new Master of the Blade, had been European Kendo champion and British national champion and had been trained in Kenjutsu in Japan, by two past Masters of the Blade. Dominique Rose, nee St Clair, was also going to be arriving, along with Zakariah St Clair, her father. They would have most of the team leaders with them who had been at Cumbria and had fought Salah El-Din. The younger Knights were excited to meet the Cumbria heroes in person.

The six-Knight recon team had not eaten a hot meal in days, or had a fire to give them warmth. Days ago, they had applied the dark camo cream to break up their facial lines, and it had stayed on their worn and tired faces ever since. They used hand signals to communicate, and, if they spoke, it was only in base camp and always in low whispers. Being located in a valley between mountains meant sound travelled further than normal — they didn't take chances. They were a disciplined group. They were a small group, but that was about to change; many more Knights were about to arrive as Operation Mairano was now in play.

Place: An open meadow 43 miles from the recon team's base camp

The cargo and personnel transporter plane landed in the only possible landing place within the target location that wasn't an official airstrip. It had taken Courtney, Bertram and most of their team in the control room many days to find a suitable location. It had to be away from prying eyes, didn't require the landing site to have major re-construction to it, and it would allow the Templars to land without killing everyone on board. They thought they had found it but couldn't be 100% sure!

The flight path for landing had to be low. The plane skirted the canopy of the forest, almost brushing the tops of the trees as it came into land. Air currents swirled up underneath it, making it hard to steady the plane. The pilots kept the nose of the plane down as they dropped the elevation. Next, full flaps and then the landing gear came down. They'd had to wait to clear the trees before they could engage the landing gear. The meadow, now a few feet below them, was tucked in between two forests and a wide, angry river. It was a bumpy landing but the two Knights, both ex RAF pilots, got them down safely – although they let out a hefty sigh of relief once the plane had come to a complete stop. They killed the engines. The quad propeller plane groaned to a silent state. One of the pilots hit a switch to his right and a green light came on in the fuselage, the signal for the Templars to disembark.

Nineteen Knights made their way off the plane. They were 43 miles from the recon team's base camp. Guards were quickly posted around a 300-yard perimeter circle of the plane. The new Sergeant at Arms was in the fuselage. He disengaged the rear door lock. It lowered slowly on its hydraulics. Knights drove the three trucks off the back of the plane, watching the directions and commands given by the Sergeant at Arms. Everyone and everything got off the plane safely. One of the trucks was packed with all their kit and auxiliary equipment. Knights started to embark on to the other two trucks. It took just 12 minutes to offload the Knights and all of their equipment, two minutes less than Billy Jack, their new Sergeant at Arms, had allowed for. He was responsible for all military equipment; this also included weapons, munitions and transportation. He was now living the job Luther had told him about and he was loving it.

Billy Jack had jumped straight into the role. The Templars

came calling and he had answered. He had been in charge in Scotland, making sure the extraction team would have all the kit they needed. It had taken Billy, Luther, Cameron and Zakariah two days of detailed planning to make sure they took the minimum load because of weight on the plane. They hoped they would have more people flying back than flying out, so they also had to allow for the additional weight of the captive Knights.

Once they had finished all of the off load, Billy Jack would be staying with the two pilots to guard the plane and to cover the return of the extraction and recon teams.

The Knights made sure their weapons were primed and ready. Most carried automatic weapons, with 30-round magazines and 100 rounds in webbing pouches; plus, sidearm hand guns with 30 rounds. Dominique carried her Heckler Koch .40 and a pump-action 12-gauge shotgun, designed for smaller shooters. It had a seven-shot magazine and a specially modified handgrip stock. Inside her shoulder rig, she also carried a backup gun with a 13-round magazine.

Amongst the Knights was one bomb disposal expert – like Navy Seals, Templars always took at least one on most missions to detect and clear any IEDs, to make sure their entry and exit routes were clear. There were two snipers, one carrying a McMillan TAC-338A rifle, and the other a MK13 bolt-action sniper rifle, which used larger calibre rounds. One doctor and one medic were in the group because they didn't know what shape Sabath and his Knights would be in. In total, it was a 19 strong mission team for Operation Mairano. Everyone dressed in black, the only insignia on their clothing was the baussant, the black and white chequered war banner of the most revered and secret fighting force: the original warrior monks.

Luther made the hand signal; he held his hand up and circled it above his head twice: time to go. They turned on the engines and three trucks moved forward.

"Good luck," Billy called to Luther. "Bring them home safe."

"I will," Luther said, as he jumped into the cab of the lead truck; he was really glad he had another former SAS solider with him.

Cameron walked over to Billy and stood beside him. "It's been a strange week, Grandad. One minute I'm giving lectures about how bad the Templars were in the thirteenth century, and you had eased nicely into your slippers and armchair routine, and next, well, next we are standing in the middle of makeshift runway in Romania armed to the teeth."

Billy smiled. "Your dad would be so proud of you, Cameron."

"No, Grandad," Cameron said, "your son would be so proud of you."

The Templars reached the coordinates an hour later. They turned off the road and drove along an old logger's track in the forest, brushing the trees with the khaki canvas covers of the trucks. Three miles later they came to a stop in a small clearing. The Templars hid the trucks and covered them with branches and bracken – they were now well out of sight. They took up cover positions in five-person tap formations, lying on the ground in a circle, their guns ready. Each Knight had one foot pressed against the person next to them. It was their communication system should a firefight break out. During their training, they were taught that when gunfire starts, it's deafening, and oral commands get lost in the commotion and din. A tap of the foot would let everyone know to watch their section leader for visual commands. The section leader would tap first, then within seconds all eyes are on them.

A noise came from out of the forest. Feet tapped feet and Luther raised his hand in a fist – all stop, quiet. Two fingers pointed to his eyes and then he pointed to the location where the sound had come from.

Easy, Luther thought; he didn't want any of the younger Knights to get jumpy and start firing.

Then came a voice from the trees. "Mairano." It was the Russian.

"What does Mairano mean?" one of the Knights asked Dominique, in a low whisper.

She smiled. "It's an anagram of Romania," she said.

"Mairano," Luther called back to the Russian.

The Russian appeared from out of a thicket, followed by two other Knights. He had left one Knight to cover base camp and two were hunkered down in the OP. He looked tired; they all looked tired.

The Russian, Zakariah, Dominique and Luther all shook hands – the Russian never hugged. The others stood back slightly while these eminent Knights greeted each other. There was reverence for the Knights that been at the centre of so many missions, and whilst St Clair discouraged it, that handful of Knights had almost legendary status with some of the younger Knights.

The Russian led them back through the thicket from where he had just come and towards base camp. "Watch our six," he whispered to his two Knights. They both hung back and took up the rear.

Base camp was just 1000 yards away. Once there, the recon Knights made sure the visitors were given some light rations – they used up all of the existing rations because they would not be returning to base camp, so everyone got a little of something. Base camp was fully packed away and ready for decamp and withdrawal.

The Russian laid out a hand-drawn map in front of them and Dominique, Luther, Zakariah and Cameron all gathered round him. Scotland was also watching because every Knight wore a body camera on their chest webbing, relaying pictures back to the control room in the castle in Scotland; over forty screens stacked five abreast and eight high were displaying live footage.

"Bertram?" the Russian said into his mic, which dangled from his ear piece.

"Yes, Mr Russian Klymachak." Bertram's voice came over their ear pieces.

"Are you seeing this?"

"Dope, Mr Russian Klymachak."

259

"Dope." Zakariah sidled up to Dominique and whispered, "What is he talking about?"

"It's their gangster rap thing, again," she said. "It means yes, or cool. Bertram was an introvert before he met the Russian; now he's become an ambivert, both an extravert and introvert, depending on where the Russian is. It is the oddest friendship. You know Bertram calls him every morning at the same time to check if he needs anything."

"Cute," Zakariah said.

"Thank you for confirmation, Bertram," the Russian said. "Payne," he continued, "if you can have eyes on this it will help."

"I'm with you," Payne St Clair said through their ear pieces.

"This is the town," the Russian began, pointing to the position of the town. "As you know from the site reps we've sent, we think most of the buildings are not used; in fact, they look like they are ready to fall down. This means we have to make sure no one goes into them for cover when this all starts; they are more likely to get killed by falling timbers than a bullet if they go in there. We've had eyes on what lies outside of town on its three sides, so we got the layout pretty much all figured out, and on the surrounding terrain on those three sides. Problem is the far side, back end of town, which is due north from our OP. That was our blind spot until yesterday, although it's still a big problem."

The others closed in a little.

"We are here," he pointed. "Two miles away and directly south of the town. Our OP is in a direct line from our base camp here, to the town. It's about one-mile away from here, and one mile away from the start of the town." He pointed to the observation post on the map.

"The terrain on the right side, the east side, is pretty much scrub and small rocks, until you get to the foot of the mountain, *Muntele Gri*. So, that's a tough route for us to use to get in there, but it also means that it's a tough route for them to use to get out. So, that way is pretty much dead to us. All it has going through it is an old mule track leading out of the town and up into the mountain that the old timers used to ferry supplies up to their mines. So, an eastern attack point is not an option. Opposite, on the west side, well, that's mainly meadow grass and hillocks for about a five-mile stretch, then there's a large forest. No road and no cover in or out, just five miles of openness. We'd be spotted easily, no matter how low we crawled. So, no good for us and again, no escape route for them."

"Which leaves the back end out of town, straight north," Luther said, "your twelve o'clock from the OP. How does that look?"

"From the OP we don't have a clear view of that at all; it was an unknown. It's been giving us issues ever since we got here. There is no way of getting there to check it out without being seen. Scrub and open space on the right of the town, then mountains and meadows with short grass meadow to the right, all open ground. We thought about trekking out of here and going the long way around, a big semicircle and then cut in at the back end. However, that's about a three-day walk if you're going to stay in cover and we have no idea what's out there on the semicircle: locals, lookouts; we know there are bears and wolves."

The Templars looked at each other; they were concerned glances. A blind spot: not what they wanted to hear.

"But," the Russian continued, "Jose here figured it out." He pointed to one of his Knights. The Knight smiled and they all looked at him approvingly.

"Yesterday, Jose went out early in the morning and made for the edge of the forest on the west of town. Took him nearly nine hours to get there, tough yomp. We agreed a time when he would start intermittently shooting. Jose's plan was simple. We needed them to think a local was out hunting wild boar or pigeons, so they wouldn't get too spooked but most of their eyes would be on the west. At the same time, we launched our drone, one of Bertram's stealth sky-eyes, on the east side. We flew it towards the mountain, practically hugging the mountain's face until we got to the back end of town and far enough back to risk hovering and seeing what's there."

"Smart move, Jose," St Clair's voice came over the coms. Jose looked really pleased at the Grand Master's praise.

"Pretty smart indeed," Luther repeated and nodded to the Knight. Jose was almost unable to hold back a great big grin because now Luther Jones had praised him. Many of the younger Knights considered Luther to be the ultimate warrior Knight and many looked to him for guidance. He had been in the SAS for 15 years; saved Dominique in South Africa, in 1996; he was stocky, he was fearless; he epitomized a warrior Knight.

"What did we get?" Zakariah asked the Russian.

"Bad news, just bad news," the Russian said. "At the back end, behind the last building on the left, are three jeeps and a lightweight military personnel vehicle; it'll carry about twenty men."

"How many hostiles you figure are in there?" Dominique asked.

"We figure around twenty to twenty-five. In addition to the lousy news about their backup transport, there is also a track out of the backend of town that leads straight north into a forest; it would take them about eleven minutes to drive into perfect cover. If Romania lacks one thing, it sure isn't trees. Perfect cover, perfect escape route for them."

"We need to change the plan," Cameron said. He hadn't spoken until then.

"Everyone," Zakariah said, "this is Cameron, Cameron Jack. He is the new Master of the Blade and he will be leading Bravo team; they will cover the extraction team: team Alpha led by Luther."

"What are you thinking, Cameron?" St Clair asked over the coms.

"We need to change the plan," Cameron said. "It won't work, not now we know this. The backend is wide open."

"Well," Zakariah said, "you're the ex-Intelligence Corps officer; what are you thinking? How we going to get there?"

"Fly," Cameron said.

"Fly?" Zakariah, Luther and the Russia said almost simultaneously.

"Fly," Cameron repeated. "Thanks to Bertram and Billy and their foresight, we can fly in."

No one said a word; they were all waiting for Cameron to explain his idea. The other Knights had stood up and were now gathered around, intrigued to hear the plan.

"Luther," Cameron began, "you go in as planned with Alpha team. It looks like you'll have cover to within about five hundred yards of the town, but I'm afraid that 500 yards is all open ground. There is no way of getting over that fact. Given that fact, and given the equipment we have and the time pressure," Cameron looked around, "because the longer this many people stay here, the more likely we will be discovered, there is only one way I know to mount an attack and extraction that stands a chance of succeeding."

"Damn," Luther said, more to himself than anyone else: he had just figured out what was coming.

"Crawl to the five hundred-yard point," Cameron continued, "when you are there and ready, give the rest of us the signal. Then—"

"Stand, fire and charge." Luther said. "We shock and awe them. When you have no other option, but you do have the element of surprise, it's a classic SAS aggressive tactic."

"They won't know what's going on and they'll panic," Cameron said. "You are only exposed for five hundred yards of open ground; then you have the buildings for cover. Zakariah, you take Bravo team and lay down cover fire for them on their entry and exit. You'll be in position before Alpha team start their charge.

"I'll take a new team and go east towards the mountains, then cut along north towards the back of the town and will mount an attack from the rear." He paused, then said over the coms, "Bertram, you with me?"

"Yes, Sir, I got you. Brilliant, sir."

"Tell them, Bertram," Cameron said.

Bertram started, excitedly. "Mr Jack and I, not this Mr Jack, well, that Mr Jack because Mr Jack is with the plane and so he's not here, he's there but actually—"

"We're going to need to sort this out when we get back," Zakariah said to Dominique; "his explanation of having two Jacks could start to expand into days."

Courtney came to the rescue. "Bertram, let's say young Mr Jack and older Mr Jack."

"Ah," Bertram said, "splendid, thank you, Miss Courtney. After seeing the images that Mr Russian Klymachak has been sending through, Mr older Jack asked us if we had parajets. These are different from paragliders because they have propeller blades, about four feet high. That is attached to a cyclone engine, all connected to a body harness. Everything is connected to an elongated, 12-foot long parachute through hand control rigging. The whole thing weighs about forty pounds.

"Strap the harness on to your torso, start the engine with a pull cord, lean forward slightly and start running. The parachute rises and the wind catches it and will lift you into the air and at the same time you can fly in any direction you want and over any kind of terrain."

"Thank you, Bertram," Cameron said. "We will take off before the shooting starts. We will time it to make sure that, as we approach the town, Alpha and Bravo teams start firing; this will mask our approach. Bertram, we have about a mile before we need to mask the sound. Allowing for average body weight, webbing, weapons, ammunition, average wind and elevation, what do you calculate?"

Bertram needed no time at all to make the calculations. "One mile per one and three-quarter minutes. So, allow ten seconds for take-off, it will take you about five minutes; allow for wind and elevation and weight, you need five point five minutes. Alpha team need to start their charge and Bravo team need to start laying down cover fire, two point five minutes into your flight to distract your enemy and keep you safe up there. I suggest, if I may Mr younger

Jack, as you pass the end of town, just past the church, you hit the release button on the harness and the whole kit will fall off, propeller blade, engine, harness and of course, your parachute, because it's attached. Then, you need to pull the ripcord on your reserve parachutes, and then turn back towards the town. If there is enemy fire, you can engage them before you hit the ground because you won't have the burden of the all the equipment."

It went quiet. Everyone was running through Cameron and Bertram's plan. They all thought the same; it seemed really risky for the Knights who would be hanging in the air like turkeys over a kill zone, but if they got the timing right, it could work.

St Clair broke the silence. "Cameron, you're getting thumbs up from the folk at this end. Nickolin," he said, "your thoughts?"

The Russian nodded. "I think it'll work. I like it."

"Luther," St Clair asked "and the rest of the plan: what do you and the team think?"

"They just told me we have four parajets in the truck. So, that's Cameron and three other Knights. I suggest, Cameron, you take Knights that have been here all along. They will be dialled into the terrain and have a better feel for the place. You will be going in blind so you will need any sixth sense they have built up whilst being here this long."

Cameron nodded in agreement.

"So, Cameron and his team hit the back end of the town. Take out the transport and cover any possible get away from that end. We send one of the snipers out forty minutes before we go in; they can sabotage the water supply at the foot of the mountain. It's a hard trek but doable. This will draw one, maybe two of them, out, so fewer to worry about. Then, she can fall back to the graveyard; she will have a clear shot to take them out when we charge the town."

Both snipers were woman; both wanted to take the assignment. Luther spoke to them. They decided that Marie-Claude would do it. She would take out the water supply and then take up

265

position in the graveyard. She left immediately; the other sniper went with her and covered her as she left base camp and headed north east towards the water supply.

"I'll take Alpha team of five Knights," Luther continued. "Plus, I'll have Dominique, Rafael to cover any IEDs on the way in and the doc, so that's nine counting me. Zakariah takes Bravo team, he'll have five Knights; one will be our other sniper. The best position looks to be the left side of town. The first two buildings, an old store and a mule barn and stables. You should have enough cover there. Zakariah, remember Marie-Claude will be opposite you in the graveyard. You will have the exit route covered but you will have to watch cross fire

"Nickolin sets up in the OP to cover our fall back, with one of his Knights.

"Our coms operator stays at base camp, along with the medic, who sets up a field tent for any trauma casualties, in case the Doc has to do some quick field surgery before we get out of here. We have no idea what state they will be in and what our casualties might be."

"So," Dominique said, "that's two at base camp, two in the OP, six for Bravo, nine in Alpha team, one in the graveyard and four for the air."

Everyone fell silent. They were each thinking about their individual assignments, the kit they would need, mentally checking and double-checking.

"That's our tally too, Dominique," St Clair said. Then his voice went serious. "Can everyone hear me?"

"They can," said Dominique.

"Knights, pay attention to your enemy because your enemy are always the first ones to discover your mistakes first. You will have to stay hidden until everyone is in position. They will know that a two-man team is a kill team, any more than that and it's an extraction team. As soon as they see numbers, they will know you have come for their prisoners. So, please stay out of sight as long as

266

you can. We need to get to Sabath and the others as quickly as possible, before they start killing prisoners. If we can shock and awe them, it buys us about five to ten minutes at the very most, to get our Knights out of there. Now, let us pray for our brothers and our success today." St Clair led them in a short prayer.

The Knights then broke away into their teams for their final briefings. The medic, helped by the coms Knight, set up the temporary trauma position.

Cameron Jack started to walk out of camp and back towards where they had left the trucks. Dominique looked over to him.

"I'm going to try and learn how to fly one of those things," he called back. "I've got about fifteen minutes; wish me luck." Three worried looking Knights followed him.

Time: 4 p.m. in Romania; 9 a.m. in Panama; 3 p.m. in Scotland

St Clair's mobile phone buzzed. He answered it. The controller put him straight onto Morgan Clay.

"It's nine a.m. here in Panama," Clay said, "and they've just opened the offices. All hell's broken lose here. Wolf and I are initiating our exit plan right now, we leave in 12 minutes."

"They discovered the break in then?" St Clair asked.

"And some. I got a call a few minutes ago, we've all been called in to the office for questioning, I think I'll give it a miss. There are police sirens going off all over the city, we can hear them from here, but there must be at least ten police cars and a couple of ambulances."

"A bit excessive for a break in?"

"It's for the lift shaft."

"Lifted shaft?" St Clair asked confused.

"There are bodies in there. I guess they must have found them."

"I'm guessing Wolf?" St Claire said.

"He saved my life again, Payne. The break-in got rough. We

must have tripped something, I don't know but we had a visit from three armed henchmen and they were not there to ask us to leave. Wolf took care of them."

"You give him my best and tell him I'll see him soon." St Clair had a special bond with John Wolf. When Wolf's father, Grey Cloud, was murdered, it was St Clair who took the young Indian boy under his wing and paid for his education. He became a surrogate father to him and made sure that he and his family were well supported.

"What's your plan, Clay?" St Clair asked him.

"John Edison has arranged a biplane. We fly out to sea, we then land off the coast of Venezuela, then we transfer onto a charter yacht, which John has hired from Caracas. He has five of his Knights on board with him waiting for us, just in case we run into any trouble. We then sail for his place. It's a long way, and it will be slow but it will keep us at sea for a number of days and out of sight. No one will be able to trace us to Bermuda. If we use the airports, they will have them well covered."

"God speed my friend," St Clair said.

Clay hung up and he and John Wolf drove to the docks, boarded a charted sea plane and left Panama behind them.

St Clair got back on the coms to the team in Romania. He said three words, "Templars go green." Then he got off the coms so his men had the channel. He stood in the control room, Jonathan by his side, watching the screens as the Templars started to head out for their starting points. They saw Cameron and his men strap into their harnesses and check their equipment and rigging. Bertram sat in front of the communications computer that managed the coms. He watched for frequency and signal strength fluctuations and made ongoing corrections to keep the coms clear and strong. He made sure everyone could hear and all could be heard. Courtney sat next to him, monitoring a dozen other computer screens. She was also in contact with Billy Jack and the pilots, relaying events as they unfolded;

although they could hear on their coms, they could not see. She would also tell them when their passengers were about five miles out from their position and how many there were. The rest of the control room staff were all busy on their computers.

Place: Inside a building in the disused mining town

Sabath was now aware of everything around him. He still felt acutely nauseous but his head had now cleared. He had figured out that his nausea was not because of the iodine smell, or the disinfectant; it was his health. His body was terribly weak, his breathing shallow; it felt worn down with fighting whatever had been happening to him. Above him, Tarik hung motionless on the crane hook. Sabath closed his eyes and said a prayer.

He opened his eyes and looked around, he could now see 11 beds in room. They were all occupied with men: sick looking men and he guessed he looked the same. They were all connected to saline drips and the same white machine he was now attached to again. Now he recognised it; it was a dialysis machine.

The man that had sat on the chair in front him was back. The doctor was standing next to him, reading the dials on his dialysis machine and making medical notes on a clipboard. The two men that had been playing with the scorpion were standing around, and they were armed. There was another man there, a tall, imposing man.

"I want the Seer," Zivko said, learning in towards Sabath. "I want the priest."

Sabath struggled with the dreadful cramps his body was experiencing.

"Ah," Zivko said. "Your blood is poisoned, like mine." He lifted his sunglasses and wiped his eye and Sabath saw the empty eye socket. "I have taken your blood and given you mine. Your organs have rejected it but we wanted your blood to clean ours. All the blood," he pointed to the other poor souls in the other beds. We clean it through the machine," he said, looking at the dialysis machine, "and then we put it back in you. Then we take it from your arm and we give you ours."

What he didn't say was that his blood was highly compromised and almost toxic, as he strived to purify it over the years using all sorts of experimental applications, poisons, and diluents pumped into his body. His body had not fared well from the experiments but, as they had been going on for some 70 years, there was some tolerance in his body, however, not for the poor souls they transfused his blood into. Like all of the other 'subjects' that Zivko and his doctors had bled, injected, experimented on, Sabath's organs were failing and his body shutting down. That's why they kept them all in comas for ten days at a time, then brought them out of it for three days, then induced the coma again because they could manage the organ functions better.

Sabath looked at the tall, imposing man standing next to the one-eyed man. He looked familiar but he couldn't place him. His face was distinctive. He searched his memory; he couldn't forget a man that looked like that, but from where? He seemed to recall seeing a security photo of his face, but why, he thought?

"I know you," Sabath said wearily as it came to him. It was the description a young child had given of him, of this man, in addition to a fuzzy security camera photograph he had seen. It was the same man. Now he knew, but he was confused. *But how could that be,* he thought. *How could it be him? He only looks 30 years old, the description was ... now I remember, it was in 1986. How could that be? That was 26 years ago. He would only have been about four years old. Who gave me the description?* He thought about it, then remembered. A ten-year-old child had given the Templars the description in 1986, to go with the fuzzy security camera photo. The ten-year-old child was Dominique St Clair, Zakariah's daughter and Payne St Clair's niece. It was the man that had kidnapped and murdered her mother, Sophia. *But there's something else,* he thought.

He struggled. Then the horror of it all came flooding back to him. It was the man who had slaughtered his Knights in the industrial unit, in Abu Dhabi. The man who had slaughtered his Knights in the 4 x 4s. The African stood by the one-eyed man in the chair and Sabath now knew from his posture towards him, that the one-eyed man was the real person in charge.

Zivko's mobile phone rang. He looked at the number displayed on the screen and grunted. He answered the call. "This is Zivko," he said curtly in his gravelly whisper. He listened, his face showed no emotion. "How much do they know?" he asked.

The man at the other end of the phone was a partner in a law firm in Panama. He had the unenviable job of calling their client and telling him that their offices had been broken into and files had been copied, which would reveal details about a number of his investments and shell companies and could compromise his anonymity.

Zivko hung up and then told Bo Bo Hak to prepare to leave in 15 minutes. Then immediately Zivko left the building.

Prior to that call, two men had already headed out to the water source. They thought it had been exposed and ripped apart again by an animal, because there was no water coming through to the town. They were armed with 9mm hand guns only.

She had them in her sights the second they broke the line of the town and headed out onto the open scrub.

As they walked, they thought they could hear an engine; it was distant. A farmer maybe, a tractor, a chainsaw in the forest? They didn't look up; they looked across towards the trees. They saw nothing.

Zakariah, one of the snipers and four Knights crawled past the OP and then veered left. They kept as low as possible. They headed for the first disused building on the left side of the town as a cover point. From there they had a firing arc that covered the road running through the town. Once in position, they formed a semicircle, knelt on one knee, held their weapons to their shoulders, clicked their safeties off and waited. Everyone breathed deep and slow to lower their heart rates — they had crawled on their stomachs a long way and they were breathing hard. They all knew that firing a weapon with your chest heaving up and down does nothing for accuracy.

The men occupying the town, the hostiles, were not expecting anyone; they had not seen anyone for weeks, other than when the supply truck came in, and, even then, it was the same guy that always drove the truck.

They had become sloppy and guard duty meant they could relax a little because they would not be under the watchful eye of the Ghost – Zivko – or his crazy African right-hand man. Most of them were mercenaries, a few were local criminals; all of them killers. There were ten men inside the main building with Bo Bo Hak. One was a South African doctor, he'd been struck off the register years ago for malpractice. With him were three orderlies, and between the four of them they kept Sabath and the other 11 males they had restrained in hospital beds, alive: just. The other six men were thugs, all armed with machetes and hand guns. Three men were posted at the top of the town in a sandbagged position that covered both the south approach and the north approach to the town. In the last building on the left, the old bunk house, five men were on rotation and resting from duty. In the church, three men kept the generators running and controlled their supplies. Along with the two men who had gone off to check on the water supply, Zivko had 23 men, plus himself and Bo Bo Hak.

Zakariah and his team had a clear view down the main track; it was around 400 yards long. His sniper set up so that she had a clear line of sight to the building where they thought Sabath was being kept. Over the other side of the road, in the graveyard about 300 yards away, Marie-Claude still had the two men in her sights as they ambled off towards the mountain; they were in no hurry to get there and no hurry to get back.

* * *

Cameron and his team were now in full flight. They were managing to head in the right direction but it was hairy. Thankfully, there was no wind; had there been, they would have struggled to stay on course. Cameron had found a user manual with one of the packs. He read it out loud to the Knights as they started to strap in. The manual was pretty thick; he only read the 'glossary' and 'fault finding and possible solutions' sections. It was a page and half: it covered the basics of take-off; how to go up, and three tips on turning.

Now they were flying. He had torn out the one and a half pages he had read from the manual and was now holding the instructions in his hand, trying to read them and yelling out instructions to the other three Knights. He'd temporarily switched off his mic because he didn't want to dominate the coms for everybody else. However, the wind was rushing so fast up there that he had to shout to be heard. It was trial and error – with big errors likely being met by a fast- approaching ground.

Back in Scotland, the pictures they were seeing from the airborne Knights were mostly of the sky. The sound they were hearing were the words "what, I can't hear, what?" And from Cameron's body cam all they could see was a page and half of instructions flapping about in his hand as he was hanging onto them in the wind for all he was worth.

St Clair shook his head. "Oh, my good Lord," he whispered to Jonathan. "This could be the shortest membership of our Order we've ever had. Pray for them."

"I haven't stopped," Jonathan replied.

Luther looked up and saw Cameron and the Knights precariously flying above. He knew it was time to go. They were now dangerously close to the point when someone in the town might hear them. Timing was everything.

Luther and his team of Dominique and seven Knights had also

crawled along the ground. They were within about 500 yards of the town and ready to break cover.

Luther stood up and his team followed. He called through the coms, "for Sabath and his Knights; let's get them back."

Then, all hell broke loose.

Marie-Claude heard the gunfire. She looked and saw Luther and Alpha team running towards town in vee formation and firing off rounds. Wood splintered and glass shattered as the rounds hit the buildings. She fixed her cross hairs on one of the men she'd been watching, took in a breath, let half of it out and slowly squeezed the trigger of her MK13 bolt-action sniper rifle.

The large calibre round struck its target and the man fell to the ground. She pulled the bolt back, ejecting the casing. She pushed the bolt forward and a new round was now in the chamber and ready. Again, she breathed in slowly, exhaled half the air out and squeezed the trigger. The second man fell. She rolled onto her back, cleared the weapon, reloaded and then aimed her rifle at the town to help Bravo team cover Alpha team.

Luther and his team did not run. The nine Knights walked at a fast pace in vee formation, with Luther at the head, weapons firing as they passed each building; scanning the foreground and the buildings in front of them. They had the covering fire of Bravo team and heard the shots coming from Marie-Claude. Luther made straight for the last but one building on the right-hand side of town, the last one before the church: This was the target building. No one needed to say anything; they had trained for days and were totally tuned in to the moment. Rafael was the only one out of vee formation; he was off to the right looking for IEDs.

A man appeared from behind one of the buildings on the right; he'd been in a hidden sandbagged position with two others but left it to see what was happening. He took aim and opened fire on Luther's team. A Knight fell dead.

Zakariah's team suddenly opened up on the man and he took 11 bullets in the chest. They tried to scan every building, every space between the buildings but Zakariah knew that they did not have clear lines of sight; others could be lying in wait between the buildings. They held their aims and stayed vigilant, trigger fingers ready.

Luther's team had moved forward another 50 yards when two men suddenly opened fire on them. They were from the sandbagged position. One had a semi-automatic weapon but the other had an L7A2 machine gun and he started laying down heavy fire on Luther's team. They had to break formation and dive for cover. They were now spread out and pretty much pinned down. Whilst Rafael and five other Knights returned fire, and kept the focus on the hostiles, Luther, Dominique, the doctor and one other Knight eased round the back of one of the buildings and made their way gingerly towards the target building.

Inside the building, Bo Bo Hak knew what was happening as soon as he heard the gunfire, but his men did not. His thugs outside were ill-disciplined and totally ineffective as most of them ran around in confusion. Inside the target building, he ordered his men to the back end of the room. They were crowded around the windows to see what was happening. He took out his machete and plunged it into the back of one of his men. He now he had their full attention.

"Him," he said, pointing to Sabath. "He goes church, now," he barked. "Make him ready." The doctors and the orderlies ran over to Sabath's bed. Bo Bo Hak wanted the collateral just in case. He'd guessed they had come for the Templar; he heard the amount of gunfire and knew it was an extraction team. "Them," he said, pointing his machete towards the people in the other 11 beds. "Make them dead, all."

Cameron and his team had made it to the far end of town. They hit the release buttons on their harnesses and their kit fell to the ground, engines still whirling as they dropped. For a split second they felt as if they were suspended in the air, then gravity grabbed them. They fumbled furiously for their ripcords, found them, then their reserve parachutes opened. Below them three men had run out of the church and were making their escape towards the forest at the back end of town. They saw the Templars soaring in from above and they started running.

Cameron and the Knights landed, detached their reserve chutes – their weapons at the ready, safeties off. He turned to two of the Knights and pointed to the three men running away. "Take them out, Jose, and I will get the vehicles, then cover the back end." The vehicles were 50 yards away. The two Knights made off after the three men running towards the forest, and Cameron and Jose headed for the vehicles.

The door burst open in the target building and Dominique and Luther appeared in the doorway, weapons ready. Behind them the doctor and one other Knight followed. They quickly surveyed the room. There were ten hostiles inside the room, at the far end; one was on the floor, he was already dead. Hanging in the middle of the room they saw the butchered body of Tarik, strung up on a crane block. Scotland saw the same image through their body cams. The body was swaying and slowly rotating. Every Knight who saw it, said a silent prayer and made the sign of the cross over their chests: they would never forget what they saw.

Shots rang out and the Templars pulled over metal lockers, beds and mattresses and dived for cover. A Knight took a bullet to the head and then Luther took a bullet to his right arm. He switched to firing with his left. They were now three against ten: they were outnumbered and pinned down and barricaded in near the door.

Most of the hostiles were at the back of the room, also taking cover. The Templars now realised that the building was being used as

276

a make-shift hospital; there was medical equipment and supplies everywhere.

On all but two of the beds lay dead bodies. The bed sheets were stained red with fresh blood – their deaths had only just happened. Two men with machetes were hacking and finishing off the other two. Neither screamed as thankfully they were still in induced comas

Dominique raised her head slightly and scanned the room; she saw André Sabath lying in a bed just ten yards away from them. She barely recognised him; he seemed conscious. He was gaunt and thin; he looked gravely ill. A man in a white gown stood by him, three others wearing green hospital gowns all busied themselves around him, trying to keep low. They were taking tubes out of Sabath's arm. The man in the white coat, had a stethoscope to Sabath's chest whilst another gave him an injection. Domonique looked for a way to get close to Sabath.

From the back of the room a man moved and caught her eye. He was a big man and was holding a machete in his right hand. There was something familiar about him. She froze. An overwhelming feeling of sickness ran through her stomach. It churned. It was as if her brain was trying to play catch up with her basic senses. Then something triggered in her brain and bad memories from over 20 years ago flooded back like a dam bursting. She saw the image of her mother screaming as she was being beaten and dragged away by the same man now standing at the far end of the room. She reeled back and screamed. The man with the machete moved towards her and she to him.

"Murderer!" she screamed at him. "You killed Sophia, you killed my mother."

"Ah, woman in the Italy, Seer woman," Bo Bo Hak barked. "Not me, I kill her not. Azrael, my father, he took her; he made her bleed; he made her dead. I am Bo Bo Hak, I will take new Seer. I will take Priest. I will bleed him."

Dominique threw her firearms down and drew her Katana

277

sword from the scabbard attached to her back and hidden beneath her long, black leather coat. The man had just threatened to kill Jonathan, her husband, her soulmate and friend. She wanted this man's death to be up close and personal. "Over my dead body," she screamed at him. "Now raise your blade and prepare to die."

"I make you bleed, bitch," he said. Then he shouted to his men. "She mine, no guns. My blade."

Back in Scotland they all looked at Jonathan. He was white. St Clair put his hand on his shoulder. "Do you want to go into another room, Jonathan?" he asked.

"No, I'm staying right here." He moved forward and touched the TV screen showing the pictures from Dominique's body cam. Then he whispered, "I'm with you; you go get him."

St Clair spoke to Rafael, and the rest of the Alpha team. "Rafael, Knights, what's your status?"

Rafael was out of breath. "Three wounded, they are out of the fight. It's just me now, I'm afraid. We are pinned down by the same machine gun post as Bravo team. I am trying to keep theses Knights alive, sir.

"Zakariah," St Clair called, "can you get to them? Luther needs help; they are majorly outnumbered inside that building and pinned down and Rafael can't help them?"

"We can't move. We in the same situation as Rafael. They have us pinned with that damn machine gun. If we move, I'll get all my Knights killed, Payne; I've already lost one Knight. The only way out is to go around and that would take too long. I can't help them from here. Can someone get to my daughter? Can someone help Luther and his team?"

From over the coms they heard Cameron call in. "I'm on it; I'll be with Luther in twenty seconds. Hang on in there, Luther; I'm coming."

Then, Marie-Claude came over their ear pieces. "Sniper one here, I'll take the machine gun—"

278

Luther cut her off. "Stay where you are, Marie-Claude; you'll never make it."

"Already on my way, sir. Marie-Claude out."

Bravo team saw her rise from her position in the graveyard and start to run forward. The second sniper, with Bravo team, turned to Zakariah. She didn't say anything; the look on her face said it all.

"Damn it," Zakariah he said. "Okay, okay. Go. Keep low and keep to the backs of the buildings. Don't you go getting yourself killed, you hear me, Knight? I'll never forgive you if you go and die on me today. Now go and help your friend."

She smiled, nodded and then she was gone, amidst a hail of machine gunfire.

Cameron ran to the target building. He was approaching it from the north end. He peered through one of the windows and saw how much trouble Luther and his team were in. One Knight dead. Luther's right arm bloody, with the Templar doctor next to him applying a field dressing to it. Dominique was walking up the centre of room with no firearms, just her sword. She was heading straight for the African who looked mean. He was holding a machete and Cameron knew straight away that he would be too powerful and too skilful for Dominique – he had 'that' feeling. The same feeling when two strangers in a crowd recognise something about the other that connects them: an experience, a tragedy, an ability. He just had the sense that this guy was altogether in another league.

At the back of the building were two large double doors that had been used to crane heavy machinery in and out of the work shop in the old days; they had been boarded up a long time ago. So, his only way in was the window.

Dominique swung her sword at the African but he knocked it away: he was strong and he was skilful. He smiled. "Daughter of woman Seer, I bleed you now."

279

Luther jumped on the coms again. "Zakariah, what's your status? Has it changed? I'm out of options here."

"Same position, I'm afraid," Zakariah said. "We are still held down by machine gunfire. Sniper One is on route towards the machine gun holding us down, Sniper Two has gone to help her. Hang in there, Luther; as soon as they take out the machine gun, we'll be with you."

"Even if we can get to Sabath," Luther said, "and Cameron gets in, we won't be able to carry him out. We don't have the manpower."

"I'll do it." It was the Russian's voice over the coms. He left the OP and ran as fast as he could run towards the target building, via the back end of the buildings. Zakariah and the rest of Bravo team laid down cover fire for him; Rafael tried to help but he was nearly out of ammunition. Marie-Claude had stopped when she heard the Russian and she also covered him all the way.

The Russian ran hard. André Sabath was the one who had saved his father back in Paris, saved him from certain death from Mother Russia. He owed the man a debt of honour, but, more than that, André was his friend and no one, not even an enemy in a greater number and with the tactical advantage, was going to stop him saving his friend.

Dominique was now cut off from both Luther and the doctor, who were pinned down behind metal lockers and mattresses. She was fighting hard. The thought of her mother, Sophia, kept her going but she knew she was losing the fight with the African. She didn't have the skill to beat Bo Bo Hak and she no longer had her firearms as an alternative. She knew her sword was not going to be enough.

Dominique remembered the face of the man that took her mother, the scarred face of an evil murderer. The image bolstered her resolve. She got up and raised her sword again. Bo Bo Hak swung his machete and the sword fell from Dominique's hands – he was too powerful and he had full height leverage. She was exhausted but she was a 7th Dan in karate. She pulled her leg around in a wheelhouse-style kick and struck him. He teetered slightly, then regained his balance. She sprang at him again, leading with her elbow; it hit his jaw. He brought his left fist down and caught her on the side of the face. She fell back and bounced hard against a dialysis machine. He stepped forward with a grin on his face. Sabath tried to move; he tried to help her, his god-daughter, but even though they had removed his restraints, ready to move him, his muscles refused work.

Jonathan and the rest of the Knights in Scotland were watching the fight through Dominique's body cam. They saw through Luther's camera that each time Luther tried to take aim at the African, a hail of bullets rained down on his position.

"Cameron, please help her." This time it was Jonathan's voice over the coms.

There was a crash of glass. Cameron Jack had launched himself through a side window, protecting his eyes and face with his arms. He landed near to Dominique. "Get Sabath," he called. He drew his Katana, bowed towards the African, opened his stance and raised his sword. The sword that had been given to him by Hinata Satō-san in Japan. It was the same sword that the Cathar, Father Jacque Durand, had used on the dusty road to Carcassonne, to save the life of their first Seer, the daughter of Joan of Arc. The sword that had belonged to every Master of the Blade since. He turned to Bo Bo Hak and said, "You ready to try me, big guy?"

The Russian was at the door and saw where Luther and the doctor were. They couldn't help. He had a pistol in each hand. He reloaded them. He needed to draw the fire away from Luther and the doctor so they could move into a better position. He started towards the men at the other end of the room, firing at them furiously. Moving from left to right, taking cover, then moving, cover and moving. He had drawn their fire.

Luther stood up and shouted, "Where our brothers go, we all go." He started moving towards them; the Templar doctor moved forward too. They made it ten yards and took out two hostiles. Luther took a bullet in his right side; it went straight through but he was down. The doctor made it to his side. They both returned fire as best they could.

Outside, a group of five hostiles were banging and pushing against the double doors at the back of the building. They had been resting in the bunk house after rotation and slow to go outside and see where all the firing from coming from.

Luther heard them. "I need eyes on the back of the building; we have more hostiles trying to get in. It doesn't look like it would take much to break it open."

Jose's voice came over the ear piece. "You have five hostiles. I don't have a clear shot."

"Don't move, Jose. Stay put but if they break through, then start firing," Luther said.

Billy Jack had left the pilots to guard the plane and he was running through the forest towards the gun battle as fast as he could.

Inside the building, the Russian took two shots to the chest and stumbled. He was quick to his feet again and moved forward yet again towards Sabath. He then took another bullet to the upper arm, but he was now with Sabath. He threw his knife at the man in the white coat, Zivko's doctor. He had taken refuge under the next bed. The knife bedded into his forehead. The three orderlies started running to the back of the room with the other hostiles.

Dominique was now beside the Russian at Sabath's bed. She leaned over to Sabath and stroke his forehead. "It's okay, André. It's okay now, we're here."

St Clair saw his friend on the screen and just said, "Oh my God," when he saw how gravely ill he looked.

Bo Bo Hak spun his machete around and brought it down at a diagonal angle to slice the head of the man in front of him, Cameron Jack.

However, Cameron was onto him before the machete blade had travelled three inches; he read the move like a book. This shook Bo Bo Hak.

Cameron then sidestepped, crouched and uncoiled like a cobra and brought his sword onto the forearm of Bo Bo Hak and cut him. He fell back against the wall and shouted in rage. Bo Bo Hak had never been cut like that before, despite all the machete fights he'd been in.

Three of Bo Bo Hak's men had moved forward and jumped in front of Cameron, their machetes aloft. Cameron spun round to face all of them. They hacked and wielded their machetes with wild arrogance. Three to one, the odds, they thought, were with them. They were wrong. Whilst they attacked Cameron with ferocity, Cameron fought with majestic grace and extreme accuracy. He fought them with Kenjutsu.

Bo Bo Hak's walkie-talkie sounded; it was Zivko. "We leave now."

Bo Bo Hak didn't want to leave; he wanted to finish off the man six feet away, the man he had been fighting. He wanted to test himself against a man that knew Bushido; the man that fought like a Samurai and fought with a Samurai sword. The voice came over the walkie-talkie again, the strange, eerie voice of his master. Bo Bo Hak jumped out of the same window that Cameron had crashed through, and made for the church.

Zivko was waiting for him in the bulletproof Range Rover that the recon team hadn't seen because it was always kept hidden in the church. Bo Bo Hak jumped in the driver's seat and started the car. He revved the engine and then the Range Rover burst out of the side of the wooden church and headed for the forest, cover and escape.

Jose watched them as they sped off. Halfway along the track the Range Rover halted. Jose saw the two Knights Cameron had sent to shoot the three escaping hostiles running back to the fire fight in the town. He saw the smoke from the gun first, and then he heard the two shots — sound traveling slower than light. The Range Rover roared off again and the bodies of two dead Knights lay by the side of the track.

With Bo Bo Hak gone, the dynamics of the firefight were beginning to change, as some of the hostiles were looking for a way out. Despite being far superior in numbers, they had never fought such as a determined enemy before. They were thugs against battle-hardened warriors.

Finally, the Templar doctor had reached Sabath. He finished disconnecting the tubes from Sabath's arms and checked Sabath's vital signs. "My Lord, he said, looking at the ashen and beaten body of Sabath connected to the white machine. "It's a dialysis machine."

"Why?" the Russian asked.

The doctored looked around at the medical equipment surrounding Sabath's bed, and the beds of the others. "Looking at the equipment they have been using, and the configuration of the inlet and outlet tubing, it looks like … it looks like they've been transfusing André's blood to someone and then putting that person's blood into André but it makes no sense. We have to get him out of here. He's not well, not well at all; all his vitals are down. We have to get him out or he will die," he shouted.

Just then another salvo of bullets rushed past their heads.

Sabath opened his eyes and saw the Russian. "By God's grace, brother." He tried to smile but was in tremendous pain.

The Russian put his arms underneath Sabath and lifted him off the bed. "Where our brothers go, we all go," he whispered to Sabath. Just then two more shots hit the Russian in his left lower side and one that took out his body camera and imbedded itself in his chest. The low thuds were followed by his low grunt as the pain hit him, again. He straightened up. "Let's go," he called.

In Scotland there was silence, then Courtney said, "That's five … that's five bullets he's got in him."

Next to her Bertram had tears in his eyes; he could not believe what was happening to his friend.

The Russian had Sabath in his arms. The doctor held the saline drip up high and moved alongside Sabath. Dominique had their back and was laying down cover fire against the hostiles, with the Russian's guns.

Another hail of bullets rained down and the Russian stumbled. He held onto Sabath and they fell to the floor. The doctor and Dominique crouched down on their knees and kept low. One of the orderlies had made his way round the other side of the room and was trying to escape through a window. He saw them on the ground and raised his gun. The Russian was the largest target, so he fired. It hit the Russian in the stomach.

The Russian crawled, bleeding, groaning, dragging Sabath along the floor. The doctor and Dominique were on their hands and knees, desperately trying to get Sabath out.

Cameron was toe-to-toe with three of Bo Bo Hak's men. Their machetes flying in wild movements and an unconventional attack thrust made it hard to defend against. Cameron was eight feet away from the Russian, Dominique and the doctor, and stepping ever backwards so he got closer to the door and farther away from the hostiles at the far end of the room. His Katana sword cut through the air with tremendous speed and laser-sharp accuracy. His assailants were breathing hard. Cameron Jack's breathing controlled; he fought with pinpoint accuracy. They tried to cut him, to stab and slice at his body. His sword fighting was an orchestrated flow, the way he had been taught in Japan. He blocked, twisted, turned and spun like the master swordsman he was.

Luther called to them that they had to go; the back doors were about to give way, then they would be overrun.

Cameron Jack cornered the three assailants. He caught one on the arm. He bent slightly, then pirouetted on the balls of his feet and when two assailants were lifting their machetes and leaving their midriff exposed, he stood up and at the same time drew his Katana blade across their stomachs. They fell, dying.

The other man tried to breakaway. He was confused and ran for the door, towards Sabath, the Russian and Dominique – he just wanted to get away from the man with the Samurai sword and certain death. Cameron saw him run and hurled his sword at the hostile and it landed in the square of the man's back, a second before Luther's bullet penetrated his skull.

Now they were all together at the far end of the room and Luther barked at them to get Sabath out. Jose had now made his way round and was there to help. Dominique, the doctor and Jose carried him out. Cameron had retrieved his sword, wiped the blood from his blade on the dead man's shirt and was now covering their exit by laying down fire.

Marie-Claude and the other sniper had finally made it into position. They were at opposite sides of the town and in their sights were two hostiles, one with a high-calibre belt-fed machine gun. They both steadied their breathing. Then, in a whisper over the coms, "Take the one on your left; I have the one on your right. On my three. One, two three." Two shots fired in unison and both hostiles lay dead.

The Russian was sitting on the floor, slightly slumped forward, bleeding very badly. He knew the door at the far end of the room was about to give way and the hostiles would then rush them, and they wouldn't be able to get Sabath away. His mighty strength was leaving him.

"You got to get up, Nickolin," Luther said. "They will be through that door any second now."

Cameron Jack stood in front of them, protecting them, facing

286

the barricaded door. Blood seeped from a head wound and a machete cut to his left leg. He wiped the blood and sweat from his eyes.

"Nickolin, we have to go." Luther begged him again, but Luther already knew that it was too late for the Russian.

The Russian took out his phone from his pocket and held out his hand for Luther's phone. They looked at each other, their eyes locked. Luther was shaking his head, he didn't want to give it to him.

"It's ok," the Russian whispered." He leaned forward and took Luther's phone from his belt. He placed his thumbs on the two-small black, indented buttons on the side of the phones.

Outside, Zakariah rose to his feet. "Machine gun is out," he said over the coms. "We're on our way."

"Too late," was Luther's reply. "Stay where you are; this place is about to blow. Cover our exit."

It was all quiet on the coms as everyone tried to catch their breath. They heard Luther say blow, and one person in Scotland instantly knew what that meant. Then, over the coms, Bertram's voice. He was crying. "Please, Mr Russian Klymachak … please don't press them; don't do that."

"What's the flash to bang, Bertram?" the Russian asked, staring intently at the splintering wood of the double door at the far end of the room.

"Twelve seconds, but you won't have time, Mr Russian Klymachak. Please don't press them, please."

"You go now," the Russian whispered to Luther. He was now struggling to speak because blood was entering his throat. "You go, Luther, and get my friend André back to safety. You get him home." He held the two phones in his hands.

"Damn it," shouted Luther.

"*Fartres Sumus*," the Russian said to Luther in Latin. *We are brothers.*

"*My brat'ya'*," Luther repeated the sentence in Russian.

The Russian smiled. "Your Russian's coming along, my brother, but now you need to go. I have enough rounds to put down cover for about ten seconds." He fought to get his breath from the pain and the blood. He fought not to fall unconscious.

The door split and bodies started to pile in; the existing hostiles found new courage now that the others were arriving. They started to charge down the room.

The Russian looked down at his wounds. People had always thought him aloof, hard and even stubborn. He never said much. His body hard and hands like leather; six feet five tall with short-cropped black hair with hints of grey and a deep scar over his left eye, remnants of a knife fight with three Zeks in his first year at Perm 35. However, Nickolin Klymachak had not always been so aloof, so distant. In 1986, whilst still fighting the war in Afghanistan, his young wife – whom he'd left back in Russia – was finally persuaded to take their two children from Russia to her parents' home until he returned: her parents' hometown, in northern Ukraine, was called Chernobyl. In 1986 two huge central reactors exploded in Chernobyl and Nickolin's wife and two children perished within a few months; it was a slow and painful death for all three. The authorities never told him until a year later. It changed Nickolin Klymachak forever. He refused to blow up an Afghan village, full of villagers, and then spent the next four years awaiting trial from Mother Russia: he was given a 15-year jail sentence.

Luther looked at him for the last time. He knelt down and kissed him on the cheek. "Go be with them, go be with your wife and your children, my friend." Luther rose to his feet, put his fist to his heart and then he and Cameron Jack left. The pictures from Luther and Cameron's body cams showed them running out of the doorway and into the open.

Luther called over the coms, "Knights go red." The call sign for emergency, pull back.

The screen showing the inside of the church was blank and

static. The Russian's body camera had been destroyed by a bullet. Everyone in Scotland was motionless; they were devastated and couldn't believe what was happening. They stared at the Russian's blank screen. Then the coms crackled.

"Bertram, Bertram, you there?"

Bertram fought back the tears. "I am, Mr Russian Klymachak."

"Would you stay with me?"

Bertram was crying again. "I … I would be honoured to, Nickolin."

There was the sound of lots of gunfire and shouts. After a few seconds it then went silent.

The explosion tore the room apart and everyone in it.

Chapter 15
Yuletide & Old Enemies

Date: 25th December, Christmas day 2012
Place: a remote castle in Scotland

It had been nine months since the mission in Romania.

It was bitterly cold; a frosty white blanket of snow stretched out as far as he could see. He stood on the battlements of the castle, his favourite place to go to be alone; to think when he was troubled; or just to remind himself of how blessed he was. The castle had been a sanctuary for the Templars over the years. Semi-isolated from civilization, the castle stood in hundreds of miles of bleak Scottish wilderness, accompanied on three sides by bracken-covered hills and by a dense meandering spruce forest on the other. A magical place in summer; a desolate and barren place in the winter. He looked out over the snow-covered scene he had stood and looked at thousands of times. He breathed in deeply, then watched his breath escape into the frosty air.

He took out his phone to call Jonathan. He mouthed Jonathan's name at the screen and the phone made the call. *Clever lad, our Bertram*, he thought.

Jonathan answered. "Merry Christmas," he said.

"Merry Christmas to you, too," St Clair replied. "How you coping without her?" Dominique was away in New York.

"I'm good, thanks. I spoke to her late last night to wish her Merry Christmas; well, late last night for her, early this morning for me. She gave me a lot of specific instructions about the food she had left me, where it was, how I should cook it. Also, a list of chores; apparently, I have been promising to get these done for ages. In America we call it a 'honey list'; she calls it the 'wait for ever list'."

St Clair laughed. "She'll never change. I'm not married, never have been, but if you want my advice, you'll complete at least two thirds of the list before she gets back."

"I think you're right," Jonathan said. "I'll dig out my hammer and nails."

"Sorry we had to ask her to go but we really did have an emergency," St Claire said. "Father Angelo Fugero is the Vatican representative in New Jersey. The Vatican gave him our contact details. I got the call early yesterday from him. Did Dominique tell you why she was going?"

"No," Jonathan replied.

St Clair knew she would not have said anything anyway; that's the rule. No one tells anyone anything about any operation unless they are part of the operation or mission team. The strict rule is governed by the simple statement: 'need to know'. It also ensures the safety of those on an operation or mission, and finally the safety of the rest of the Templars: if they don't know, they don't know.

"You might need to know now, Jonathan," St Clair told him, "because I think I am going to have to bring you in on it. The Vatican has a secret—"

"The Vatican has many secrets; perhaps too many," Jonathan interrupted.

"They do indeed," St Clair smiled, "but this one is one of the special ones. One of the very special ones. This one concerns the specific contents of a reliquary. What do you know about relics in altars?"

"I know what we all know, Catholic churches have a relic of a saint hidden them. Normally the relic is placed in the church's altar, in a space or compartment or they put the relic in a box, a reliquary box, and that's normally placed in the altar. Most often it is a small bone fragment of a saint, or maybe hair. It could be something that a saint possessed, a piece of clothing, or a possession they were associated with. The passage in the Bible says, 'When he broke open the fifth seal, I saw underneath the altar the souls of those who had been slaughtered because of the witness they bore to the word of God.' Revelations 6:9."

"Well," St Clair said, "the Vatican has been hiding one of the most sacred altar relics in a place no one would ever think to look."

"Outside the Vatican?" Jonathan asked.

"Very much outside the Vatican," St Clair replied. "They decided this one was safer hidden in the small township of Brick, in Ocean County, New Jersey, in the States. It has a small population of around eighty thousand, the Vatican City has a population of around a thousand. However, and here's the reason they do it, whilst the Vatican may only have around a thousand people there, they receive approximately ten million visitors to St. Peter's Basilica every year. So, every day, around fifty thousand people visit that place. Around twenty thousand people visit the Sistine Chapel every day in the summer. It is a security nightmare for them and so they decided a long time ago to move a lot of their most sacred and revered objects to places around the globe that no one would ever guess would hold anything of such value. The Roman Catholic church had the skull of John the Baptist."

"Wow," Jonathan said, surprised.

"It was kept in a small catholic church in Brick," St Clair continued, "hidden within the church's stone altar in a steel safe with a digital code key. Plus, the altar has a secret door. In the safe they kept the head of John the Baptist inside a bronze reliquary box. Apparently, it has been there since nineteen thirty-two. Until it was stolen just two days ago. Three people were killed in the process."

292

"That's terrible news," Jonathan said. "I'm going to walk the dogs quickly and then I'm coming in; I'm coming to the castle." He paused for a second or two. St Clair heard the rattle of the dogs' leads as Jonathan prepared to go out to walk them on the beach and brave the blustery winds and snow flurries. "By the way, St Clair," Jonathan said, "I wanted to say something to you, something I've been giving a lot of thought but have only realised this past week or two. I thought, because I wasn't involved in Romania, that it wasn't about me, but I was wrong, wasn't I?"

St Clair looked at the land stretched out before him. "It was all about you, Jonathan; it always was. It was all about the Seer and always will be."

"I get that now," Jonathan said, "and I think I understand why. And I think I know why I have not been able to understand the Ark more; why we have been frustrated with our progress. You see, I think I finally know what the Ark is, what it's for, and I believe you already know what it's for. If I'm right, this means it will cause the greatest event since the birth of Jesus Christ." Jonathan paused a little. This was the first time he heard it said out loud; the first time he had said it out loud. It had been thoughts in his head; now those thoughts had become words. "And based on that, then I also know what one of the ten prophecies will say, probably the next prophecy in line, the fourth prophecy."

St Clair was smiling again but Jonathan couldn't see him. They had been together for four years and St Clair had hoped every day of those four years that Jonathan would one day see the plan, the brilliant celestial plan and what that meant they had to do. He waited for Jonathan to speak: he waited with bated breath.

"The fourth prophecy is about me, St Clair; it says I am the last of the Seers. There will not be another one?"

"The third prophecy, you remember," St Clair began, "was: 'A Knight will fall. A new Seer will come from the house of God and the fallen Knight will return'. You are right, Jonathan; the fourth prophecy reads: 'He is the last of them. Keep the Seer alive. He is the key to opening the Ark but enemies are at your gate." St Clair heard Jonathan whistle his dogs, then he called them.

"Cleo, Simba, come on, dogs, beach time." Then he said, "St Clair, I will be there within two hours."

As soon the Templars had got André Sabath back to safety, they moved him into a private hospital in the Lebanon, so that he would be near his family and they him. He was gravely ill but, despite this, he debriefed St Clair and the others. He told them about the loss of his Knights in Abu Dhabi and what had happened. He also told them that it was the Abaddons who'd held him. He told them Zivko's name and described him. He confirmed he seemed to be their leader. This also confirmed Morgan Clay's suspicion that Zivko Gowst, the man they called the Ghost, had funded the Abaddons and had been doing so since 1955.

After all the fighting had ended, the Templars had gone back into the disused mining town to look for enemy survivors – there were none. However, they did find the same tattoo on every body, three moons on the underside of their right wrists and they then knew for sure that they were Abaddons.

They searched the buildings to try to discover what they had been doing there. The building they stormed was pretty much incinerated in the blast but the doctor saw it before it had been blown up and gave them a detailed account of the equipment and what he thought they were doing there. He believed they had been using it to syphon blood from their captives, always men. They would remove their blood, clean it and then transfer the blood into someone else. In reverse, they put that person's blood back into the captives. He said that Sabath's symptoms suggested that the blood pumped back into him had a high toxicity level; it had attacked the organs and caused irreparable damage. Sabath confirmed the person receiving their blood was Zivko.

In the church, where Zivko's escape vehicle had been hidden, they'd found a germ-free plastic isolation room. It looked like someone, who they presumed was Zivko, spent a lot of time in there. The doctor, from the charts he discovered, calculated that Zivko spent up to five hours each day in the isolation room. In addition to that, they found liquids and creams, which they analysed. The conclusion was that Zivko's skin was being treated, two maybe three times per day, with a lotion of Aloe Vera, Llama milk, bees' honey and antiseptic components, like chlorhexidine gluconate, hexachlorophene, boric acid, Lugol's iodine and formaldehyde. Sabath had told them that the smell of Zivko Gowst was distinctive, overpowering, ghastly and resembled the smell of a mortuary; it was the same smell when the Templars entered the germ-free plastic isolation room. They concluded that the mining town was being used as a medical treatment centre for Zivko Gowst, and, besides Sabath, all of the other captives were local, poor people who, if missed, would not be a priority for the authorities.

All this new intel, the debriefing by André Sabath and what they found in Zivko's camp was a major break for the Templars, but it had come at a heavy cost. They'd lost five Knights, including Tarik. They had also lost Nickolin Klymachak, the man they fondly called the Russian. Romania cost them six lives and four wounded, which included Luther Jones who led Alpha team. Whilst none of the wounds were life-threating, it took months for some of them to heal before they could return to duty. They lost eight of their Lebanese Knights, who had flown down to Abu Dhabi to support André Sabath. A total of 13 dead and whilst they had killed 20 hostiles in Romania, the Templars had taken its heaviest loss in nearly 50 years.

Sabath had been gravely ill for months. His body had been starved of his good blood and replaced with toxic blood, in Zivko's unhinged pursuit to purify his blood and reverse his albinism and all of the side effects he was now suffering in old age. Sabath's organs had been badly damaged. The bad blood had attacked his nervous system: his body was slowly destroying itself. Four months after Romania, André Sabath started to lose feeling in his limbs and his movement slowly ceased altogether. By November he was completely paralysed and needed a ventilator to breath and 24-hour clinical care. He was fitted with a computer that detected the movement of his eye lids: it was the only movement he had left and the only way he could communicate with the outside world.

St Clair had just finished speaking with Jonathan. He was still on the battlements. He shuddered with the cold. His mobile phone rang. It was the controller in Islington. "It's André's wife, Lillia, for you." André Sabath's wife rang St Clair every two days with updates about her husband.

"Thanks, Tiff," St Clair said to the controller, then added, "oh, by the way, Merry Christmas." He stamped his feet to remove the snow from his shoes. "Are you doing anything today?" he asked.

"I'm going to put some fresh flowers on Harry's grave and spend some time at the grave. Then I will be with Proctor tomorrow and we are going back to the village to pay our respects to the other graves."

"Harry Gannan was a good man, he never let you down, did he?"

"He never did."

"Well, say a pray to Harry for me, wish him Merry Christmas and Merry Christmas to you again, Tiff.

"You too, Payne," the controller said. "Here's Lillia for you."

The phone call was not a happy one; he could tell she had been crying.

"I'm sorry to have to tell you, Payne, but André passed away this morning," she began.

"I'm so sorry, Lillia," he said.

"It's okay, Payne; we've been expecting it for months." She took a breath. "He is not in pain any more. He's in a better place. The

296

hospital called me an hour ago to tell me, and I went in to see him. He looked at peace." She started to cry again. "Do you know what he'd done, Payne, without any of us knowing? He'd done all his Christmas shopping online, by blinking. He has seven grandkids and four kids and they all got their presents from him; none of us knew he'd done it. They all arrived this morning. It must have taken him weeks but I think he was determined to buy his kids and grandkids presents, as he's done every year since the day each one of them was born." She managed to hold back her tears now. "I know you will let everyone know. I'll let you know and the rest of his brothers, about his funeral arrangements once we have them sorted out and I would like you to give the eulogy."

"It would be my absolute honour to speak about my friend. And I'm here, we're here, if you need anything, anything at all," St Clair said.

"I know you are," she said; "you always are and bless you for it. He loved you, you know. Along with spending time with his kids, he loved the time he spent with you. I know he died in pain but I think he died a happy man because of the life he led, because of you and his brothers ... because of what you do."

They said their goodbyes and André Sabath's wife hung up. She returned back to the living room, a living room that was full of her children and grandchildren.

St Clair made his way down the dimly lit, spiral stone stairs. The draught from an open embrasure made his breath visible as he exhaled. He sent out the message via his phone about André so that everyone would know at the same time. The he went to his room and changed.

Fifteen minutes later he paused outside the castle's chapel. He checked his dress, adjusting his white surcoat, centralising the distinctive red cross of the Templars. He breathed ruefully. In his mind he saw his friend, André Sabath. A lifelong friend, a brother in arms, a Templar, a Knight. He smiled at the image of his friend laughing, then he went inside the chapel.

297

Payne St Clair, the Order's Grand Master, knelt at the foot of the cross and altar. He made the sign of the cross on his chest. He knelt in silence. He was a proud man; he personified reverence and dignity but today he was a sad man.

The old, arched door creaked and Bertram crept into the chapel. He too was in full Templar ceremonial uniform. He smiled at St Clair. "May I?" he said pointing to a seat next to his Grand Master.

"Of course." Bertram knelt and made the sign of the cross. "How are you doing, Bertram?" St Clair asked. "I hear you changed your name; someone told me you added Nickolin's name?"

"I did, Mr St Clair, by deed poll. My name is now Bertram Hubert Klymachak De'Ath."

"Well," said St Clair, "that's a fine sounding name. I'm sure Nickolin would be proud you thought of him and proud you will now carry it with you."

Just then the door opened again and Courtney, Zakariah, Billy and Morgan Clay came into the chapel, again all dressed as 13th-century Templars. They were followed by John Edison, one of the Nine Worthies. Twenty other Knights joined them. They were all wearing their ceremonial dress; they had heard about the passing of André Sabath.

Jonathan was out walking the Ridgebacks, Cleo and Simba, on the beach. It was windy and the sky was full of flurries of snow. He was on his own; he saw Elaine Wall, their dog-walking, dog-minding friend.

"No Dominique today?" she called to him, as she approached him somewhat windswept. The four dogs greeted each other with great gusto and headed off to the sea a hundred yards away and to a game of chase the wave.

"She has a presentation to deliver," he said, "in Qatar, for the Ministry of Education. No Christmas there." He smiled.

"Ah, that's a shame" she said. "But I am glad I've caught you, Jonathan. A man was on the beach earlier this morning when I was down here for my morning walk and asked me if I knew you; of course I said yes. He gave me this mobile phone." She pulled a cheap-looking mobile phone from her coat pocket. "He asked me to give it to you. He said it was yours. You'd left it behind somewhere; can't remember where he said."

Just then the phone she had given him started ringing. Jonathan hadn't left his phone anywhere; it wasn't his phone. He looked around the beach line and the rough common land surrounding most of the beachhead. He answered the phone. He knew the voice. His heart started pounding. He started rattling the change in his pocket and wishing Dominique was there.

"I hear that some of your friends had a rough time in Romania?" the voice at the other end of the phone said.

Jonathan didn't respond. The dogs – Dusty, Nell, Cleo and Simba – started barking and his heart jumped again; he thought they had spotted someone. He turned around but it was only a piece of washed up seaweed they had obviously convinced themselves needed a warning bark or two.

"I'd gone by the time you all got to Abu Dhabi, long gone. I was listening to the stupid Yemeni talk all the time on his phone, so I knew what you were planning." Salah El-Din's voice was as clear as if he was standing right next to Jonathan. "We should make a partnership, priest, the Templars and I. We got off on the wrong foot four years ago; I think we just had a natural collision of interests."

"A collision?" Jonathan said. "You killed me."

"Maybe but your God, He should have treated you better, priest, then you would not have been there."

"He did," Jonathan said.

"How?" the Arab criminal asked him.

"I was dead, then I wasn't."

"Why would your God do that?" Salah El-Din asked him.

"Perhaps to teach me that faith means nothing unless it's tested," Jonathan said.

299

"And you have faith now, priest?"

"I do," Jonathan said.

"And now we have a common enemy."

Jonathan took out his own phone from his jacket pocket and hit the red button: As Bertram had put it: "hit red for emergency ... it means can't call, can't speak, come and get me. Help. It's like the red pull cord in a retirement home for the elderly."

"I want to talk to the leader of the Templars. I want to talk about a pact against our common enemy, the Abaddons. I will call again, priest."

The dogs barked again. This time Dusty had the seaweed in his mouth. "You should teach that dog not to eat that seaweed, it looks awful," Salah El-Din said. Jonathan turned around sharply, searching desperately for the sight of a figure watching them.

Elaine now moved a little closer to him. "Are you okay, Jonathan?" she asked.

"I really don't know, Elaine," Jonathan said, "but we need to get off this beach."

THE END

Printed in Great Britain
by Amazon

64052153R00184